**Praise for #1 *New York Times* bestselling author
Sherryl Woods**

"Sherryl Woods always delights her readers—
including me!"

—#1 *New York Times* bestselling author
Debbie Macomber

"Woods is a master heartstring puller."

—*Publishers Weekly*

"Woods employs her signature elements—the
Southern small-town atmosphere, the supportive
network of friends and family, and the heartwarming
romance—to great effect."

—*Booklist*

Praise for Jo Ann Brown

"Jo Ann Brown writes with an eye for conflict and a
heart filled with love."

—Charlotte Hubbard,
author of *Christmas Comes to Morning Star*

"Brown is a gifted writer who makes unforgettable
characters that invite the reader to join them on
their journey."

—*Publishers Weekly* bestselling author Marie E. Bast

With her roots firmly planted in the South, #1 *New York Times* bestselling author **Sherryl Woods** has written many of her more than one hundred books in that distinctive setting. Her Chesapeake Shores books have become a highly rated series success on Hallmark Channel and her Sweet Magnolias books have recently been released as a much-anticipated Netflix series. Sherryl divides her time between her childhood summer home overlooking the Potomac River in Colonial Beach, Virginia, and Florida's east coast.

Jo Ann Brown has published over one hundred titles under a variety of pen names. A former military officer, she enjoys taking pictures and traveling. She has taught creative writing for more than twenty years and is always excited when one of her students sells a project. She has been married for more than forty years and has three children and two rambunctious cats. She lives in Amish Country in southeastern Pennsylvania. She enjoys hearing from her readers. Visit her at www.joannbrownbooks.com.

#1 *New York Times* Bestselling Author

SHERRYL WOODS

KATE'S VOW

HARLEQUIN
BESTSELLING
AUTHOR
COLLECTION

**HARLEQUIN®
BESTSELLING
AUTHOR
COLLECTION**

Recycling programs
for this product may
not exist in your area.

ISBN-13: 978-1-335-00817-6

Kate's Vow
First published in 1993. This edition published in 2023.
Copyright © 1993 by Sherryl Woods

His Amish Sweetheart
First published in 2016. This edition published in 2023.
Copyright © 2016 by Jo Ann Ferguson

For questions and comments about the quality of this book, please contact us at CustomerService@Harlequin.com.

Harlequin Enterprises ULC
22 Adelaide St. West, 41st Floor
Toronto, Ontario M5H 4E3, Canada
www.Harlequin.com

Printed in U.S.A.

CONTENTS

KATE'S VOW

Sherryl Woods

Chapter One

One more hour of paperwork, Kate Newton thought wearily. One more hour and this horrible week with its endless confrontations and sad, bitter stories of marriages gone wrong would be over. By Friday afternoons, what had once seemed challenging had lately become draining. It seemed she could hardly wait anymore to leave the office behind. That in itself was more troublesome than she cared to admit. High-priced, barracuda divorce attorneys were supposed to thrive on a steady diet of late hours and endless work. And until recently Kate had reveled in every minute of it.

She sighed as she stared at the piles of depositions and court documents still on her desk. She was suddenly struck by an unprofessional and almost irresistible urge to shake a few of her clients and tell them to wise up, drop their divorce petitions and fight for their marriages. Just the thought of doing something so completely out of character shook her. What the devil was wrong with her lately?

The buzz of her intercom provided an almost welcome interruption of her introspection, even though at this hour on a Friday it almost certainly promised disaster.

"Yes, Zelda," she said to her secretary, whose mother had been fascinated by F. Scott Fitzgerald and his flamboyant, nutty wife. Zelda Lane had taken the whole Fitzgerald mystique to heart and was every bit as colorful as her namesake. She was also, thank goodness, incredibly efficient.

"There's someone here to see you," Zelda said. Her voice dropped to a whisper. "He says he's a prospective client."

Something in Zelda's tone put Kate on alert. "Okay, what's the deal?" she asked irritably. "I don't have any appointments on my calendar. Is this one of those arrogant sons-of-bitches who expects to barge in and get first-class treatment?"

Her secretary uttered a sound that might have been a muffled hoot of laughter. "I don't think so, boss. I think this is one you ought to see."

Kate sighed. Unfortunately Zelda's instincts were usually worth exploring. "Does this prospective client have a name?"

"David Allen Winthrop," she said.

Kate heard a muffled exchange, then Zelda added, "The third. David Allen Winthrop III."

Kate knew all about men who were so precise, so full of themselves and their own importance. They were the kind she normally preferred to take to the cleaners in a divorce proceeding.

"Send him in," she said, already plotting her strategy for putting the bozo in his place with a stern lecture on busy schedules and the courtesy of making appointments.

Her office door swung open to admit the redheaded Zelda, whose expression hovered between amusement and anticipation. In a woman with her zany, off-beat sense of humor, that was yet another warning signal. Kate should have slammed the door on her secretary and the as-yet-unseen prospective client, sneaked out the back door and headed for a long weekend of much-needed relaxation in Malibu.

She watched the doorway expectantly, her gaze leveled just above Zelda's shoulder. The movement she saw, however, was waist high. She glanced down. Her mouth dropped open in astonishment. Her would-be client was about ten years old.

She blinked at the kid, whose sandy hair had been slicked back neatly. His face, with its smattering of freckles across the nose, had been scrubbed clean. His gray blazer and navy slacks looked as if they had come off the junior rack at Brooks Brothers. The stylish effect was completed by a perfectly knotted tie and a white dress shirt. Either this kid's summer camp had a rigid dress code or he was practicing for Wall Street at a very early age.

Judging from his earnest expression that whatever had brought him here was deadly serious to him, Kate held out her hand and formally introduced herself. "I'm Kate Newton, Mr. Winthrop. What can I do for you?"

Huge brown eyes regarded her somberly. "I'd like a

divorce." He said it in the same unemotional tone with which he might order vanilla ice cream, even though everyone knew he'd really prefer chocolate.

Kate's composure slipped a notch. "Excuse me?"

Uncertainty flickered in his eyes for just an instant. "That's what you do, isn't it? You handle divorces?" His voice began to regain a little of his earlier confidence. "I read all about your last case in the paper. It sounded like you were good. A little rough on the husband, but generally quite good."

Kate was struck by the unexpected insightfulness from a pint-size analyst who should have been playing *zap-bang* computer games.

"Thank you, but I'm afraid I don't quite understand. You seem—" She fumbled for a word that wouldn't offend his determined dignity. She settled for blunt. "It's just that most people who get a divorce are a little older. Who exactly do you want to divorce?"

If this kid was married, she was giving up law, moving to a ranch in Montana and raising sheep. She wanted nothing further to do with the human race.

"My father," he said.

His tone was filled with such regret that Kate felt something deep inside her shift. Maternal instincts she'd never known she possessed roared to life. "I think we'd better talk, Mr. Winthrop. Why don't you have a seat over there on the sofa? How did you get here, by the way?"

"I'm supposed to be at a movie. Our housekeeper will pick me up."

Kate followed him to the conference area in her office and took a chair across from him. "Okay, then, why do you want to break things off with your father?" She absolutely refused to use the word divorce again.

"Irreconcilable differences," he said in that formal tone that gave Kate the creeps.

"I see." She nodded sagely and tried once more to gather her composure. Zelda's expression of barely controlled mirth wasn't helping. She glared at the secretary. "You can leave us now."

"Sure, boss. Could I bring you something? A soft drink, perhaps?" she said to the boy with as much deference as she would display toward an heiress. Zelda had had lots of practice with heiresses, but none that Kate was aware of with kids.

"Coffee," he told her, then added as if it was an afterthought, "with a lot of cream, please. And three sugars."

Kate, who drank her special-blend Columbian coffee black to savor the taste and aroma, cringed. Still, she couldn't help admiring a kid who was so determined to present a mature impression. Impression, hell, she corrected. This boy was more polite than half the men she knew. He was sitting soldier-straight on her sofa, even though the position looked awkward. His feet didn't quite reach the floor. There was none of the fidgeting that had driven her crazy with all of her sister's kids. The kid was so self-possessed, it was downright disconcerting.

When Zelda had delivered the coffee, Kate regarded her prospective client soberly. "Okay, why don't you tell me what this is all about?"

"I think it's fairly straightforward," he said, as if he'd been studying court documents for the proper wording. "My father and I don't get along."

"In what way?" she asked, genuinely fascinated now

by both his demeanor and his claim. What would send a boy to a divorce attorney? Insufficient allowance? Strict discipline? A parental drug problem? Abuse? God forbid it was the latter.

"We never see each other anymore," he said, and then his lower lip trembled dangerously. "Not since my mom died."

Kate swallowed hard against the unexpected lump that formed in her throat. It was at least the size of a boulder. Her associates would be astounded at the rare display of emotion in a woman with a reputation for going for the jugular no matter how many tears were shed in the courtroom.

"When did your mom die?" she asked gently when she could form the words.

"Six months ago. It's been very hard on my dad," he said as if he'd heard that said by a zillion adults making excuses for a thoughtless parent.

"I'll bet it's been hard on you, too."

Those huge brown eyes, suddenly brimming with unshed tears, met hers. "Sometimes," he admitted in little more than a shaky whisper. A tear spilled down his cheek. "But I'm trying really hard to be brave for my dad's sake."

"Do you and your dad talk about it?"

He shook his head. "It makes us both too sad."

Kate suddenly wanted to leave her Century City office, go straight into Beverly Hills or Bel Air or whatever upscale part of town this man lived in and strangle him. No doubt he was hurting. Even without knowing the details of Mrs. Winthrop's death, she could imagine how devastating it must have been for her husband. She must have been very young, and that was never

easy on anyone. But he had a son—a son who, for all
his grown-up pretenses, was still a little boy who was
hurting desperately inside. Kate recognized that kind
of pain. She was at a complete loss about how to deal
with it. The one thing she did know was that David
Winthrop's way wasn't it.

"What would you do if you got a divorce?" she asked.

For only the second time since his unscheduled arrival, he appeared uncertain. "I was hoping maybe you
could find someone who might adopt me. Maybe with
some brothers and sisters, a mom and dad. You know,
like a real family," he said wistfully. "Do you think you
could find anyone like that? I wouldn't be any trouble.
I promise."

"Maybe it won't come to that," Kate said as a furious determination swept through her. David Allen Winthrop, Jr. or the second or whatever the hell this boy's
father called himself was about to get hit with both bar-
rels of her mighty indignation. She would make him
feel like slime. She would negotiate a settlement for
his precocious, lonely son, if it took a hundred hours
of her extremely well-paid time. Pro bono. No charge.
The mother and brothers and sisters were beyond her
control, but by the time she was done, David would have
his father back, she thought resolutely.

She held out her hand. "I will be happy to represent
you," she said as she formally shook his hand. She was
already thinking of a precedent-setting case recently in
Florida that might provide her with ammunition.

Now that the deal had been struck, however, Davey
looked uneasy. "You have to tell me about your fee
first," he said. "I know you're probably expensive, but I
have an allowance. I don't spend much of it. I have fifty

dollars saved now. Is that enough, at least to start?" He held out some crumpled bills. A few pennies trickled to the floor, indicating the savings had been stashed in a piggy bank.

Kate extracted one dollar from the bills. "This is enough to put me on retainer," she said, refusing to hurt his pride by declining any payment at all. "I'll have Zelda give you a form to sign, saying you want me to be your lawyer. That will make everything official."

He looked doubtful. "You got a lot of money in that case I read about."

"It was a percentage of the settlement. We can make the same arrangement, if you like."

"You mean my dad would have to give you money when I get the divorce?"

"Something like that."

"He won't like that."

"They never do," Kate said dryly. "But the court will see to it."

In this case there would be no court and no settlement, if she had anything to say about it. In fact, she figured one stern lecture and some healthy outrage ought to fix things right up. Surely the boy's father wasn't being intentionally cruel. He was probably just a little misguided. Misguided could be straightened out in no time. It usually required no more than a determined logical assault.

"I'm very proud that you chose me to represent you," Kate said. "I will be in touch. I promise." She picked up one of her cards and scribbled on the back. "Take this. If you need me, call. I've given you my home number and my car phone."

He tucked the card carefully in his pocket. His already grave expression grew even more worried. "Will it take long? School starts soon, and if I'm going to have to go to a different one, I'd like to start with everyone else."

"I'm hoping it won't take long at all. You give Zelda your dad's address at work and your phone number at home. I'll get started today."

He hesitated at the door. "What if he gets mad and kicks me out before you can find anybody to adopt me?"

"You don't need to worry about that," she promised.

"But he might," he said, as if this man he obviously adored was likely to turn out to be a tyrant.

Kate didn't believe that for an instant, but she could see that he was genuinely worried about the prospect. With a rare impulsiveness she told him, "If he tries, you can stay with me until this is resolved."

His eyes brightened for the first time. "Do you have any kids?" he asked hopefully.

"No." It was something she'd never really regretted until now. At this moment she wished with all her heart that she could wave a magic wand and provide this kid with a ready-made family.

"Don't you have to ask your husband?"

The ingenuous question made Kate's hackles rise, but she merely shook her head. "No."

"Then that'd be okay, I guess."

In the last few minutes Kate had discovered that her dream child, one that skipped over all the messy stages, wasn't nearly as appealing as she'd thought. David Winthrop personified such a miniature adult. Yet she found that she wanted badly to reach out and muss his hair and tug that tie loose until he looked more like a carefree kid. She wanted to see him smile and to hear him laugh. She wanted to hug him and tell him that everything was going to be okay.

Even so, she held back. She had a feeling David Allen Winthrop, for all his self-possession, was holding himself together by a thread. She would do nothing that might offend the pride and dignity he wore like a protective cloak.

One thing was for certain—she'd never felt such a gut-deep need to make a case turn out right.

"Go home," Dorothy Paul told David Winthrop, scowling ferociously. Her plump, naturally cheerful face softened the impact of the scowl.

"It is Friday night," she reminded him. "The weekend is just beginning. Enjoy it. Go to the beach. Take your son to Disneyland. Go to a ball game."

"Are you through?" David asked, frowning back in annoyance. Obviously he'd given his assistant too much latitude. She thought she had the right to pry like some self-assigned mother hen.

"No, I am not through," she said, ignoring his exasperation. "You're working too hard. You have been ever since Alicia died."

"That's enough!" he snapped. The mere mention of Alicia's name brought back too many painful memories of those last days and weeks before her death. He couldn't relive that time. That was one of the reasons he slept fitfully, usually on the couch in his office. If he allowed himself to crawl back into the bed they had once shared so joyfully, he had unbearable nightmares about her suffering.

His longtime assistant regarded him patiently. "See

what I mean? You would never use that tone with me
if you weren't exhausted."

"I am using that tone with you because I am rapidly
losing my temper."

To his regret, the look she shot him was full of pity,
not fear. "David," she began in that gentle, mothering
tone that was always a prelude to a lecture.

"Not tonight, Dorothy. Please. I'm beat."

"So, go home."

"I can't. I want to finish this one last sketch for the
set for *Future Rock*."

"What makes you think you know what Mars actually looks like?" she said, coming close to peer over
his shoulder.

"I don't, at least not from personal experience," he
countered. "But neither do you, so my guess is as good
as anyone's."

"How many movie set designs have you worked on
in the last six months?" She didn't wait for his reply.
"I'll tell you. Four. That's more than you did in the past
two years."

"I'm building a reputation. I'm in demand. You
should be grateful. It allows me to pay you an exorbi-
tant salary to keep this office running smoothly."

"You're hiding."

"Dorothy!"

To his deep regret, she ignored the warning note in
his voice. "I will not shut up. I have watched you hiding out in this office long enough. It's time to start living again. If not for your sake, then think of Davey."

David ran his fingers through his hair. "Look, I know
you mean well, but I have to handle this the best way
I know how."

"By working yourself into a state of exhaustion? By ignoring your son?" she said.

"I couldn't have said it better myself."

The unfamiliar feminine voice, filled with derision, cut into their conversation.

Startled, David turned to stare at the slender, dark-haired woman standing in the doorway. Her wide-set eyes were flashing fire. Her mouth, which no doubt would be described as lush by advertising standards, had taken a disapproving downturn. She was wearing one of those power suits, dark and businesslike. A flash of hot pink silk at the neckline teased suggestively. He doubted she realized the provocative effect. She struck him as the type who would have disapproved of it.

He completed his survey and decided there wasn't a hint of vulnerability to soften all those hard edges. All in all, she was the kind of woman he genuinely disliked on sight. The exact opposite of Alicia, who'd been warm and gentle and compassionate, all soft curves and femininity.

"Who the hell are you?" he demanded ungraciously. "We're closed."

"Then you should have locked the door," she shot right back, clearly unintimidated by his lack of welcome.

He headed for the door to the workroom. "Dorothy, take care of this. I'll be in back," he said, retreating from the woman and from the unsettling effect she was having on him.

The woman looked ready to leap into his path. Dorothy, damn her, was practically racing for the opposite door.

"See you," his assistant said. "Like you said, we're closed. It's the weekend and I'm out of here."

"You're fired."

She beamed at him. "In that case, don't forget to clean the coffeepot before you go. You know how you hate it when it gets all cruddy after sitting all weekend."

Poised in midflight, David stared after his traitorous assistant. Then he regarded the unexpected visitor suspiciously.

"Are you a reporter?" There had been a lot of them lately, trying to sneak an advance look at the designs for *Future Rock*, which was being touted as the most ambitious futuristic drama since the advent of all the *Star Wars* films.

"No."

"If you're looking for a job, I don't have any available. Dorothy handles everything around here."

"Then I don't envy her," the woman retorted sympathetically.

David dealt with snippy, feminist women like this all the time, women who'd had to claw their way to the top of a sexist entertainment industry. Normally he gave as good as he got. Today he was simply too worn-out to try.

"Lady, obviously you have some sort of ax to grind," he said wearily. "Get it off your chest and leave me alone. I have work to do."

"Don't we all," she countered. "I'll bet mine is less pleasant than yours."

"Then I suggest you get it over with and leave us both in peace."

An odd expression, mostly anger, but touched by sadness, flashed across her face then. David suddenly began to wonder if it was going to be so easy to find peace again, once she'd said whatever was on her mind. He was bothered by a nagging memory of what she'd said when she walked into his office. It had been something that suggested she knew more about him than a stranger should. A reference to Davey?

"I'm here representing your son," she said.

The statement confirmed his recollection but added a startling twist. "My son," he repeated weakly. Then in a rush, he demanded, "Is Davey okay? What the hell do you mean you're representing him?"

She ignored his tone and slowly withdrew a piece of paper that for all the world looked like a legal document. She held it out. Heart thumping, he snatched it from her grasp. When he'd read it through, he regarded her in astonishment. As indignation washed through him, he waved the paper in her face.

"This says that my son has retained you as his legal counsel."

"Good. You can read. That will make things easier."

The cutting remark sailed right past him as he tried to focus on the meaning of the legal document in his hand. He finally met her gaze again, indignation suddenly tempered by genuine bewilderment. "He's a ten-year-old boy, for God's sake. What does he need a lawyer for?"

"Because, Mr. Winthrop, your son would like to file for a divorce." She waited just long enough for that incredible piece of news to sink in, then added, "From you."

Chapter Two

David couldn't have been more stunned if someone had told him that his futuristic sets, all products of a vivid imagination, were accurate depictions of far-off planets down to the last alien being and barren detail. He also felt a powerful surge of helplessness and anger that a total stranger knew more about what was going on in his son's head than he did. Why in God's name hadn't he seen this coming?

Of course, he consoled himself, it was entirely possible that this woman was making the whole charade up. He clung to that premise because it allowed him to retort with a heavy dose of sarcasm.

"You know, lady, I've heard of ambulance chasers in your business, but taking advantage of a ten-year-old boy is outrageous. I could have you brought up on charges."

She didn't bat an eye. He had to admit that impressed him. And worried him.

"What charges?" she inquired with disconcerting calm. "I'm looking after my client's interests. Last I heard, that was what lawyers get paid to do."

"Paid? Now we're getting down to it, aren't we?" he said, almost sorry that this woman was the low-down vulture he'd first predicted her to be. "What's it going to take to get you off your high horse and out of my life? Name your price."

The derisive question brought a furious spark to those incredible, vivid eyes that were the shade of whisky shot through with fire. He couldn't seem to look away, fascinated despite himself by the immediate, passionate response that was evident before she said a word.

"How dare you!" she said, stepping up until they were toe to toe. In her high-heeled pumps, with her chin tilted up defiantly, their eyes were almost level.

"This isn't about money," she said slowly and emphatically, as if she wasn't entirely sure he could grasp plain English. "It isn't about me taking advantage of anyone. It's about a little boy's relationship with his father and, frankly, Mr. Winthrop, I'm beginning to see why he wants out."

Noble words, spoken with conviction. Hurled smack in his face, in fact. David recognized the technique. She was invading his space, trying to intimidate him. She was probably a real hellion in a courtroom, he thought with surprising admiration. Perhaps elsewhere, as well. A little shiver of awareness cut through his own outrage. Analyzing that unexpected reaction kept him from listening too closely to the accusations she was leveling at him, until one snagged his attention.

"…and neglect."

Neglect? He simply stared at her. "I do not neglect my son," he said in a low, furious tone that matched hers for righteous indignation. "He is fed and clothed. He has every toy, every opportunity a boy his age could possibly dream about. He's got more computer games than FAO Schwartz. He plays baseball, football and soccer. He has an Olympic-size pool in the backyard. If he expresses an interest in anything, he's signed up for lessons. Our housekeeper spends more time driving him around town than she does taking care of the house. He goes to the best private school in all of Los Angeles."

"I'm delighted your housekeeper is so dutiful. But frankly, for all the attention you've been paying him yourself, I'm surprised you don't have him in boarding school," she snapped back, clearly unimpressed by everything that had come before.

He cringed at that. He actually had considered boarding school at one point during Alicia's illness, but she had protested vehemently, had made him promise that Davey would never be sent away from home. He regarded this woman—Kate Newton, according to the paper she'd handed him—as if she were some sort of witch for having zeroed in on his single biggest weakness as a parent, his desire to deal with his anguish in his own time, in his own way…alone. And his ardent wish to spare his son from having to cope with one single instant of his own dark depression.

"I think you'd better go now," he said with quiet resolve, refusing to give in to his desire to shout at the top of his lungs. There was a tremendous temptation to take out months of pent-up frustration and grief on a woman he'd just met, because she was tearing open all of the raw wounds that time had not yet healed. He gestured toward the door. "You can show yourself out, I'm sure." He started for the workroom in back.

"We're not through," she retorted, staying right where she was. The low, natural command in her voice halted him in his tracks.

He turned slowly to face her. "I think we are, Ms. Newton. I've heard just about enough of your outlandish accusations. This business about representing a ten-year-old in a divorce proceeding against a parent is garbage. Any court in the country would laugh you out the door."

"Sorry. A child in Orlando won in a similar case just last fall. I'm surprised you didn't read about it. It was in all the papers." She glanced around, apparently taking in the elaborate, futuristic sketches pinned to the cork-board walls for the first time. "Of course, perhaps you don't live in the real world with the rest of us."

"So that's it," he said, finally beginning to get a glimmer of understanding about what had driven this woman to charge into his office like an avenging angel. If it wasn't money, then it had to be publicity. In the long run, one well-placed story in the Los Angeles paper and picked up by the wire services and networks would equal money in the bank.

He shook his head in disgust. "God knows how you zeroed in on Davey, but you probably took some innocent remark he made and latched on to it because you knew the case would generate a lot of publicity. Are you that desperate to get your career off the ground?"

Instead of lashing back with the fury he'd half expected, she simply laughed. To his bewilderment, the amusement seemed genuine. And the sound of that laughter did astonishing things to his pulse rate, stirred it in a way that all that yelling had not.

"Mister, I don't need the publicity," she retorted bluntly. "I get more than my share. That's how your son chose me. He read about my last case in the paper. As for the validity of the agreement David and I have, you have the retainer he signed. I think under the circumstances it would hold up in court." She shrugged. "But if that's not good enough for you, go home and ask him what he wants, ask him why he felt the need to retain a lawyer in the first place. At least, that's one way to assure that the two of you actually sit down and have a long-overdue conversation."

The sarcastic barb hit home, just as she'd obviously intended. Suddenly filled with despair as he realized that this situation wasn't going to evaporate, that she genuinely believed she was in the right, he felt all the fight drain out of him. "You're really serious about all this, aren't you?" he asked wearily.

"You bet I am. I don't like seeing a kid sitting in my office telling me that he and his father have quote, irreconcilable differences, unquote."

David sank down in a chair and regarded her miserably. "He said that?"

"That and a whole lot more," she retorted without a trace of sympathy. "It's been my experience, and Lord knows I've handled enough custody disputes, that kids don't make this sort of thing up. Even so, I'll give you the benefit of the doubt. Is there any truth to his claims? Have you been neglecting him? Shutting him out?"

He struggled with the answer to that one. "I suppose he might see things that way," he admitted eventually, not liking what that said about him as a father. He'd wanted desperately to believe that Davey didn't need him right now, because he wasn't at all sure he had anything left to give.

"Is there another way?" she asked. "What's your perspective?"

"My wife…" He couldn't even bring himself to complete the sentence aloud.

"Davey told me she died," she said, finishing it for him. She said it with the first hint of gentleness she'd displayed since storming into his office.

He regarded her in astonishment. "He actually told you that?"

"Does that surprise you?"

He nodded. "He never talks about it."

"He says it makes you both too sad."

The thought that Davey had recognized his anguish and shared that with this woman penetrated all the barriers he'd slid into place months before Alicia's death. To his amazement, he found himself saying more than he had to anyone in all these long weeks, the angry, tormented words spilling out before he could censor them.

"My wife's death was agonizingly slow and painful," he said. "It was horrifying to watch. It wasn't easy on any of us. I tried to protect Davey from the worst of it. So did Alicia. She insisted on being away from home, in a hospital, for the final weeks. Davey was only allowed to see her when she had her good spells. Those became increasingly infrequent."

"So even before she died, Davey already felt cut off from his mother," she said.

Phrased that way, it sounded like an accusation.

"We both felt it was best for him," David said stiffly.

"How do you protect a child from the fact that his mother is dying?" she asked quietly. "I still think about my father's last days. It's been years since he died and I was an adult when it happened, but I still remember his illness, how frightened I was at the prospect of losing him. I can't block out those thoughts because they might be painful. I know that eventually the good memories will begin to overshadow all the others. Why wouldn't Davey feel the same way?"

She paused for breath and regarded him evenly. "Why wouldn't you?"

David ignored the question because he had no answer for it. He was more fascinated by what she had just revealed about her own feelings. He had a hunch it was far more than she usually shared. He suspected that she, like he, tended to keep a tight grip on messy emotions. It struck him as all the more surprising, then, that she had taken Davey's side with such passion.

His impression of Kate Newton altered slightly. Perhaps she did really care about what happened to Davey, perhaps she was more capable of empathy than he'd given her credit for.

Then again, despite her disclaimers, perhaps she was simply meddling for the potential publicity a case with him at its center would generate. His might not be a household name, but the films he'd worked on were as familiar as those of Spielberg or Disney.

"Look, I appreciate your coming here and telling me about Davey," he said in an admittedly belated attempt to sound gracious and cooperative. "I'll have a talk with him. We'll work it out. Just send me the bill for your time."

She shook her head. "It doesn't work that way. Davey hired me. He has to fire me."

David felt his irritation climb again. Was there no getting rid of this pesky woman, even after he'd conceded that she'd made her point? "No document signed by a kid his age would be legal," he argued. "Drop it. You've done your job."

"I'm not referring to the legalities," she said stubbornly. "I'm discussing moral obligations. I took his case. I'll see it through."

He started to protest, but she cut him off. "I'm sure you mean well, Mr. Winthrop, but I have an obligation to my client. I hope you will talk to Davey. I hope you will work things out, but until he tells me the case is closed and he no longer wishes to divorce you, I'll be sticking around."

She stood up and headed for the door. David was about to breathe a sigh of relief, when she turned and faced him. She glanced pointedly at her watch. "It's nearly eight o'clock on a Friday night, Mr. Winthrop. If you meant what you said, shouldn't you be going home to your son?"

Kate thought the meeting had gone rather well. She'd served up a healthy combination of threats and guilt. With any luck David Allen Winthrop would take a good, hard look at himself and change his ways. He'd certainly looked shaken once he realized that she wasn't going to vanish without a fight, that she was taking his son's claims seriously.

Over the past ten years she had developed a keen eye for an adversary's weaknesses and strengths. As much as she'd been inclined to dislike him on sight, David oking guilty. "I met this lady today. I guess you know out that, huh?"

"Ms. Newton," David said, trying not to sound angry. ow could he blame Davey for taking desperate mea-res? It was his fault his son had gone to see a lawyer.

"Yeah. She said she talked to you." Davey regarded im worriedly. "You're not mad, are you? I had to see er, Dad. I had to."

David hunkered down until they were eye to eye. Are you so upset with me that you really want to leave ome and find a new family?" David asked, unwilling o concede even to himself how much that hurt.

"I guess," Davey said, shifting from foot to foot un-asily.

"Why?"

Davey's expression suddenly turned belligerent. 'You're never here anyway. It probably doesn't even matter to you what I do."

David sighed. "Oh, Davey," he said, his voice filled vith regret. "It matters. I promise you, son. What you o will always matter to me. You're the most precious art of my life."

"Then how come you never spend any time with e?"

Months of hurt were obviously summed up in that e damning question. David found himself reacting f he were under siege. "I do spend time with you," ountered too sharply.

Davy shook his head. "Not like you used to. You're ys too busy. You haven't been to one single game mmer. Most of the time you're at the office. Even you're here, it's like you don't even see me. You're s telling me to be quiet and stuff."

Winthrop had struck her as a man who possessed a great deal of inner strength. He also was a man in pain. She had never known anyone who'd loved so deeply, whose grief was plainly written in the depths of his dark, al-most midnight black eyes. Hopefully she had forced him to examine the price his son was paying while he struggled with his own suffering.

But she had meant what she'd said; she would be sticking to him like a burr until she was certain that her client had his father back again.

She was surprised by the shaft of anticipation that shot through her as she contemplated that prospect. When was the last time she'd even noticed a man in a sexual way? Months? A couple of years? She thought she'd pretty well buried her libido under a schedule that would wilt a well-trained athlete. The fact that she'd been at least marginally aware of David Winthrop's rug-gedly handsome features and the snug fit of his jeans was downright startling.

That worrisome bit of self-awareness was still nag-ging at her when her car phone rang just as she turned onto Pacific Coast Highway heading up to her summer retreat in Malibu.

"Ms. Newton, this is Davey. You know, Davey Win-throp."

"Hi, Davey. What's up?" she asked, trying not to let on that she'd recognized the faint trace of fear in his voice. "Are you okay?"

"Yeah, I guess," he said, his voice flat.

"Davey, what's wrong?"

"I was just thinking, about the case and all. I think my dad is going to be really, really mad when he finds out. Maybe it would be a good idea if I came to live with you now."

She breathed a sigh of relief. So, that's all it was. Regret. She'd never met anyone seeking a divorce yet who didn't struggle with regrets the instant the decision had been made and the first steps taken. The calls came with such frequency that even Zelda had grown adept at all the necessary reassurances.

"Sweetheart, I just saw your father. I don't think he's mad at all." Except at me, she thought to herself. She probably should have crossed her fingers as she boldly lied. "In fact, I think he'll probably be home any minute and that things will start getting back to the way they used to be."

"Really?" Davey said, his voice suddenly filled with excitement. "You mean it?"

"I can't swear to it," she cautioned, "but I think so. Why don't you and I talk on Monday and see how the weekend went, okay?"

"Geez, yes," he said, sounding more like a high-spirited kid again. "I think I hear his car right now. 'Bye, Ms. Newton! Oh, yeah, thanks!"

As the phone thunked in her ear, Kate prayed she hadn't gotten his hopes set too high. If David Winthrop hurt that sweet, savvy kid again, he'd have to answer to her.

As David stepped out of the four-wheel-drive wagon that Alicia had insisted they needed to haul Davey and his friends around, his son came barreling through the front door. The huge, old Bel Air house had once belonged to some star of the silent-movie era, according to the real estate agent, who'd probably tacked an extra

half a million on to the price for that bit ᴏ overpriced as it had been, David had seen t of pleasure that a tie to the glamorous Holl had put in Alicia's eyes, and he'd signed without a second thought.

They had moved in six months before t had been diagnosed. For those six months hi been deliriously happy redecorating, puttin sonal stamp on every room.

David watched his son, and for an instant almost believe that Kate Newton's visit had bᴇ dream. His son looked healthy, vital and eve exuberant as any other ten-year-old. Until he ca shadows in his eyes. Then he knew that there w measure of truth in what the attorney had told him, and his heart ached.

"Hi, Dad! Did you eat yet? Mrs. Larsen i pot roast. She says it's almost ready." A worri creased his brow. "That's your favorite, isn't her it was. She said you might not get home dinner and that everything would go to wa made it anyway."

"Pot roast is definitely my favorite," blinking hard against the tears that alwa when he saw so many reminders of Ali The same reddish blond hair, the same eyes, the same scattering of freckles acr that same crooked smile, flanked by what he now knew about Davey's so ful, impish smile nearly broke his your day?"

The smile faltered slightly. "Oka

"Because I'm working. I have to earn a living," he said, fully aware of the defensive note that had crept into his voice but unable to contain it. Kate Newton had touched off a spark of guilt in him. Davey was fanning it into a roaring blaze.

"Yeah, I guess," Davey said, sounding defeated. He started for the stairs.

"Where are you going? I thought you said dinner was almost ready."

That steady gaze met his. "I don't think I'm very hungry anymore."

As David stared after him, his son plodded up the stairs as if he carried the weight of the world on his narrow shoulders.

Chapter Three

"So, boss, how'd it go with your new client?" Zelda inquired on Monday afternoon when Kate finally reached the office after a long, frustrating morning in court. Zelda grinned. "Filed his divorce papers yet?"

Already irritable, Kate wasn't amused by her secretary's lighthearted attitude. She put aside the stack of messages on her desk and scowled as she searched for the Winthrop file. "It's not a joke, Zelda. Not to me and certainly not to Davey."

Zelda looked hurt by the reprimand. "I know that. But you have to admit it's pretty unusual. You're not really going through with it, though, are you? He's just a kid. That Orlando case might have set a precedent, but I doubt the courts are going to start granting divorce decrees for disgruntled kids the way they do for adults."

"In some cases, they may be justified," Kate said,

thinking of the way David Winthrop had deliberately distanced himself from his son. She wasn't at all convinced he could mend his ways, even if he genuinely wanted too. She'd never much believed in behavioral changes brought on by the threat of legal action, either. They seldom lasted past the final court date.

"You didn't like Davey's father much, did you?" Zelda guessed.

Kate didn't waste time reminding her that she wasn't the one who had to like David Winthrop. He was Davey's father and it was obvious the boy loved him. Her own reaction wasn't all that clear-cut. "You sound surprised," she said.

"It's just that I've read about his father. He sounded like an okay guy. He's some bigwig in the movies. I think he's even won an Oscar."

Kate glanced up from the notes she'd made after her meeting with David Winthrop. "He has? For what?"

Zelda shook her head in dismay. "For a woman born and raised in Hollywood, you don't know zip about the movie business, do you?"

"Who has time for movies? Just tell me. What does David Winthrop do?"

"Set design, sometimes on those comic-book action pictures, but mostly on the big sci-fi movies. His newest one has everyone in town talking. I think it's called *Future Rock*. Every reporter in town is trying to sneak a look at his sketches."

Kate recalled all the designs pinned to his office walls. "Oh, yeah, I guess that's what he was working on when I was there Friday night."

Zelda's turquoise eyes grew round. "You actually got into his office? You saw the designs?"

"I suppose," she said, unable to work up nearly as much excitement over those as she had over the unusually dark and mysterious color of the man's eyes. Still she made a mental note about David Winthrop's professional life. Surely the fantasy worlds he created would be fascinating to a ten-year-old boy. Perhaps those could provide a bridge between him and his son.

"So what'd they look like?" Zelda demanded, perching on the corner of her desk, her face alight with curiosity.

Kate shrugged. "I didn't pay much attention."

Zelda groaned. "Do you realize what it would do for my social life if I could say that I know someone who saw those designs?"

Kate chuckled. "Well, that much is true."

"Sure, but who'd believe me if I couldn't even describe one? Come on, boss, surely you can remember some little detail."

"Afraid not."

Disappointment washed across her secretary's face. "What's he like?" she asked finally. "I mean, really. Be objective."

Kate glanced up again. "Objective about what?"

"David Winthrop," Zelda said impatiently.

"He's…" She searched for a description that would satisfy Zelda's curiosity without stirring her overly active imagination. She didn't dare say anything about the way the man's temper had riled her. She couldn't mention that she'd been intrigued by the sorrow in the depths of his eyes. She settled for *pleasant*. To be honest, the description was far from accurate, but it was definitely innocuous enough to suit her purposes.

"Pleasant," Zelda repeated incredulously. "What

does that mean? Dinner is pleasant. Mediocre movies are pleasant. Men are either fascinating or dull or out-and-out creeps."

Kate laughed. "Those are my only choices?"

"In my experience."

Zelda had vast amounts of experience, which she was willing to share in the form of anecdotes or advice. "Given that, I'd have to say fascinating," Kate conceded, thinking of the layers to David Winthrop that she'd suspected, but hadn't begun to plumb and probably never would.

Zelda's eyes lit up. "Okay, now we're getting somewhere. So you did like him, after all?"

"I didn't say that."

"Sure you did. No man has climbed beyond dull on your rating system for ages now."

Unfortunately Zelda's perceptiveness was sometimes a pain in the neck. So was her tendency to think that Kate's social life was fair game for discussion.

"Zelda, the man is our adversary. We represent his son."

"What does that have to do with whether or not he's a hunk?"

"I did not say he was a hunk," Kate protested.

"You said fascinating. That's close enough."

"Zelda, don't you have work to do?"

"Sure. I always have work to do," she said, not budging.

"Then go do it," Kate prodded.

"Oh," she said, her eyes blinking wide. "Sure." She made it as far as the door before she turned back. "It's a good thing your new stepfather doesn't know about this David Winthrop, huh?"

"What is that supposed to mean?" Kate demanded, though she knew perfectly well what Zelda was getting at. Brandon Halloran had taken a personal interest in her future not ten seconds after he and her mother had spoken their wedding vows. Given his meddling ways, Zelda was right on target. Brandon would latch on to the news of Kate's *fascination* with David Winthrop and start making plans for a wedding.

Kate's gaze narrowed. "He will not hear about this from you, will he?"

"Me?" she repeated innocently. "Never. Of course, the man does seem to have a real nose for romance. You told me how he plotted to marry off his grandson. I'd be real careful what you tell him about your current caseload."

"Brandon and I do not discuss my caseload. He and my mother are on their honeymoon. If we discuss anything at all, it's which European capital they intend to visit next."

"Oh, I guess he doesn't bother to ask you because he's already pumped me for all the information he wants," Zelda added slyly.

Kate's heart plummeted. "He what?"

"Don't worry, boss. I am very discreet."

Kate scowled at her. "See that you are or you will be very unemployed." The last thing she needed was Brandon Halloran taking an active interest in her love life. In fact, she didn't especially want her new stepfather involved in any aspect of her life. She'd had a wonderful father she'd adored. She didn't need a replacement.

For the next three hours Kate returned urgent phone calls, delegating those less pressing to Zelda. At four-thirty, she packed up her briefcase and walked out of her office. "I'm gone for the day."

Zelda regarded her with open astonishment. "It's only four-thirty."

"I have to visit a client."

Her secretary glanced at the appointment book in front of her. "Which client? It's not in here. Boss, how do you ever expect the accountant to keep the billing straight if you forget to write things down on the calendar?"

"This isn't a billable appointment. I'm going to see Davey Winthrop."

Zelda propped her chin on her hand and contemplated her boss with a look that was openly speculative. "Oh, really?"

Kate glowered at her. "I'll check in for messages about six. Don't beep me unless it's an emergency."

"You got it. I don't suppose you're planning to have a cozy mediation meeting between father and son over a snack of milk and cookies?"

"No. I'm sure your hotshot set designer will still be in his office. I'm out of here. Call Davey and let him know I'm on my way."

She found him waiting on the front steps, wearing a neatly pressed cotton shirt and jeans with creases so sharp they could have sliced through butter at the very least. His expression was thoroughly dejected. The weekend had obviously not gone nearly as well as she'd hoped. She took a seat beside him.

"How you doing?" she asked.

"Okay," he said without looking up.

"How'd things go with your dad?"

He glanced at her then. "Not so good. I think he was mad at me for talking to you."

"What makes you say that?" she asked, infuriated by the thought that David Winthrop might have taken her visit out on his son.

"We started to talk when he got home Friday night, but then he got mad and then I got mad." He shrugged. "Nothing's changed. Not really. He acted like everything was all my fault. I think he's really mad about what I did. I knew he would be."

"He was probably more embarrassed than mad. Sometimes grown-ups don't want other people to know about their troubles."

"I guess."

"Did you do anything together?"

"Not really. He stayed at home, though. I guess he's trying."

Staying at home didn't sound like much to her. He obviously wasn't trying hard enough by Kate's standards. "Why don't you and I have dinner together?" she suggested impulsively. "Do you have plans?"

His expression brightened. "Really? You can stay?"

"Absolutely. We'll work out a settlement plan to propose to your dad. Will your housekeeper mind if you invite a guest?"

"Heck no. She always makes a ton of stuff anyway, just in case Dad comes home. He almost never does," he added forlornly.

Mrs. Larsen gave Kate a thorough once-over when Davey introduced them. The lines in her face suggested her mouth was always turned down in a perpetual frown. Still, she was polite enough when she was told that Kate had been invited to stay for dinner.

"I hope you don't mind," Kate said.

"There's plenty," Mrs. Larsen responded succinctly. She scowled at Davey. "Young man, have you washed your hands?" she demanded, hands on ample hips.

Davey grinned, not put off in the least by the older woman's brusque tone. "You ask me that every night."

"Because you never wash until I do," she retorted. "Now get along with you."

When Davey had gone, Kate asked, "Are you sure you don't mind my staying?"

"It'll be good for Davey to have company," the housekeeper said grudgingly. "The boy's alone too much. He eats in the kitchen with me most nights, but I'm afraid I'm not much company by that hour. I like to watch the news and, tell the truth, I'm pretty worn out after taking him this place and that all day long. I'm sixty-five. I don't have the stamina I once did."

Kate sensed this was the start of a familiar lament. "I'm sure a boy Davey's age is always on the go."

"Indeed," Mrs. Larsen said. "Summertime's the worst. It's hot as the dickens here in town, and the boy's into everything. In my day, a child's friends all lived in their neighborhood. Davey's are scattered all over the county." She shook her head, clearly disapproving of the changes in society.

"How do you think Davey and his father get along?" Kate ventured cautiously.

"I'm not one to gossip, miss," Mrs. Larsen replied sternly.

"I'm sure," Kate agreed. "But I am trying to help Davey. To do that I really need to know what you've observed. You're closer to the two of them than anyone."

The housekeeper appeared placated by the explanation. "That's true enough," she said. "I suppose since it's for Davey's sake, I could tell you what it seems like to me. I've been with the family since Davey was a toddler. The two of them adore each other. Always have. That's why it's been so sad, seeing how Mr. David spends all his time at the office these days. He claims it's because he's got more work than he can handle, but the truth of it is that he just can't bear to be in this house."

"You mean since his wife died?"

Mrs. Larsen nodded. "This place was Miss Alicia's choice. Her touch is on every room. I doubt he's admitted, even to himself, how much that bothers him. Asked him once why he didn't move after she was gone. He liked to bit my head off." She shook her head sorrowfully. "I haven't said another word about it. He'll snap out of it one of these days. It'll just take time."

"And in the meantime, Davey's suffering," Kate murmured, more to herself than the housekeeper.

When Davey came back and they were seated at one end of the huge, formal dining room table, Kate suggested they draft a schedule of the time Davey wanted his father to spend with him.

"And he'll have to do what I ask?"

"We'll negotiate," Kate explained. "But yes, I think he'll agree to most of it."

Breakfast every morning, he suggested, glancing at Kate for approval. She nodded and made a note. An hour each evening before bedtime. Saturday and Sunday afternoons. One all-day outing a month on a weekend. The requests seemed pitifully small and yet it was clear from the hopeful gleam in his eyes that they would mean so much to Davey.

As Kate drew up the list, she used her own childhood as a model, then modified that optimum to allow for David Winthrop's current emotional state. It would be pointless to demand that he correct everything overnight. If she could get him to commit to making small changes, the big ones would come eventually. Coaching one of those teams his son was on, perhaps. A weekend fishing trip. An honest-to-goodness vacation.

Kate thought back to the special relationship she had shared with her father. He had always been there for her and Ellen, cheering them on in sports, encouraging them with their schoolwork.

Only recently had she discovered that he hadn't even been Ellen's natural father. Yet he had never openly differentiated between the two of them. If Kate and he had shared a special bond, he had done his best to balance that by spending extra time with her sister. She couldn't imagine what life would have been like if he hadn't played such an integral role in their family.

To Kate's growing irritation, David Winthrop still wasn't home by Davey's bedtime. Mrs. Larsen found them in Davey's playroom, a huge, cheerful room filled with games, long-neglected stuffed animals, a rocking horse, sporting equipment and a state-of-the-art computer. The colorful storybook murals on the wall had obviously been painted with loving attention to detail. Davey had confirmed that his father had done them.

Mrs. Larsen observed Kate and Davey silently from the doorway for a moment before saying firmly, "Bedtime, young man."

"But I have company," he protested, glancing up from the Monopoly board. "Besides, Ms. Newton owes me a bundle. I've loaned her a lot of money and I'm about to foreclose on her last property."

Mrs. Larsen gave Kate an understanding look. "The boy's destined to be a real estate mogul."

"He's sneaky," Kate added. "Had me in hock up to my eyeballs before I realized what he was up to."

The housekeeper's mouth curved faintly in what probably passed for a smile. "Then it's definitely bedtime. We adults have to stick together. Davey, I'm sure Ms. Newton understands that rules are rules around here."

"I certainly do," Kate said with obvious gratitude.

Davey grinned. "You just don't like losing."

"Nope," Kate agreed. "Never have."

He regarded her hopefully. "Could you tuck me in? I don't really need anyone to do that," he added quickly. "But I thought maybe you'd want to, since you don't have any kids of your own."

Kate swallowed hard, touched by the bravado that masked a cry for affection. "I would be happy to tuck you in."

"I have to take a shower first, but I won't be long. You won't leave, will you?"

Kate cast a look at the usually stiff housekeeper and discovered that her eyes were surprisingly misty. Sensing no disapproval from that quarter, she shook her head. "I'll wait right here," she promised.

When Davey had gone, Mrs. Larsen regarded her somberly. "The boy misses his mother. What you're doing for him is a real nice thing," she said stiffly.

She walked out before Kate could respond. Kate wondered if she knew the real reason Kate was around or if she'd simply been referring to her agreement to remain to tuck the boy in.

When Davey came in a few minutes later, he was

wearing pajamas, and his damp, sandy hair was slicked back. He showed Kate his room, pointing out pictures of his softball and soccer teams, the trophy he'd won for football. "We were champions," he told her as he smothered a yawn.

"I'll bet your dad was really proud," Kate said.

Davey shrugged. "I guess. He didn't get to the game. He had to work."

"Things like that happen sometimes," Kate told him, thinking of how many times she had put social engagements on hold because of a backlog of work. It wasn't the first time it had occurred to her that she might have been every bit as distracted from parental responsibilities as David Winthrop, and without the recent loss of a spouse as an excuse.

"I'm sure he wanted to be there," she said, mouthing the platitude in the faint hope that it would reassure Davey.

"He never even asked about it," Davey retorted, then sighed. "I guess he just forgot." He glanced at Kate. "Do you ever wish you had a kid like me?"

Kate felt an odd and definitely unexpected twinge of yearning deep inside. "Yes," she said. She meant it only to reassure him, but as she spoke she realized with amazement that it was true. Right this instant she did wish she had a child who cared whether she was home at night, a child who wanted desperately to share the excitement of accomplishments, a child who would give meaning to an existence that had recently seemed to lack focus.

She smoothed his hair and smiled as his eyelids fluttered closed. "Yes," she said again softly. "I wish that I had a boy just like you."

* * *

It was nearly one in the morning when David finally trudged wearily into the house. He'd meant to get home earlier, but somehow the work had been so engrossing that he'd never even noticed the time.

Who was he trying to kid? He hadn't been able to bear the thought of spending another night trying to figure out how to form a new bond with his son. The weekend had been sheer torture. Davey's patient, hopeful glances had filled him with an intolerable level of guilt and left him wishing that parenthood came with an instruction book. It had never seemed difficult when Alicia was alive. She had planned outings. She had been the driving force that had filled the big old house with laughter.

He walked into the den, tossed his jacket on the back of a chair and poured himself a drink. Only then did he notice Kate Newton, sound asleep in a wing chair in front of the French doors opening onto the patio.

He stood over her, indulging this odd fascination she seemed to hold for him. She was wearing another one of those power suits, this one in a pale gray. A ruffle of ice blue silk edged the deep V neckline. She had kicked off her gray high heels and sat with her legs tucked under her. A slight breeze fanned the cloud of black hair that fell in curling wisps against her cheek. For the first time since he'd met her, she looked utterly feminine and vulnerable. Desirable, he thought, recognizing the sharp awakening of his senses with amazement.

As if she'd been aware of the wayward direction of his thoughts, she snapped awake, blinked and immediately began hunting for her shoes. David grinned as she jammed her feet into them. Cinderella fearful of having to deal with a prince? He held up the decanter of brandy.

"Would you like a drink?"

She shook her head. He shrugged and poured his own, then sank down in the chair opposite her.

For a moment he simply relished the blessed silence and the unexpected, but surprisingly welcome companionship. Then finally, knowing that the topic couldn't be avoided forever, he asked, "What are you doing here?"

"I had a business dinner with my client."

He regarded her in disbelief. "You had dinner here, with Davey?"

"There was no one else around to eat with him," she said.

There was no mistaking the note of censure. "Mrs. Larsen is here," he retorted.

"I'm sure Mrs. Larsen is a lovely woman. I know she's a terrific cook. But she is sixty-five years old and she prefers to eat in the kitchen alone with the TV blaring."

"How would you know that?"

"She told me herself."

David sighed in defeat. "I don't know what you want me to do. I have a career."

"No one's career takes that much time," she countered sharply.

Something in her voice alerted him that even she found a certain irony in that statement coming from her. "Not even yours, Ms. Newton?"

"I don't have a son at home who needs me."

He regarded her curiously. "Who do you have waiting for you at the end of the day?"

"At the moment, my mother's cats. She's off on her honeymoon."

"And as we all know, cats are pretty independent, so you can stay out as late as you want."

"We're not talking about me, Mr. Winthrop." She reached for a piece of paper. "Davey and I drew up a list of ideas."

"Demands."

She shrugged. "Whatever. I think they're reasonable."

David couldn't help being more intrigued than ever by the woman who was championing his son. He'd made a few calls over the weekend, checked her out and discovered that she had exactly the high-profile reputation she'd claimed. He'd also learned that she always represented the woman. He had a feeling there was a story behind that.

"How come you never take the man's side?" he asked, watching closely for her response.

"Because men usually have powerful allies in court, including a good many of the judges. I like to even the odds."

"Why'd you choose this kind of law? Were you getting even with some man who did a number on you?"

Though she didn't answer, he could see by her startled expression that he was right. "Who hurt you so badly, Kate Newton?" he asked. He'd formed the question first out of mild curiosity. Only after it was spoken did he suddenly realize that he genuinely wanted to know.

"It's an old story and hardly relevant," she said indifferently, though there was a faint flicker of pain in her eyes.

"If you're planning to meddle in my life, then I think everything about you is relevant."

"I wouldn't need to meddle if you'd just agree to the terms I've outlined."

He declined to accept the paper she held out. "I never deal with business matters this late. I like to look papers over carefully when I'm fully alert. In this case it would probably be a good idea to have my own lawyer examine them. Who knows what a woman with an ax to grind against men might try to do to entrap me," he said slyly. "Of course, if I knew a little more about you, perhaps that wouldn't be necessary."

She looked disconcerted by the subtle innuendo he'd allowed to underscore his taunt. "Another time," she said, plunking the paper on the table beside him and practically bolting for the door.

Surprised somehow by the skittish response, David followed at a more leisurely pace. "I'll hold you to that."

Outside, striding across a lawn already damp with dew, she slowed down just long enough to remind him, "I expect your response to our requests within the next few days."

"You'll have it tomorrow," he said, then, probably as much to his own amazement as to hers, he added impulsively, "Over dinner."

She halted in her tracks. Her gaze narrowed suspiciously. "With my client?"

David found himself grinning at discovering yet another flaw in that suit of armor she wore. Kate Newton might have the upper hand in a courtroom, but here, on his turf both literally and figuratively, he could clearly rattle her. He realized it delighted him in some indefinable way.

"If you insist," he said, making it an unmistakable taunt.

Clearly refusing to be daunted, she squared her shoulders. "I do, Mr. Winthrop. I most definitely do."

"Then, by all means, Ms. Newton. We will have our chaperon along."

He heard her indignant intake of breath as, chuckling, he turned and went back into the house. For some reason he felt better than he had in ages.

Chapter Four

Normally Kate spent her weeknights at her Century City apartment, only blocks from her office. The location saved transportation time, which was especially critical given the kind of jam-packed schedule she maintained. But after leaving David Winthrop, she was thoroughly wide-awake, far too wired to sleep.

Surely someone with her analytical capabilities could figure out why. It wasn't just the disturbing conversation they'd had before she'd left the house, she decided finally. It was the way she'd felt when she'd awakened to find him studying her so intently. There had been a cozy intimacy, a sweet tenderness to that moment that had struck a responsive chord somewhere deep inside her. Combine that with the way she'd felt when she'd kissed Davey good-night and she could be heading for emotional disaster.

In an attempt to derail herself from that track and to rid herself of that disconcerting sensation, she found herself driving the entire winding length of Sunset Boulevard, emerging finally on Pacific Coast Highway. She turned toward Malibu.

But as she drove along the dark coastal road, nearly deserted at this hour, she couldn't seem to shake the somewhat astonishing reaction she seemed to be having to David Winthrop and to his son. Was she suddenly going through some sort of mid-life crisis? True, her emotions had been topsy-turvy for weeks now, but this sudden maternal yearning and this unexpected awakening of her senses were so entirely out of character she had no idea what to make of them.

She knew all about marriages, the bad ones, anyway. By the time she met most couples, they were engaged in bitter acrimony, all positive aspects of their love wiped out by pain and anger.

By contrast, she'd always considered her own parents' marriage idyllic. Only recently had she discovered it had been more a marriage of convenience. She had been stunned by the revelation that while her father had adored her mother, her mother had secretly harbored a lifelong love for another man, Brandon Halloran. Worse, from Kate's perspective, her father had known about it, had accepted the bargain, willing to play second best to a memory.

All of that had only served to confirm her jaded view that even the best marriages represented nothing but a series of bad compromises. So, with every last illusion destroyed, why was she suddenly experiencing these faint stirrings of need to get involved in a relationship that could only lead to emptiness and pain?

Maybe it was a simple matter of lust, she consoled herself. She was a healthy, active woman whose hormones had been ignored for too long. Perhaps they were simply reminding her of that. And David Winthrop happened to be in the vicinity when the awakening occurred.

That had to be it. That was something she could understand. That was something she could control. She nodded in satisfaction as she parked in the garage of her modest Malibu beach house. She had no intention of indulging those wayward hormones, but it was good to know what she was battling here. She would be on her guard, especially around David Winthrop.

She winced as she recalled how easily he'd detected her motive for insisting that Davey join them for dinner. She might have protested for a month that her client had a perfect right to sit in on their meeting, but neither she nor David would have believed that was all there was to it. She wanted a chaperon, just as he'd accused in that amused tone of voice. And they both knew that the only reason she felt that way was because she was attracted to him and feared that attraction.

In the living room of the beach house, after opening the sliding glass doors to the pounding of the Pacific's surf, she dug through a stack of magazines she subscribed to mainly to have on hand for weekend guests. The most recent issues of a slick, monthly film magazine were buried amidst news weeklies, women's magazines and upscale architecture and gourmet periodicals. Kate flipped through, looking for any mention of David Winthrop or his set designs. Maybe she'd stumble across something that would cast him in such a negative light it would kill this stirring of fascination she felt.

She was skimming the last issue in the stack, one over a year old, when she turned a page and saw his face staring up at her. Eyes alight with excitement, he was standing in the interior of a comic-book world created for a blockbuster that had been released at Christmas. In his denim shirt and jeans, he looked every bit as handsome as the actor who'd played the superhero. In fact, she decided with careful objectivity, he was probably even more attractive with his natural, rugged masculinity, his careless hairstyle, the faint stubble of a beard on his cheeks. He appeared to be a man unaware of his looks, just confident in himself.

What struck her even more, though, was how alive he looked. Enthusiasm had chased away the shadows in his eyes. He seemed perfectly comfortable and happy in this make-believe world of primary colors and cartoon-style structures. It occurred to her, given the date of publication, that the picture had probably been shot before his wife's death, perhaps even before her illness had progressed to its terminal stages.

Kate touched her fingers to the laughing curve of his mouth and wondered if she would ever see this relaxed, lighthearted side of David Winthrop. She had a feeling if he was disturbing her equilibrium now with just a glimmer of his charm, he would be devastating if he ever turned the full force of that smile in her direction.

She was still holding the magazine when she finally fell into a restless, dream-filled sleep in which a larger-than-life hero bearing an uncanny resemblance to David Winthrop saved her from mythical dragons.

What the hell had he been thinking of? David wondered as the dinner hour approached on Tuesday night.

The very last thing he wanted to do was have dinner with a woman whose avowed intention was to separate him from his son. Finding her in his living room in sleepy disarray the night before had momentarily blinded him to Kate Newton's real character.

After she'd gone, he'd looked over that damnable list she'd given him. Couched in legalese, it ordered him to adhere to a militaristic schedule of meetings with his son. He hadn't a doubt in the world that she intended to see that the timetable was enforced.

Dorothy poked her head into his office for their end-of-the-day consultation on the status of all his projects. "You're looking even grumpier than usual," she observed cheerfully as she came in and closed the door. "What's the problem?"

"Kate Newton is the problem," he complained without thinking.

"Who's Kate Newton?" Her eyes lit with sudden awareness. "I don't suppose she's that beauty who stormed in here on Friday night?"

He'd done it now. She'd pester him until she knew every last detail. "The same," he admitted, hoping that would be enough to satisfy her curiosity.

"You never did say what she wanted."

"No," he said pointedly. "I didn't."

Dorothy scowled at him. "I can't help if you clam up. Now who is she?"

"My son's lawyer."

Her eyes widened. "Uh-oh," she said, settling into a chair and putting aside the clipboard with its timetable for the various stages of the *Future Rock* set designs. "Let's hear it."

"Shouldn't we be going over that schedule?"

"In a minute. Now, talk."

David sighed and handed her the latest handwritten document with its list of demands for parental attention. Dorothy read it and nodded approvingly.

"So, what's the big deal?" she asked.

"The woman is trying to legislate my life."

"I've been trying to do that for years. You don't let me get under your skin. What's different about this woman? The fact that she's young and gorgeous and single, if the lack of a wedding ring is any indication?"

He regarded her in amazement. "You noticed whether or not she was wearing a ring?"

"I'm always on the lookout for single women for you. My goal in life is to see you happily involved again," she said complacently.

Those words, coming from a woman with Dorothy's determination, sent a shudder of dread through him. He decided she needed to understand that Kate Newton was not the woman for him.

"Did you even read that thing?" he demanded. "If I'm not careful, she'll be telling me which jobs to take."

"Maybe that would keep you from taking on too damn many," Dorothy shot right back. "Somebody has to slow you down. I'm certainly not getting through to you. And that agent of yours would have you working twenty-four hours a day just so his piece of the action would climb."

"Dammit, don't you see? She's trying to separate Davey and me."

"From the looks of this, I'd say the opposite is true," she countered in that logical, reasonable tone that made him want to chew nails. "David, all she's asking is that you spend more time with your son. What's so terrible about that? You and Davey used to spend all your spare time together. It's no wonder he's feeling neglected."

David sighed and rubbed his temples. His head was pounding. "I know," he admitted.

Dorothy regarded him curiously. "Are you sure there's not something more to your reaction? Are you feeling the slightest bit disloyal to Alicia because you're attracted to this woman?"

Leave it to Dorothy to nail it, he thought ruefully as he recalled the regrettably powerful and very masculine response he'd had to Kate Newton the night before. For one brief instant there, he'd actually found himself flirting with her. And enjoying it!

Almost the instant her car had pulled out of his driveway and he'd turned toward the house, he'd been weighed down by guilt. He'd vowed on the spot to call this morning and cancel the dinner invitation. He'd worked himself into a state over the paper Dorothy held, using indignation over that as an excuse for bowing out.

She regarded him sympathetically. "You're a widower. You have been for six months now. Being attracted to a woman is not a sin," Dorothy told him gently, obviously operating on the assumption that she'd guessed the truth. "Come on, boss. Alicia wouldn't want you to stop living. You know that. She'd want you to grab whatever happiness you can find."

Happiness in the form of Kate Newton, an attorney with ice in her veins? He struggled just a little with the concept. And yet, she definitely represented living. Everything about her suggested that she was vibrant and exciting and passionate, even if a little too driven and rigid for his taste. For a time she might make him feel alive. She might chase away the memories of death and mortality. But then what?

David sighed. "I know that's what Alicia would want," he said, agreeing bleakly with his assistant. "But sometimes living is just too damned painful."

The conversation with Dorothy had accomplished one thing, though. David decided against canceling the dinner with Kate and Davey. It would have been the cowardly way out and probably would have added ammunition she could use later, if she pursued this damnable divorce.

With his stomach tied in knots, he approached the informal restaurant she'd chosen in Century City. He blamed the upset on trepidation. The truth of the matter was, though, that it was probably anticipation that had him nervously pacing the outdoor mall as he watched for Kate and Davey to arrive. She had insisted on picking up his son, almost as if she feared he might exclude the boy at the last minute. The realization that she obviously felt she needed protection from him cheered him slightly. It evened the playing field a bit.

When he spotted the pair at last, his heart seemed to climb into his throat. Still the consummate professional, she was wearing a bright red suit accessorized with a twist of chunky, expensive gold at the neckline. Her hair had been pulled back into what had probably started as a neat style. Now stray wisps had tugged free to create wayward curls.

And, though she looked as if she were dressed to step into a courtroom or the pages of a career woman's magazine, the expression on her face as she listened to Davey was what stunned him. She looked genuinely entranced, that generous mouth of hers curved into a smile, her eyes bright with amusement. Whatever his son was saying obviously delighted her. When she laughed, the pure, musical sound carried to him, and he regretted more than he could say that he hadn't been in on the joke.

He walked slowly toward them, feeling like an outsider. When she glanced up and saw him, the sparks in her eyes didn't die as he'd anticipated. Instead, her smile broadened to include him, a touch of sunshine that warmed him.

Basking in that smile could be dangerous, he thought for a fleeting instant, and then he simply responded to its sheer magic. Cares slid away and for this moment, his family was whole again, untouched by sorrow, united by love and laughter. He was a man used to living in a world that made fantasy seem like reality. He realized with a start that he wanted this particular illusion to last more than he'd wanted anything in a very long time.

"Hey, Dad, did you know that Kate has a house at the beach?" Davey said excitedly. "She said we could use it sometime. Wouldn't that be great?"

David met her gaze and wondered at the generosity. "It would be great," he agreed. "But I'm sure Ms. Newton likes to get away herself on the weekends."

"We could all go together," Davey said eagerly. He glanced at Kate. "Is there enough room?"

"Sure," she said.

Despite the quick response, David caught the sudden uneasiness in her eyes. He doubted if her impulsive offer had taken into account this possible turn of events. Lazy days, sun-kissed sand, sparkling blue Pacific…and the two of them. It was the most seductive arrangement he could imagine. If dinner had made her nervous, he could just imagine her reaction to this proposal.

He couldn't resist giving her a long, level, considering look that left no doubts about the provocative direction in which his imagination had roamed. The color that crept into her cheeks almost matched her suit.

"I'm starved," she said in a breathless rush. "Shall we go inside? I made the reservation for seven."

Over their meal, it was Davey's chatter that filled the silences. David hadn't felt quite so tongue-tied in years. As for Kate, he had the feeling she had deliberately withdrawn in an effort to encourage conversation between father and son. Either that or she was still in shock over his deliberately flirtatious glance earlier. He was a little shaken by it himself.

"Shouldn't we discuss this proposal you two have made?" he asked finally, drawing the paper from his pocket.

Davey glanced nervously toward Kate. "It was just some ideas," he mumbled.

"Breakfast every morning?" David read. "I thought you liked sleeping in, during the summer."

"Yeah, I guess."

"Why don't we agree that we'll have breakfast together on the weekends, at least until school starts? Then we'll aim for every day."

Davey's expression brightened. "You promise?"

"I'll put it in writing," David agreed with a pointed look at Kate. "Now, about bedtime. I think I can arrange my schedule to be home on time most nights. I'll even try to make it for dinner."

"Every night?" Kate inquired.

David shook his head. "I have to be realistic. Let's

aim for two nights, plus weekends." He regarded her evenly. "Do you plan to be around to check up on my follow-through?"

"It's my client you have to satisfy, not me. If he tells me you're living up to the agreement, that will be good enough for me."

"Too bad," he found himself taunting. "I'd try harder if I knew I'd find you all curled up in my chair the way I did last night."

She scowled at him. "Keep reading. There are more requests."

"Ah, yes, the once-a-month outings." He glanced at Kate and couldn't resist another attempt to provoke that embarrassed tint in her cheeks. "Why not start with that visit to the beach?"

"Yeah!" David chimed in enthusiastically.

Kate looked stunned.

David regarded her innocently. "Are you busy this weekend?"

She swallowed hard. "This weekend…" Her words faltered. Then her chin came up and she shot him a determined smile. "This weekend would be fine."

No sooner had she agreed than David wondered if he'd lost his mind. Not three hours earlier he'd sworn to stay as far away from this woman as he possibly could. Now he'd committed himself to spending an entire weekend in her company. It was only minimal consolation that she didn't look any more thrilled about the prospect than he did. Only Davey looked ecstatic.

Suddenly David wanted to get out of the dark restaurant and into the twilight and fresh air. "Why don't we have ice cream for dessert?" he suggested. "We can get cones outside."

"All right!" Davey said. "Can I go now?"

"Sure. Just don't go anywhere else. Get the cone and sit at one of the tables right there. We'll be out as soon as I've paid the bill."

Davey grabbed the money his father held out, then took off.

"I could go with him," Kate offered, glancing a little desperately in the direction Davey had gone.

"No. Actually, I wanted a minute alone with you."

Troubled eyes met his. "Oh?"

"I wanted to apologize. I backed you into a corner."

"Yes," she said bluntly. "You did." She shook her head. "No. I made the suggestion in the first place. I guess I just thought you and Davey would go there alone."

"We could still do that," he offered reluctantly. "We would have more fun, though, if you were there. At least, I know I would."

She studied him intently. Obviously she had caught something in his voice, something he hadn't intended to convey with the mildly provocative comment.

"You say that almost as if you're afraid to be alone with your son," she said finally. "It's not the first time I've noticed that. Were you always so uncomfortable around Davey?"

Startled by her insight, David sighed. "No," he admitted. "We used to do a lot of stuff together. But ever since Alicia died, I don't know what to say to him."

"He's a person. Talk to him about school. Talk about the weather."

"That would be faking it. We both know the one thing we should be talking about is his mother."

"Then for God's sake, talk about his mother," she

said with obvious impatience. "Do you know how desperately he needs to share his heartache with you?"

Raw anguish ripped through him as he struggled with what should have been a simple request. He deliberately took his time counting out money to pay the bill. Then he cast one quick look into Kate's eyes and caught the lack of comprehension.

"I can't," he said simply and walked away, leaving her staring after him.

Chapter Five

Kate wanted to sit right where she was until hell froze over. She wanted to do almost anything, in fact, except walk out of the restaurant and join Davey and his father. She wasn't sure she could bear seeing that expression of anguish on David's face.

Worse, to her amazement and regret, she realized that for a few brief moments she had allowed herself to indulge in the fantasy that this was her personal life, not her job. Unlike all those business dinners she had four and five nights a week, sitting here with David and his son tonight had given her a small hint of what it might be like to be part of a normal, ordinary family.

Then Alicia's name had entered the conversation and reality had intruded with the force of a hurricane-strength wind.

That's what happens when you lose your objectivity, she chided herself. She had set herself up like a ten-pin in a tournament of bowling champions. There was no way not to get knocked down. The irony, of course, was that it had been a fantasy which might never have crossed her mind a week ago, before a desperate, lonely boy had walked into her office.

Forcing herself to put her own bruised feelings aside, she left the restaurant and went in search of her client… and his father. She found them sitting at a table in front of the ice-cream counter. The last rays of sunlight filtered through an evening haze. A breeze had kicked up, chasing away the last of the day's dry heat. Davey's expression was glum. His father's, if anything, was even more morose, an echo of her own feelings.

It had certainly turned into a swell evening, Kate thought miserably. She forced a smile. "Where's my ice cream?" she demanded, feigning a fierce scowl. She glanced at David. "You don't have any, either. Did Davey eat all they had?"

The weak joke didn't even earn a halfhearted smile.

"I was waiting for you," David said. The response was politely innocuous, but there was a questioning look in his eyes as if he wasn't sure what to make of her teasing or the strained note behind it. "Name your flavor."

"Heath bar," she said at once. "How about you? I'll get it." She wanted another minute to gather the composure that seemed to slip a notch every time she looked into David Winthrop's eyes. To her relief, he didn't argue with her.

"Cherry Garcia."

"Cone or dish?"

"Cone," he said.

When she came back to the table with the two ice-

cream cones, Davey and his father were engaged in a
tense discussion that broke off the minute she arrived.
She handed David his cone and sat down, concentrating
on the rapidly melting ice cream. She tried to catch all
the drips before they slid down the cone toward her already sticky fingers. It was hopeless. She glanced over
and saw that David was having the same problem. As
he caught a drip with the tip of his tongue, he gazed into
her eyes and smiled. Kate's heart thumped unsteadily
at the innocently provocative gesture. She had to force
herself to look away.

It was several minutes before she realized that Davey
hadn't said a word since she'd joined them. She glanced
at him. His arms were folded across his middle and, if
anything, his expression had turned mutinous.

"What's the deal, kiddo?" Kate inquired, wondering
what on earth they'd fought about.

He glanced at his father with a belligerent look, then
said, "Dad says it was rude that we invited ourselves to
your house. He doesn't think we should go."

Relief and dismay shot through Kate in equal measure. Then she caught the unhappiness in Davey's eyes
and forced herself to put her own conflicting emotions
aside and focus on his feelings. He'd already suffered
more than enough disappointments in his young life.
No matter how trapped she'd felt earlier, she wouldn't
add one more by reneging on the invitation. She looked
directly at David.

"I want you to come," she said.

His expression told her nothing, but he nodded finally as if he, too, was aware that his son needed the
promise of this weekend to be kept. "If you insist," he
responded, his tone as cool and unemotional as her own.

Kate stood up, anxious to escape the escalating tension that seemed to be choking off her ability to breathe. "I really need to get some work done tonight, if you two will excuse me." She met David's gaze. "I'll call you about this weekend."

When she looked back as she turned the corner, father and son were sitting silently exactly where she'd left them. It was becoming increasingly obvious that she could throw the two of them together all she wanted, but getting them to have a real relationship again just might be beyond her control. There weren't many things in her life about which that could be said. She discovered she didn't like it.

The phone was ringing when Kate walked into her apartment. She debated letting the service pick it up, then decided that would only delay the inevitable. Whoever it was, she would wind up having to call them back.

She grabbed for the phone on its third ring. "Yes, hello."

"Kate, it's Ellen," her sister said unnecessarily. "Are you okay? You sound out of breath."

"I just ran in the door," she said, wishing she had let the phone go on ringing after all.

Ever since she had learned the whole story behind Ellen's conception, Kate had felt awkward around her older sister. Half sister, she corrected. Now their mother was married to the love of her life, Ellen's natural father, Brandon Halloran. Ellen, after her initial shock and anger over years of lies and deception, seemed to have adjusted beautifully to having a new father. In fact, she was all caught up in the drama and romance of their mother's separation from Brandon and his intensive search to find her again. Despite everyone's best efforts, however, Kate couldn't help feeling like a resentful outsider.

"I tried to get you earlier," Ellen said. "I wanted to ask you to dinner."

"Sorry," she said, thinking of the unanswered messages she'd allowed to accumulate because she couldn't think of what to say to Ellen these days. "I couldn't have come anyway. I had dinner with a client."

"You work too hard."

"What else is new?" Kate stated with a shrug, kicking off her shoes and wiggling her toes in the cool plush carpet. There was something pleasantly sensuous about the act. "That's the kind of business I'm in."

"Ever think about getting out?" Ellen asked. "Getting married? Settling down?"

"No," Kate said, though less firmly than she might have a few weeks or even a few days ago.

"You should. Dealing with all those unhappy people all the time can't be much fun. Anyway, how about tomorrow? Just you and me and Penny," she suggested, referring to Kate's precocious niece, who displayed every indication of turning into a damn fine trial lawyer herself, if her nosy interrogations into everyone else's personal lives were any clue. Kate didn't think she was up to that sort of teasing scrutiny.

"I really can't, Ellen. This week is jammed up."

"This weekend, then," her sister suggested. The casual persistence was underscored by a hint of genuine dismay over Kate's constant excuses. It was evident Ellen saw right through them.

"I'm having a client out to the beach," Kate said, phrasing it in the most innocuous way she could think of. "Maybe next week." To shift her sister's attention to something else, she asked, "What have you heard from Mother?"

There was a hesitation, as if Ellen wanted to call her on making yet another excuse, but then she sighed. "She phoned this morning from Rome. Can you believe it? Our mother is turning into a world traveler at this stage in her life. Isn't it great?"

"Great," Kate echoed, suddenly feeling even more depressed. "Look, I've got to run. I have a ton of paperwork to get through tonight. I'll be up until all hours."

Ellen didn't respond for a full minute. If it had been anyone else, Kate might have hung up. Instead, she waited.

"Kate, we're going to have to talk about it one of these days," Ellen said finally.

"I don't know what you mean," Kate said stiffly. "Good night, sis."

She hung up hurriedly and then faced the fact that in one way at least she and David were very much alike. Neither of them seemed able to face the painful truths in their lives.

At five o'clock on Thursday Kate sat at her desk, staring at her calendar and trying to work up the courage to place the call to David Winthrop that would finalize their weekend plans. Zelda found her with her hand in midair over the phone.

"Don't you dare get on that phone again," her secretary ordered. "We have things to discuss, and I've been trying to catch up with you all day."

Grateful for the reprieve, Kate sat back. "What's up?"

"The Winthrop case. What's happening?"

It was the last thing Kate wanted to discuss, especially with Zelda. "Things are moving along," she said evasively. "The father has agreed to spend more time with Davey."

"The father," Zelda mimicked. "Last I heard, the man had a name."

"David," Kate said dutifully.

"Do you have another meeting scheduled with the two of them?"

"Actually, that's what I was calling to arrange when you came in."

"Don't let me stop you, then," Zelda said, though she didn't budge from right where she could listen to every last word of Kate's end of the conversation. Apparently her finely honed instincts for gossip were operating in overdrive.

"Haven't you ever heard of privacy?" Kate grumbled.

"I've had four roommates. What do you think?"

Kate rolled her eyes.

Zelda observed her lack of action and quickly put her own particular spin on it. "If this call were going to, let's say, Jennifer Barron, would you have this same problem about me being in the room?" she inquired, referring to another of Kate's clients.

"You've made your point," Kate retorted. "Now leave."

"Not until you explain why you want to talk to David Winthrop in private."

"If I felt like explaining, then I wouldn't need the privacy, would I?"

Zelda grinned. "Fascinating." She moved reluctantly toward the door. "How about if I leave this open just a crack? I probably couldn't pick up every word."

"I don't want you picking up any words," Kate retorted.

"It gets better and better. You know I could call and schedule the appointment for you. It would save you the trouble."

"Zelda, there are at least a dozen executive secretaries in this building alone who could replace you in less time than it's taking you to leave this room," Kate warned, fully aware that they both knew she was grossly exaggerating. No one could replace Zelda. The threat lost a little of its oomph because of it, but Zelda dutifully closed the door. All the way.

Kate called David's office. She immediately recognized the voice of the woman who answered. It was the same one she'd met the first night she'd charged in there.

"Hi, it's Kate Newton. Is Mr. Winthrop available?"

"Why, Ms. Newton, hello," the assistant said in a tone that rivaled Zelda's for openly friendly curiosity. "I'm Dorothy Paul, his assistant. He's in the back using the chain saw. He'll never hear me buzz. I'll have to get him. Do you mind waiting or shall I have him call you back?"

"I'll wait," she said, unable to hide a grin at the image the woman had raised by mentioning the chain saw. It was fortunate Kate knew what David did for a living. The reference might be very disconcerting for anyone who didn't.

She heard an intake of breath and realized that David's assistant was still on the line.

"Before I get David, I hope you won't mind me butting in, but I wanted you to know that I think you're good for him." She laughed. "He'll kill me for telling you that."

Kate chuckled despite herself. "Actually, I think you couldn't be more wrong. He thinks I'm a nuisance."

"Exactly," Dorothy said. "No one else has braved that don't-bother-me front he puts on."

"Except you," Kate guessed.

"I am fifty years old, fifteen pounds overweight and happily married. He has never looked at me the way he looks at you."

"With disdain," Kate retorted. "I should hope not."

"No. With fascination," she insisted. "Don't give up on him."

Kate felt it important that she clear up Dorothy Paul's misconception about her relationship with David. "I don't think you understand. Our dealings are strictly professional."

The woman chuckled. "Yes. That's what he says, too," she said, her skepticism evident. "I'll get him now."

While she waited, Kate told herself that she had successfully squelched any personal fascination with David Winthrop. There was no reason at all to view the coming weekend as anything more than three acquaintances relaxing and getting to know each other better. It was not the first time she had invited clients or colleagues to visit the beach house. That was one of the reasons she'd bought it in the first place, in fact.

David's grumbled hello sent goose bumps scurrying over her flesh. The effect immediately put an end to any illusions she might have been manufacturing about him being any other business associate.

"I promised to call about the weekend," she said, sounding as if she were the one who'd had to dash for the phone.

"Right," he said matter-of-factly. "This really isn't necessary, you know."

"I think it is."

"Okay, then. What works for you?"

"Can you get out there about seven or seven-thirty tomorrow night? I'll pick up some steaks and we can barbecue on the deck."

"We'll be there. Don't worry about wine or beer. I'll bring that. Anything else you'd like me to bring?"

"No. I keep it pretty well stocked. There are plenty of games and things for Davey, too. There's even a basketball hoop over the garage, if you want to play."

"You entertain a lot of kids?"

"My sister's girls."

"They play basketball?"

"No," she retorted. "I do."

He chuckled. "Now there's a challenge if ever I've heard one."

"Take me on, if you dare," she shot back, then hung up while their shared laughter was still ringing in her ears. Suddenly, despite the loud clang of warning bells, she could hardly wait for the weekend to arrive.

She called Zelda back into her office. "Can you clear my calendar for tomorrow?"

"Any particular time?"

"All day."

Zelda's mouth dropped open in astonishment. "The whole day? Are you sick?"

"No. I just have some things I need to do. I thought I'd take a long weekend at the beach to catch up."

As if she'd already linked Kate's request with that call to David Winthrop and sniffed romance as a result, Zelda immediately grabbed the appointment book and scanned the entries. "You don't have anything in court. No depositions. It looks to me as if I can reschedule your appointments."

"Do it," Kate said, ignoring the speculative gleam in her secretary's eyes. Going to Malibu first thing in the morning would give her a chance to make sure the house was in order.

It would also give her time for a long run on the beach, maybe a swim. Hopefully a little exercise would put an end to all these ridiculous fantasies before the object of those fantasies turned up.

Chapter Six

Running didn't help. Neither did swimming. By seven o'clock on Friday night, Kate was as jittery as a teenager on her first date. Why, she wondered, had an intelligent, cynical woman become attracted for the first time in years to the one man least likely to offer himself heart and soul to a relationship? A man whose behavior toward his son represented the epitome of irresponsibility, if not outright neglect?

She tried telling herself it wasn't attraction so much as determination to help Davey in any way she could. If that meant she had to insinuate herself into his father's life to assure that David and his son forged a new bond, then that's what she would do. She almost believed the explanation. It sounded noble, professional, compassionate. And, in fact, that much really was true. However, despite all the claims she'd made to Dorothy Paul, it wasn't the whole truth by any means.

It was the lost, faraway look in his eyes, she decided after careful analysis. That sorrow hinted at a depth of emotion that some part of her desperately wanted to experience, at the very least wanted to comprehend. And maybe, in some small measure, it was his unavailability. Perhaps she was merely responding to the challenge of conquering that had appealed to men and women from the beginning of time.

The sun was sinking in a rare clear sky when she heard a car pull into the space next to hers along the narrow beachfront road that forked off Pacific Coast Highway. Barefoot and wearing loose white pants and an oversize rose-colored sweater, she walked along the side of the house to the back and opened the gate. She was just in time to see Davey bound around the trendy four-wheel-drive wagon parked next to her expensive low-slung sports car. The ultimate Hollywood, two-car family, she thought wryly, one practical vehicle, the other fast and sexy.

"This place is the best," Davey announced, his eyes sparkling as he bounced up and down on his sneakers as if he couldn't quite wait for the starting gun in a race.

She grinned at his exuberance. "You haven't even seen it yet."

"But I can tell already. Dad says you have a basketball hoop. Can I play? You and me against him, okay? He said you had games, too. What kind? Maybe we could play Monopoly after dinner."

Kate grinned at his nonstop plans. "If you think I'm playing Monopoly with you again, you're crazy, kiddo.

You're obviously destined to be some sort of real estate tycoon. My ego can't take that kind of bashing."

Just then David emerged from the car. He was wearing the same style of snug jeans he always wore, topped by a polo shirt in a soft jade green. Somehow, though, he already looked more relaxed, as if he had caught some small measure of his son's excitement.

He surveyed her from head to toe, a surprisingly approving glint in his eyes. That glint told Kate she'd made a mistake when she'd dressed, after all. She'd thought the loose-fitting clothes would be less provocative.

"I suspect your ego could withstand all sorts of assaults," he taunted.

The surprisingly lighthearted comment seemed to set the tone for the day. Kate's mood shifted from anxious to something closer to anticipation.

"Surely losing a game to a mere boy wouldn't be enough to shatter your self-confidence," he added.

"Has your son ever bankrupted you twenty minutes into a game of Monopoly?" she inquired dryly.

"Afraid not. I taught him everything he knows."

Kate scowled as both males grinned unrepentantly. "How about cards? I'm very good at rummy."

"We have a whole long weekend to discover all the things at which you excel," David retorted, his speculative gaze leveled on her.

Whatever distance he'd managed to put between them the other night went up in flames. The innuendo sent a shiver straight down her spine. Kate wasn't sure which startled her more, the fact that he'd said it or her own immediate and unmistakably sensual response.

He glanced at her car, and his eyes lit up with an excitement that almost matched Davey's for the house. "Obviously one thing at which you excel is your taste in cars. This is a beauty."

He touched the finish with a certain reverence. Kate found herself envying the sleek metal bumper. He leaned down and peered inside.

"What's it do?"

Kate assumed he was referring to speed. "On our freeways?" she said dryly.

"Yeah. You have a point." With obvious reluctance he turned away from the car. "Davey, have you got all your things?" he asked.

For the next few minutes, they were busy unloading the car and settling the two guests into their rooms.

"If you're hungry, I have dinner set to go," Kate said as the long, empty evening stretched ahead of them. She wanted to cram those hours with activity so that lingering glances could be kept to a minimum, so that these little thrills of pleasure that shot through her at having the two of them there wouldn't escalate into something more. There had to be some way to keep the weekend from ending with her yearning for things that could never be.

"Can we wait?" Davey begged. "I want to see the ocean. Please."

David shook his head. "You'd think you'd never seen the Pacific before."

"It's been a long time, Dad. A really long time. It was before…" His voice trailed off and his father's face went still.

Kate leapt into the sudden silence. "I think a walk on the beach would be the perfect way to work up an appetite. Let's go before it gets too dark."

With Davey running on ahead of them, Kate fell into step beside David. He'd shoved his hands into the pockets of his jeans. The sea gulls circled lazily overhead and a fine mist blew into their faces as they strolled by outrageously expensive homes crammed on the edge of a cliff. Most clung to just enough land to qualify as a homesite, with massive pilings shoring up the bulk of the house. Kate shivered as she considered what was bound to happen one of these days when a violent storm struck.

"Cold?" he asked, misjudging the cause of her trembling.

"No. I was just thinking of what a bad storm would do to this property. Actually, I like chilly nights like this," she confessed. "It's so miserably hot in the city this time of year that I find this thoroughly refreshing. Some nights there's enough briskness in the air to justify a fire. That's always seemed really decadent to me somehow."

He studied her intently. "You love it out here, don't you?"

She nodded. "You sound as if that surprises you."

He shrugged. "I would have thought the rhythm of the city suited you more."

She laughed. "I love that, too. I guess I'm just greedy. I want it all. I want days that are so crowded with work I can't even find time to breathe, and then I want leisurely, do-nothing days that require nothing more than plunking into a chaise longue with a good book and a view of the ocean."

"Be honest," he said. "When was the last time you really had a relaxing, do-nothing day?"

Kate searched her memory. She couldn't think of one, at least not recently.

"Stumped you, didn't I?" David said.

His laughter caught on the wind. He seemed delighted by the discovery that she apparently never followed the exact advice she was giving him.

"I don't have a son around who needs my attention," Kate reminded him.

"Is that the only reason for time off? What about just restoring your own energy, pampering yourself?"

"No time," she admitted.

"Then perhaps this weekend will turn out to be a lesson for both of us," he said, his expression softening. "Now tell me what else you would do, if you really took a vacation. Mountain climbing? That seems like the sort of challenge that would appeal to you."

"Afraid not. I prefer my dangers to come in the form of unexpected evidence. What about you? Mountains? Seaside?"

"No real preference. I live in a world of make-believe most of the time. Always have. I guess what always kept me grounded in reality in any way at all was family. It didn't seem to matter where we were."

"Were you an only child?" she asked, studying him with new perspective.

He regarded her with obvious amazement. "Now, how would you guess a thing like that?"

"It's always seemed to me that an only child might spend a lot of time making up fantasy worlds. Am I right?"

"You're right. And the make-believe worlds kept me from being lonely. Maybe that's why I retreated into one job right after the other once Alicia died. Those worlds are safe, protected. And they're mine to control. I can make them be anything I want them to be."

Control, she thought. There it was again. It seemed to be something they were both intent on having in their lives. "But you have a son, and he didn't get to go along," she reminded him.

"No," he said regretfully. "I suppose he didn't."

She thought she heard real sincerity in his voice and saw an opportunity to forge yet another connection between him and his son. "Could I make a suggestion?"

He grinned at her hesitance. "Nothing's stopped you before."

"If it's still too painful for you to live in the real world full-time, couldn't you take Davey into your world occasionally? I'm sure he would be fascinated to see the sets you create coming to life on a soundstage. He'd probably be the envy of all his friends for getting a sneak peek at movies that are already being talked about."

To her relief he exhibited absolutely no resistance to the idea. In fact, he pounced on it.

"Would you come along?" he asked lightly. "Would you be interested in seeing my worlds?"

"If you and Davey wanted me to."

He shook his head. "That's not what I asked. I asked if *you* wanted to come along."

"Yes," she admitted, leaving it at that. She didn't want him to see how very curious she was becoming about everything that made him tick. She pushed for a firm commitment, knowing just from what she'd observed of him so far that once he'd made one, he wouldn't back down. "Next week?"

"I'll set it up." His gaze was suddenly warm and approving. "I'm beginning to think it's entirely possible that I had you pegged all wrong," he said slowly, stop-

ping and turning to face her. He reached out to brush
the windblown wisps of hair from her face.

Kate's breath snagged in her throat. "Meaning?"

"I thought Davey was just another high-profile case
for you, but you honestly care about his feelings, don't
you?"

As he spoke, his thumb almost absently caressed her
lower lip. Even if she'd been able to form a coherent
thought, she wouldn't have risked speaking and breaking that gentle contact. She nodded finally.

"Why?" he asked, lowering his hand to his side with
obvious reluctance. He looked almost as shaken as she
felt.

Kate shrugged, unable to form a clear response. "I
don't really know," she said finally. "He touched me in
a way no client has before. I suppose all the people I
usually represent are old enough to bear some responsibility for whatever plight they find themselves in. At
least they chose their spouse. Davey didn't get to pick
his parents. I figure he got a raw deal losing one at such
a young age. I couldn't bear to see him losing the other
one, especially when it didn't have to be that way."

David's gaze lingered and then he nodded. "Point
taken."

She regarded him intently. "I hope so, David. I really hope so, for Davey's sake and for yours. It seems
to me you have a pretty terrific kid."

"Yeah," he said, his gaze fixed on the boy who was
playing tag with the waves up ahead. "Yeah, I do."

David wasn't sure what name to put on the feeling
that was stealing through him. Peace? Contentment?
Maybe even a smidgen of anticipation?

Davey had trounced all over both him and Kate playing Monopoly. David blamed it on being distracted. He hadn't been able to keep his eyes off Kate all evening. Now, with an exhausted Davey tucked in, they were alone. Each of them had retreated into work, after a flurry of nervous apologies.

He glanced over at her again. Her cheeks were pink, flushed first by their brisk walk on the beach, then by the color that rose every time she sensed him staring at her. Her hair was carelessly tousled in a way she would never have allowed it to be in the city. Whatever makeup she'd worn earlier had faded, until only her natural beauty showed through. Her bare feet, the toenails painted a soft, feminine shade of rose, were tucked under her. Her lips, curved down in a thoughtful frown as she concentrated on some legal paperwork, suddenly seemed exceptionally kissable. The script he'd been sent for an upcoming feature film couldn't begin to compete for his attention.

He fought against an onslaught of guilt. Dorothy's words came back to him, a reminder that Alicia would never begrudge him a future filled with whatever happiness he could seize for himself and his son. Still, a lawyer? Especially one with a go-for-the-jugular reputation?

And yet all night he had been forced to reassess Kate Newton. She'd been constantly surprising him, both with her compassion for Davey and with her insights. Now, as she sat curled up in a chair, she presented yet another image. Quiet, serene and approachable. All evidence of the prickly, consummately professional attorney had been softened, tempered in this comfortable environment.

Even the house had surprised him. He'd expected something huge and new, a showcase, something so modern and sterile that he would have worried about leaving fingerprints on all the glass and chrome.

Instead, the house was small compared to the newer monstrosities jammed on either side. The decor was an attractive blend of wicker and overstuffed cushions covered in a sturdy, simple Haitian cotton. Every piece of furniture invited relaxation. Colorful pillows added to the cozy allure. To a man sensitive to the uses of color and design, the house offered up the perfect casual, homey beachfront ambience. He wondered if her apartment in the city was the same or offered a contrast to suit her professional persona.

Suddenly he realized that she was regarding him intently.

"I thought you were working," she chided. "Instead, you seem lost in thought."

"That is how I work," he reminded her with a grin, not entirely willing to confess that he hadn't thought of work in quite some time now.

She shook her head. "Of course. I forgot. Is the script any good?"

Now she had him. "I'm not far enough into it to tell yet," he hedged.

"How will you know if it's something you want to work on?"

"If the images start to come."

"And they haven't yet?"

"Not for the movie," he said, surprised a little himself as the faintly provocative words slipped out.

"So, you weren't working," she accused, her eyes

dancing with merriment, the golden sparks lighting them from within. "What were you thinking about?"

"Are you sure you want to know?"

"I wouldn't have asked if I didn't."

"You."

"Oh," she said, her voice suddenly whispery soft, even though she didn't look nearly as startled as he'd expected her to.

"No more questions?" he prodded.

"Sure," she said, lifting a bold gaze to clash with his. "Elaborate."

"I was wondering if your apartment in the city suited you as well as this place does."

A startled expression crossed her face. "I never really thought about it."

"Let me guess, then. Very elegant. Very tasteful. Very expensive. Maybe a few Oriental touches, along with some European antiques. The finest wood."

She laughed. "Have you been peeping in windows?"

"Nope. I just know where all the top decorators hang out."

"What makes you think I didn't choose that for myself?"

"You wouldn't waste the time." Her expression told him he was right.

"And this place?" she challenged.

"This, I think, you did yourself. I think you picked things because they appealed to your sense of color and touch or maybe just for fun," he said, glancing at a colorful child's pinwheel that had been used instead of flowers in a tall vase in one corner.

"A gift from my youngest niece," she admitted. "It was accompanied by an automatic bubble gun. She thinks I'm too stuffy." She hesitated, then added, "I get the impression that you think that, too."

"Does it matter to you what I think?" he asked, allowing his gaze to linger warmly until he sensed the color rising in her cheeks again. It felt good to engage in this sort of flirtatious bantering with a woman again, especially with one who seemed almost as new to it as he was.

There was an instant's panic in her eyes before that stubborn chin of hers tilted up a notch. "Yes. I think perhaps it does," she admitted, leaving him almost speechless at the rare hint of vulnerability she'd displayed.

Such candor deserved an honest response. David considered his answer carefully. "My impression of you is changing by the minute," he said slowly. "I'm beginning to think you are a rather remarkable woman, Kate Newton."

She looked startled and pleased. "Really?"

"Definitely remarkable," he said as he rose to his feet and walked across the room. He held out his hands, and after an instant's hesitation she placed hers in them. He drew her up. "I don't know what the hell is happening here, but I don't think I can wait one more minute to kiss you."

Her eyes widened, but she didn't pull away, seemingly every bit as mesmerized as he was. Stunned by the force of his need after months and months of abstinence, he slanted his mouth over hers.

Her lips were every bit as soft and yielding as he'd imagined. The texture was like satin, warmed and rumpled by a night of steamy sex. The taste? Sweet, with an intoxicating hint of the wine they'd had with dinner. It had been so long since he'd kissed anyone other than his wife that the sensations felt totally new, more vivid and soul-stoppingly pleasurable than anything he remembered.

He drew back and looked into her eyes, saw the faint stirring of passion and sensuality, that startled look of amazement that told him she was as taken aback as he by whatever was happening between them. Unwilling to let those feelings fade when they'd only just discovered them, he scooped up handfuls of that luxurious, silky black hair as he framed her face and settled his lips over hers once more.

There would be time enough tomorrow and the day after that and on into the weeks ahead for all the regrets that were bound to follow.

Chapter Seven

Thank God for Davey, Kate thought as she sat across the breakfast table from David in embarrassed silence. For a woman not easily rattled, those kisses the night before had shaken her in ways she'd never imagined possible. She'd been awake half the night thinking about them. At least Davey's presence prevented a morning-after analysis of the mistake in judgment they'd made by allowing the intimacy of those kisses.

Why the devil hadn't she thought to set ground rules for herself, as well as him? Possibly because it had never occurred to her that David viewed her as anything other than a prospective adversary in a battle over his son's future. She wondered for one fleeting instant if those kisses had been part of some low-down, scheming tactics to throw her off guard. She dismissed the idea almost as soon as it had formed. Nothing she'd seen thus far had suggested that David was anything but a man of real character, albeit one who'd lost sight of his priorities for a brief time.

None of that explained her own behavior. She had wanted him to kiss her, had practically set the stage and invited him to, with her taunting remarks. She never did things like that. Never!

Davey looked from Kate, who was sweeping scrambled eggs from one side of her plate to the other without lifting so much as a forkful to her mouth, to his father, who was crumbling a piece of toast in a similarly distracted manner.

"You guys are acting weird," Davey declared.

He was right on target. Kate glanced up, found her gaze clashing with David's, and forced her attention to his son. "That's because we're both in a state of shock after the way you stole every piece of property we'd accumulated last night," she improvised, rather well she thought.

"Stole it!" he exclaimed indignantly. "I bought it. Can I help it if you managed to go bankrupt trying to stay out of jail and paying off rental charges every time you landed on my property?"

"Your overdeveloped property," Kate retorted. She shot David a conspiratorial glance. "Next time, I say we demand zoning laws."

"Rigid zoning laws," David agreed. "And I personally intend to check those dice today to see if you tampered with them. Nobody should have the run of luck you had."

Davey's eyes danced with impish laughter. "You had luck, too, Dad."

"Oh, really?"

"Yeah, rotten luck."

His father glowered at him, but with obvious underlying affection. "Just for that, you're on kitchen duty. Kate and I are going for a walk on the beach. You can come join us when these dishes are done."

"But I have a dishwasher," Kate protested, though Davey didn't seem to regard being relegated to doing the chore as any sort of punishment.

"And Davey can load it," David countered. He held out his hand. "Let's go."

Kate regarded that outstretched hand as if it represented more danger than a crate of TNT. The last time she'd allowed even such an innocent touch, she'd found herself in an embrace that had taken her breath away. To avert a repeat performance, she grabbed up her dishes and put them on the counter, as close as she could get them to the dishwasher without undermining David's order. She caught the unmistakable gleam of understanding in his eyes as she tried to sashay out the door with no hint of the turmoil she was in.

Outside, with the morning fog still hanging over the ocean, she jammed her hands in her pockets and set off at a brisk pace. She reminded herself sternly that she was a woman who took on powerful men in court all the time without the least trepidation. She reminded herself that David Winthrop was no more powerful, no more threatening than any one of those adversaries.

And then he put his hand on her shoulder and proved her wrong. She felt a jolt of electricity that went clear to her toes. Some dangers obviously had nothing to do with intelligence, courtrooms or adversarial relationships. Some dangers, it seemed, came from within. This man had an innate ability to shake her up with the simplest gesture, the slightest contact. Apparently ignoring those reactions wasn't going to make them go away.

"I'm curious about something," she said eventually.

"Oh?"

"Why did you kiss me last night?"

"Surely a woman as bright as you are can figure that one out," he said, amusement written all over his face. He didn't seem nearly as distressed by what had happened as she did.

"Never assume anything," she shot right back, the comment as much an explanation for her behavior as it was a challenge to him.

"Why does any man kiss a woman?" he asked with a great display of patience. "Because he finds her attractive."

Attraction, she thought. An inexplicable chemistry. She could deal with that. She was attracted to him, too. That didn't mean they had to *do* anything about it.

"Are you suggesting that anytime someone is attracted to another person, they should have free rein to act on those impulses?" she inquired cautiously just to be sure those ground rules weren't an absolute necessity.

That increasingly familiar tolerant smile crept across his face. "Assuming we're talking consenting adults here, Ms. Attorney, I'd have to say yes," he said.

"Then it could happen again?"

"Oh, I'd say that's almost a certainty." He regarded her intently. "Does that make you nervous?"

Now she was caught in a big-time dilemma. She believed in truth and honesty at all costs. She also believed in preserving some measure of dignity. "Me?" she hedged.

"There's no one else around who looks as jumpy as

a Junebug," he observed, giving an exaggerated glance around the deserted beach just to prove his point.

Kate drew in a deep breath. "Okay, let's be honest here."

He looked disgustingly fascinated by the prospect. "By all means," he taunted.

"I can understand your wanting to kiss me." She glanced at him, then away. "You know, the chemistry thing."

"Given your intelligence, I'd be surprised if you couldn't."

"Would you give me a break?" she asked impatiently. In court, the judge would probably charge him with contempt for all the snappy rejoinders. She was stuck with appealing to his sense of fair play. "I'm trying to make a point here."

He held up his hands in a gesture of surrender. "Sorry."

"Okay, then. I can understand one kiss, as an experiment, so to speak."

"Two," he corrected, not even trying to contain that damnable grin. "I distinctly remember two."

Kate did also. Even if she'd been able to bury the fiery memory of one of them, it appeared likely he intended to remind her at each and every opportunity. How had she so badly misread David Winthrop? She'd never guessed that all that sorrow had dimmed the soul of a scoundrel. She'd wanted to draw him out of his self-absorption for his son's sake, not reawaken his slumbering libido for her own.

Of course, who was she to say it had been slumbering? Davey was the one he'd been ignoring. For all she knew, those nights he spent away from home had

ought to be in analysis," he said dryly. "Do you
w anyone who's not in some sort of recovery pro-
m or obsessed with bloody true-crime cases?"

No one I know is in a recovery program. That's
they read so many of those books. They swear
cheaper than analysis and just as effective. As for
true crime, a lot of my clients are in the entertain-
t industry. They're always looking for movie ma-
al," she explained, then added as an afterthought,
course, I can't swear that some of them aren't con-
ring techniques for murdering their spouses at the
e time. I try to head that off by getting them very
e settlements."

You obviously perform a great public service, in
case."

he grinned. "I do try." She glanced at the thick, dog-
d book he was carrying. "What are you reading?"

My beach book," he said without the least hint of
ogy. "I've been reading this for years. I usually
age about fifty pages per vacation. The rest of the
I don't have time for it."

Must not be a terribly compelling plot, if you can
aside for long periods of time," she noted.

aval history. That's the great thing about reading
y. Once it's recorded, not much changes. I could
his up ten years from now and it would still be
te, just farther in the past."

r a man whose life revolves around whimsy and
believe that's an awfully staid approach to read-
terial."

ance," he reminded her. "Isn't that exactly what
been trying to remind me about? We all need a
lance in our lives."

been spent in the consoling arms of some woman. She
scowled at the thought, even as she dismissed it. If she
was certain of nothing else, it was that David was every
bit as loyal to his wife's memory as he had been to Alicia when she was alive.

"Hey," he said jovially. "One kiss. Two. Who's counting? No need to get testy."

"I am not testy," she said in a tone that contradicted
the statement. "Look, all I'm trying to say is that I have
a responsibility to my client here. I think there's a real
conflict of interest in our…"

Involvement? She wasn't about to even hint at the
word. *Kissing?* That sounded absurd, given the way he'd
downplayed the activity as little more than a scientific
experiment that might need to be repeated indefinitely
until some theory or other was proved or disproved.

"Our what?" he prodded.

"I think we should keep our distance," she blurted.

"From an ethical standpoint."

She beamed, delighted that he'd caught on so quickly.
"Yes, exactly."

Brown eyes, devoid of so much as a hint of amusement now, studied her intently. "Hogwash!" he said
softly, stepping closer and framing her face with his
hands.

The warmth of his hands against her skin sent that
all-too-familiar, insidious heat flooding through her.
She glared at him indignantly and stepped out of reach.
"What's that supposed to mean?"

"I thought you intended to be honest."

"I am being honest."

"Hogwash!" he repeated even more adamantly.

The word was really grating on her nerves, especially

since it was about as accurate as any she could think of for describing the wimpy speech she'd just given.

"Kate, if you have a problem with me touching you, you'll have to spell it out in a way that doesn't mock *my* intelligence. There is no danger whatsoever of a few kisses influencing the way you handle Davey's case. In fact, if you were being totally honest with me and yourself, you'd admit that the closer you and I become, the more influence you'd have over my relationship with my son."

"But then I'd be open to charges that I'd manipulated you," she said, desperately grabbing at straws.

"Charges by whom?"

"You."

"Not me," he denied. "I don't manipulate so easily, as you'll discover as time goes by." He allowed that to sink in, then added, "Along with a good many other things."

"What?" she said blankly, wondering how she'd lost control not only of this conversation, but quite possibly of her entire life.

"There are a great many things you'll get to know about me," he explained. "Given time."

How much time did the man think this case was going to take? she wondered. She'd hoped to have him and his son on track by the close of the weekend, if only to assure a return of her own equanimity.

"I think we've gotten off track here," she told him firmly. "This weekend isn't about you and me. It's about you and Davey." She turned on her heel. "I'll send him out."

Unfortunately Davey was already out and happily engaged in building a sand fortress with two boys from

farther along the beach. That meant Da[ ] approximately fifteen seconds after Ka[ ]

"Shall I go drag him away from his [ ] he and I can share some quality time?" h[ ] a hint of mirth sparkling in his eyes.

Since she didn't have a guidebook [ ] thing, Kate had to go with instinct. A [ ] wanted David otherwise occupied, it ap[ ] out of luck. Sending him off to intrude o[ ] wouldn't accomplish a thing, except to f[ ] grudging contact. If Davey was content [ ] his father was nearby, wasn't that good [ ]

"There's a ton of books inside. Grab o[ ] she conceded. A man engrossed in a goo[ ] not be ogling her the way he was now.

"I brought one with me," he said. "[ ] take a look at what you keep on hand a[ ] shelves say a lot about a person."

"Then these will present a very con[ ] she retorted. "My collection represents [ ] tic tastes of previous guests."

Undaunted, he retorted, "Better yet [ ] tell a person by the company she keep[ ] side with a determined glint in his ey[ ]

He was back in half an hour, not n[ ] for her to become so absorbed in th[ ] was reading that she wouldn't noti[ ] truth of the matter was that she'd r[ ] ing paragraph five times without [ ] istering. Obviously, whether she l[ ] Winthrop was more fascinating.

"What's the verdict?" she ask[ ]

"A woman with this particular[ ]

"True," she conceded, and wondered yet again if this wasn't a lesson she needed very much to learn, as well. Perhaps, she thought for the second time that day, perhaps fate had delivered Davey Winthrop into her life not just because of what she could do for him, but for what he and his father might do for her.

Kate was standing under the hot spray of the shower Saturday night, when she heard someone knocking loudly on the bathroom door.

"Kate, phone," David bellowed. "It's long distance from Rome."

Oh, dear Lord, she thought at once. Her mother! And *David* had answered the phone. As she turned off the water and reached for a towel, she could already imagine the mile-long list of questions his presence would arouse.

She pulled on a thick, terry-cloth robe and wrapped her damp hair in a towel. Then, and there was no way around it that she could think of, she opened the bathroom door to face David and her mother, in that order. For the moment he actually seemed less daunting, though a gentleman would have left her bedroom once he'd announced the call. He was lingering in the doorway, arms crossed, an appreciative gleam in his eyes.

"Go away," she murmured as she reached for the phone.

He winked, but he did go away. In fact, she heard the hang-up click of the receiver on the living room phone before she'd even had a chance to say a breathless hello to her mother.

"Darling, how are you?" Elizabeth Halloran asked. "And who was that charming man?"

"Charming?" Kate repeated, hearing the distinct clang of warning bells.

"Absolutely. He asked all about our trip when I told him I was calling from Rome. He said he'd been here. He even remembered a little restaurant that he highly recommended. I think Brandon and I will try it tomorrow. Now, who is he?"

"It's a long story."

Apparently her mother knew her well enough by now to realize that further probing would be useless. "Well, I'm just delighted that you're seeing someone. Brandon will be, too."

"I'm not *seeing* David. He's a client, actually the father of a client."

"Oh," her mother said with obvious disappointment. "Then I'm sure he's probably too old for you anyway, dear. That's too bad."

Kate decided against trying to explain, since her mother seemed willing to forget whatever romantic fantasy she'd been dreaming up since David had picked up the phone. She was incredibly grateful for the reprieve.

"Are you and Brandon having a good time?" she asked.

Her mother sighed dreamily. "Darling, it's the vacation of a lifetime. I can't tell you how happy he has made me. Wait until you see all the pictures."

"When are you coming home?" Kate asked, trying not to let a wistful note creep into her voice.

"Not for a while yet, dear. Brandon insists on going to Athens next, then Paris and London. After that, we'll see how exhausted we are."

Kate heard a murmured argument, then Brandon's voice. "Katie, don't you go badgering this woman to come home when I've finally got her to myself after all these years," he teased. "Now what's this I hear about a man being at your place when you're in the shower? What are his intentions?"

She realized the inquiry was vintage Brandon. "I don't think he has any intentions, at least where I'm concerned."

She heard another murmured comment by her mother, then Brandon's deep chuckle and a low retort that had her mother laughing.

"Your mother says he's too old for you anyway," Brandon said. "I just reminded her I'm old, and I wasn't such a bad catch."

"Ah, but you're one of a kind," Kate teased him, finding that despite her reservations, she couldn't help liking the man who was making her mother so happy. "If I could find someone like you, then maybe I'd find marriage more appealing."

"You just sit tight, then, young lady. As soon as I get home, I'll find you somebody who'll treat you the way you deserve to be treated."

Since she didn't have an answer to that except to scream a fervent *no*, Kate muttered a hurried goodbye and prayed that this honeymoon would turn out to be the longest one on record. Knowing Brandon's penchant for meddling, though, he might very well get it into his head to cut it short just to fix up her love life, especially if he sensed it would make her mother happy to see her settled.

She was still sitting on the edge of her bed contemplating the horror of that prospect, when David tapped on the partially opened door and stuck his head in.

"Is that what you're wearing to dinner?" he inquired hopefully.

She glowered at him. "We're casual out here, but we usually do insist on clothes," she retorted. "I'll be ready in a few minutes."

He regarded her quizzically. "Want to tell me why you were looking so sad just now? The call wasn't bad news, was it?"

"Not unless you consider the prospect of a stepfather arranging a marriage for me to be bad news."

David looked incredulous. "You're joking, right?"

"You don't know Brandon. He's getting worried that he'll have a spinster stepdaughter on his hands. If I'm not careful, when they get to Greece he'll provide a herd of sheep and a grove of olive trees as a dowry in return for some suitably old-fashioned Greek husband for me," she said with what was probably only minimal exaggeration. "He'll drag him home along with the more conventional souvenirs."

David gave her a thoughtful look, one that suggested he was considering whether she was worth more or less than that herd of sheep and an olive grove.

"If it comes to that," he said finally, "you tell him to speak to me first. I'll take you without the sheep. I think there's a law against them in Bel Air anyway."

She scowled at him. "I'll keep your generous offer in mind," she retorted dryly.

"On the other hand," he said, "I could use a good dairy cow."

Kate threw her silver hairbrush straight at him. It didn't do a thing to squelch his amusement, but it did get him to close the damned door.

Chapter Eight

Because she did so much weekend entertaining during the summer months, Kate kept a standing reservation for four at Alice's Restaurant on the Malibu Pier for every Saturday night. She called only to cancel or to enlarge the size of her party. She liked the food. She liked the people. And she loved the view, especially in summer when an eight o'clock reservation virtually guaranteed a spectacular sunset display except on the foggiest evenings. On Sundays when she had guests, she took them to Geoffrey's for brunch in the lovely garden setting on a cliff overlooking the sea, but on Saturday night she liked the crowded, lively ambience of Alice's.

Though the staff and many of the regular customers were used to seeing her here, she noticed a few raised eyebrows and speculative glances when she walked in with David and Davey.

Everyone knew that Kate Newton never dated. The painful love affair responsible for her solitude had long since ceased to be a topic of conversation, but it hadn't been forgotten. At the time, almost everyone in certain Hollywood circles had seen the irony in the famed divorce lawyer being caught up in what had nearly become a highly publicized palimony scandal with the creep suing her. Knowing Kate as well as he had, however, had led Ryan Manning to settle out of court and slink off to prey on other unsuspecting women.

As a result of all that thoroughly dissected past history, had she been with David alone, everyone would have guessed him to be an exceptionally handsome colleague or a client and gone back to their dinners.

Davey's presence changed all that. Kate rarely entertained children, other than her nieces. She wasn't regarded as the maternal type, probably because of her cutthroat courtroom reputation. To see her here with father and son, especially this particular father and son, was clearly cause for fascination.

All during dinner people found excuses to drop by the table, angling for introductions, hoping to pinpoint the exact nature of the relationship. Some, she knew, genuinely hoped that she'd found a new, satisfying romance. Others had recognized David and no doubt knew the details of his tragic loss. They clearly wondered if his days of mourning were past.

Kate guessed there would be no fewer than half a dozen calls by Monday morning, at least one of them from a gossip columnist from one of the film industry trade papers. She could barely wait for the meal to end, so she could escape the unspoken speculation.

Davey, however, insisted on dessert. And David

wanted coffee. Kate wanted to scream with impatience, but didn't dare. Then she would have to explain exactly why she was suddenly so uncomfortable.

"Kate? Coffee?" David asked as the waiter jotted down the order.

"Please," she said, though she couldn't think of anything she wanted less. But if she had to sit here, she wanted something to do.

"You can have some of my dessert," Davey offered generously. "I probably won't eat it all."

"Right," his father said skeptically. "You never leave me so much as a crumb."

"Because you always say you don't want any and then you start sneaking in with your fork, and before I know it, it's all gone. Then you call me a pig."

Kate relaxed slightly as she chuckled at Davey's indignation. Watching him, she felt a powerful, deep emotion that was entirely new to her. His usually neat hair was windblown. His cheeks and arms were tinted pink from too much sun. He had a scrape on one elbow from falling on the sand during a volleyball game. He had a streak of ketchup on his chin. He was so exhausted he could hardly keep his eyes open, but he looked the happiest she'd ever seen him. He looked like a kid again. The messy, energy-draining kind. The kind she'd always sworn she wanted no part of.

So why did she feel so contented? Why did she look at Davey and feel this gut-wrenching tug of tenderness stealing through her? True, Davey was a pretty extraordinary boy. He was bright, funny and compassionate. He was certainly bold beyond his years. In short, he had a lot of the same traits she'd had at the same age. Her niece, Penny, was similarly precocious. Kate wondered if her own kids would have turned out to be nearly as interesting. Maybe she ought to be grateful she knew kids like Penny and Davey and not even consider testing her own luck with the gene pool.

A rational plan, one she'd embraced long ago, when work had been a demanding, satisfying lover. Tonight, however, Kate wasn't feeling rational. She looked at Davey and his father and wished with all her heart that her life had taken a different track. She sighed at the realization that it was rapidly getting too late to change directions, especially now that she'd been on this lonely course for so long.

"You look as if you're a million miles away," David said, interrupting her disturbing thoughts. "And wherever you are doesn't look like a very happy place."

Kate was startled that he could read her so easily. She must be growing too comfortable with him. Usually she kept her guard up better. It was tiring, but necessary. One of the first lessons she'd learned as a lawyer was never to show her hand in a courtroom. She'd adopted the same unrevealing mask in her personal life, as well.

Until now.

"Is mind reading one of your talents?" she inquired more irritably than the observation merited.

"It doesn't take much talent when an expression is as easy to interpret as yours was. What were you thinking about?"

"Independence."

"The city or the state of mind?"

"Very funny."

He didn't react visibly to the trace of sarcasm, but his tone was definitely more sober when he asked, "Okay, what exactly were you thinking about independence?"

Kate hesitated to say it aloud. It would sound too much as if she were dissatisfied with her life, and she wasn't. Not really. She was just in a mood, an oddly disturbing mood that she couldn't seem to shake.

"Kate?" he prodded.

She saw that he wasn't going to let the topic drop. "I suppose I was thinking that independence isn't all it's cracked up to be. Sometimes it's very taxing."

He regarded her quizzically, obviously waiting for more.

"Actually, I suppose I was envying you," she confessed, surprising herself with the honesty of the admission. It was the sort of revealing comment she normally would have avoided at all costs.

Astonishment filled his eyes. "Me? Why?"

"You have a career you obviously love. You have your son."

As if he wasn't quite sure how to respond to the rare confession, David glanced at Davey. "A son who is asleep on his feet."

"Am not," Davey said sleepily, his eyelids drooping even as he uttered the denial.

"Maybe we should get the check," David suggested, snagging the last bite of his son's cake. His gaze caught hers. "We can finish this discussion at home."

Home, she thought with raw yearning that hit her like a bolt out of the blue. Until David had used the word, she'd never imbued it with so much meaning. Now she saw that the house she loved so much was just that, a house. It wasn't until just tonight that she'd realized that for the past twenty-four hours it had felt more like a home. Laughter and contentment and warmth had spilled into the rooms.

She sighed heavily. Would she ever feel quite the same way about it, now that they had been there to show her what having a marriage and a family could be like? Or would this odd dissatisfaction and emptiness only be magnified?

"There's nothing to discuss," Kate said, desperately wanting to put an end to the topic before yet another layer of her defenses could be stripped away. As midlife crises went, it appeared she was plunging headfirst into a real doozy.

David was up at the crack of dawn on Sunday. He made a pot of Kate's fancy coffee, then took a mug out onto the deck and tried to analyze Kate's retreat the previous night.

She had begun pleading exhaustion the minute they hit the house. Given the shadows in her eyes, he might have believed her if he hadn't seen her light burning and heard her restless pacing long after she'd supposedly gone to bed. He'd guessed then that she desperately wanted to avoid completing the conversation she herself had begun at the restaurant.

She was a real study in contradictions. There had been times this weekend when he'd felt the barriers between them—his and hers—beginning to slip away. He'd enjoyed watching her with Davey, seeing the genuine enjoyment she seemed to get from probing his lively mind. She obviously liked his son. She treated him like a person, rather than a child, and Davey responded to that respect as any kid would.

Davey had wanted Kate to tuck him in before she fled to her own room. And Kate had figured prominently in Davey's prayers, joining his father, his mother and Mrs. Larsen for special mention. Though she had rapidly blinked them away, there had been no mistaking the tears that sprang into Kate's eyes when she'd heard. Right after that she had practically bolted for her room.

Sitting on the deck, sipping his coffee, David admitted that the weekend had been good for him. He felt more relaxed now than he had in months. He and Kate had fallen into a surprisingly easy rhythm of camaraderie. That sense that he was being disloyal had stolen over him only once or twice, mainly after he had kissed Kate on Friday night and then Saturday when he'd wanted badly to kiss her again just to prove that the first time hadn't been a fluke.

So, he thought, it was just possible that he was going to go on living, no matter how hard he'd tried to bury his emotions along with Alicia. Anything more than that—falling in love, for instance—still seemed beyond him. Perhaps he would never again experience that head-over-heels sensation that had engulfed him the first instant he had laid eyes on Alicia. Maybe things a man had felt at twenty weren't possible at thirty-five.

And yet there was an oddly erratic beat to his heart when Kate Newton walked into a room. It was only a glimmer of what he recalled of those early days with Alicia, but the chemistry was unmistakable just the same. He could leave her today and slam the door on that feeling or he could encourage further contact, explore the sensations and give them time to flourish.

If she'd let him. She, it seemed, was fearful not only of commitment, but of all the stages leading up to it.

He closed his eyes, seeing her as she had been when she'd climbed out of the shower to take that overseas call the night before. He sighed as he recalled how beautiful and sensual she'd looked with her face scrubbed clean, her skin glowing and soft as satin, her slim body given fascinating curves by the added bulk of that terry-cloth robe that shaped itself to her damp flesh. It had taken every ounce of restraint he possessed to resist a quick tug on that robe's loosely tied belt to expose the alluring woman beneath. Even now, just the memory stirred his blood and sent it rushing through him.

While those provocative memories were still taunting him, he thought he imagined the scent of lily of the valley. Then he heard a faint whisper of sound and realized Kate had padded out to join him, her feet bare as usual, her endlessly long legs encased in denim. On top she wore a faded, misshapen UCLA sweatshirt. She settled onto the chaise longue next to his. He opened his eyes and turned toward her.

"Good morning."

She gave him a sleepy smile in return. "You're up early. Couldn't you sleep?"

"Actually, I slept better than I have in ages," he admitted. "The salt air and activity were obviously just what I needed."

She nodded. "I'm glad." She drew her knees up and rested her chin on them. Occasionally she lifted the mug of coffee to her lips, obviously content with the silence and perhaps even with the companionship. Suddenly David wanted to understand what she was feeling, if the weekend had meant anything at all to her.

"Kate?"

"Umm?"

"I find myself in a quandary."

Still she didn't glance at him. "Oh?"

"You could at least act sympathetic," he chided. "I'm

not a man who's used to not knowing how to handle something."

"I'm sure," she said, looking not one whit more sympathetic.

"What I'm trying to say here is that I'd like to see you again."

"I'm sure we'll be running into each other all the time," she said, her expression deliberately cool, not giving him an inch, even though he was laying his damned soul bare. To add to the insult, she said, "Given Davey's suit and all."

David lost patience. "Dammit, I'm not discussing having an occasional polite meeting to discuss legal affairs."

"I am."

She had never seemed more distant. He found it infuriating. "Why?"

"Because that's the way it has to be."

"Are we back to the ethics thing again? Or is this because you have no desire to see me on a personal basis? If that's it, Kate, just spit it out and I'll back off."

She turned then, and he could see the conflicting emotions warring in her eyes. She blinked and turned away. "That's not it," she said finally.

"Then for God's sake, explain it to me. It's been a long time since I dated. Maybe all the rules have changed."

"I suspect it's been even longer since I dated, and as far as I know the rules are the same. Given the lack of recent experience for both of us, I think maybe we're grasping at straws here, trying to fill a void in our lives. A couple of kisses don't mean anything, no matter how enjoyable they were."

"What about the walks? What about the talks? What about playing games with Davey? In my book all of that adds up to two people who are compatible, who have things in common, who are mature enough not to expect bells and whistles."

She gave him a wry smile. "Bells and whistles may not be mandatory in your book, but I figure that's what gets two people through the rough patches."

David recalled the passion Alicia had always stirred in him and knew Kate was right. Tempestuous passion and gentle, enduring love went hand in hand in the strongest relationships, forging an unbreakable bond. The memories of the glorious passion he and Alicia had shared were what he had pulled out and held dear when times had gotten tough. Was he any more willing than Kate to settle for less?

He gazed at her intently. "I think perhaps I hear a distant bell ringing," he said softly, unable to hide the wistfulness behind the claim. "Shouldn't we try to find it?"

She reached over and touched her fingers to his and all at once the peal of bells seemed more distinct. Her gaze searched his.

"We've both been bruised in very different ways, you more recently than I," she said gently. "Let's not rush into something."

He curved his fingers around hers, liking the way her hand fit in his, liking even more the protectiveness that was stealing through him. "A slow stroll, then," he suggested as their gazes caught and held.

She drew in a deep breath, then slowly exhaled, her shoulders visibly relaxing. When she nodded at last, David felt something burst free deep inside him, and for the first time in a very long time he was filled with hope.

* * *

The weekend ended for Kate with the same mix of anticipation and trepidation with which it had begun. She was anxious to see them go. She was torn by the unexpectedly powerful desire to have them stay. Her talk that morning with David had opened up all of the delicious possibilities of the future. It had also stirred all the warning signals of the past. By the time they actually began to load the car she was as limp as a dishrag from dealing with all of the conflicting emotions.

"This was the best weekend of my whole life," Davey declared.

Kate mussed his hair, which he'd brushed back neatly after his shower. "I'm glad you had fun, kiddo."

Suddenly his lower lip quivered. His arms circled her waist and he buried his head against her. "I love you, Kate," he said, his voice muffled.

She felt her throat constrict so tightly that not a single sound could squeeze past. She hugged him tight. "You'll come back," she said when she could finally speak, wishing she dared to lay her own emotions on the line as easily, wishing she even understood what they were. She made the promise of a return as much for herself as she did for Davey. She looked up and saw David watching her, his own eyes suspiciously moist.

"That's right," he said briskly. "We'll be back. And Kate's going to bring you over to see the set for *Future Rock* this week, aren't you, Kate?"

It was the first she'd heard of any specific plan, but she nodded. "Absolutely. Just think, Davey, you and I will get a chance to see something that's the biggest secret in all of Hollywood."

Davey released her then and swiped at the damp

traces of tears on his cheeks. His smile wobbled just a little. "You mean it, Dad?"

"Of course I mean it. Kate and I will compare schedules tomorrow and pick a day."

Davey made a fist. "Yes," he said as if he'd just won a victory. He climbed into the wagon and belted himself in. Kate closed the door, then turned to find David waiting for her behind the car.

"Thank you," he said.

"You're welcome."

"I'll call tomorrow."

She nodded.

He stepped closer and cupped the back of her head. Slowly, so slowly that Kate's pulse was thundering with anticipation, he lowered his head and touched his lips to hers. Cool as a breeze, quick as the fleeting brush of a butterfly's wings, the kiss was over almost before it began.

And yet she heard the very distinct, if distant, sound of bells.

Chapter Nine

When Kate returned from court at noon on Monday, a full week after her fateful weekend with David and Davey, she found her sister waiting in the conference area of her office. She felt her stomach begin to knot, but she managed what she hoped was a breezy, unconcerned smile as she stepped behind her desk. Even an amateur psychologist would have seen the significance of placing that defensive barrier between her and her sister.

"Ellen, what are you doing here?" she asked, trying unsuccessfully to keep an edge out of her voice.

"We're having lunch," Ellen said in a tone that brooked no argument.

Kate's gaze shot to her, then faltered. "Lunch?" She glanced pointedly at her appointment book. "Oh, dear, I'm sorry if you came all this way hoping to catch me free, but there's an appointment on my calendar with a client."

"Not a client," Ellen declared. "Me. I had Zelda put me down."

There was a stubborn set to her chin that Kate recognized from years of butting heads with her older sister. Though Ellen had been a dreamer and a romantic, when that strong will of hers finally asserted itself, even the indomitable Kate listened.

She glared at Kate. "And don't you dare yell at Zelda for doing it without consulting you. Now put down your briefcase and let's get out of here. I've made reservations at a place that'll probably charge by the minute if we show up late."

Kate gave a sigh of resignation as she accepted the futility of arguing. "You always were the bossiest big sister of anyone we knew," she grumbled.

Ellen shot her an unrepentant grin. "I know. Too bad I let you get the upper hand in recent years. Otherwise, maybe you'd be married by now and I could stop worrying about you."

"Don't you dare start on that," Kate warned as she followed her from the office. She shot a furious look at Zelda on her way to the elevator. For once her secretary seemed amazingly absorbed in her typing.

Ellen had heavily tipped one of the parking valets at the office building to keep her car waiting at the curb. Kate reluctantly climbed in. Now, with no car of her own, she would be totally at Ellen's mercy. She'd have to listen to every last word of whatever lecture or probing interrogation her sister had in mind.

Ellen drove the few blocks into Beverly Hills and whipped into a parking garage as if she made the trip to Rodeo Drive daily, rather than once a year, if that. She had chosen a restaurant just off the famed shopping street. Not until she and Kate were seated did she say another word. Kate was content to let the silence continue as long as possible.

Ellen ordered a glass of wine. Kate ordered bottled mineral water. She wanted a clear head for whatever was to come. When their drinks arrived, they ordered lunch. Ellen took her first sip of the Chardonnay, set down her glass and faced Kate. "Okay, let's hear it."

"Hear what?" Kate evaded. She hadn't arranged this confrontation. She saw no reason to be the first one to put her cards on the table.

Ellen looked disgusted by the evasiveness. "For a woman who can make any bigwig in Hollywood sound like a cross between Attila the Hun and the Marquis de Sade in a court of law, you show an amazing inability to verbalize your own anger," she said, her own slow-to-boil temper clearly flaring. "Now, who exactly are you mad at? Me? Mom? Brandon? The whole damned world?"

Kate winced, not so much at Ellen's furious tone, but at the evident hurt behind it. "I'm not mad at anyone," she said stiffly.

"Oh?" her sister retorted with obvious skepticism. "I have asked you to have dinner with us at least a dozen times since Mom's wedding. You've found an excuse every time, most of them so flimsy they're embarrassing."

Kate refused to meet her sister's gaze. "I'm very busy. You know that."

"Right. But you've always found time for family before. You were the one who went crazy every single

'time you couldn't get Mother on the phone. You dropped
everything, insisted I meet you and went tearing over
there. Then that time I called you when I was worried
about Mother after she and Brandon had a falling out,
you showed up within minutes. You even canceled some
big tennis match."

"That was different."

"How?"

"She's our mother, for heaven's sake. And we didn't
know what was going on. Her phone was off the hook
for hours that one time. Then when you called, you
made it sound as if she were about to leap off the top
of a skyscraper. That's hardly the same as some casual
dinner invitation."

Hurt flared again in Ellen's eyes. "I'm family, dammit. Didn't it occur to you that I might need you?"

Kate couldn't help thinking about David's with-
drawal from Davey at a time when he'd been desperately needed. She recalled her own impatience with that
behavior. Wasn't she guilty of the same thing? Still,
even though she felt ashamed of her selfish behavior,
she regarded her sister evenly.

"Are you still family?" she said softly, hearing the
unspoken torment behind that simple question, but unable to hide any longer the fact that she felt as if she'd
been cast adrift.

Ellen looked as if she'd been slapped. "How could
you even ask such a thing?"

"Because it seems to me that you have a new family
now. You, Mom and Brandon. That's where you should
be spending all your energy, not worrying about me."

For the first time Kate could ever recall, Ellen looked
utterly defeated. "Do you think all of this has been easy

on me?" she whispered. "My life's been turned upside down, the same way yours has. More so, in fact." She regarded Kate miserably. "Don't you see? I finally understand why all those years we were growing up I felt that Dad loved you more."

Astonishment and dismay swept through Kate. "I had no idea," she said, stunned by her sister's admission. "Dad always treated us the same."

"No," Ellen said angrily. Then she drew in a deep breath. "Oh, he tried. I know that. But I saw the way he looked at you. I could see how proud he was of everything *you* accomplished. It hurt, Katie, especially because I didn't know why I was never good enough."

Reluctant sympathy made Kate's heart ache, but she couldn't cope with Ellen's old wounds now. Her own were still too fresh. She knew she had to get away before she made an absolute fool of herself by bursting into tears—for herself and for her sister and the past that had come between them. She threw her napkin onto the table and stood up. "I'm sorry, Ellen. I can't talk about this anymore right now."

"Kate," Ellen pleaded.

"Not now. I'm sorry," she said, squeezing her sister's hand, hoping Ellen could find some way to understand, some way to forgive her.

She fled, leaving Ellen staring after her, her eyes shimmering with unshed tears.

Outside, Kate muttered a curse over the lack of a car, then decided it was just as well. Maybe on the walk back to Century City the solitude and exercise would clear her head. She knew that she had hurt Ellen, but she hadn't been able to stop herself. All of the pain of feeling like an outsider had boiled over under her sister's attempt at kindness.

Kate didn't want Ellen's pity. She didn't want anyone's pity. She just wanted a family of her own again. Knowing that Ellen might have subconsciously felt that way for years only made the anguish greater.

When she stormed back into the office, not one bit calmer than she had been when she'd left the restaurant, Zelda was on the phone. She quickly hung up and followed Kate into her office.

"I hope you're satisfied," Zelda said, staring at her indignantly. "That was your sister. You left her in tears."

Kate regarded Zelda coldly. "My personal life is none of your concern."

Her secretary's eyes widened at the sharply spoken reminder, but at least she clamped her mouth shut, whirled and walked out.

Terrific, Kate thought. Now Zelda was mad at her, too. How many people could she manage to alienate in one day? And what else could possibly go wrong? When her phone buzzed, she snatched it up and growled a greeting.

"Uh-oh," David said. "Did I catch you at a bad time?"

She drew in a deep breath. She was disgustingly glad to hear his voice, even though she should be furious with him. He'd promised to call the week before about arranging that studio tour for Davey. He hadn't. Even so, she wasn't up to challenging him about it right now.

"Sorry," she said wearily. "It's been a bad day."

"Tough case?" he inquired sympathetically.

Kate almost laughed. If she told him the real reason for her foul mood, he'd question whether she had any

business at all setting up rules and regulations for anyone's family life.

"No," she responded finally. "Just a family matter."

"No problem with the honeymoon couple, I hope."

"No. They're fine as far as I know. Look, I really
don't want to talk about this," she said dismissively.
"Did you have a reason for calling?"

"I did, but it seems my timing's a little off. I was
hoping to lure you out to the studio. My schedule's
pretty jammed up. That's why I haven't gotten back to
you before now. I was thinking maybe tomorrow or the
next day. Davey's been bugging me ever since we left
your house. Frankly, I think he's more anxious to see
you again than he is to see my sets. I had to promise to
call you today. I figured if I didn't, he'd have you filing more papers."

Kate chafed at the dutiful note in his voice. He
sounded harassed. When he added, "If you can't make
it, I'll understand," she knew he wouldn't just understand, he'd be grateful for the cop-out.

"Ah, but will Davey?" Kate said wryly.

Even though David sounded as if he'd be just as
happy if she turned him down, Kate couldn't help the
anticipation that swept through her. She glanced at her
calendar. Both days were crammed with appointments.
However, she considered Davey's case a priority. At
least, that's what she told herself when she said, "I think
I can clear Wednesday afternoon if we make it late."

She heard the pages of his appointment book flip.

"How late?" he asked.

"Four-thirty. I know that'll put us smack in the middle of rush hour when we finish up, but I don't think I
can get out to the valley before then."

"I guess that would work," he said slowly. After another beat, he added, "We could have dinner afterward, so you won't have to worry about the traffic heading home."

Kate caught the slight hesitation in his voice, the evident strain. Clearly he had mixed feelings about this entire invitation. She wondered if he would send Davey back home alone the minute he'd seen the sets if she didn't intervene and agree to prolong the evening by joining them for dinner.

To be perfectly truthful, though, she wanted to accept for her own sake, as much as Davey's. The lure of those feelings of contentment she'd experienced over the weekend was too powerful to resist. Especially today, she longed to feel that kind of connection to another human being again.

"Dinner would be great," she said. "Now tell me which studio and soundstage. Should I pick up Davey on the way?"

"If you don't mind, that would really help me out," he said, then gave her directions. "I'll be looking forward to it."

"Me, too," Kate said, realizing as she hung up just how much.

Trying to substitute Davey and David for the family she felt she'd lost was a very bad idea, especially since David clearly had misgivings about a simple tour of his set and dinner. She recognized the dangers with every fiber of her being. And yet, at this moment, the prospect of seeing the two of them again definitely brightened an otherwise dreary, depressing day.

From the moment they walked through the door of the huge soundstage on the lot in Burbank late on

Wednesday, Kate felt as if she'd wandered into another world. Beside her, Davey's eyes were wide with awe. David, regarding everything with a critical possessive eye, looked as if he was perfectly at home.

"Wow!" Davey said. "Dad, this is totally hot."

That pretty much summed up Kate's own reaction to a landscape so barren, so otherworldly that she expected to be greeted by an alien at any second. "Definitely hot," she echoed.

David glanced at Kate, a smile tugging at his lips. "Do you suppose that means cool?"

"Or awesome," Kate responded.

"I wish they'd hand out translations of current slang at PTA meetings."

"Just go by the look in his eyes," she suggested. "Can't you see how impressed he is by all this?"

David's gaze clashed with hers and sent a little frisson of awareness tripping through her. "And you?"

"I'm a little awed myself," she admitted. "And a little worried. Are you sure you're of this world? You make this look very real, as if you might have been to this place on your last vacation."

"Just research and imagination, I'm afraid." He held out his hand. Kate took it. "Let's go take a look at the spacecraft. I had a field day with all the gadgetry. Even wrangled a trip to NASA headquarters to see what's actually in use in our current spacecraft. There's nothing in here that's beyond the range of scientific possibility."

As Davey raced on ahead of them, David called out, "Careful of the wires."

The floor was crisscrossed with cables, and the air was filled with the sounds of hammering and shouts as construction crews put the finishing touches on the sets inside the cavernous soundstage. Technicians were running checks on the hot spotlights, creating pools of glaring light.

Despite the unfamiliar surroundings, with her hand clasped firmly in David's, Kate felt the same tantalizing sense of belonging again. She was able to shove her worries aside, at least for a time. Perhaps there was something to be said for living in a fantasy world, even one as alien as the one David had created.

As they stepped through the doorway into a shiny, metallic room filled with blinking lights and an intimidating array of controls and levers, she suddenly wished they could launch this stage prop into another dimension where the demands of the real world no longer had a hold over any of them.

David tugged the door closed behind them, and for just an instant, Kate thought her wish might be granted. Then she saw how soberly he was regarding them.

"Now, look, you two," he warned. "I want to remind you that everything you're seeing today is top secret, okay? The producer wants all of this to make a big splash a few weeks from now when production begins. No leaks."

"I promise, Dad," Davey said solemnly. "Can I push these buttons?"

"Go for it," David agreed with a laugh.

Suddenly they were inundated with shrieking buzzers and clanging bells. The strobe lights flashed with blinding intensity. The noisier and brighter it got, the happier Davey looked.

"It's like being inside a computer game," he announced excitedly.

"Just wait until you see the special effects," David told him. "The man doing them is the best in the business." He watched as Davey touched every surface, fingered every button, then asked, "Think your pals will like it when they see it on-screen?"

Though his tone was casual, Kate detected a hint of insecurity in his eyes. Whether he was willing to admit it or not, he wanted Davey's approval every bit as much as Davey sought his. Her heart ached over the distance between them, an emotional gap that never should have happened between father and son.

Just as it never should have happened between sisters, she thought sadly.

"They'll love it," Davey declared. "Do you think someday I could maybe bring them here?"

"After we've finished shooting the movie," David suggested. "How's that?" He glanced at Kate and seemed to reach a decision of some sort. "You'll have a birthday around that time. Maybe we could have the party here."

Davey could barely contain his excitement. "You promise?"

After an instant of unmistakable uncertainty, David rested his hand on his son's shoulder. "That's a definite promise."

As Davey went exploring again, Kate studied David intently, marveling at his change in mood since they'd talked on the phone on Monday. Then, he'd seemed almost reluctant to see her again, so much so that she'd been certain he'd had second thoughts.

Apparently he caught her scrutiny and somehow guessed the cause. "Kate, I'm sorry about the other day."

"Oh?" she said, not wanting to give any hint that she was even aware of the distance in his voice when they'd talked.

"Things were crazy around here. I couldn't see how I could fit this in at all, but Davey was bugging me." He gazed at her. "I shouldn't have called when I was feeling pressured. I'm sure it sounded as if this were the last thing in the world I wanted to do."

"You didn't sound overly enthusiastic," she admitted.

"I'm sorry. I just want you to know it didn't have anything to do with you or the things I said at the beach. Forgiven?"

"There's nothing to forgive."

His gaze locked with hers. "You sure?"

She smiled slowly. "I'm sure."

He grinned. "Terrific. Now how about some dinner? I promised you food, and you look as if you're faint with hunger."

"It's not that bad," she responded with a laugh, suddenly feeling more carefree than she had in days. "But I did miss lunch so I could take off early this afternoon."

"So what appeals to you when you're starving? Italian? Steak? Seafood? Mexican?"

"Hamburgers," Davey chimed in as he joined them.

"Hey, this is Kate's choice, remember?"

Davey's face fell. Then he glanced at her slyly. "I'll bet she likes hamburgers, too."

"Actually, I do," she confessed. "How about Hamburger Hamlet?"

David shook his head. "And I was prepared to pop for something outrageously expensive."

She grinned at him. "I'll hold you to that another time. Right now this sounds like heaven."

"Okay, then. The one on Beverly Boulevard?"

"Perfect. It's right on the way home."

Davey tucked himself into her side. "Can I ride back with you, too?"

"Actually, I'd like to hitch a ride, too," David said, his expression all innocence, his mood once more bordering on that wicked, flirtatious tone of their weekend at the beach. "I had one of the assistants drop me off here this afternoon."

Kate's eyebrows rose. "And what would you have done if I'd had to take off and left you stranded?"

He grinned back at her. "There's always Mrs. Larsen. Or Dorothy."

"Mrs. Larsen hates to drive all the way out here, Dad," Davey reminded him. "She gets real nervous on the freeways, and she gets lost on the other roads."

"True, but she'd do it in an emergency."

Kate chuckled. "And you consider the failure of a sneaky attempt to hitch a ride in my car an emergency?"

"No, but I would probably suffer irreversible psychological damage if you'd ducked out and left me, and *that* would be an emergency. Besides, you agreed to dinner and I doubt you go back on your promises."

Kate caught the subtle message and gave him a wry look. There was a decidedly wicked twinkle in his eyes as he gazed back at her. Whatever reservations he'd had about this outing had clearly been shoved aside.

"You're a fraud," she accused as she led the way past row after row of huge, tan soundstages to her car. "You've been angling to get behind the wheel of my car from the minute you saw it in the driveway up in Malibu. Admit it."

His expression brightened at once in a way that reminded her of Davey. "You'll let me drive?"

"By all means," she said, handing him the keys.

"You won't see any evidence of its power and speed in bumper-to-bumper traffic, but enjoy yourself. Davey and I will squeeze into the passenger seat."

"You do realize, then, how ludicrous and impractical a car like this is in Los Angeles?" he said as he smoothed a hand over the bright red finish. "I don't think anyone's been able to drive over twenty on the freeway in years."

"It's not quite that bad, but what about your car? I suppose you consider that tank practical?" she countered. "When was the last time you needed four-wheel drive to get to the office?"

He laughed. "Touché."

They continued to battle wits over dinner. By dessert Kate had almost forgotten the lousy way the week had started. She even pushed to the back of her mind the guilt that had been nagging at her ever since she'd walked out on Ellen. She needed time to get used to the idea that Ellen understood firsthand what Kate was going through now. She hoped an end to the estrangement was in sight. She would find some way to make it happen—to apologize to her sister.

By the time she dropped her companions off at David's office, her spirits were higher than they had been since their weekend in Malibu. And she was increasingly confident that Davey and David were beginning to rebuild their old rapport. Life, she decided, was not half-bad. She hummed happily all the way home.

Then she opened the door to her apartment and discovered her mother and Brandon in her living room. Though they both looked tanned and relaxed, they did not seem like the ecstatic couple she'd been hearing from for weeks now. And judging from the concerned looks they instantly shot her way, their unhappiness was directly related to her. For an instant she almost regretted having given a spare key to her mother.

When she caught the distinctive scent of raspberry tea, she knew things were serious. That's what her mother always brewed especially for Kate…and only in emergencies.

Chapter Ten

So much for that exhilarating mood she'd been in when she'd left David, Kate thought regretfully. She stifled a groan and plastered a welcoming smile on her face instead.

"Hello, Mother," she said, dropping a kiss on her mother's cheek. "Brandon. You look terrific, but what on earth are you two doing here? Last I heard you were headed for Florence or Paris or someplace."

Brandon shrugged, his sharp gaze studying her intently. Kate detected no anger in the look, just worry.

"Your mother seemed to feel we were needed here," he explained.

"But why?" Kate asked guiltily. "We just talked, a little over a week ago. Everything's fine here."

"No, it is not," her mother said. Those blue eyes of

hers sparked indignantly. "You and Ellen are on the outs, and I want to know why."

Kate regarded her with dismay. "She called and told you that? Why would she deliberately set out to ruin your honeymoon?"

"She didn't deliberately set out to do anything. I called. She was upset. Penny got on the phone and with some urging on my part, she finally explained why. I had no idea you and Ellen were quarreling, and over my marriage of all things."

Kate poured herself a stiff drink, then glanced at them. "Want one?"

Brandon shook his head and looked at her mother. "Lizzy?"

"No," she said impatiently. "I want to know what is going on between my daughters."

When Kate remained stonily silent, Brandon stood up and walked over to where she was staring out the window, her back to the room. He put his hand on her shoulder and squeezed. Tears sprang to her eyes, but she blinked them away, praying he wouldn't see them. As much as she wanted to dislike Brandon Halloran, it seemed he wasn't going to let her.

"Kate, you know I'd do anything in the world to make your mother happy, but this is one thing I can't do. You're the only one who can tell her what's wrong and what we can do to help. I hope you will," he said so gently and with such genuine compassion that Kate felt like a spoiled brat for hurting them. How had she allowed things to get so out of hand? Had she secretly wanted her mother to come home as proof she still cared? Lord, she hoped she wasn't that selfish.

She sensed that Brandon had gone back to her mother's side, heard a low murmur of conversation and then the sound of her front door closing.

"Darling," her mother said quietly.

Kate turned and saw the look of anguish on her mother's face. She saw something else as well: understanding.

"Darling, I know you're feeling left out," she said, proving that with a mother's intuition she had guessed what was at the root of Kate's uncharacteristic behavior. It also explained why she had turned up here, rather than at Ellen's. "What can I do to show you that you are still very much a part of my life and of this family?"

Tears spilled freely down Kate's cheeks. "Look, I know this is ridiculous," she said, brushing irritably at the tears. "I'm a grown woman. I shouldn't be so hung up on things staying the way they always were."

Her mother smiled. "Oh, Kate, you always were too hard on yourself. Change is always hard to accept at first. Why do you think it took me so long to say yes to Brandon, even when I loved him with all my heart? I knew how it would disrupt all our lives."

"But you have a right to be happy," Kate insisted, voicing the rational thought that had struggled with her emotional reaction from the outset.

"Yes, I do, but not at the expense of my girls." Her mother shook her head. "I thought Ellen was the one who'd have trouble with this, not you. I should have thought more about how you would feel. You think I betrayed your father, don't you?"

"No," Kate said, too quickly, judging from her mother's skeptical expression. She considered the question more carefully, then repeated her answer. "No. Not really. You and Dad were open with each other.

He knew how you felt." She looked at her mother. "He did, didn't he?"

"Yes, and he understood. Darling, your father was a wonderful man, a good father, and I am very sorry he is gone. We had a happy life together, and because of him, I have you. That alone would have made our marriage worthwhile."

Kate sighed and felt some small measure of relief steal through her. "I really needed to hear you say that," she admitted.

"Oh, baby," her mother whispered, her voice catching. "How could you possibly doubt how much I love you?"

Those words echoed sentiments she'd heard from David only days before, the same mix of disbelief and anguish and gut-deep caring of a parent. The parallels between his situation with Davey and her own experience were stronger than she'd realized. And she, like Davey, wanted nothing more than reassurance that their world was still secure. It seemed even someone as self-assured as she was would never outgrow that need to feel connected, loved.

Her mother held her arms wide and Kate stepped into them. The hug, combined with the words, reassured her of something she never should have doubted. Even though Ellen was the child of her mother's love for Brandon Halloran, there was still room in her generous heart for Kate. There always would be.

When their tears were dried and her mother had made another pot of raspberry tea, Kate said, "Now tell me about this fantastic honeymoon, Mom. When are you going to take off again?"

"We don't have a set plan. I think we should stick around here for a while, though."

Kate regarded her with renewed guilt. "Not on my account, please. I'm fine now."

"Are you really, Kate? I'm beginning to think Brandon's right. You need a focus in your life, something more than work. You need a husband."

"I need a trip to the French Riviera more." The snappy retort didn't pack the conviction it might have a week or two ago. Her mother clearly caught the change.

"So," she said casually. "Tell me again about the man who was out at the beach house for the weekend."

Kate regarded her suspiciously. "What have you heard?"

"Heard?" her mother said innocently. "You told me yourself he was the father of a client."

"And you immediately dismissed him as being too old for me. What's changed? I can tell by that gleam in your eyes that you've heard something."

"Actually, I believe Zelda did fax an item over to Rome."

"An item?" Kate said blankly. "What item?" Then she recalled the square clipped out of the middle of one of the trade papers the week before. Zelda had been amazingly evasive when she'd asked about it.

"It mentioned that you and David Winthrop were seen dining together at Alice's along with his son."

"I told you that much."

"No."

"Well, I told you they were at the house."

"You didn't tell me the man's name, dear. If you had, I would have known that the man you were entertaining is one of Hollywood's most eligible bachelors."

"How would you know a thing like that?" Kate demanded, knowing that her mother paid very little attention to the film industry.

"Actually, Brandon made a couple of phone calls," she announced cheerfully. "He seemed quite impressed."

Kate covered her face with her hands. Oh, dear Lord. It was her worst nightmare come true. "Mother, call him off," she begged.

Her mother regarded her smugly. "I don't think so, dear. You're inclined to drag your heels about these things. I think this time, perhaps, you could use a little nudge."

"No nudges," Kate protested. "No meddling. No circumspect investigations. Please."

She could tell from her mother's expression, however, that her pleas were falling on deaf ears. She figured she and David had about another twelve hours while Brandon recovered from jet lag. After that, she suspected there would be no holds barred. Dear heaven, what had she let the man in for?

The definite chill in Kate's office had nothing to do with the air-conditioning. Zelda had been in a snit for over two weeks and, Kate was forced to admit, for good cause. She owed her an apology. Now that her personal life was getting back on a more even keel, it was past time she gave her one.

The door opened and Zelda stood framed in the doorway. "Mrs. Mason is here," she announced without setting foot over the threshold. Her voice held that same distant, icy note that had been giving Kate shivers since the previous week.

"I'll see her in a minute," Kate said. "Come in. I'd like to speak to you."

Zelda took one cautious step inside.

"All the way in," she said dryly. "And close the door."

Zelda reacted as if she were being asked to sign her own death warrant.

"Oh, for goodness' sake," Kate said impatiently. "I'm not going to fire you."

"There are worse things than being fired," Zelda replied huffily.

"Like being yelled at when you were only trying to help?"

Her secretary's eyes widened. "For starters," she said.

"I'm sorry," Kate apologized. "I've been a mess ever since Mom's wedding. I can't really explain why, but that's no excuse for taking it out on you."

"You mean because you and Ellen are only half sisters?"

With a sinking sensation in the pit of her stomach, Kate regarded her in astonishment. "How in the world did you know that?"

"Your sister explained."

Irritation flashed through Kate, followed almost at once by resignation. It was Ellen's story to tell or to keep secret. Obviously she'd needed an ally in her battle to get past Kate's hostility and had trusted Zelda enough to share the information with her. As thrown as she might be feeling at this instant, Kate knew that Ellen's trust had not been misplaced. For all of her offbeat personality, Zelda was as loyal and discreet as she was compassionate.

"I see," Kate said slowly. "Then you understand why I've been unusually stressed out."

Zelda shook her head. "Not really. But if you were feeling so bummed out, why didn't you just talk about it?"

Why, indeed, Kate thought. Wasn't that the advice she parceled out almost hourly to her clients before she agreed to handle a divorce? Wasn't that what she'd been advocating that David and Davey do? Talk out their problems, discuss what was on their minds honestly, and when that didn't work, keep talking until it cut through the barriers. She tried to analyze her reluctance to follow her own advice.

Perhaps it had something to do with a lifetime of feeling in control, of feeling absolute certainty about her place in the scheme of things. She'd always credited her parents for giving her that kind of self-confidence by creating a secure environment, filled with love. The discovery that her world was not at all what she'd thought it to be had caused her to question everything about how she fit in. Nothing had prepared her for the loneliness and desperation of that kind of uncertainty.

The blow had also thrown into doubt everything in her universe. Subconsciously she'd apparently put family on a back burner in order to pursue her career, confident in the stability of their love. When that confidence had been shaken, her priorities had been turned topsy-turvy. Talking about it would only have made it seem more real.

"I guess I was hoping that with time, the feelings would go away," she admitted to Zelda. "I suppose I even felt guilty for begrudging Mom her happiness and Ellen her new father."

Zelda gazed heavenward. "Do you hear that, Lord? The woman is human." She regarded Kate with a shake of her head. "Must have been a rude awakening, huh?"

"You mean Ellen's news?"

"No. I mean discovering that not every single thing in life is within your control."

Kate grinned ruefully. "Yeah," she admitted. "It was. Anyway, I am sorry for taking my mood out on you. Now send Mrs. Mason in."

Zelda nodded. "By the way, Davey called from school. He wants to come by when he gets out. I told him you could fit him in. Okay?"

Kate frowned. "Did he say what it was about?"

"No."

"How did he sound?"

"Like he'd lost his best friend."

Kate muttered a curse and wondered what had happened in the week since she'd last seen Davey and his father. With one of her cases going into court this week, she'd been swamped with preparations and hadn't checked on them. Besides, she'd been so sure that the tension between them was easing and that David understood the importance of rebuilding that relationship. Even as she thought about their fragile rapport and its need for nurturing, it occurred to her that she had some bridges to mend herself.

As if she'd read her mind, Zelda said, "By the way, don't you think you should reschedule that lunch with Ellen?"

"I could almost swear I did not hire you to be my conscience," Kate retorted.

"No," her secretary agreed. "It's a bonus."

Kate laughed. "Call her. Set it up. See if Mom wants to come along."

"Perfect," Zelda said approvingly. "Then maybe she'll relax and finish her honeymoon."

"Is there anything about my family life you don't know?"

"Not much," Zelda said cheerfully. "I'll send Mrs. Mason in."

As it turned out, Mrs. Mason was less in need of legal counseling that she was of a friendly ear for her complaints about the philandering Mr. Mason. Kate suggested she make notes for a tell-all memoir that would embarrass the jerk so badly he'd never want to show his face again at Musso and Frank's, the old film industry hangout on Hollywood Boulevard which had managed to maintain its character despite other changes to the neighborhood. Mrs. Mason's eyes lit up at the suggestion.

"I think I'll buy one of those little tape recorders on the way home," she said, then added with a certain amount of glee, "Just seeing me with one of those ought to terrify him."

Personally Kate thought the bill for a month at a fancy health spa would terrify him more, but clearly Mrs. Mason wanted public revenge more than expensive relaxation.

No sooner had the middle-aged woman gone off in search of a tape recorder than Zelda announced Davey's arrival. To Kate's regret, the boy who walked into her office looked much as he had on his first visit. Too neat. Too polite. Too lonely.

"Hi," she said. "What brings you by?"

"I just wanted to visit," he said in a dull tone. He regarded her uncertainly. "Is that okay?"

"Of course it's okay. My favorite client can always be squeezed in." She watched as he paced the room, looking at pictures, touching the small bronze sculptures she'd chosen as decorations. He seemed particularly fascinated by her Remington cowboy. "How are things at home?" she asked finally.

"Okay, I guess."

"Davey," she said insistently, waiting until he turned to face her. "The truth."

"I thought it was going to be better," he said finally. "I really did. Especially after we went to the beach and everything."

"And the studio," she said.

His chin lifted stubbornly. "But I had to remind him and remind him about that."

"Sweetheart, it was only a week or so after the trip to the beach. Even the very best parents in the whole world can't plan special outings like that for every single day." It was a reasonable excuse, but she could see from Davey's expression that he didn't care about grown-up logic.

"He missed my first ball game, too."

"Did you remind him?"

Davey shrugged and Kate guessed that he hadn't, that he'd wanted his father to come through on his own.

"It's going to take time to work all this out," she told him. "It won't happen overnight."

"I know, but we had a list for all that other stuff. Like breakfast. We were supposed to have breakfast together on the weekends until school started. When I got up Saturday, Dad had gone to the office. Sunday he was out in the yard telling some guy how he wanted him to cut the grass or something. School started Monday, and he hasn't been there for breakfast once." Those brown eyes, which telegraphed his hurt feelings, stared at Kate. "I don't think he likes spending time with me."

Only recently having resolved her own feelings of insecurity, Kate could sympathize, even though she knew he was every bit as wrong about his father as she had been about her family. At least she had been old enough to understand what was going on at an intellectual level, even when she hadn't been able to overcome the hurt. Davey was only ten.

"What would you like me to do?" she asked, wanting him to sense that he had control over the steps she was taking. He needed desperately to believe that at least one grown-up was taking him seriously. Hugs and platitudes wouldn't do it this time.

"Maybe we should go ahead with the divorce."

Kate regarded him seriously, her heart aching for him. "Now let's think about that a minute. Your dad promised to make some changes, didn't he?"

"Yeah, but he's not changing at all."

"No," she corrected, "he did make some. Shouldn't we give him the benefit of the doubt, maybe a little more time?"

"I suppose," he conceded grudgingly. "But then what do we do?"

"I'll talk to him, if you like. I'll remind him that we have a binding, legal agreement, and that he has an obligation to live up to the terms of that agreement."

"But what if he doesn't?"

"Then you and I and he will sit down and discuss the alternatives."

"You mean the divorce," he said dully.

Kate went over and pulled him into a hug. "Sweetheart, I can almost guarantee it will not come to that," she said firmly. Not if there was a way in hell she could prevent it, up to and including personally supervising every single activity David was supposed to be sharing with his son.

"How'd you get here?" she asked Davey.

"Mrs. Larsen brought me. She thinks I went to a movie with my friends, though. I'd better go back over so I'm there when she comes to pick me up." He regarded Kate hopefully. "You'll talk to Dad?"

"Today," she promised. "And I'll call you later."

His expression brightened and he hugged her back finally. "Thanks, Kate."

"You bet, kiddo."

The minute he had left, she buzzed Zelda. "Call David Winthrop and tell him I want to see him in my office." She wanted him on her turf this time. Her *professional* turf, so there could be no mistaking the seriousness of her intentions. This was not a place where they could get sidetracked by easy charm and distracting kisses.

"When?" Zelda asked.

"Today."

"But it's already after four."

"That's okay. I'll wait until he can get here. Don't take no for an answer."

She paced until Zelda buzzed her back.

"He'll be here at six-thirty. Is that okay?"

"Yes. Thanks, Zelda."

"Want me to stick around to take notes?"

"Nope. It won't be necessary," she said, then changed her mind. "Actually, if you don't mind staying, I think it would be a good idea for Mr. David Winthrop to catch on that we're playing for keeps with this."

"I'll wait," Zelda said in a tone that suggested that she was at least as interested in getting a look at David Winthrop as she was in being a dutiful secretary.

David showed up five minutes early. He did not look overjoyed at having been summoned across town at the conclusion of one of the hottest September days on record. He looked mussed and exhausted and irritated. For about ten seconds Kate actually felt sorry for him. Then she remembered why he was there and gathered her resolve. She couldn't let her skittering pulse and sympathetic reaction affect her obligation to Davey.

"Would you mind telling me what is so all-fired important that it couldn't wait until tomorrow?" he demanded. He glared at Zelda, who scowled right back at him. "And what is she doing in here?"

"She's here to take notes. I want this conversation on the record."

He glowered at her. "For what?"

"So I can demonstrate to the court that there was an attempt at mediation."

"The court?" he repeated incredulously. "Have you lost your mind?"

Despite her determination to remain objective and impersonal, she couldn't help identifying with what he must be feeling. Mixed in with the anger was no doubt a good bit of humiliation at having his relationship with his son under public attack. Figuring she'd made her point about the seriousness of the situation, she glanced at Zelda. "You can go. I'll make notes and you can type them up tomorrow."

"Are you sure?"

Kate nodded. When Zelda had gone, she looked at David. "I hope you appreciate the fact that I shouldn't have done that. I thought it might be more constructive, just this once, if you and I talked alone."

"About what?" he snapped, still clearly defensive and obviously feeling besieged. Whatever chemistry had sparked between them in the past appeared to have given way to pure resentment. She couldn't help regretting that and wondering if there would ever come a time when things would be simple.

"We need to discuss your son," she retorted firmly. "Remember him?"

He groaned and sank into a chair. "Not this again." He shoved his fingers through his already tousled hair. "I thought we'd resolved this."

"So did I," Kate said evenly. "Unfortunately, Davey stopped by to see me today. According to him, nothing seems to have changed."

"How can you say that? We spent a whole damned weekend with you. We toured the studio."

Kate winced at his beleaguered tone.

"What the hell do you want?" he demanded. "I'm on a tight deadline. I'm doing the best I can."

Actually, he sounded about at the end of his patience and his energy. Kate's resolve wavered under a flood of empathy. She'd had stretches of weeks, even months, exactly like this, with no time even to pause to catch her breath. She could identify completely with the tension he was obviously under and, for that matter, the choices he had made.

"Are you really trying?" she said, but more gently. She owed it to Davey to get the point across, no matter how much she might relate to David's dilemma.

"Yes, dammit. You have no idea what it's like getting crews to bring this job in on time, dealing with a director who's had a sudden brainstorm that changes the set for one entire scene, handling a producer who's going ballistic over the budget. I'm at the end of my rope here. I don't need you adding to it."

The last of Kate's indignation on Davey's behalf faltered. She looked into David's tired eyes and saw a man just struggling to survive.

"I'm sorry," she said, resisting the urge to walk over and massage away the obvious tension in his shoulders. "But we do have a problem here. Davey doesn't understand all this. All he sees is that you made promises and now you're not keeping them." At the risk of incurring another explosion, she added, "It's not as if he has anyone else at home he can depend on."

His expression went absolutely still. "Don't you think I know that?" he whispered.

He regarded her with such absolute misery that something inside her shifted. She couldn't think of any way to respond that wouldn't jeopardize the stand she had to take for Davey's sake. Instead, she waited and listened as he struggled to find his own way out of the mess.

He started to pace, stopping to finger the same objects that had intrigued Davey only hours earlier. Holding the Remington sculpture, he faced Kate. "I don't know what else I can do, not now, anyway. Once this job is over, I can slow my pace down some, make more time for Davey."

Kate recognized the excuse and the well-meant, but probably empty promise. "Will you do that?" she asked. "Or will you bury yourself in just one more project and then one more after that? I'm familiar with the pattern. I do it myself all the time. It's a great way to avoid living."

He scowled at her. She didn't allow herself to waver, even though she badly wanted to recapture their personal rapport for reasons that didn't bear too much scrutiny under the circumstances. Finally some of the anger eased out of his expression. He regarded her ruefully. "Sounds as if you've been engaging in a little self-discovery yourself lately."

"Painful, but true," she admitted. "Actually, I owe some of it to you. I recognized some of my behavior in what you're doing. They always say recognizing what you're up against is the first step toward change."

He grinned and carefully placed the sculpture back on the credenza. "So you did read those pop psychology books your guests left behind after all?"

"A few," she conceded. "Look, no one knows better than I how difficult it is to choose family over work, but it has come to my attention lately that I've made some lousy choices. Isn't it just possible that you have, too?"

"Oh, I'd say it's a dead-on certainty," he agreed without batting an eye. "But, Kate, that doesn't mean I know how the hell to change, not when I'm in the middle of a professional commitment. If I screw this up, my reputation for being on time and on budget will never be the same. This industry can be unforgiving."

"Surely there's room for compromise." She held up the paper he'd signed. "You make the changes one step at a time," she reminded him. "Isn't that what they say?"

He sighed heavily. "So I've heard."

"We can go over this, modify it so that it's more reasonable, given your commitments for the next few weeks. It's better to give Davey some realistic expectations than to have him constantly disappointed by your failure to live up to these."

As she spoke, she realized that he was studying her intently. She lifted her eyes to his and their gazes locked. Electricity arced between them in sufficient voltage to light a soundstage.

"How about dinner?" he said. "Do you have plans? We could work out these modifications."

Kate wanted badly to accept. She wanted to pursue the sensations that had the atmosphere in the room suddenly charged. She wanted to be held and kissed and…

"No," she said with great reluctance. Pleased by his obvious disappointment, she added gently, "You do have plans, though. Go home to your son."

"Could I persuade you to come along?"

"As a buffer? I don't think so."

"I was thinking more as a friend."

Kate's heart seemed to stand still. She knew how badly they both needed a friend right now, but not tonight. Davey came first.

"Because we are friends," she said with an unexpected mixture of certainty and definite anticipation, "there will be other nights."

He nodded finally. "I suppose you're right."

He stood up and Kate walked with him to the elevator. When the doors opened, he leaned down and gave her a quick kiss. The touch of his mouth was warm and feather-light, but it was a commitment nonetheless, a promise that the time was coming when they would explore these fresh, new feelings that were blossoming for both of them even under these trying circumstances.

"Thanks," he said. "Despite my rotten attitude, I know that Davey's fortunate to have you in his corner."

Kate reached up and touched his cheek. "Don't forget that he's lucky to have you for a father, too."

He regarded her ruefully. "I thought you just finished telling me what a lousy job of parenting I was doing."

"Right now," she said gently. "Not always. If you hadn't been such a great father before, he wouldn't be missing you so much now."

"Thank you for saying that," he said. Then, just as the elevator doors slid closed, he added, "I hope you know what an incredibly special woman you are, Kate Newton. I really mean that."

Kate sighed. Thanks to him and Davey and her own family, she was just beginning to remember that she had a worth that extended far beyond her value as an attorney.

Chapter Eleven

When David walked into the house, he found Davey seated alone at the huge dining room table, looking so forlorn that David felt his heart wrench with guilt and dismay. No little boy should ever look that sad.

"Hey, pal," he said. His breath caught at the expression of happiness that instantly brightened his son's face. How had he forgotten that this was what mattered? How had he lost sight of the wonder of having Davey regard him with such open adoration?

"Dad! I didn't know you were coming for dinner."

"Sorry I'm late. Where's Mrs. Larsen?"

"In the kitchen. She wanted to watch the news and her game shows. Sometimes I watch with her, but it's pretty boring. I told her I wanted to eat in here."

"By yourself? Why not in the den, so you could watch a video or something?"

"Mrs. Larsen says the den's no place for food. That's why we have a kitchen and a dining room," he said in a tone that precisely mimicked the housekeeper's.

Suddenly angrier than he had been in a very long time, David forgot about his own meal. He pulled out a chair and sat down. He studied his son's neatly combed hair, the spotless shirt he was wearing. He'd always assumed such things were an indication of what good care the woman was taking of his son. Now he realized what Kate had meant when she'd told him weeks earlier that the housekeeper was rigid, even though she clearly cared a great deal for Davey.

"What else does Mrs. Larsen say?" he said tightly.

"She says lots of stuff," Davey said with a shrug. "She has rules for just about everything. I'll bet she never had any fun when she was a kid."

"How about shooting some baskets with me?" David said impulsively. Suddenly he badly wanted to see his son flushed with excitement and messed up from having exactly the sort of fun Davey assumed the housekeeper had missed in her childhood.

"Now?" Davey replied, his eyes lighting up. He glanced at the generous scoop of baby carrots and broccoli untouched on his plate and his face fell. "I haven't finished my vegetables. Mrs. Larsen says beta…beta-something is an important vitamin."

"To hell with your vegetables," David said, thinking that Mrs. Larsen said entirely too much. "Let's go."

Davey started for the stairs.

"Where are you going?"

"I have to change into my play clothes."

"You do not," David said firmly, as he unbuttoned his shirt and tossed it on the dining room chair. Fortunately he was wearing jeans and sneakers. "Not tonight, anyway. Where's the basketball?"

"In the garage."

"Good. I'll get it and switch on the outside lights." He grinned at his son. "I hope you've been practicing, because I'm feeling very lucky tonight."

Davey giggled as he darted past him. "Dad, you're terrible, except at free shots."

"Terrible?" David retorted indignantly. "I'll show you terrible, you ungrateful little monster."

They thundered through the kitchen, startling Mrs. Larsen, whose mouth immediately turned down into a disapproving frown. She opened her mouth, but before she could say a word, David gazed at her evenly and said, "You and I will have a talk later. I think some changes are in order around here."

Eyes wide with astonishment and instantaneous anxiety, she stared after him. David felt only minimally guilty for disrupting her meal and her routine. He felt worse about making her anxious. Though his first ill-tempered instinct had been to fire her, he realized that would be unfair.

Over the years Mrs. Larsen had been good to all of them. In fact, she had been a real saint during Alicia's illness, treating her as tenderly as if she'd been her own daughter. She was older, and no doubt a firm hand and rigid rules were her way of coping with an energetic boy. Hopefully he could make her see that a more moderate approach of discipline was called for.

As he and Davey played basketball, he realized exactly how much his son had improved since the last time they'd been on the court. Not only was he quick on his feet, but his shots were increasingly sure, despite whatever pressure David put on him. He was also sneaky as the dickens when it came to blocking his father's shots. They called the game at nine o'clock, when they were tired and sweaty and dead even.

"Enough," David cried, collapsing onto the grass beside the half court that backed up to the garage.

"Chicken," Davey accused. "I had the ball. One more minute and I would have won."

"Probably so," David conceded with a laugh, wondering how his son had developed such a fierce competitive streak. Kate would no doubt say the boy had inherited it from him. But he hadn't always been that way. He'd only become driven since Alicia's death. Perhaps with Kate and Davey prodding him, to say nothing of Dorothy, he could get his priorities back in order.

He ruffled Davey's damp hair. "Think how humiliating it would have been for me to lose. Give your old man a break."

"You want a drink?" Davey asked. "I could bring us a pop."

"Wonderful," he said gratefully.

When Davey returned with the cans, he sat down next to his father. "I think Mrs. Larsen is really worried," he said, sounding genuinely concerned about the housekeeper. "You're not really mad at her, are you, Dad?"

"No, not really. I just want to talk to her about relaxing a few rules around here."

"Good," Davey said, "'cause she's not so bad. It's not like she's really mean."

David regarded his son proudly. "You're a great kid to stand up for her."

Davey shrugged. "She's not like a mom or anything,"

he said carefully. "But she bakes pretty good cookies and stuff, and she'll usually take me places to see my friends. I think it makes her nervous, though, when they come here. She's afraid we're all going to fall in the pool and drown."

"Is that why you don't have your friends over so much?"

It was a long while before Davey answered. "Not really," he said.

"Why, then?"

"I like to go to their houses better," he admitted finally.

David thought of the way his own home had always been the center of his boyhood activities. He'd wanted that for Davey, too. He wondered why it hadn't happened that way. Then he recalled the way things had been during Alicia's illness, how quiet they'd tried to keep things for her. Had Davey stopped inviting his friends over then? Or was the answer as uncomplicated as the choices of entertainment available in his friends' homes?

"Do they have more stuff to do?" he asked, though he couldn't imagine any child having more toys than his son.

Davey shook his head, his gaze focused determinedly on a smudge on his sneakers. He rubbed it intently.

Puzzled by Davey's sudden reticence, David prodded, "Son, what is it?"

Those huge brown eyes that could break his heart finally met his.

"Most of them have a mom and a dad," he said wistfully. "It's really nice."

The pain that cut through David then was worse

than any heart attack, worse than the anguish he'd felt
the day Alicia had died. He reached over and gathered
Davey close. Skinny arms circled his neck, the rare
gesture all the more precious coming from his too-big-
for-hugs son.

"I'm sorry, Davey," he whispered, his throat clogged
with emotion. "God, I'm so sorry."

After a while he felt tears fall onto his chest, but he
had no way of knowing if they were Davey's or his own.

David got Davey into bed, then showered, put on
pajama bottoms and a robe for Mrs. Larsen's sake and
went in search of the housekeeper. He found her in her
room, still dressed, still looking as if she feared dis-
missal.

"Mrs. Larsen, I apologize if my behavior earlier worried you."

"I try to make allowances," she said primly, following him into the kitchen. She pulled out a chair and sat
down heavily, obviously expecting the worst.

David wondered guiltily how many allowances had
been made in the months since Alicia had died and the
burden for caring for his house and his son had fallen
on Mrs. Larsen's sturdy shoulders.

"You've done a wonderful job around here," he reassured her. "I really don't know what I would have done
without you. But I am concerned about Davey."

The relief that had flickered in her eyes gave way to
defensiveness. "What's he been telling you?"

"Nothing, I promise you. I just have the feeling that
perhaps it's time we were a little more lenient with him.
He needs to learn to take responsibility for his actions. I
think you've laid a solid foundation for that, don't you?"

"But he's still just a boy," she protested. "He needs guidance."

"Exactly. He needs guidance, not military discipline. Perhaps we could loosen the rules just a little. If I'm not home, for example, and he wants to eat in his room or the den, I think a tray could be prepared, don't you?"

Though she looked horrified by the very thought, she nodded. "I suppose, though there's bound to be a mess."

"Then he'll have to clean it up."

She gave an approving bob of her head. "I suppose that would do."

"And I'd like you to encourage him to invite his friends here. I know it's asking a lot. Ten-year-old boys tend to be noisy and rambunctious, but I think it's only reasonable that Davey pay them back for having him over so often. I'll try to make sure that I'm home when they're here, too."

An idea from his own childhood occurred to him. "Maybe next weekend he could even have a sleepover, if you wouldn't mind baking an extra couple of batches of those cookies he likes so much. I'll order in pizza and soft drinks."

The prospect of the deafening commotion a group of ten-year-olds could create was almost as daunting for him as it was for Mrs. Larsen, but he was determined that she not be the only one making changes around here. He would try to manage some without Kate's insistence, though he couldn't deny he wanted her approval.

Mrs. Larsen's gaze softened just a little. "If you don't mind my saying so, sir, I think that's what he really needs, a bit more of your attention."

"So I've been told," David said ruefully. "That's all

for tonight, Mrs. Larsen. If you run into any problems, please talk them over with me."

"Yes, sir," she said. She started back for her room, then turned around. "It's good to see you taking an interest again, Mr. David."

He sighed. "Thank you, Mrs. Larsen. I should have done it long ago."

When she had gone, he went into his den and sank into the wing chair where he'd found Kate a few weeks earlier. For the first time in ages, he was pleasantly worn out, rather than gut-deep exhausted. He also saw how right she'd been about how much Davey needed him. He'd have to tell her that the next time they spoke.

Why not tonight? Impulsively he picked up the phone, glanced at the card attached to the legal papers Kate had given him and dialed her number. The service picked up.

"Is it urgent, Mr. Winthrop?"

He figured it was at least as urgent as her demand to see him earlier. "Yes."

"I'll have her call you."

It was less than five minutes before his phone rang. The smoky sound of Kate's voice made his heart leap in a way that was altogether astonishing. It seemed when she wasn't infuriating him, she was turning him on.

"I wanted to thank you," he said, even as he listened to the unspoken explanation for the call echoing inside him: *I wanted to hear your voice.*

"For what?"

"For the best night I've had in a long while." *For caring.*

"With Davey?" she said.

"Yes." *And with you.*

"I'm so glad." There was a note of genuine happiness in her voice. "What'd you do?" she asked, as if she were eager to hear every single detail.

"Played basketball until we dropped."

"Who won?"

"No one. I had sense enough to call the game when we were tied."

"You mean before he beat you?" she taunted.

"That's what he said," he grumbled. "I think you two are in cahoots."

"Yes, we are," she admitted with a laugh.

David sighed. "I'm glad," he told her. "I can't promise things will change overnight, but I am trying, Kate."

"That's all I can ask."

Suddenly there were so many things he wanted to say to her, so many things he wanted to discover about this woman who'd bulldozed her way into his life. Realizing that he was genuinely beginning to care, he waited for the onset of guilt, but it didn't come. Once more he saw that tonight had been a real turning point in his life. He owed her for that, for opening him up to living again.

"I'll see you soon," he said. He kept to himself the one thing he wanted to say above all others: *I can't wait to hold you in my arms to see if there really are miracles.*

"See you soon," she echoed.

It was a full minute before either of them actually broke the connection, as if they were both reluctant to go back to their own lonely, isolated worlds again.

Even though Kate felt reassured by her meeting with David and his late-night call, she recognized that the changes she was asking for were not likely to happen overnight without a little nudge every now and then. She was very good at nudging.

She started by calling the house every morning at seven o'clock to remind David that he was supposed to stick around to have breakfast with his son. Of course, hearing David's sleepy, sexy voice at that hour of the morning did delightfully wicked things to her frame of mind for the rest of the day, as well.

If David was bothered by her blatant interference, it never once showed in his voice. In fact, the conversations lengthened day by day, touching on their own plans for the day, exploring the latest news. Kate soon felt she knew his schedule almost as well as she knew her own. Too often she found herself glancing at the clock during the day and recalling where he'd said he'd be.

But despite the closeness she was beginning to feel, despite the unexpectedly satisfying warmth of feeling as if she was some small part of his life, neither of them made any overtures to get together. It was just as well, she told herself. Her schedule was jammed from dawn until way past dusk, just as it had always been. It seemed the advice she'd been quick to give him hadn't affected her own behavior at all.

Then, when she'd been calling for just over a week and least expected it, David suggested she stop by and join them for breakfast. "The weather's beautiful on the terrace in the mornings. It's a great way to start the day," he said, as if he'd just made the discovery and couldn't wait to share it.

She was torn between accepting and duty. "I have to be in court at nine."

"Tomorrow, then. It's Saturday. No excuses. Besides,

your client asks about you all the time. Could be he's already tired of my company."

She laughed at his deliberate sneakiness. "And I thought I was a master manipulator. Okay, I'll be there. Just promise me that Mrs. Larsen won't make oatmeal. Davey told me it's like cement."

"It could hold buildings together during an earthquake," David agreed. "Okay. No oatmeal. We'll see you about eight."

"Sounds good." She'd started to hang up when she heard his voice.

"Kate?"

"Yes."

"Good luck in court."

She was already feeling exceptionally lucky.

On Saturday with the weatherman calling for record heat again, Kate chose a bright yellow sundress that reflected her cheery mood when she dressed to join David and Davey for breakfast. She spent an extraordinary amount of time on her makeup, assuring herself that it looked natural. The irony of that did not escape her. She spent less time on her hair, knowing that the wind would play havoc with whatever style she attempted. She refused to put the top up on the car just to save a hairdo, especially on a day made for a convertible.

As she drove to David's, her pace leisurely despite the deserted roads, she anticipated the changes in his rapport with his son. She could hardly wait to see how much progress they'd made. Then, uttering a little sigh, she confessed to herself that she could hardly wait to explore the changes she had sensed in her own relationship with David. Every phone call had had an increas-

ingly provocative undercurrent, no matter how mundane
the actual topic.

Mrs. Larsen greeted her at the door, her expression
perfectly bland, though Kate was almost certain she
caught a surprising twinkle in the housekeeper's eyes.
Perhaps Mrs. Larsen had a touch of romance in her
soul after all.

"Mr. David is on the terrace," she said. "Follow me."

"And Davey?"

"He spent the night at a friend's. I'm not sure exactly
what time he's expected back."

Kate's step faltered. Davey wasn't here? Wasn't the
whole purpose of this visit to give her a chance to be
reassured about how much better he and his father were
getting along? She hadn't realized until just that instant
how much she had been counting on Davey to provide a
buffer between her and his father. His presence would
have guaranteed that everything would remain pleasantly impersonal, even if her own common sense had
taken a nosedive.

As she followed Mrs. Larsen onto the terrace, David
rose to greet her from the table that had been set beside
the pool. He was wearing a bathing suit and an unbuttoned shirt. He'd obviously just been for a swim. His
hair was curling damply, and droplets of water sparkled
on his lightly tanned skin. She found her gaze locking
on the very masculine expanse of bare chest as her pulse
accelerated faster than her car ever had.

David's gaze swept over her. The expression in his
eyes was so warmly appreciative that Kate had to swallow hard against the nervousness that seemed lodged
in her throat.

"You look absolutely ravishing," he said softly.

His tone set her pulse off again. To counteract the suddenly provocative tenor the morning was taking, she lifted her chin and regarded him indignantly.

"I thought Davey was going to be here," she said.

"He was, but a friend called last night and invited him over. He really wanted to go."

"Why do I have the feeling you practically shoved him out the door?" she grumbled.

She noticed that he didn't bother trying to deny it.

"Because you know that I've been wanting to be alone with you for quite some time now," he said.

"I don't know that," she argued, futilely hoping to salvage some of the distance that she needed to keep her emotions safe.

"Liar," he accused.

Then, as if he sensed that she might yet bolt, he relented. "Sit down, Kate. Juice and coffee are on the table. Breakfast should be out any minute. We're having French toast stuffed with cream cheese and orange marmalade. I trust that sounds suitably decadent."

Kate's mouth watered. "Decadent? It sounds suicidal."

"We'll swim off the calories," he promised as Mrs. Larsen placed plates laden with delectable-looking food in front of them.

"This many calories?" she asked skeptically.

"We have all day to work them off."

Her gaze darted to the pool and back to him. "I didn't bring a suit."

"Not a problem," he said in a way that sent her imagination running wild. Finally he grinned and added, "There are suits in the pool house, if you really insist on wearing one."

"Oh, I really insist," she muttered breathlessly, though she was more taken than she liked to admit with the idea of skinny-dipping under the blazing sun with this man. She was scandalized by the effect he seemed to be having on her without half trying. What on earth would happen if he ever put his mind to seducing her?

"Kate?" he said softly.

"Yes?" Her fork clattered against the plate as she met his gaze.

"Don't be afraid of what's happening between us."

"Is something happening?" she asked, retrieving the fork and holding it in a deathlike grip.

"I'm not sure when or how it happened, but it is for me. I can see in your eyes that it is for you, too."

Kate wondered just what he was feeling. Lust? He'd probably been celibate for a long time. They'd been thrown together a lot lately, shared a couple of steamy kisses. He'd probably jumped to all sorts of wicked and incorrect conclusions as a result. She tried to give herself time by taking a bite of the food. It was probably delicious. It could just as easily have been sawdust.

"David, I understand that you've been lonely," she began finally.

"This has nothing to do with loneliness," he retorted patiently.

"No. I think it does. It's natural…"

"Yes. It is natural," he interrupted, not allowing her to put another spin on the attraction. "Look, I'm not rushing into anything here. Lord knows, I have been lonely. But I have also fallen in love once before in my life. I know how that feels, too. We discussed this once. Those bells, remember?"

Kate shot a startled, desperate look at him. "Love,"

she repeated, her voice wavering. She pushed the plate aside. All interest in food had fled. What she needed was a drink. Too bad he hadn't served mimosas. Champagne and orange juice would have smoothed over this jagged nervousness she was feeling.

"Don't panic," he said, his expression amused. "I'm not jumping to any conclusions. I've just made a conscious decision to open myself up to the possibilities."

"You sound like somebody contemplating having their astrological chart done for the first time, part skepticism, part hope."

"Exactly." His smile faded and his gaze clashed with hers. "Can't you at least meet me halfway on this?"

"Halfway?" she repeated, as if there were a spot on the lawn he could pinpoint. She knew she was beginning to sound half-addled, but she wasn't prepared to leap into something even halfway as an experiment. That's how people got badly hurt.

"It's been the obligatory half hour since we finished eating. At least, you haven't touched a bite in that long," he taunted. "We could make that halfway point in the pool."

Kate wasn't wild about getting into a bathing suit or into a pool with a man who'd declared his intention to explore the way he felt about her. But at least a trip to the pool house might give her a few minutes to gather her composure and remind herself—quite sternly, in fact—that she was not in the market for a quick tumble in anyone's bed.

Her body, she noticed with some regret, seemed to have other ideas.

Chapter Twelve

As Kate headed for the pool house to change, David decided he definitely needed a dip in the pool to cool off. For a woman so damned determined not to be provocative, she'd had his temperature rising from the minute she'd strolled onto the terrace looking as cool and refreshing as a tall glass of lemonade.

Of course, he admitted candidly, it was entirely likely that any one of the bathing suits she chose from the supply on hand would be even more disturbing than that dress, which had simply bared her shoulders and swirled around her like a pool of sunlight. Just the anticipation stirred an arousal that not even the cool, turquoise water of the pool could counteract. Clearly it was payback time for months of celibacy. His body was reminding him with throbbing urgency that he was still very much alive.

He started to swim long, hard strokes that had his taut body slicing through the water. He completed one lap, flipped and went back the other way. He'd done nearly twenty exhausting laps, when he finally stopped. Breathless, he clung to the edge of the pool. It was a full minute before he glanced up, saw Kate standing hesitantly before him and felt every nerve ending in his body clamor for just one thing. It wasn't a quick game of water polo.

Dear Lord, what was he about to do? he wondered desperately as his gaze locked on the unrevealing one-piece bathing suit that still managed to entice like the most daring bikini. The sedate neckline didn't dip too low, but that didn't matter. There was no way it could hide the lush fullness of her breasts, something her usual power suits managed to disguise. The cut of the bottom wasn't especially high on the sides, but it still revealed long, shapely legs and hips that were meant to cradle a man. The slick black material fit like a second skin. David's pulse took on a staccato rhythm. He was afraid if she stood there one more instant, his rampaging hormones would lead them both into more trouble than they'd bargained for.

"Dive in," he urged. "The water's wonderful."

"Not too cold?"

Not that he'd noticed, he thought wryly. He shook his head. "Take the plunge."

If she caught the unintended double entendre, she didn't show it by so much as the flicker of an eyelash. She simply walked to the edge at the deep end, lifted her hands in a diver's stance and cut into the water with barely a ripple to disturb the sparkling surface. Not two seconds later, she came up sputtering, goose bumps already rising on her pale-as-cream skin.

"It's like ice, damn you!" she said and swam toward him with a gleam of mock ferocity in her eyes.

David couldn't help laughing at her indignation. "Just the thing for a hot day, don't you think?"

"It's not hot yet," she pointed out as she drew closer. "Maybe by noon this would feel terrific." As if to emphasize how cold it was, her teeth began to chatter. "S-see what I mean?"

"What you need is a little exercise," he announced. "It'll warm you right up. I'll race you to the end of the pool and back."

"You're on," she agreed with that devilish glint back in her eyes.

She pushed off. The fact that her first kick landed squarely in his midsection was probably just an accident, he told himself as he took off after her.

Kate was good, he realized as he caught her, then found her matching him stroke for stroke. She was also a fighter and she didn't necessarily play fair. More than once she managed to tangle her legs with his just enough to throw him off, while she swam confidently on. When they'd finished two laps, she grinned at him as she executed a tight flip and muttered, "Again?"

She didn't wait for his response. She was a half lap ahead by the time he could reverse directions. He was too much a competitor to lag behind for long, though. He pushed his endurance to catch and then pass her. Several laps later, they were both clinging to the side trying to catch their breath.

He looked into her eyes and found himself mesmerized by the light shimmering in their depths. That brilliant spark lured like a lantern in the darkness. Without thinking, just reacting to a deep, yearning need, he tucked one hand around the back of her neck and drew her closer. He felt the shiver that raced over her. When his lips claimed hers, she shuddered. He felt her cool skin turn warm under the persuasive touch of his mouth, the gentle teasing of his tongue.

There was an instant as his hand settled at the curve of her hip when her body tensed as if she might push him away. David's breath seemed to lodge in his chest as he waited for her decision. And then, when he wasn't sure he could bear another second of indecision, she relaxed and melted against him. Her hands slid up his chest with slow, teasing deliberation, then locked behind his neck as she turned her head to angle her mouth under his, open to the invasion of his tongue.

David groaned. Her skin was warm and cool at once, the fire inside chilled by the pool's water. Slick with moisture, her body felt the way it might have after long, sensuous hours of lovemaking. As that thought struck him, he wondered that steam didn't rise around them.

His hands skimmed along the material of her bathing suit, learning the shape of her, discovering that the layer of fabric tantalized, even as it thwarted flesh-on-flesh contact. He could feel the hardening of her nipples as he caressed her breasts, could feel the way she seemed to move into his touch, rather than holding back. The subtly sensuous movements almost drove him crazy.

He sensed then that Kate was a woman who would hold nothing back when it came to giving and receiving pleasure. A woman like that would be more vulnerable than most and a great tide of tenderness washed over him when he realized the rare gift she was sharing with him, the risk she appeared willing to take with her own peace of mind.

He framed her face with his hands, his gaze locked on hers, trying to see into her soul. He tried to judge one last time if he had misread things, if she truly was with him all the way on the desires that were throbbing deep inside, crowding out everything else. He saw only a need that matched his own. Whatever doubts she might have about them, about the future—and if he had dozens, she was bound to have more—she had committed herself to following his lead. She seemed more than ready to explore the sensations that were as old as time, yet as sparkling new as if this were the first time in their lives for each of them.

"Kate?" he said softly.

Those dark eyes of hers blazed back at him, filled with life, luring him into a world of powerful need and thrilling sensation, drawing him from the past into the present, into this one, single moment in time. Deep inside, something slowly shifted, eased, freeing him forever from the past, blessing his decision to move on.

He knew, though, that if they ventured further—he and this warm, passionate woman he held—for him there would be no turning back. To him, making love had always been a commitment, a promise, and for reasons he couldn't have explained if he'd tried, he knew that was as true for him now as it had ever been. It didn't seem to matter that Kate was only weeks past being a stranger. It didn't even seem to matter that she was a declared adversary. In fact, he was stunned to discover that it felt so right that his choice this time was Kate, a woman so unlike Alicia. She was harder, more fiercely competitive, more passionate about everything.

And then he looked more deeply into her eyes, those windows to the soul, and saw the anxiety, the wellspring of gentleness, the yearning. So, he thought, as he captured her mouth once more, it wasn't so surprising after all.

The surprise came when he carried her from the pool and, still dripping wet, into the master bedroom suite. It came when she declined slow, gentle touches and set a pace that was just shy of desperate, a frenzied claiming that left them in a tangle of wet bathing suits and pushed them into a fevered, urgent release that rocked the bed and left them both gasping for breath.

"Dear Lord," he said, when he could finally gather breath to say anything at all.

Kate, her hair a dark tangle against the pillow, her skin flushed and damp, merely smiled. It was a contented Mona Lisa smile. Had she been a cat, David thought with amusement, she would have been purring. Even her slow, lazy, sensuous stretch spoke of satisfaction and bore no hint of the self-consciousness she had displayed earlier. This Kate was all woman and reveling in it.

"It occurs to me that you should wear a tag warning of danger," he teased, still pleasantly startled by her complete and generous sharing of her body. "I'm stunned."

"I must admit to being a little stunned myself," she said, laughing with him. "Two hours ago I would have sworn that I didn't want this to happen, that I wouldn't allow it to happen."

Having felt much the same way, David circled his arms around her and settled her against his chest. He smoothed her hair away from her face. "What happened to change your mind?"

He felt the slight shake of her head.

"I'm not sure," she said, her breath whispering against his overheated flesh. "Suddenly it just felt right, as if it would be absolutely foolish to resist when I wanted to be held like this more than anything."

"By me?"

Her gaze, filled with surprise, met his. "Of course by you." She pulled away and she studied him more intently. "What about you? Is this what you had in mind when you lured me over here?"

David searched his heart for the answer to that. The quick, easy answer was no. The truth seemed much more complicated. "Although I've denied it for weeks now, I think I've wanted you from the first moment I set eyes on you."

"You thought I was an uppity bitch when you first laid eyes on me," she reminded him.

"Always the biggest challenge," he retorted, chuckling at the indignation that flared in her eyes. He touched her lips, which were threatening to curve into a smile despite her best efforts to stop herself. "Ah, Kate, you've made me laugh again."

"And yell," she said. "Don't forget the yelling."

He pressed a kiss against her forehead. "The point is you've made me feel things again. For a very long time, I wasn't sure that was possible."

She sighed and settled more comfortably in his arms. "Right this instant, almost anything seems possible."

"Yes," he murmured. "It does."

He heard her breathing slow into a quiet, steady rhythm. He swept a hand down her spine, stopping eventually on the curve of her bottom. He was fascinated by the unexpectedly easy intimacy between them. He'd expected if the time ever came when he brought another woman to this bed, he would be battling ghosts.

Perhaps that explained Kate's aggressive, urgent lovemaking, he thought with sudden understanding. She hadn't wanted him to have time to think. She had wanted him so caught up in what was happening between the two of them, in the perfect fit of their bodies, in the demanding need, that there was no time for second thoughts. If that had indeed been her intention, he owed her for making this step easier for him to take.

"Ah, Kate," he murmured, even though she wasn't awake to hear him. "You are, perhaps, the most enchanting, complex woman I have ever known."

How the hell was she supposed to extricate herself from this mess, Kate wondered when she awoke. She was not thinking of the tangled sheets and bathing suits currently holding her captive in this bed, either. She was referring to the fact that she had ignored her best intentions and behaved like an absolutely wanton woman the very first time David Winthrop had so much as given her a come-hither glance.

Okay, so it had been more than a glance. It had been a couple of those bone-melting kisses, but the point was the same. Her resolve, based on pretty sound, rational thought, had vanished like a puff of smoke. Poof! Gone! And she'd convinced herself that she was a woman ruled by her intellect rather than her hormones, she thought wryly. What a joke that was.

She blinked open one eye and dared a glance at the man against whom she was currently snuggled up. He was drop-dead handsome, she thought with a sigh. And sexy. Even now, when regrets were stampeding through her at a hundred miles an hour, she wanted him. She wanted him to look at her the way he had earlier, as if she were the most desirable woman on the face of the earth. She wanted him to touch her again with that mixture of reverence and fascination that turned suddenly urgent. She wanted to be swept away on a tide of glorious, magical sensation one more time.

And then she wanted to go home and pretend it had never happened, wipe it from her mind, go on living as if something cataclysmic hadn't just happened to her. It was very important that she be able to do that, too. She didn't have a doubt in the world that a man who hadn't been able to push grief aside for the sake of his beloved son was hardly ready to embrace a new relationship.

As for her, everyone knew she had chosen to go through life alone. It was less complicated, less hurtful. There might be a real shortage of peaks, but there definitely were no miserable valleys, either. She'd plunged into the lowest valley of them all with Ryan and vowed never again.

She stroked her fingers along David's smooth jaw. It was too bad it had to be this way, she thought regretfully. The peak they had just attained without half trying had been one damned fine peak.

She closed her eyes and wished they could linger this way forever, suspended in time. Suddenly she felt him nuzzling against her, felt his mouth, warm and wet, surround her nipple. The deep, sucking sensation sent a live current jolting through her. Regrets fled. Common sense fled. Only need, sweet and wild, sliced through her as she felt her body waken beneath his slow, lazy caresses.

Hands roughened, probably by one too many close encounters with chain saws, skimmed over her flesh, teasing, setting her ablaze. She twisted and bucked as fingers reached wetness and invaded in a slow, rhythmic movement.

"When you come awake, you really come awake, don't you?" she murmured, fighting the all-consuming sensation that threatened to sweep her over the edge before he had joined her.

"Don't fight me," he whispered back, the strokes more intense, deeper, more demanding.

She let go then, let the flood of feeling wash over her, through her. Then, just when she thought she would spin free, the touches slowed, taunted. Wild now with need, she pleaded silently, gazing into eyes darkened with passion.

"You want me?" he asked in that husky, low-down, sneaky tone that conjured images of the back-seat scrambling of adolescence, the hunger to try everything.

She wanted to say no, wanted to say she didn't need anyone, ever, but it would have been a lie. Right now, this instant, she couldn't bear the thought of one more second without him inside her, without that full, throbbing sense of completion.

Breathless, she rose instinctively toward him, hips lifting off the bed as she admitted between gasps, "I… want…you."

Satisfaction broke over his face as he joined her then with one powerful thrust. Even then, even when she felt she would explode with sensation—skin sensitive, fire in her veins—he took his time. He led her to the edge and back again and again, each time a little higher, the ride a little wilder until at last she felt the sweet waves of a shuddering climax consume first her and then him.

It was a long time before either of them spoke, before either of them could move. Kate was content to be held in his arms, her body still joined with his in the most intimate way possible. As long as they were together like this, she wouldn't have to decide whether to go or stay.

It was David who moved eventually, brushing a kiss on her bare shoulder as he left the bed and padded into the bathroom. She heard the shower go on and then, before she realized he'd returned, he had scooped her once again into his arms.

In the steamy bathroom she regarded the shower skeptically. "I'm not sure I trust you where water's concerned. Maybe I'd better test this myself before I plunge in."

He grinned. "It's warm. I promise," he said, standing her on her feet at the edge of the huge sunken tub. He grabbed a towel and headed for the door. "You go ahead. I'll pull on my suit and go for another swim."

Startled and disappointed that he wouldn't be joining her, she warned herself not to show it. "How can you possibly have that much energy to spare?" she said, too cheerfully. "I'm drained."

"I'm not sure I do. If you hear me yell, I trust you'll come save me."

She gave him a considering look, then forced a grin. "Yeah, I suppose I would."

He chuckled and left her then. Uneasy and unable to explain exactly why, Kate didn't linger under the steamy spray, even though it felt wonderful. Something inside nagged that she and David ought to be talking about what had happened, not suddenly ignoring it. She sensed that his retreat in that bed a few minutes earlier had been more than just physical. There had been something in his eyes, a shadow of regret perhaps, that reminded her that she should have heeded all those warnings to stay away. She toweled herself dry, then remembered that her clothes were still in the pool house.

Wrapped in the oversize towel, she started to walk back into the bedroom. Then she saw David standing beside the bed, head bent, shoulders slumped. A man in real torment. At first she wanted to run to him, but then she realized what had captured his attention so completely. He was holding a silver-framed picture in his hands. She'd noticed it herself earlier on the bedside table. It was his wedding picture.

She could feel the sting of tears in her eyes as she imagined the agony of regrets churning through him now. Reminded that the past few hours had been only an interlude, she felt her heart ache far more than it should have, given all the stern lectures she'd given herself lately. Obviously, intellectually knowing something was a far cry from the gut-wrenching pain of experiencing it emotionally.

It shouldn't have mattered. She had never wanted anything from any man, least of all this one. Clutching the towel together as she debated what to do, she finally admitted to herself that she had lied.

It was a lie that was going to cost her dearly.

Chapter Thirteen

If nothing else over recent weeks, Kate had learned a couple of valuable lessons. Nothing ever got solved by shoving it into a closet and ignoring it. Her own problems with her family, and Davey's problems with his father, were proof of that. The wounds had festered far longer than they'd needed to.

With that in mind, she crossed the bedroom until she was standing next to David. Careful not to brush against him, she said quietly, "She was very beautiful."

A sigh shuddered through him. Without turning to look at her, he said, "Yes. She was." He opened the drawer of the nightstand beside the bed and started to put the picture inside.

Pushing her own feelings firmly aside, Kate stayed his hand. "Don't."

His gaze, dark with anguish, clashed with hers. "It's

time to let go of the past. Isn't that what you've been telling me for weeks now?" he said angrily, slamming the drawer closed, the picture inside.

"Yes," she said evenly, opening the drawer and taking it back out. She placed it carefully in its former spot on the nightstand. "There's a difference between moving on with your life and locking the past away as if it had never happened. What message would it send to Davey if he saw that his mother's pictures had all been shoved away out of sight? He's already afraid to mention her for fear of upsetting you."

For the space of a heartbeat, he looked taken aback. Then, if anything, his eyes flashed even more stubbornly. "Surely one of those pop psychology books at your house has a chapter on grief," he said sarcastically. "Perhaps you should look it over. I suspect it says that everyone handles grief in his or her own way."

Kate tried not to lose her temper, but he was so damned bullheaded and irritating. "That's true," she shot back. "But you're not *handling* it at all."

She thought for an instant he might lash back at her, hoped for it, in fact.

Instead, he simply said coldly, "What would you know about having your life shattered? You're always in control, always so certain of what you should be doing, what everyone should be doing. I'm sure you refuse to allow any little ups and downs."

Kate winced at the unflattering image. All too recently, however, his description would have been on the money. After her breakup with Ryan she had sought control, prided herself on it. But that hadn't always been the case, and she had paid heavily for that mistake, just as it appeared likely she would pay again for having fallen in love with a man who wasn't ready to give himself to anyone.

"You're wrong," she said. "You see, a long time ago I fell in love with a man I was sure was the man of my dreams. We were in law school together, but he dropped out, decided that there were other ways he could help the poor and downtrodden. I thought it was the most idealistic decision he could have made. I was very proud of him."

She watched David for a reaction. His expression was stony, his gaze directed at the floor. She plunged on anyway, hoping something about the rarely told story would get through to him.

"It didn't stop me from finishing school, though. He thought I would join in his fight, but I didn't. I had always wanted to go into a big law firm. I had wanted to be a powerful divorce lawyer, not because I wanted the money or the fame, but because I wanted to be there for women who gave everything to a marriage and then, it seemed to me, were always getting taken when it came time for a settlement."

She smiled ruefully as she thought about what had happened after that. "We lived together. I volunteered with some of his causes at first, but then my own career took off, and I had less and less time. He took it personally, accused me of selling out. Finally he told me he was leaving. I guess by then I wasn't all that surprised, but that didn't stop it from hurting."

Now at last David was watching her intently. "There's more, isn't there? What happened then?"

"A few days later, while I was still mourning our lost dreams, I received some legal papers. He was filing for palimony. He wanted a cut of everything I'd earned. He figured it was his due for letting his career take a back seat to mine."

The disgust was evident in David's expression. "How the hell would he figure that?"

"It's amazing how facts can get twisted to suit someone's purposes," she said with a shrug.

"Did you give him what he wanted?"

"I wanted to rip his heart out. I wanted to drag him through the entire legal system and show the world what a lousy creep he was. I was persuaded it wasn't in my own best interests. We settled out of court. Pragmatically I know it's what I had to do to avoid a scandal that could have hurt my career, but it's a decision I still regret."

She met his gaze. "I'm sure you're wondering what this has to do with you and Alicia, but I am trying to make a point. What happened with Ryan made me angry and bitter. Ironically, it probably made me an even better divorce lawyer. It gave me my go-for-the-jugular edge. At any rate, I allowed it to color every choice I've made—or not made—about relationships. In other words, I stopped living, and for all the wrong reasons."

She reached up and touched his cheek. "You have happier memories. You know how wonderful love can be. That won't change if you move on with your life. It won't be a betrayal of Alicia. If anything, it will be the opposite, a testament that what you shared lives on in you."

His expression instantly hardened, deliberately shutting her out. "I really don't want to discuss Alicia," he said adamantly. "I'm going for a swim."

He walked off and left her staring after him. Kate saw then that for all of their closeness that day, for all of the physical intimacy, one very real barrier stood between them. Alicia.

Until David could deal with his grief, until he could bring his memories into the open and discuss her with Davey or Kate or anyone else, a part of him would remain locked away and unreachable. It wouldn't matter what he believed about having moved on.

If she tried to force David to discuss Alicia with her, he could easily call her motives into question. Urging him to have those same conversations with Davey, however, was another matter altogether. Davey needed to talk about his mother, he needed to remember those times before she got sick and he needed to share his grief not with Kate, not with strangers, but with his father.

And no matter the cost to her, she was going to see that it happened. Bringing Alicia's name into the open so the healing could begin would be her final gift to the two of them.

From a chair in the shade beside the pool, his head throbbing, David watched Kate slip from the bedroom to the pool house wrapped only in a towel. Even after making love to her twice already this morning, he wanted her again. His body, primed by recent reality rather than distant memories, responded like an adolescent's, with hard, urgent need.

Unfortunately, given his behavior not ten minutes earlier, effectively telling her to mind her own business, he doubted she was going to be too anxious to accommodate this sudden need he had to hold her in his arms again.

When Kate emerged from the pool house, he fully

expected her to mumble a polite goodbye and take off. Instead, she strolled over as if nothing, *nothing*, had gone on between them. She poured herself a glass of orange juice and sat down opposite him as if she'd just dropped in to chat about the weather. Puzzled, he waited for the verbal knife to be unsheathed and aimed at his belly. He watched her uneasily.

"Expecting Davey soon?" she asked.

"Any minute now."

"Good."

"You going to stick around?"

"If you don't mind."

He shook his head. "I don't mind." What he minded was this sudden, cool inanity, but he couldn't think of a blasted way to end it. Actually, he could think of one way. He could finish the conversation she had tried to start inside. Given that alternative, he opted for silence and watched as Kate slipped farther and farther away, lost in her own thoughts.

He glanced up and saw Mrs. Larsen bustling toward them. If she had any clue about what he and Kate had been up to, it didn't show in her stoic expression.

"I thought I'd clean up these dishes if you're finished," she said. "Need to get things done around here if Davey's going to have those boys over tonight."

He glanced at Kate. "I don't need anything else. How about you?"

"Nope," she said, giving Mrs. Larsen a smile. "Thank you, though. It was a lovely breakfast."

The housekeeper nodded. "You staying for lunch?"

"I would like to see Davey," Kate said, glancing at David.

Which caught him between a rock and a hard place.

He wanted her out of here so he could get his equilibrium back, maybe even figure out what the hell she was up to now. At the same time he wanted her to stay, so these thrilling new off-balance sensations would last. "By all means, stay," he said. "Davey would be furious if I let you get away before he sees you."

If Mrs. Larsen sensed the undercurrents, she ignored them. "I'll be fixing something around one o'clock, if that's okay."

"Something simple," David said. "I know you're baking all those cookies for tonight."

"Yes, sir," she said and lumbered off with the tray of breakfast dishes.

"So, what's happening tonight?" Kate inquired.

"Davey's having a sleepover. Eight of his friends are coming. I've given Mrs. Larsen the night off. Otherwise, I'm afraid she'd quit."

Kate's expression turned wistful. "I think it sounds like fun."

David regarded her skeptically. "Fun?"

"Sure. Ghost stories. Games. Lots of cookies."

"Don't forget the pizza."

"Pizza and cookies," she said, nodding approvingly. "Every kid's dream menu."

"You know," he said slyly, "if you play your cards right, you could wind up as a chaperon."

Instead of backing down instantly as he'd anticipated, she hesitated. Then, slowly, she beamed, as if the whole idea genuinely appealed to her. "You wouldn't mind?"

"Mind?" he said, refusing to examine the consequences of having this woman in his home overnight...

in a guest room. "I'd welcome the prospect of adult conversation."

"Not from me. I intend to tell ghost stories, too." She looked uncertain. "Do you think Davey will object?"

"To your being here or to your sitting in on the ghost stories?"

"Either one."

"I think he'll be ecstatic to have you around. As for the ghost stories, it depends on whether you know any really scary ones."

"I think that between now and tonight, I ought to be able to dream up one that'll have them all hiding under the beds. What about you?"

"Forget the ghost stories. I was thinking of spending the entire evening under the bed with earplugs."

"No. No. No," she said, her eyes unexpectedly alight with laughter. "You have to get into the spirit of this."

"Just how many sleepovers have you hosted in your time?"

"Only one, for my youngest niece. It was for her thirteenth birthday. It wasn't any fun," she said with obvious disgust. "All they wanted to do was practice using makeup and styling each other's hair."

Startled by her genuine indignation, David suddenly found himself laughing with her, letting the tension finally ease away. "Oh, Kate, you really are something."

"I trust you'll remember that the next time I irritate you," she said.

"Do you intend to irritate me often?"

For an instant, she looked nonplussed, a little sad. "No." She stood up suddenly. "If I'm going to spend the night, I'd better go home and change and pick up a few odds and ends."

"I thought you were staying for lunch."

"I'll try to get back, but if I don't make it, tell Davey I'll be here tonight."

Suddenly David didn't want to be left alone with his thoughts. "Why don't I drive you? I can pick up the soft drinks for tonight."

She hesitated, then nodded finally. "Sure."

On the way through the house, he stopped to tell Mrs. Larsen they were going out. "Anything else you think we need for tonight?" he asked her.

"Extra toothbrushes," the housekeeper suggested. "Kids never remember their toothbrushes."

The instant they were outside, Kate met his gaze. "Don't you dare buy extra toothbrushes. Half the fun of staying out overnight is not having to do all those things your parents are always insisting you do. Nobody's teeth will rot between tonight and when they go home tomorrow."

He grinned back at her. "Does that mean if you and I stay out overnight one of these days, you'll want to break all kinds of rules?"

"Oh, I think we've already broken about as many rules as we're going to," she said quietly.

Something in her voice stunned David into silence. She sounded as if she'd looked into the future and no longer saw them together. The very thought of losing her sent a chill through him.

The din from the family room echoed through the entire house. Kate slapped a throw pillow to either ear and went in search of David.

"Whose idea was this?" she demanded loudly when she found him.

"What?" he shouted back.

His voice barely topped the sound of some musical group that relied heavily on bass. Kate could feel the whole house vibrating. She stepped close and plucked the earplug from his ear.

"I asked whose idea this was."

"Yours, I think," he said. "You wanted my son and me to get closer. I think you wanted to be nearby to observe the bonding."

"If this is bonding, it's not all it's cracked up to be," she grumbled. "They don't even know we're here."

"I'm sorry about the ghost stories," he said sympathetically. "I know you were really counting on telling them."

Kate grimaced. When she had suggested telling ghost stories, nine boys had stared at her uncomprehendingly. Davey had informed her privately in an undertone that that was baby stuff. "I guess I caught them two or three years too late."

"You could tell me one," David suggested. "Or I could tell you about the next Stephen King picture. It's a guaranteed spine tingler."

Kate shrugged. "It wouldn't be the same. Is there any pizza left?"

"Are you kidding? That went ten minutes after the delivery man dropped it off. Too bad they don't give you a discount if you can eat it faster than they can deliver it." He held out a hand. "Come with me, though. Mrs. Larsen left a secret stash of roast beef sandwiches for us."

Kate sighed. "Wonderful."

He poured them both mineral water and put the plate of sandwiches on the kitchen table. Kate watched the fleeting look of dismay that crossed his face and wondered if he was thinking again that this was something he should have been sharing with Alicia. When he sat down across from her, though, his gaze was free of whatever had been troubling him.

She, however, couldn't shake that bleak mood so easily. It reminded her once more that the memory of tonight was all she would have left soon. She had to force David and Davey to face their grief and when she did, David wouldn't thank her for it. Maybe someday, but certainly not now. And yet she had no choice. David would be living only half a life as long as a part of himself remained buried with Alicia.

So she would have this one night of feeling as if they were a family and in the morning she would do what had to be done and then she would move on and try to put her own life in order. Alone, as usual. She had to blink hard against the sting of tears.

She looked at David and forced a smile. "Davey's having the time of his life," Kate said, determined to put on a brave front so that he would never know how much it hurt her to know that even when they were most intimate Alicia had come between them, would always be there between David and any woman, unless she found a way to free him. "Is this the first time he's ever had a sleepover?"

"Yeah. I must say I wasn't sure what to expect," he confessed. "When I was a kid, I occasionally had a friend over, but never a whole gang like this."

"But I imagine living in a college dorm is a similar experience," Kate said.

"Maybe. I didn't live in a dormitory. I lived at home."

"Me, too," Kate said wistfully. "I wanted to go to a really good law school and that meant going to one within commuting distance. I couldn't have afforded to go away to one of the Ivy League schools."

"Did you feel you missed out on a lot by living off campus?" David asked.

She nodded. "The social things, yes. I don't suppose it really mattered, though. I met Ryan my sophomore year, and that was that."

"Do you suppose you fell into a pattern with him because you didn't have an opportunity to meet a lot of other students socially?"

Kate considered the question thoughtfully. "You may be right. We met in the library. Just a couple of studious loners, I guess."

"And here you are with me, another loner."

"A loner, maybe," she said. "But not a misfit. I think that was Ryan's problem. He *prided* himself on being a social outcast. Trying to live a normal life with someone like that creates a real strain. I think I was beginning to resent that even before he walked out."

"Maybe he anticipated that you were getting ready to cut him loose and wanted to beat you to it. The palimony business was his way of making you notice he was going."

"A last bid for attention?" she said, surprised by his perceptiveness. "Could have been, I suppose." She met David's gaze. "It doesn't seem to matter anymore."

It was ironic, she supposed, that this had been his gift to her. After all this time she had finally left the past behind. She was no longer afraid to love again.

And now she had to let go of the man who'd made that happen.

Kate awoke in the guest room the next morning with sunlight streaming through a window and a ten-year-old asleep beside her. As soon as she rolled over, Davey's eyes blinked wide and a grin spread across his face.

"Hi, Kate."

"Hey, sleepyhead, what're you doing in here?"

"I came in to check on you after everybody left this morning. You were still asleep. I guess I was pretty sleepy, too, so I lay down." He regarded her uncertainly. "Was that okay?"

"Absolutely," she said, thinking of how wonderful it felt to have this child trust her so completely, to have him take her into his heart the way he had. This was yet another of those moments she would hold close through the years. A child's love was so simple and straightforward. It was only between grown-ups that the emotion got complicated.

Suddenly the rest of Davey's explanation struck her. "You said everyone's gone?"

"Yeah, a while ago."

"What time is it?" she asked, reaching for her watch.

"Probably eleven o'clock," Davey guessed.

"Closer to noon," Kate said with a groan. She hadn't slept this late in years. "Is your dad up?"

"I don't think so. He looked pretty beat when he finally went to bed."

"Indeed he did," Kate agreed, thinking of his half-asleep kiss at the guest room door sometime after four this morning. He'd missed her lips. The kiss had landed in the vicinity of her nose. "Well, since Mrs. Larsen isn't here, suppose you and I go clean up and fix breakfast."

"The guys helped to clean up," Davey said, bounding out of bed. He frowned. "I think we probably need to vacuum, though. Mrs. Larsen will have a heart attack if she finds popcorn stuck under all the cushions."

"To say nothing of pepperoni and cookie crumbs."

He grinned. "Yeah, that, too."

Actually, the boys had at least put the furniture back into upright positions and replaced most of the cushions. They'd even lugged the trash into the kitchen. Three garbage bags full.

"Not so bad," Kate observed, bending down to retrieve the green pepper she'd almost squished into the carpet. "Where's the vacuum?"

"I'll get it," Davey said, dashing off and returning with it a few minutes later.

"Okay, I'll run this, if you'll get a rag and dust. You go first so that all the crumbs are on the floor when I start."

While Davey got the cleanup started, she made a pot of coffee and fought against the feelings of belonging that kept sneaking up on her. It was almost impossible to resist the magical allure of believing that this was her house, that Davey was her child and that the man still asleep upstairs was hers, as well.

But that couldn't be, she reminded herself. Not until the past was well and truly buried. And after she said what she had to say this morning to make that happen, David might never forgive her.

She refused to let anticipation of the confrontation to come ruin these last precious moments, though. She was humming as she ran the vacuum from room to room with Davey darting ahead of her, turning it into a game, making her laugh.

Suddenly she looked up and spotted David standing in an archway, his jeans riding low on his hips, his chambray shirt hanging loose. His cheeks were stubbled with the beginnings of a beard. His hair was mussed.

It was a sexy, masculine look that had her whole body crying to march back into his room and tumble into bed with him.

"Good Lord, what's all this racket?" he murmured in a husky, sleepy voice that teased her senses.

"It's the morning after," she told him.

"After what?" he grumbled. "Did somebody set off a bomb in here? You've been making that infernal racket for hours now."

"Just trying to live up to Mrs. Larsen's high standards," she said, pushing the vacuum into one last corner. She beamed at him as she switched it off. "All done now."

"Thank God."

"You don't do well in the morning, do you?"

"I do wonderfully well when morning comes after a night of sleep. This morning came after sleep deprivation that could have been used to elicit military secrets from the enemy."

"Well, pull yourself together, buddy. I am about to make some of my world-famous pancakes."

"World famous, huh?"

"They would be, if this weren't a secret recipe. Now move it."

He mumbled something about twisted personalities as he stumbled back toward the master suite. Davey peeked around a doorway. He grinned. "He's always cranky before he has his coffee."

"Then by all means take him some coffee," she suggested. "I just made a fresh pot."

While Davey did that, Kate fixed breakfast. She found silverware and napkins and, when Davey returned, sent them outside with him. "Fork on the left, knife and spoon on the right," she reminded him as he dashed off.

David reappeared just as she was about to pour the pancake batter onto the sizzling hot griddle. He smelled of soap and some sort of minty mouthwash. No aftershave. Just the pure masculine scent of a man who'd freshly showered. She decided that all those manufacturers of sexy shaving lotions were wasting their time. There was nothing more alluring than this.

He propped himself against the counter and observed her in a way that was thoroughly disconcerting. "Don't mind me," he said when she stood there with a spoon in one hand, poised over the bowl of batter.

That was like asking the tides to ignore the moon, she thought grumpily, but she ladled the batter onto the griddle and listened to the satisfying sizzle. "If you're going to stick around in here, grab that plate," she said, flipping the golden pancakes over and fighting an unexpected urge to cry. How was she going to walk away from this? The temptation to try to hold on tight, to compromise and accept just a small part of David's heart, was almost too great.

When David had the plate in hand, she scooped up the first batch of pancakes. He took them and started for the door.

"Hey, where do you think you're going?"

"I've got mine. I'm going to eat."

"Oh, no, you don't. Come back here. That plate's for all of them."

"But these'll get cold."

"Not if I keep adding warm ones on top. Now stand still. Here's another batch."

She flipped at least a dozen onto the plate before

she shooed him out of the kitchen. "Share those with your son."

He leaned down and dropped a kiss on the end of her nose. "You look cute all dusted with flour."

Kate groaned and rubbed at the offending flour as he walked out the door. She turned one last batch of pancakes onto another plate and followed.

All during breakfast, she couldn't keep her glance from straying first to David, then to the pool, and then to the master bedroom just beyond. He seemed to be studiously avoiding exactly the same kind of survey. Occasionally their gazes caught and Kate felt an embarrassed flush creep over her.

Unfortunately, she couldn't help thinking about the way yesterday morning had ended, as well. She glanced at Davey and then at his father. Drawing in a deep breath, she made a decision. Putting this off wouldn't solve anything. It might give her a few more memories, but the agony of leaving would be just as inevitable.

"Davey, I'll bet your mom would have liked seeing you with all your friends last night," she said casually.

Davey's eyes widened, and his gaze darted to his father. He mumbled something under his breath.

Kate determinedly pressed on. "David, don't you think Alicia would have liked having all the kids stay over?"

He glared at her. "What the hell are you trying to do?" he muttered finally. He shoved his chair back as if he was about to take off.

"I'm trying to have a perfectly normal conversation."

"Not now," David insisted, scowling at her furiously.

"Yes, now," she retorted stubbornly. "Davey, what's the one thing you remember most about your mom?"

"She was…" he began and then his voice broke off as he stared guiltily at his father.

Kate kept her gaze pinned on David, willing him to respond. Finally he swallowed hard.

"She was what, son?" he said in a voice that was barely above a whisper.

"She smelled like flowers and she was pretty and fun," he said softly. Tears welled up in his eyes.

"Yes, she was," David replied, his own face ashen.

Davey was staring at the table. "I miss her, Dad. I'm sorry but I really miss her."

Tears spilled down Kate's cheeks as she waited. Her hands were clenched into fists in her lap. Please, she murmured silently. Please.

Finally, his voice choked and gruff, David said, "I miss her, too, son."

Davey's sobs broke then, and he scrambled into his father's arms. David's gaze clashed with hers, his expression filled with something very close to loathing. Then he murmured something to Davey and refused to look at her at all.

Numb with her own pain, Kate left them like that, grabbing her bag from inside the guest room and hurrying to her car. She waited until she was down the hill before she pulled to the curb and allowed her own tears to fall freely.

Chapter Fourteen

The ache in Kate's heart wouldn't go away. Time and again she told herself that she'd done what she had to do. She had pushed David and Davey into talking about Alicia. Surely their relationship was mending more rapidly now. And that, after all, was the only reason she'd involved herself in their lives in the first place.

At least, that was how it had started. Somewhere along the way she had fallen in love. She had taken father and son into her heart, allowed them to become woven into the fabric of her life. No matter how frequently she told herself that letting go was for the best, it didn't stop the hurt. She'd expected David not to forgive her, but his absence was painful just the same, even worse than she'd anticipated.

She was going through the motions of living, consuming raspberry tea by the potful as if that could soothe the pain. She was going into court, presenting strong cases for her clients. She was consoling others still struggling with the decision of whether to fight for a marriage or leave. Far more often than she might have only weeks ago, she encouraged them to fight. To ward off the memories, she kept her calendar booked from early morning until late at night.

Despite the crammed days, her life was emptier than ever. For the first time in years, she found herself re-evaluating her own needs and expectations based on a different set of priorities. It was a process she'd begun just before meeting David. He had only served to mag-nify the changes that were needed if she was ever to find real happiness. In pushing him toward the one thing that really mattered, bottom line, she had discovered it for herself, as well.

As she sat in her office at the end of the day, lost in thought, she tried to put a positive spin on the muddle her life seemed to be in. Taking stock was good. She owed David Winthrop a debt of gratitude for forcing her to engage in some heavy-duty soul-searching.

Unfortunately, she didn't much like what she saw. All the success suddenly seemed shallow without some-one with whom to share it. She knew her mother was proud, knew that Ellen on occasion even envied her ca-reer. Her peers respected her. Her clients thought she walked on water. None of it seemed to matter. No, that wasn't quite right. It didn't seem to matter as much. She wanted the balance of a personal life, someone like David with whom she could share her problems and her successes, someone who would be there to console her or rejoice with her.

Stop hedging, she lectured herself in disgust. She

wanted to share her life with David Winthrop, not just someone like him. She wanted him to show her the way to feel so deeply that not even death could break the bond.

Late on Friday night, Kate stared at the pile of work on her desk and contemplated yet another lonely, work-filled weekend. This was the path she'd chosen, she reminded herself sternly as she shoved papers helter-skelter into her briefcase.

"It's going to take you half the night to sort those out," a low, husky voice commented from the doorway.

Kate's gaze shot up. Pleasure seemed to vibrate through her. "David!"

He regarded her somberly. "Hello, Kate."

She hoped he couldn't hear the sudden thundering of her heart, wished she weren't quite so aware of it herself. As she hungrily searched his face, she noted the tiredness in his eyes, the lines in his forehead. For a man whose life should have been back on an even keel, he looked miserable. Nor was there any hint of anger. That puzzled her.

"What brings you by?" she asked, not allowing herself to hope.

"We need to talk."

She shook her head, denying the need. "I don't think so."

"Don't you even want to know how Davey and I are getting along?"

"Of course, but..."

"Then have dinner with me."

She couldn't go through this again, couldn't get so close to him and to Davey only to have Alicia come between them again. She snatched at the first, most obvious excuse. "I have plans."

He shook his head. "No, you don't. I checked with Zelda."

"She doesn't keep track of my personal calendar."

He smiled ruefully. "Kate, you don't have a personal calendar. Now stopping arguing and let's get out of here. I made a reservation."

Her chin rose stubbornly. "You should have called first."

"I did."

"You didn't talk to me."

"No, I didn't. I figured you'd already written the final farewell scene when you walked out of my house a couple of weeks ago. You're too obstinate to admit that it could have a very different ending."

Her gaze challenged his. "David, why are you doing this?"

"Because *I* don't think things are over between us. I think they're just beginning."

"You're wrong," she said, fiercely trying to protect herself from the anguish of parting all over again. Pride and determination had gotten her away from his house the first time. She wasn't sure either was strong enough to be tested again.

"Are you saying you don't…?" He hesitated over the choice of words, his gaze searching hers. "Are you saying that you don't care for me? Do you want me to believe that the way you've involved yourself with Davey and with me was the same way you'd treat any other case?"

Kate couldn't bring herself to lie. But she did hedge.

"Of course you weren't just another case. I do care for you and for Davey. I always will. But that's where it ends."

"Why?"

Couldn't he see that she wouldn't settle for less than what he'd shared with Alicia? "Caring is not the same as love. We both deserve bells and whistles."

He chuckled and lifted his gaze heavenward in disbelief. "I guess you weren't in that bed with me a few weeks back, then," he observed wryly. "I've heard magnificent, centuries-old church bells that chimed with less intensity."

"You're just grateful because I helped with Davey."

"Kate, what I feel is a hell of a lot more powerful than gratitude." He pinned her with his gaze. "I am very close to wanting to strip those damned, conservative clothes off you, so I can take you right on top of your desk just to prove how wrong you are."

Blood roared in Kate's ears, and fiery anticipation danced through her. "That's just sex," she said dismissively, but her voice was oddly breathless.

David grinned. "Yes, it is. Hot, steamy, hungry sex. We do it damned well, Kate." He stepped closer and cupped her chin, his gaze locked with hers. "Don't we?"

Her breath snagged. She closed her eyes, trying to block out the images he'd aroused. She couldn't. They filled her head. They filled her heart. Memories, she reminded herself firmly. They were just memories. They would fade in time.

But this was now, and David was flesh-and-blood real. His sly, potent virility was casting a spell over her this instant. Kate wanted to believe, but she didn't dare. Believing led to heartache, pain even worse than the agony she was feeling at this moment. Her gift to him was the freedom to move on. Nothing more.

"Please," she pleaded. "Don't try to make this into something it isn't. You've just gotten used to having me around the last few weeks. You don't need me. Not really."

"Yes, I do," he said softly. "Davey and I both need you and I will prove that if it takes me forever to do it."

Then with a faint sigh, he leaned down and touched his lips to hers. The gentleness of that touch shook her far more than the persuasive command of which she knew he was capable. The tenderness shattered resolve and chased away rational thought. She could almost believe then that he'd meant what he said. He needed her. It was a start, but no matter how hard she tried to believe it was enough, she knew that she wanted more. She wanted his love.

"Why won't you take the man's calls?" Zelda demanded days later. "He's beginning to drive me crazy."

"I pay you to deal with persistent, unwanted callers."

"Unwanted? I don't think so," she said smugly.

"Zelda, if you are not very careful, I will introduce you to my new stepfather and tell him I'm worried about the state of your love life," Kate warned.

Zelda's laughter bounced off the walls. "Is that supposed to scare me?"

Kate frowned. "It terrifies me." In fact, she was flat-out horrified that Brandon would somehow learn that she was no longer seeing David Winthrop and would set out to do something about it.

"I wouldn't mind having someone rich and successful and intelligent look around for the right guy for me," Zelda said dreamily. "Brandon Halloran probably travels in much more interesting circles than I do." She regarded Kate with a disapproving look. "You realize that you're avoiding the real problem here."

"Oh? What problem is that?"

"You're scared," she accused. "Knee-shaking, pain-in-the-gut scared."

"Maybe so," Kate conceded with a sigh. "Maybe so."

Not five minutes later, Zelda buzzed. "Call on line one."

"Who is it?" she asked, but she was talking to herself. Filled with trepidation, she stared at the flashing light on her phone. Finally, because she absolutely refused to be ruled by cowardice, she gingerly picked up the receiver. "Hello."

"Hi, Kate, it's me," Davey said.

She breathed a faint sigh of relief. "Well, hi, yourself. How're you doing?"

"I'm okay," he said, and for once Kate believed him. She could hear the change in his voice. "I called to invite you to a ball game."

"Me?" she asked, inexplicably pleased. This was the first time she'd talked to her client since that day at the house. She thought he'd probably become so caught up in reestablishing his relationship with his dad that he'd forgotten all about her.

"Yeah. And guess what? I'm going to play quarterback."

"Davey, that's wonderful." At least, she thought it was. He certainly sounded as if it was.

"Will you come? I haven't seen you for a really long time."

"I'm sorry. I've been really busy, but I've missed

you a lot. Now about the game, shouldn't you be asking your dad?"

"Oh, he's already promised to come, but I want you, too."

She couldn't go. It would hurt too much. But when she hesitated, he added, "All the other kids will have their moms there."

Kate felt as if the floor had dropped out from under her. "Oh, Davey," she whispered, her voice choked. How could she resist a plea like that, especially when it appealed to the yearning deep inside her, as well?

"Okay, I'll come," she said finally, after considering and rejecting every single logical reservation she had about going.

"Thanks, Kate. You're the greatest."

"Where and when?"

He gave her directions to the field. "It's six o'clock tonight."

Tonight? Kate thought, suddenly panicked. How could she slam all her defenses into place that quickly?

"You won't be late, will you?" Davey asked worriedly.

"Not if I can help it," she promised.

As soon as she'd hung up, however, she regretted making the commitment. How was she going to get through an entire evening pretending that she was no more than a casual acquaintance, when Davey seemed hell-bent on having her fill in as his mother?

"You going to that game?" Zelda inquired from the doorway.

Kate's gaze shot up. "What do you know about that?"

"A little birdie told me," her secretary announced smugly.

"A little birdie or a grown-up birdie?" Kate inquired suspiciously.

"Sorry. Confidential," Zelda retorted. "Enjoy yourself. You'd better get going if you plan to change and be there by six."

"Don't I have an appointment at five?"

"Postponed until tomorrow."

Kate sighed. She should have guessed. "Any other plots afoot that I should know about?"

Zelda shook her head. "Nope. This is my last nudge. From now on you're on your own."

"Thank God," Kate said fervently. Ironically, though, the reassurance didn't bring nearly as much comfort as it should have.

There were at least a hundred parents in the bleachers when Kate arrived. Her gaze zeroed in on David as easily as if he'd been wearing neon. He lounged at the end of a row, his gaze focused first on the field, then shifting to search the parking lot. The sun shot his hair with gold.

As soon as she stepped out of her car, a smile spread across his face. That slow, lazy smile should have been outlawed in polite society. To her regret, it warmed her down to her toes.

"Hi," he said when she neared the stands. "I wasn't sure you'd come."

"Davey told you I'd be here?"

"Actually, I suggested he call." At her look of dismay over the low-down, sneaky tactics, he added quickly, "It didn't take any persuasion, Kate."

He held out a hand and helped her up. To Kate's dismay—and relief—he didn't let go, not until her hand had been warmed by the contact, not until half the people around them had taken note of the possessive gesture.

"Has the game started yet?" she asked, unable to keep the shaky note from her voice.

"They've run one series of plays. The other team couldn't convert on third down. We have the ball."

"English, please," she demanded.

His eyes widened. "Kate, haven't you ever been to a football game before?"

She shook her head. "Afraid not."

"But you went to UCLA," he protested.

"I spent all my time in the library. I told you that."

"What about now? We have two professional teams in this area."

"And I have season tickets for both. I give them to clients."

"Dear Lord."

She frowned at him. "Davey said he's the quarterback. Is that good?"

David laughed. "It is if he completes his passes."

Kate tried to concentrate on the game after that. She wasn't always absolutely certain what was going on, but she took her cues from the fans and from the man seated beside her. He spent most of the game muttering advice under his breath. The advice was clearly meant for Davey.

"Why aren't you shouting at him like everyone else?"

"I won't put that kind of pressure on him. He's a kid. He should be enjoying the game. If he asks me later, I'll tell him what I thought he could improve, but I won't badger him while he's out there. He's doing the best he can."

He shook his head and glanced around them. "Listen to the way some of these parents carry on. It's a wonder their children sign up to play at all."

Kate listened to the shouts around them more closely and decided—totally objectively, of course—that David was quite possibly the best parent in the stands. But that was no real surprise. She'd always believed in the strength of his relationship with his son. She was glad that she'd come, if only to see that the bond between them had been fully restored.

With the score tied at ten, Davey went back on the field with less than a minute to play. Kate found herself on her feet, cheering as hard as anyone around her. She glanced up and caught David watching her and shrugged.

"I guess I got a little caught up in the spirit of things."

"Don't apologize. That's the idea," he said, just as Davey threw something that David described as a Hail Mary pass.

The boy it was meant for stumbled, then lunged into the air, arms outstretched. Kate's breath caught in her throat as she waited for that ball to come down. It seemed to linger on his fingertips for an eternity before he gathered it close and fell forward over the goal line.

The parents in the stands went wild, including Kate. She threw her arms around David. "Did you see that? Did you see how Davey's pass went straight into that boy's arms? What a pass!"

"Give the receiver a little credit," David teased.

"Well, sure, but it was Davey who got the ball down there. The ball didn't even wobble. What an arm!" she said, echoing the praise she'd heard around her.

David's tolerant smile finally penetrated her exuberance.

"Sorry," she apologized.

"For what?" He touched her cheek with his fingertips. "Do you have any idea what it does to me to share this with you?"

Kate felt the salty sting of tears in her eyes and tried to look away, but he wouldn't let her.

"We were meant to be like this," he insisted. "You and me and Davey. We could be a real family, Kate."

A family. The words seemed to echo in her heart. Oh, how she wanted that. But she refused to allow herself to hope. Before she could utter a denial, Davey came racing toward them. He was caught up in his father's hug.

"You were terrific, son."

"Thanks, Dad. Did you see, Kate? That pass was the longest one I've ever thrown. Ever!"

She smiled at his excitement. "I'm really glad I was here to see it."

"I think a celebration is in order," David said, his gaze on Kate, pleading with her not to spoil things for Davey.

Because she wanted one last memory to tuck away with all the rest, she nodded slowly. "A celebration sounds terrific."

But Davey, it seemed, had his own plans for celebrating with his friends. David didn't seem nearly as surprised by that information as he might have been.

"I guess it's just you and me, then," he said, linking Kate's arm through his as Davey ran off to join his friends. "My place? We can raid the refrigerator."

He made it sound so incredibly casual and spontaneous that Kate couldn't find the words to refuse. "Sure," she said finally. "I'll follow you."

"Why not ride with me and I'll bring you back to your car later?"

Which would effectively strand her at his house until he had used every bit of persuasion at his disposal to convince her that they had a future, she thought. No, thanks! She smiled. "I think I'll drive."

He shrugged. "Whatever. I'll meet you there, then."

Kate followed him up the winding narrow road into Bel Air. By the time they reached the house, the lights of Los Angeles were spread out below as if stardust had been sprinkled on the valley floor. At the house David poured them each a glass of wine and led the way onto the terrace so they could take full advantage of the view. The awareness sizzling between them was almost palpable.

"I'm glad you came," David said quietly.

"I didn't want to disappoint Davey," she said.

"I'm not talking about the game, Kate," he said with a touch of impatience. "I'm talking about here. Did you not want to disappoint me, as well?"

She sighed. "I'm not exactly sure why I came. I should have known that sooner or later you'd force us back into the same conversation."

David slowly put his glass aside and with his gaze locked with hers, he took her glass and set it on the table. "No conversation, Kate."

Kate's heart thumped unsteadily as he pulled her into his arms. Damn it all to hell, she didn't even try to resist. She went willingly, yearning for the feel of his body pressed into hers, hungering for his lips to plunder hers. With a little cry that was part pleasure, part dismay, she opened her mouth to the invasion of his tongue. The fantasy world spread out below them seemed to reach up to draw them in.

This, Kate told herself, this was what she was giving up. She could feel David's heart thundering beneath her palm, the scratch of his faintly stubbled skin against her cheek, the hardness of his manhood pressed against her. Each sensation was distinct and separate. Each blended into a thrilling swirl of desire that swept through her and left her dazed with need.

Why couldn't she just accept this moment? Why couldn't she take whatever part of David's heart he had left to give and be satisfied?

Because she'd seen what he was capable of giving, she admitted finally. And she wanted it all, wanted the full power of his love and attention. She couldn't share it with a ghost.

"No," she said, far too late, when her body was crying out for satisfaction. "David, no."

His jaw clenched with anger, he stepped away. He picked up his glass, finished the wine in one gulp, then drank what was left of hers. Only then did he allow his gaze to clash with hers. Kate shuddered at the hot fury in his eyes.

"Why?" he bit out.

"I'm not in the mood."

"Dammit, I am not referring to sex. I'm talking about us."

"There is no us."

"Then I'll ask one more time, why?"

For Kate the answer was simple. One word. "Alicia."

He regarded her incredulously. "Kate, for God's sake, Alicia is dead."

"But you haven't stopped grieving for her. If I doubted that before, your reaction just now to the mention of her name was proof that it's the truth."

David shoved his hand through his hair and began to pace, leaving Kate to stand alone in the chill air, shivering. Finally, when he turned to face her again, his expression was anguished.

"No," he corrected softly. "It's not grief. It's a lot of things, Kate, but not grief."

Stunned by the note of despair in his voice, she stared at him incredulously. "But what, then?"

"Guilt. Anger, maybe."

"I don't understand."

"I was glad when she died, Kate," he said, looking heartbroken by the admission. "Glad! What kind of creature does that make me? What kind of father could I be when I wanted my son's mother to die? I wanted to see her suffering over with. I wanted desperately for things to get back to normal."

A sigh shuddered through him. "Only when she was gone did I see that they never would be normal again. And that made me angry, at her, at God, at myself. Every single time you attributed me with this noble passion, this gut-deep sorrow, I felt like a fraud."

She reached out to him, but he shook her off.

"No, let me finish. Don't get me wrong. I loved her. She was an intelligent, beautiful, gentle, lovely woman. But in the end, she wasn't even Alicia anymore, and I hated myself for feeling that way."

"Oh, David," Kate said, her voice catching. "I'm so sorry."

He regarded her with a wry expression. "So, you see, I'm not at all the man you thought I was."

"Yes," she said firmly, "you are. What do you think grief is? It is anger and pain and a sense of loss and maybe even some guilt all rolled into one shattering emotion. Do you think you are the only person ever to be glad to see an end to a loved one's suffering? Do you think you are the only man ever to feel anger and resentment at being left alone?"

She touched his cheek, and this time he didn't withdraw. "But you will work your way through those emotions in time. I can promise you that. Just by admitting the feelings to me tonight, I think you're already well on your way."

"Am I asking too much if I ask you to go through this with me? I need you, Kate."

Need, not love, she thought dismally. "I will always be your friend," she said, because it was all she could say without showing the depth of her vulnerability. "I'm going now, but we'll talk soon."

"What about dinner?"

She shrugged. "I think food is the last thing either of us has on our minds."

She stood on tiptoe then, and pressed a kiss to his cheek. As she turned and walked away, she wondered when or if she would ever share a kiss with him again.

Chapter Fifteen

The bed trembled as if it were being shaken by an ill-tempered giant, jarring Kate awake, her heart thundering in her chest.

An earthquake! A huge one, if the rolling motion of the room was any indication. Her equilibrium went off kilter, rendering her almost as nauseous as if she'd been on the deck of a boat caught in an ocean's swells.

When she could move, she raced for a doorway and braced herself against the building's terrifying sway that had light fixtures swinging back and forth from the ceiling. Outside she could see the frantic to-and-fro movement of light poles, heard the crackle and fiery pop of a transformer before the street was plunged into darkness.

All her life she had lived with the frightening threat of earthquakes, had accepted it as part of the price for living in LA. Earthquakes were among the few things in life absolutely beyond her control. She tried to be prepared and left it at that.

Over the years she had experienced scary tremors and mild aftershocks with minimal psychological scars. She knew this terrible creaking and rocking would end, but when it did, what would be left?

This one seemed to be going on longer than usual, its force more powerful than any she could recall from recent years. She knew it had to be centered far closer than the strong quakes that had hit the desert the previous summer, nearly a hundred miles away and still terrifying.

She heard the doors on her kitchen cabinets open and slam, open and slam, followed by the breaking of glass.

With her adrenaline pumping by the time the awesome quaking stopped, she found slippers, then inched her way carefully to the kitchen, where she kept earthquake supplies. She turned on a battery-powered light, then the battery-powered radio.

"A quake estimated to be at least seven point five or greater on the Richter scale has just shaken downtown Los Angeles. Reports from Cal State indicate the quake was centered in West Hollywood. Our studios on Sunset have cracks in the walls. Studio windows popped out. We can see from here that glass is out in some downtown office buildings. Several residents in the Beverly Hills and Bel Air area have called to report smelling gas. We have reporters heading into the area now and will be back with full details as they come in. Is this The Big One? Stay tuned."

Bel Air, Kate thought, stricken. What about David and Davey? Were they okay? Their house sat high on a ridge overlooking a valley. Obviously it had weathered other quakes through the years, but if preliminary reports were talking about gas leaks and shattered glass, this could be far worse than anything it had ever sustained before. On top of the earthquake damage, gas leaks and downed power lines threatened fires.

She grabbed the phone and dialed. Only after she'd punched in the last number did she realize that there had never even been a dial tone. The line was out.

Frantic now, she grabbed a pair of jeans and a T-shirt and scrambled into them. She pulled on thick socks and sneakers, stopped for her kit of emergency supplies and bottled water and hurried into the building's hallway. It was dark as midnight.

No electricity, no elevator, she thought with dismay. She could make out the generator-powered red light above the doorway to the emergency stairwell and crept along the corridor, wasting precious time but unable to risk moving any faster. At last she reached the door and pushed it open. Using her flashlight to illuminate the stairs, she began making her way down twelve flights to the parking garage below. The trip seemed to take an eternity.

Eventually, though, she reached the car. As she sped up the exit ramp, she heard the distant, terrifying drone of sirens. Lots of sirens. She turned north on Century Park East and then she saw the glow on the horizon. Not in the east where the sun would be breaking through, but northwest. In Bel Air. Where David and Davey were. Her stomach turned over as she considered the danger they were in.

Kate was halfway up the canyon road when she hit the first crevice, a crack sufficiently wide to jar the car. There were two more beyond that, each a little wider, a little more difficult to navigate. Ignoring tire damage and the threat hinted at by the increasing severity of those cracks, she drove on until she found her way blocked by a fallen tree.

All around her she saw families dazed by the quake, standing in their yards gazing at the aftermath. One whole wing of an estate had collapsed. A tree had tumbled on top of three cars in a single bricked driveway. And still, strong aftershocks kept the earth trembling.

Bullhorns warned of potential gas leaks and advised residents to avoid using electricity or candles until utility crews could get into the area. From every yard she could hear the hum of radio reports, updated every few minutes. The announcers, too, listed the hazards that followed earthquakes, reminding listeners of precautions to be taken.

Somewhere above her the warnings were already too late. She could see the glow of a fire, stronger now, feeding on the drought-stricken landscape. The acrid smell of smoke filled her nostrils.

Images of David and Davey crowded into her head as she pulled to the side of the road and determinedly set out on foot. Just as she rounded the next bend, a fireman blocked her way.

"Ma'am, you can't go up there."

Kate stared at him, uncomprehending. "But I have to," she said simply and kept walking.

He caught her arm and held her back. "It's not safe."

Her gaze clashed with his. "But David is there and his son. I have to find them."

The fireman, a young man with streaks of soot on his already weary face, regarded her sympathetically. "I'm sorry. I can't let you do that. Wait here. We're evacuating the people from up there now."

"But what if they're injured?" she said, her voice catching on a sob.

"We'll get them out, ma'am."

Defeated, Kate walked to the side of the road and sank down on the trunk of an upended tree. Tears cut streaks down her cheeks as she kept her gaze pinned to the road and the straggle of residents making their way down from higher ground.

They had to be all right, she told herself over and over. She couldn't lose them. Whether they were her real family or not, she loved them as if they were. An image of David swam before her eyes, a teasing I-told-you-so glint in his eyes. She choked back a sob. He would come to her eventually, if only to say those words, if only to taunt her for taking so blasted long to admit something he had accepted weeks ago.

Family, she thought as the smoke seemed to surround her. Dear Lord, she hadn't given a thought to her mother and Brandon or to Ellen and her family. Chances were good, given the preliminary estimate of the quake's epicenter, that they'd received no more than the same awakening jolt she had. Still, she had to check. She thought, belatedly, of her car phone.

Reluctant to leave where she was, she realized that she had no real choice anyway. The smoke was becoming more dense by the minute, and she could see by the expression on the fireman's face that at any second he was going to insist that she move farther out of the path of danger.

She trudged back down the winding road until she reached her car. She tried first to call David, but there was no answer at the house. Because he was already moving out of harm's way, she told herself firmly. Even though she wanted with all her heart to believe that, she couldn't help envisioning him pinned under a fallen beam or trapped on the far side of the fire.

Trembling with the agony of waiting, she dialed her mother's house. "Mom?" she said and then her voice broke.

"Kate, darling, are you okay? I've been calling and calling, but your damned phone isn't working."

"I'm sorry I didn't call sooner. As soon as it happened, I saw that there was a fire over in Bel Air."

"And you started worrying about David?" her mother guessed. "Is he okay?"

"I don't know," she said bleakly. "I can't get all the way up to the house. The fire's getting worse. It's driving me crazy. I don't like sitting on the sidelines and waiting this way. I want to do something."

"Charging to the rescue," her mother said, and Kate could practically see her smile. "Oh, Katie, darling, you can't save the world."

"Maybe not," she admitted. "But I've given it a damned good shot." She hesitated. "Mom?"

"Yes, darling?"

"I think I'm ready to think about saving myself."

"Is that your way of saying you've fallen in love with David Winthrop?"

Kate laughed. "Yes, I guess it is." It was such an overwhelming relief to be able to speak the words aloud. "I love David Winthrop."

Suddenly she heard someone pounding on the window of the car and looked up to see David, sooty and rumpled, but very much alive. He was grinning at her and she knew that he'd heard, but it didn't seem to matter anymore that she'd put her heart on the line.

"He's here," Kate shouted, jubilant. "Mom, I'll talk to you later, all right?" Then, almost as an afterthought, she said, "You are okay, aren't you? And Ellen?"

"Everyone is fine, darling. Why don't you and your young man join us for breakfast? Ellen's coming, as well, with Penny."

Her gaze locked with David's, Kate barely mumbled an affirmative response before hanging up and springing out of the car.

"You're okay?" she asked when she was wrapped tightly in his embrace. She touched his cheeks, his forehead, his shoulders as if to make sure.

"Keep that up and we're going to cause quite a scene," he taunted lightly.

She lifted her gaze to meet his. "Oh, David, I was so worried about you. When I thought I might never see you again, I wanted to die."

He touched her lips with a finger. "Don't ever, *ever* say that." He held her even more tightly, his own expression mirroring her relief. "I went nuts when I couldn't reach you. Davey even had the car phone number and we tried calling that." He gave her a quelling look. "Even though I knew only a damn fool would be out traipsing around at six in the morning after an earthquake."

She ignored the criticism. "Davey's okay?"

"He's over there with a fireman. What do you think?"

She glanced across the road and saw Davey asking questions of the fireman at a clip that had put a smile on that exhausted face. Her heart filled to overflowing.

"Kate?"

"Umm," she murmured, content to be held.

"I heard what you said on the phone."

She glanced up and met his gaze. "That I love you?"

He nodded. "Did you mean it?"

There was no point in hiding the truth any longer. For better or worse, she loved him. It was time to take a risk. "Have you ever known me to say anything I didn't mean?"

"Enough to marry me?"

A joy unlike anything she had ever experienced before spread through her, sneaking up on her and bringing with it an undeniable sense of fulfillment, but still she was cautious.

"Marriage?"

He tilted her face up. "I love you, Kate," he said with slow emphasis. "Just you."

She wanted so badly to believe. "Are you sure?"

"Absolutely sure. You've made me feel alive again. You've given me back my son. Married or not, we're a family, Kate, in every sense of the word."

She knew that was true. She'd felt it herself for weeks now. She searched his eyes and for the first time there were no shadows, only hope and joy. "Yes," she said then. "Yes, I will marry you."

He swung her off her feet with a cry of such absolute delight that people all along the road turned to stare and smile. Davey came charging across the street.

"Did you ask her, Dad? Did you ask her to marry you?"

David winked at Kate. "I did."

"And did she say yes?" he asked, bouncing up and down with excitement. "She did, didn't she?"

"I did," Kate confirmed.

"All right!" Davey shouted, hugging Kate around the middle.

"We're getting married," he announced to all the observers.

In a morning bleak with destruction and marred by
fear, the news was greeted with applause.

"If total strangers are this pleased, just imagine how
my family will feel," she said wryly. "Which reminds me,
we've been invited to a family breakfast. Are you up to it?"

David brushed a strand of hair from her face and
grinned, his hand lingering to cup her chin. "I thought
you'd never ask."

When Kate and David pulled up in front of the house
she'd grown up in, she looked at the spill of fuchsia bou-
gainvillae, the Spanish tiled roof, the neat lawn, and
thought of all the years she'd thought of this house as
home. She glanced up at David, caught his smile and
felt his hand envelop hers.

"Second thoughts?" he asked.

She shook her head. "Not a one. I was just thinking
about what it takes to make a home."

"Two people who love each other," he said. "A family."

"It's taken me a long time to understand that."

"Maybe what's taken a long time was finding the
right man to make that happen," he suggested with a
devilish twinkle in his eyes.

If he'd expected her to argue, even mildly, she
couldn't. There was only one right man for her, and he
had taken an impossibly long time to turn up. Or perhaps
he'd simply waited until he knew the time was right.
Any sooner and she might not have been ready for him.

"I think everyone is going to love you," she told him,
grinning. "You're so self-confident."

"Can't see my knees shaking, huh?"

"What are you guys talking about?" Davey demanded. "I'm starved."

"Well, go inside and tell the first person you see to feed you," Kate suggested with a laugh.

Davey's eyes widened. "I can't do that." He glanced at his father. "Can I?"

David chuckled. "No, I suppose not. Come on, Kate, there's no sense putting this off."

"You realize that you have forestalled a lot of problems by making an honest woman of me before our arrival. Otherwise, you could have forgotten having a nice leisurely breakfast with my clan. They'd have been plaguing you with questions."

The possibility didn't seem to concern him. "Kate, you're dallying."

She grinned. "Yes, I guess I am." She took a deep breath. "Let's do it."

By then her mother already had the door open and her arms held wide. "Darling, it's so good to see you. I'm so glad to see for myself that you're okay." She turned her worried expression on David and Davey. "Now, what about you two? Are you okay? Kate told me about the fires."

"We're a little the worse for wear, but nothing serious," David told her. "I'm David Winthrop."

"Well, of course. I've been hearing all about you."

Kate could practically hear alarm bells clanging. She looked up just in time to see Brandon Halloran making his way to the door, his smile warm, his eyes filled with concern as he looked them over.

"David," he said, shaking his hand. "Good to see you again."

"Again?" Kate murmured, looking from one to the other for an explanation. David just smiled. Brandon avoided her gaze altogether. She tugged on David's sleeve. "What does that mean? Again?"

"I'll explain later," he said, just as Ellen swooped in for an introduction, followed by Penny.

"I wish my husband could be here to meet you, too," she said. "He got called in to work." She gave Kate a smug, sisterly look, linked her arm through David's and led him away.

Kate glanced down at Davey. "Let's sneak into the kitchen and see what's cooking."

"Yeah!" he agreed.

Kate found her mother at the stove taking up the last of an entire package of crisp bacon. She sniffed the air appreciatively.

"Should Brandon be eating this?" Kate teased as she saw the bowl of eggs waiting to be scrambled.

"I indulge him once a week," her mother said. "And today is definitely a special occasion."

"Should I be taking notes on how to maintain marital bliss?" Kate inquired idly after she'd sent Davey off with a covered plate of warm biscuits.

Her mother's sharp gaze took in Kate's expression. Suddenly she was laughing and her arms were around Kate. "Oh, darling, I'm so happy for you. He seems like a fine young man."

"Is that the judgment you formed in the last five minutes or has Brandon been indulging in a little more background checking?"

"I believe they had lunch one day last week," her mother admitted.

"They what!"

"Now, dear, we just wanted to be sure that this was the right young man for you."

Davey, back again and clearly bored with the grown-up talk, finally chimed in. "Are we ever going to eat?"

Kate and her mother laughed at his impatience. "In five minutes," Elizabeth Halloran promised her new grandson-to-be. "Why don't you go and tell everyone?"

When everyone was gathered around the dining room table, Brandon glanced down the length of it until his gaze caught with his new wife's. "I think this calls for a blessing, don't you?"

Eyes shining with love, Elizabeth Halloran nodded. The pure happiness on her face brought tears to Kate's eyes.

"Heavenly Father," Brandon began, "thank you for sparing us from today's earthquake and for bringing us all together here this morning. I thank you, too, for my new daughters, my granddaughter and for the fine young man and his son who have brought so much happiness into Kate's life. We ask your blessing on this food we are about to eat and on this family. May we always remember the importance of the love we share. Amen."

Kate lifted her head and looked around the table. At last her glance settled, first on Davey, seated across from her, and then on David at her side. "Amen," she echoed softly.

Beneath the table she felt David's hand reach for hers and close around it. She looked up into eyes that were filled with the radiance of love. Surely they shone no more brightly than her own.

A smile stole across her face. "Now," she said sweetly, "tell me all about this lunch you had with Brandon."

Epilogue

The glass walls and ceiling of the Wayfarer's Chapel high above the Pacific allowed sunlight to spill in on the small group gathered for the wedding of Kate Newton to David Allen Winthrop II. Her heart in her throat, Kate stood on the stone steps at the back of the church and waited for David to take his place before the altar.

Then she turned and smiled at Ellen. "I guess this is it."

"I guess so, little sister." Ellen kissed her cheek. "I love you and I know you're going to be very, very happy."

"Yes," Kate agreed with certainty. "Yes, I am."

"Ladies," Brandon Halloran said, gazing at them both with eyes filled with tenderness and unmistakably genuine caring. "I believe we're on."

Kate looked up at this white-haired man who had twice blessed her mother's life with happiness. No lon-

ger a stranger, once Kate had opened her heart to him,
she recognized at last that he was someone she could trust
to be there for her, just as her own father once had been.

"Brandon?"

"Yes, my dear."

"Thank you for agreeing to give me away."

"Nothing could have pleased me more than your asking," he said, patting her hand and then linking her arm
through his. Kind eyes studied her intently. "All set?"

"Just one more thing. For a time I couldn't imagine
how you could care for me the same way you care for
Ellen. Then I met Davey, and I couldn't possibly love him
any more if he were my own, just because he's David's."

His smile was gentle. "That's the power of love. It
has no limitations, my dear. Now, are you ready to begin
this new life of yours?"

She took a look down the aisle and let her gaze rest
on David and Davey. "Absolutely," she said firmly.

Like her mother just a few months earlier, she
couldn't keep the spring out of her step as she closed
the gap between herself and the man who'd brought
joy into her life and the boy responsible for bringing
them together. She glanced up and caught the look that
passed between her new stepfather and her mother, saw
the tears shimmering on her mother's cheeks.

And then her hand was in David's and the ceremony
was underway.

"I, David, take thee, Kate, a woman who has brought
new joy into my life, to be my lawfully wedded wife.
I give thanks for the day I met you. I love you for your
spirit, your generosity and the power of your love, which
encompasses not only me, but my son. Together I know
we can defeat any obstacle, meet any challenge. I want

to grow old with you by my side, and I vow that nothing will ever be more important to me than our family."

Her eyes stinging with unshed tears, Kate met his gaze. For her there was no one else in this wonderful chapel but the man who stood beside her and the God above who would bless their union.

"I, Kate, take thee, David, to be my lawfully wedded husband. Through you I have learned what matters in life. Through you I have discovered the importance of listening to my heart. I know that nothing matters more to me than your happiness and that of our family. When I look into the future, I see you by my side, sharing your strength, your commitment and your love. I vow that whatever obstacles we face, whatever challenges we must meet, we will do so together. You have my respect, and above all, you have my love."

At Kate's insistence there had been no mention of death in the ceremony. She wanted no sad reminders that love didn't always last forever. No one knew that better than David. They would concentrate on the days they had. They would make each one precious, as if it might be their last together. If they succeeded at that, if they cherished each day, when the end of their time on this earth came, they would have no regrets.

Their individual vows spoken and their hands clasped, they looked deep into each other's eyes and echoed the vows spoken at Elizabeth Newton's wedding to Brandon Halloran and at marriage ceremonies throughout time.

They began in a halting cadence, but by the end their voices soared, filling the tiny chapel with their joy. "I promise to love, honor and cherish you all the days of my life."

Outside the chapel on the slope of lawn facing the

sea, Kate and David shared a toast with their guests. Because they had planned the wedding in just days, taking the first available date at the chapel, they had kept the guest list small. In a month, when they returned from their honeymoon—the first holiday either had taken in too many years, they would hold a huge reception.

For now, though, Kate was content to be sharing the occasion with family and a handful of people who had seen them both through rough times. She stood amidst the small cluster of well-wishers and felt her heart overflowing with happiness.

Davey came up just then, his expression serious. "Kate?"

"What?" she asked, smiling at him as she thought of what Mrs. Larsen would have to say about his shirttail hanging out and the streak of dirt on the pant leg of his tuxedo. She thought he looked wonderful.

"Should I still call you Kate, now that you and Dad are married?"

Kate's heartbeat stilled, then picked up. *Let me get this right*, she prayed. "What would you like to call me?"

"I was thinking," he began, glancing around until he located his father. "I was thinking that someday, maybe not right away or anything, but someday I'd like to call you Mom."

Kate blinked hard to keep her tears from spilling down her cheeks. "Oh, Davey, I would like that very much, whenever you're ready. Until then, Kate's just fine."

He grinned. "Thanks. Can I go have another piece of cake?"

"You can have all the cake you want."

Just then David's hands settled on her shoulders. "Sure," he teased. "You can tell him that. You're not the one who'll be up with him half the night when his stomach aches."

"Mrs. Larsen won't mind," Kate said with conviction. "She loves him, you know."

"What I know, Kate Newton Winthrop, is that I love you very much and I am ready to get this honeymoon underway."

She pivoted and grinned up at him. "Me, too. Where are we going?"

"That's a secret."

"Somebody has to know." She glanced around. "Dorothy?"

His smug smile told her nothing.

"Zelda?"

Nothing.

"Brandon?"

"What makes you think I've told anybody? Maybe I want complete and total privacy for the next four weeks."

"Now that you mention it, that doesn't sound like such a bad idea."

"Sure you won't miss all the meetings and all the phone calls?"

"Are you sure you won't wish you were in some futuristic kingdom?"

"I guess we'll just have to stay very busy," he taunted.

"Very busy," she agreed. "I have some ideas."

He grinned. "I'll just bet you do. Now how about throwing that bouquet of yours, so we can get this show on the road?"

Kate sent Davey to round up the guests for the ceremonial toss. She stood on the bottom step, took one last peek over her shoulder, then tossed the bouquet into the air. Even without looking, she recognized the squeal of absolute delight.

She turned and walked back to Zelda and gave the redhead a hug, then linked Zelda's arm through hers. "Come on. There's somebody here I definitely want you to meet."

Laughing, they crossed the lawn together until they were in front of Brandon Halloran. Kate winked at him, gestured toward the bouquet clutched tightly in Zelda's hands and said, "Okay, do your thing."

Then she looked around for her husband and her stepson. Her family. When she found them at last, a sigh shimmered through her. It might have taken a long time for her to come to this moment, but she wouldn't have traded the adventure that lay ahead for anything.

* * * * *

Also by Jo Ann Brown

Love Inspired

Amish of Prince Edward Island

Building Her Amish Dream
Snowbound Amish Christmas

Green Mountain Blessings

An Amish Christmas Promise
An Amish Easter Wish
An Amish Mother's Secret Past
An Amish Holiday Family

Amish Spinster Club

The Amish Suitor
The Amish Christmas Cowboy
The Amish Bachelor's Baby
The Amish Widower's Twins

Amish Hearts

Amish Homecoming
An Amish Match
His Amish Sweetheart
An Amish Reunion
A Ready-Made Amish Family
An Amish Proposal
An Amish Arrangement
A Christmas to Remember

Visit her Author Profile page at Harlequin.com,
or joannbrownbooks.com, for more titles!

HIS AMISH SWEETHEART

Jo Ann Brown

For John Jakaitis
Thank you for helping us find our way home.

For if thou altogether holdest thy peace at this time,
then shall there enlargement and deliverance arise
to the Jews from another place; but thou and
thy father's house shall be destroyed:
and who knoweth whether thou art
come to the kingdom for such a time as this?
—*Esther* 4:14

Chapter One

Paradise Springs
Lancaster County, Pennsylvania

Esther Stoltzfus balanced the softball bat on her shoulder. Keeping her eye on the boy getting ready to pitch the ball, she smiled. Did her scholars guess that recess, when the October weather was perfect for playing outside, was her favorite part of the day, too? The *kinder* probably couldn't imagine their teacher liked to play ball as much as they did.

This was her third year teaching on her own. Seeing understanding in a *kind*'s eyes when the scholar finally grasped an elusive concept delighted her. She loved spending time with the *kinder*.

Her family had recently begun dropping hints she should be walking out with some young man. Her older brothers didn't know that, until eight months ago, she'd been walking out—and sneaking out for some forbidden buggy racing—with Alvin Lee Peachy. Probably because none of them could have imagined their little sister having such an outrageous suitor. Alvin Lee pushed the boundaries of the *Ordnung*, and there were rumors he intended to jump the fence and join the *Englisch* world. Would she have gone with him if he'd asked? She didn't know, and she never would because when she began to worry about his racing buggies and fast life, he'd dumped her and started courting Luella Hartz. In one moment, she'd lost the man she loved and her *gut* friend.

She'd learned her lesson. A life of adventure and daring wasn't for her. From now on, she wasn't going to risk her heart unless she knew, without a doubt, it was safe. She wouldn't consider spending time with a guy who wasn't as serious and stolid as a bishop.

As she gave a practice swing and the *kinder* urged her on excitedly, she glanced at her assistant teacher, Neva Fry, who was playing first base. Neva, almost two years younger than Esther, was learning what she needed so she could take over a school of her own.

Esther grinned in anticipation of the next play. The ball came in a soft arc, and she swung the bat. Not with all her strength. Some of the outfielders were barely six years old, and she didn't want to chance them getting hurt by a line drive.

The *kinder* behind her cheered while the ones in the field shouted to each other to catch the lazy fly ball. She sped to first base, a large stone set in place by the *daeds* who had helped build the school years ago. Her black sneaker skidded as she touched the stone with one foot and turned to head toward second. Seeing one of the older boys catch the ball, she slowed and clapped her hands.

"Well done, Jay!" she called.

With a wide grin, the boy who, at fourteen, was in his final year at the school, gave her a thumbs-up.

Smiling, she knew she should be grateful Alvin Lee hadn't proposed. She wasn't ready to give up teaching. She wanted a husband and a home and *kinder* of her own, but not until she met the right man. One who didn't whoop at the idea of danger. One she would have described as predictable a few months ago. Now that safe, dependable guy sounded like a dream come true. Well, maybe not a dream, but definitely not a nightmare.

Checking to make sure her *kapp* was straight, Esther smoothed the apron over her dress, which was her favorite shade of rose. She'd selected it and a black apron in the style the *Englischers* called a pinafore when she saw the day would be perfect for playing softball. She held up her hands, and Jay threw her the ball. She caught it easily.

Before she could tell the scholars it was time to go in for afternoon lessons, several began to chant, "One more inning! One more inning!"

Esther hesitated, knowing how few sunny, warm days remained before winter. The *kinder* had worked hard during the morning, and she hadn't had to scold any of them for not paying attention. Not even Jacob Fisher.

She glanced at the small, white schoolhouse. As she expected, the eight-year-old with a cowlick that made a black exclamation point at his crown sat alone on the porch. She invited him to play each day, and each day he resisted. She wished she could find a way to break through the walls Jacob had raised, walls around himself, walls to keep pain at bay.

She closed her eyes as she recalled what she'd been told by Jacob's elderly *onkel*, who was raising him. Jacob had been with his parents, walking home from visiting a neighbor, when they were struck by a drunk driver. The boy had been thrown onto the shoulder. When he regained consciousness, he'd discovered his parents injured by the side of the road. No one, other than Jacob and God, knew if they spoke final words to him, but he'd watched them draw their last breaths. The trial for the hit-and-run driver had added to the boy's trauma, though he hadn't had to testify and the Amish community tried to shield him.

Now he was shattered, taking insult at every turn and exploding with anger. Or else he said nothing and squirmed until he couldn't sit any longer and had to wander around the room. Working with his *onkel*, Titus Fisher, she tried to make school as comfortable for Jacob as possible.

She'd used many things she hoped would help—art projects, story writing, extra assistance with his studies, though the boy was very intelligent in spite of his inability to complete many of his lessons. She'd failed at every turn to draw him out from behind those walls he'd raised around himself. She realized she must find another way to reach him because she wasn't helping him by cajoling him in front of the other *kinder*. So now, she lifted him up in prayer. Those wouldn't fail, but God worked on His own time. He must have a reason for not yet bringing healing to Jacob's young heart.

Or hers.

She chided herself. Losing a suitor didn't compare with losing one's parents, but her heart refused to stop hurting.

"All right," she said, smiling at the rest of the scholars because she didn't want anyone to know what she was thinking. She'd gotten *gut* at hiding the truth. "One more inning, but you need to work extra hard this afternoon."

Heads nodded eagerly. Bouncing the ball in her right hand, she tossed it to the pitcher and took her place in center field where she could help the other outfielders, seven-year-old Olen and Freda who was ten.

The batter swung at the first three pitches and struck out. The next batter kept hitting foul balls, which sent the *kinder* chasing them. Suddenly a loud thwack announced a boy had connected with the ball.

It headed right for Esther. She backpedaled two steps. A quick glance behind her assured she could go a little farther before she'd fall down the hill. Shouts warned her the runner was already on his way to second base.

She reached to catch the ball. Her right foot caught a slippery patch of grass, and she lost her balance. She windmilled her arms, fighting to stay on her feet, but it was impossible. She dropped backward—and hit a solid chest. Strong arms kept her from ending up on her bottom. She grasped the arms as her feet continued to slide.

The ball fell at her feet. Pulling herself out of the arms, she scooped the ball up and threw it to second base. But it was too late. The run had already scored.

Behind her, a deep laugh brushed the small hairs curling at her nape beneath her *kapp*. Heat scored Esther's face as she realized she'd tumbled into a man's arms.

Her gaze had to rise to meet his, though he stood

below her on the hill. He must be more than six feet tall, like her brothers, but he wasn't one of her brothers. The *gut*-looking man was a few years older than she was. No beard softened the firm line of his jaw. Beneath his straw hat, his brown eyes crinkled with his laugh.

"You haven't changed a bit, Esther Stoltzfus!" he said with another chuckle. "Still willing to risk life and limb to get the ball."

He knew her? Who was he?

Her eyes widened. She recognized the twinkle in those dark eyes. Black hair dropped across his forehead, and he pushed it aside carelessly. Like a clap of thunder, realization came as she remembered the boy who had made that exact motion. She looked more closely and saw the small scar beneath his right eye…just like the one on the face of a boy she'd once considered her very best friend.

"Nate Zook?" she asked, not able to believe her own question.

"Ja." His voice was much deeper than when she'd last heard it. "Though I go by Nathaniel now."

When she'd last seen him, he'd been…ten or eleven? She'd been eight. Before his family moved away, she and Nate, along with Micah and Daniel, her twin brothers, had spent most days together. Then, one day, the Zooks were gone. Her brothers had been astonished when they rode their scooters to Nate's house and discovered it was empty. When her *mamm* said the family had moved to Indiana in search of a better life, she wondered if it'd been as much a surprise for Nate as for her and her brothers.

She'd gone with Daniel and Micah to play at his grandparents' farm in a neighboring district when he visited the next summer, but she shouldn't have. She'd accepted a dare from a friend to hold Nate's hand. She couldn't remember which friend it'd been, but at the time she'd been excited to do something audacious. She'd embarrassed herself by following through and gripping his hand so tightly he winced and made it worse by telling him that she planned to marry him when they grew up. He hadn't come back the following summer. She'd been grateful she didn't have to face him after her silliness, and miserable because she missed him.

That was in the past. Here stood Nate—Nathaniel—Zook again, a grown man who'd arrived in time to keep her from falling down the hill.

She should say something. Several *kinder* came to stand beside her, curious about what was going on. She needed to show she wasn't that silly little girl any longer, but all that came out was, "What are you doing in Paradise Springs?"

He opened his mouth to answer. Whatever he was about to say was drowned out by a shriek from the schoolhouse.

Esther whirled and gasped when she saw two boys on the ground, fists flying. She ran to stop the fight. Finding out why Nathaniel had returned to Paradise Springs after more than a decade would have to wait. But not too long, because she was really curious why he'd come back now.

Nathaniel Zook stared after Esther as she raced across the grass, her apron flapping on her skirt. Years ago, she'd been able to outrun him and her brothers, though they were almost five years older than she was. She'd been much shorter then, and her knees, which were now properly concealed beneath her dress, had been covered with scrapes. Her bright eyes were as blue, and their steady gaze contained the same strength.

He looked past her to where two boys were rolling on the grass. Should he help? One of the boys in the fight was nearly as big as Esther was.

"Oh, Jacob Fisher! He keeps picking fights," said a girl with a sigh.

"Or dropping books on the floor or throwing papers around." A boy shook his head. "He wants attention. That's what my *mamm* says."

Nathaniel didn't wait to listen to any more because when Esther bent to try to put a halt to the fight, a fist almost struck her. He crossed the yard and pushed past the gawking *kinder*. A blow to Esther's middle knocked her back a couple of steps. Again he caught her and steadied her, then he grasped both boys by their suspenders and tugged them apart.

The shorter boy struggled to get away, his brown eyes snapping with fury. Flinging his fists out wildly, he almost connected with the taller boy's chin.

Shoving them away from each other, Nathaniel said, "Enough. If you can't honestly tell each other you're sorry for acting foolishly, at least shake hands."

"I'm not shaking hands with him!" The taller boy was panting, and blood dripped from the left corner of his mouth. "He'll jump me again for no reason."

The shorter boy puffed up like a snake about to strike. "You called me a—"

"Enough," Nathaniel repeated as he kept a tight hold on their suspenders. "What's been said was said. What's been done has been done. It's over. Let it go."

The glowers the boys gave him warned Nathaniel that he was wasting his breath.

"Benny," ordered Esther, "go and wash up. Jacob, wait on the porch for me. We need to talk." She gestured toward a younger woman who'd been staring wide-eyed at the battling boys. "Neva, take the other scholars inside please."

Astonished by how serene her voice was and how quickly the boys turned to obey after scowling at each other again, Nathaniel waited while the *kinder* followed Neva into the school. He knew Esther would want to get back to her job, as well. Since he'd returned to Paradise Springs, he'd heard over and over what a devoted teacher Esther Stoltzfus was. Well, his visit should be a short one because all he needed was for her to say a quick *ja*.

First, however, he had to ask, "Are you okay, Esther?"

"I'm fine." She adjusted her *kapp*, which had come loose in the melee. Her golden-brown hair glistened through the translucent white organdy of her heart-shaped *kapp*. Her dress was a charming dark pink almost the same color as her cheeks. The flush nearly absorbed her freckles. There weren't as many as the last time he'd seen her more than a decade ago.

Back then, she and her twin brothers had been his best friends. In some ways, he'd been closer to her than her brothers. Micah and Daniel were twins, and they had a special bond. He and Esther had often found themselves on one team while her brothers took the other side, whether playing ball or having races or embarking on some adventure. She hadn't been one of those girly girls who worried about getting her clothes dirty or if her hair was mussed. She played to win, though she was younger than the rest of them. He'd never met another girl like her, a girl who was, as his *daed* had described her, not afraid to be one of the boys.

"Are you sure?" he asked. "You got hit pretty hard."

"I'm fine." Her blue eyes regarded him with curiosity. "When did you return to Paradise Springs?"

"Almost a month ago. I've inherited my grandparents' farm on the other side of the village."

"I'm sorry, Nat—Nathaniel. I should have remembered that they'd passed away in the spring. You must miss them."

"Ja," he said, though the years that had gone by since the last time he'd seen them left them as little more than childhood memories. Except for one visit to Paradise Springs the first year after the move, his life had been in Elkhart County, Indiana.

From beyond the school he heard the rattle of equipment and smelled the unmistakable scent of greenery and disturbed earth. Next year at this time, God willing, he'd be chopping his own corn into silage to feed his animals over the winter. He couldn't wait. At last, he had the job he'd always wanted: farmer. He wouldn't have had the opportunity in Indiana. There it was intended, in Amish tradition, that his younger brother would inherit the family's five acres. Nathaniel had assumed he, like his *daed*, would spend his life working in an *Englisch* factory building RVs.

Those plans had changed when word came that his Zook grandparents' farm in Paradise Springs was now his. A dream come true. Along with the surprising menagerie his *grossdawdi* and his *grossmammi* had collected in their final years. He'd been astonished not to find dairy cows when he arrived. Instead, there were about thirty-five alpacas, one of the oddest looking animals he'd ever seen. They resembled a combination of a poodle and a llama, especially at this time of year when their wool was thickening. In addition, on the farm were two mules, a buggy horse and more chickens than he could count. He was familiar with horses, mules and chickens, but he had a lot to learn about alpacas, which was the reason he'd come to the school today.

He was determined to make the farm a success so he wouldn't have to sell it. For the first time in far too many years, he felt alive with possibilities.

"How can I help you?" Esther asked, as if he'd spoken aloud. "Are you here to enroll a *kind* in school?"

Years of practice kept him from revealing how her simple question drove a shaft through his heart. She couldn't guess how much that question hurt him, and he didn't have time to wallow in thoughts of how, because of a childhood illness, he most likely could never be a *daed*. He'd never enjoy the simple act of coming to a school to arrange for his son or daughter to attend.

He was alive and well. For that he was grateful, and he needed to let the feelings of failure go. Otherwise, he was dismissing God's gift of life as worthless. That he'd never do.

Instead he needed to concentrate on why he'd visited the school this afternoon. After asking around the area, he'd learned of only one person who was familiar with how to raise alpacas.

Esther Stoltzfus.

"No, I'm here for a different reason." He managed a smile. "One I think you'll find interesting."

"I'd like to talk, Nathaniel, but—" She glanced at the

older boy, the one she'd called Benny. He stood by the well beyond the schoolhouse and was washing his hands and face. Jacob sat on the porch. He was trembling in the wake of the fight and rocking his feet against the latticework. It made a dull thud each time his bare heels struck it. "I'm going to have to ask you to excuse me. *Danki* for pulling the boys apart."

"The little guy doesn't look more than about six years old."

"Jacob is eight. He's small for his age, but he has the heart of a lion."

"But far less common sense if he fights boys twice his age."

"Benny is fourteen."

"Close enough."

She nodded with another sigh. "Yet you saw who ended up battered and bloody. Jacob doesn't have a mark on him."

"Quite a feat!"

"Really?" She frowned. "Think what a greater feat it would have been if Jacob had turned the other cheek and walked away from Benny. It's the lesson we need to take to heart."

"For a young boy, it's hard to remember. We have to learn things the hard way, it seems." He gave her a lopsided grin, but she wouldn't meet his eyes. She acted flustered. Why? She'd put a stop to the fight as quickly as she could. "Like the time your brothers and I got too close to a hive and got stung. I guess that's what people mean by a painful lesson."

"Most lessons are."

"Well, it was a *very* painful one." He hurried on before she could leave. "I've heard you used to raise alpacas."

"Just a pair. Are you planning to raise them on your grandparents' farm?"

"Not planning. They're already there. Apparently my *grossmammi* fell in love with the creatures and decided to buy some when she and my *grossdawdi* stopped milking. I don't know the first thing about alpacas, other than how to feed them. I was hoping you could share what you learned." He didn't add that if he couldn't figure out a way to use the animals to make money, he'd have to sell them and probably the farm itself next spring.

When she glanced at the school again, he said, "Not right now, of course."

"I'd like to help, but I don't have a lot of time."

"I won't need a lot of your time. Just enough to point me in the right direction."

She hesitated.

He could tell she didn't want to tell him no, but her mind was focused on the *kinder* now. Maybe he should leave and come back again, but he didn't have time to wait. The farm was more deeply in debt than he'd guessed before he came to Paradise Springs. He hadn't guessed his grandparents had spent so wildly on buying the animals that they had to borrow money for keeping them. Few plain folks their age took out a loan because it could become a burden on the next generation. Now it was his responsibility to repay it.

Inspiration struck when he looked from her to the naughty boys. It was a long shot, but he'd suggest anything if there was a chance to save his family's farm.

"Bring your scholars to see the alpacas," he said. "I

can ask my questions, and so can they. You can answer them for all of us. It'll be fun for them. Remember how we liked a break from schoolwork? They would, too, I'm sure."

She didn't reply for a long minute, then nodded. "They probably would be really interested."

He grinned. "Why don't I drive my flatbed wagon over here? I can give the *kinder* a ride on it both ways."

"*Gut.* Let me know which day works best for you, and I'll tell the parents we're going there. Some of them may want to join us."

"We'll make an adventure out of it, like when we were *kinder.*"

Color flashed up her face before vanishing, leaving her paler than before.

"*Was iss letz?*" he asked.

"Nothing is wrong," she replied so hastily he guessed she wasn't being honest. "I—"

A shout came from the porch where the bigger boy was walking past Jacob. The younger boy was on his feet, his fists clenched again.

She ran toward them, calling over her shoulder, "We'll have to talk about this later."

"I'll come over tonight. We'll talk then."

Nathaniel wondered if she'd heard him because she was already steering the boys into the school. Her soft voice reached him. Not the words, but the gently chiding tone. He guessed she was reminding them that they needed to settle their disputes without violence. He wondered if they'd listen and what she'd have to do if they didn't heed her.

As she closed the door, she looked at him and mouthed, *See you tonight.*

"Gut!" he said as he walked to where he'd left his wagon on the road. He smiled. He'd been wanting to stop by the Stoltzfus farm, so her invitation offered the perfect excuse. It would be a fun evening, and for the first time since he'd seen the alpacas, he dared to believe that with what Esther could teach him about the odd creatures, he might be able to make a go of the farm.

Chapter Two

The Stoltzfus family farm was an easy walk from the school. Esther went across a field, along two different country roads, and then up the long lane to the only house she'd ever lived in. She'd been born there. Her *daed* had been as well, and his *daed* before him.

After *Daed* had passed away, her *mamm* had moved into the attached *dawdi haus* while Esther managed the main house. She'd hand over those duties when her older brother Ezra married, which she guessed would be before October was over, because he spent every bit of his free time with their neighbor Leah Beiler. Their wedding day was sure to be a joyous one.

Though she never would have admitted it, Esther was looking forward to giving the responsibilities of a household with five bachelor brothers to Leah. Even with one of her older brothers married, another widowed and her older sister off tending a family of her own, the housework was never-ending. Esther enjoyed cooking and keeping the house neat, but she was tired of mending a mountain of work clothes while trying to prepare lesson plans for the next day. Her brothers worked hard, whether on the farm or in construction or at the grocery store, and their clothes reflected that. She and *Mamm* never caught up.

Everything in her life had been in proper order… until Nathaniel Zook came to her school that afternoon. She was amazed she hadn't heard he was in Paradise Springs. If she'd known, maybe she'd have been better prepared. He'd grown up, but it didn't sound as if he'd changed. He still liked adventures if he intended to keep alpacas instead of the usual cows or sheep or goats on his farm. That made him a man she needed to steer clear of, so she could avoid the mistakes she'd made with Alvin Lee.

But how could she turn her back on helping him? It was the Amish way to give assistance when it was requested. She couldn't mess up Nathaniel's life because she was appalled by how she'd nearly ruined her own by chasing excitement.

His suggestion that she bring the scholars to his farm would focus attention on the *kinder*. She'd give them a fun day while they learned about something new, something that might be of use to them in the future. Who could guess now which one of them would someday have alpacas of his or her own?

That thought eased her disquiet enough that Esther could admire the trees in the front yard. They displayed their autumnal glory. Dried leaves were already skittering across the ground on the gentle breeze. Ezra's

Brown Swiss cows grazed near the white barn. The sun was heading for the horizon, a sure sign milking would start soon. Dinner for her hungry brothers needed to be on the table by the time chores were done and the barn tidied up for the night.

When she entered the comfortable kitchen with its pale blue walls and dark wood cabinets, Esther was surprised to see her twin brothers there. They were almost five years older than she was, and they'd teased her, when they were *kinder*, of being an afterthought. She'd fired back with jests of her own, and they'd spent their childhoods laughing. No one took offense while they'd been climbing trees, fishing in the creek and doing tasks to help keep the farm and the house running.

Her twin brothers weren't identical. Daniel had a cleft in his chin and Micah didn't. There were other differences in the way they talked and how they used their hands to emphasize words. Micah asserted he was a half inch taller than his twin, but Esther couldn't see it. They were unusual in one important way—they didn't share a birthday. Micah had been born ten minutes before midnight, and Daniel a half hour later, a fact Micah never allowed his "baby" brother to forget.

Both twins had a glass of milk in one hand and a stack of snickerdoodles in the other. Their bare feet stuck out from where they sat at the large table in the middle of the kitchen.

"You're home early," she said as she hung her bonnet and satchel on pegs by the back door. The twins' straw hats hung among the empty pegs, which would all be in use by the time the family sat down for dinner.

"We're finished at the project in Lititz," Daniel said. He was a carpenter, as was Micah, but the older twin specialized in building windmills and installing solar panels. However, the two men were equally skilled with a hammer. "Time to hand it over to the electricians and plumbers. Micah already went over what needed to be done to connect the roof panels to the main electrical box."

"You've been working on that house a long time," she said as she opened the refrigerator door and took out the leftover ham she planned to reheat for dinner. "It must be a big one."

"You know how *Englischers* are." Micah chuckled. "They move out to Lancaster County to live the simple life and then decide they need lots of gadgets and rooms to store them in. This house has a real movie theater."

She began cutting the ham into thick slices. "You're joking."

"Would we do that?" Daniel asked with fake innocence before he took the final bite of his last cookie.

"Ja."

"Ja," echoed Micah, folding his arms on the table. "We're being honest. The house is as big as our barn."

Esther tried to imagine why anyone would need a house that size, but she couldn't. At one point, there had been eleven of them living in the Stoltzfus farmhouse along with her grandparents in the small *dawdi haus*, and there had been plenty of room.

Daniel stretched before he yawned. "Sorry. It was an early morning."

"You'll want to stay awake. An old friend of yours is stopping by tonight."

"Who?" Micah asked.

She could tell them, but it served her brothers right

to let their curiosity stew a bit longer. Smiling, she said, "Someone who inherited a farm on Zook Road."

The twins exchanged a disbelieving glance before Daniel asked, "Are you talking about Nate Zook?"

"He calls himself Nathaniel now."

"He's back in Paradise Springs?" he asked.

"Ja."

"It's been almost ten years since the last time we saw him." With a pensive expression, Micah rubbed his chin between his forefinger and thumb. "Remember, Daniel? He came out from Indiana to spend the summer with his grandparents the year after his family moved."

Daniel chuckled. "His *grossmammi* made us chocolate shoo-fly pie the day before he left. One of the best things I've ever tasted. Do you remember, Esther?"

"No." She was glad she had her back to them as she placed ham slices in the cast-iron fry pan. Her face was growing warm as she thought again of Nathaniel's visit and how she'd made a complete fool of herself. Hurrying to the cellar doorway, she got the bag of potatoes that had been harvested a few weeks ago. She'd make mashed potatoes tonight. Everyone liked them, and she could release some of her pent-up emotions while smashing them.

"Oh, that's right," Daniel said. "You decided you didn't want to play with us boys any longer. You thought it was a big secret why, but we knew."

She looked over her shoulder before she could halt herself. "You did?" How many more surprises was she going to have today? First, Nathaniel Zook showed up at her school, and now her brother was telling her he'd known why she stopped going to the Zook farm. Had

Nathaniel told him about her brash stupidity of announcing she planned to marry him one day?

"Ja." Jabbing his brother with his elbow, Micah said, "You had a big crush on Nate. Giggled whenever you were around him."

She wanted to take them by the shoulders and shake them and tell them how wrong they were. She couldn't. That would be a lie. She'd had a big crush on Nathaniel. He was the only boy she knew who wasn't annoyed because she could outrun him or hit a ball as well as he did. He'd never tried to make her feel she was different from other girls because she preferred being outside to working beside her *mamm* in the house. Not once had he picked on her because she did well at school, like some of the other boys had.

That had happened long ago. She needed to put it out of her head. Nathaniel must have forgotten—or at least forgiven her—since he came to ask a favor today. She'd follow his lead for once and act as if the mortifying day had never happened.

"You don't know what you're talking about," Esther said, lifting her chin as she carried the potatoes to the sink to wash them. "I was a little girl."

"Who had a big crush on Nate Zook." Her brothers laughed as if Micah had said the funniest thing ever. "We'll have to watch and see if she drools when he walks in."

"Stop teasing your sister," *Mamm* said as she came through the door from the *dawdi haus*. She'd moved in preparation for Ezra's marriage. Though neither Ezra nor Leah spoke of their plans to marry, everyone suspected they'd be among the first couples having their intentions published at the next church Sunday.

"Well, she needs to marry someone," Micah said with a broad grin. "She can't seem to make up her mind about the guys around here. Just like Danny-boy can't decide on one girl." He poked his elbow at his twin again, but Daniel moved aside.

"Why settle for one when there are plenty of pretty ones willing to let me take them home?" Daniel asked.

Esther was startled to see his smile wasn't reflected in his eyes. His jesting words were meant to hide his true feelings. The twins were popular with young people in their district and the neighboring ones. They were fun and funny. What was Daniel concealing behind his ready grin?

More questions, and she didn't need more questions. She already had enough without any answers. The marriage season for the Amish began in October. As it approached, she'd asked herself if she should try walking out with another young man. Maybe that would be the best way to put Alvin Lee and his betrayal out of her mind. But she wasn't ready to risk her heart again.

Better to be wise than to be sorry. How many times had she heard *Mamm* say those words? She'd discovered the wisdom in them by learning the truth the hard way. She'd promised herself to be extra careful with her heart from now on.

After giving her *mamm* a hug, Esther finished preparing their supper. She was grateful for *Mamm*'s assistance because she felt clumsy as she hadn't since she first began helping in the kitchen. Telling herself to focus, she avoided cutting herself as she peeled potatoes. Her brothers were too busy teasing each other to notice how her fingers shook.

Danki, Lord, for small blessings.

She put the reheated ham, buttered peas and a large bowl of mashed potatoes on the table. *Mamm* finished slicing the bread Esther had made before school that morning and put platters at either end along with butter and apple butter. While Esther retrieved the cabbage salad and chowchow from the refrigerator, her *mamm* filled a pitcher with water.

The door opened, and Ezra came in with a metal half-gallon milk can. In his other hand he carried a generous slab of his fragrant, homemade cheese. He called a greeting before stepping aside to let three more brothers enter. They'd been busy at the Stoltzfus Family Shops closer to the village of Paradise Springs. Amos set fresh apple cider from his grocery store in the center of the table.

As soon as they sat together at the table, Ezra, as the oldest son present, bowed his head. It was the signal for the meal's silent grace.

Esther quickly offered her thanks, then added a supplication that she'd be able to help Nathaniel without complications. To be honest, she'd enjoy teaching him how to raise alpacas and harvest the wondrously soft wool they grew.

As she raised her head when Ezra cleared his throat, she glanced around the table at her brothers and *mamm*. She had a *gut* life with her family and her scholars and her community. She didn't need adventure. Not her own or anyone else's. How she would have embarrassed her family if they'd heard of her partying with Alvin Lee and his friends! She could have lost her position as teacher, as well as shamed her family.

Learn from your failures, or you'll fail to learn. A poster saying that hung in the schoolroom. She needed to remember those words and hold them close to her heart. She vowed to do so, starting that very second.

As Nathaniel drove his buggy into the farm lane leading to the large white farmhouse where the Stoltzfus family lived, he couldn't keep from grinning. He'd looked forward to seeing them as much as he had his grandparents when he'd spent a summer in Paradise Springs years ago. Micah and Daniel had imaginations that had cooked up mischief to keep their summer days filled with adventures. Not even chores could slow down their laugh-filled hours.

Then there was Esther. She'd been brave enough to try anything and never quailed before a challenge. The twins had been less willing to accept every dare he posed. Not Esther. He remembered the buzz of excitement he'd felt the afternoon she'd agreed to jump from the second story hayloft if he did.

He knew he was going to have to be that gutsy if he hoped to save his grandparents' farm. It'd been in the family for generations, and he didn't want to be the one to sell it. Even if he couldn't have *kinder* of his own to inherit it, his two oldest sisters were already married with *bopplin*. One of them might want to take over the farm, and he didn't want to lose it because he hadn't learned quickly enough.

Esther agreeing to help him with the alpacas might be the saving grace he'd prayed for. If it wasn't, he could be defeated before he began.

No, I'm not going to think that way. I'm not going to give up before I've barely begun. He got out of the buggy. Things were going to get better. Starting now. He had to believe God's hands were upon the inheritance that gave him a chance to make his dream of running his own farm come true.

He strode toward the white house's kitchen door. Nobody used the front door except for church Sundays and funerals. The house and white outbuildings hadn't changed much in ten years. There was a third silo by the largest barn, and instead of the black-and-white cows Esther's *daed* used to milk, grayish-brown cattle stood in the pasture. The chicken coop was closer to the house than he remembered, and extra buggies and wagons were parked beneath the trees.

He paused at the door. He'd never knocked at the Stoltzfus house before, but somehow it didn't feel right to walk in. Too many years had passed since the last time he'd come to the farm.

"Why are you standing on the steps?" came a friendly female voice as the door swung open. "*Komm* in, Nate. We're about to enjoy some *snitz* pie."

Wanda Stoltzfus, Esther's *mamm*, looked smaller than he remembered. He knew she hadn't shrunk; he'd grown. Her hair had strands of gray woven through it, but her smile was as warm as ever.

"Did you make the pie?" he asked, delighted to see the welcome in eyes almost the same shade as her daughter's.

"Do you think I'd trust anyone, even my own *kinder*, with my super secret recipe for dried-apple pie while there's breath in these old bones?" She stepped aside and motioned for him to come in.

"You aren't old, Wanda," he replied.

"And you haven't lost an ounce of the charm you used as a boy to try to wheedle extra treats from me."

He heard a snicker and looked past her. Esther was

at the stove, pouring freshly brewed *kaffi* into one cup after the other. The sound hadn't come from her, but his gaze had riveted on her. She looked pretty and somehow younger and more vulnerable now that she was barefoot and had traded her starched *kapp* for a dark kerchief over her golden hair. He could see the little girl she'd been transposed over the woman she had become, and his heart gave a peculiar little stutter.

What was that? He hadn't felt its like before, and he wasn't sure what was causing it now. Esther was his childhood friend. Why was he nervous?

Hearing another laugh, Nathaniel pulled his gaze from her and looked at the table where six of the seven Stoltzfus brothers were gathered. Joshua, whom he'd recently heard had married again after the death of his first wife, and Ruth, the oldest, who had been wed long enough to have given her husband a houseful of *kinder*, were missing. A pulse of sorrow pinched at him because he noticed Ezra was sitting where Paul, the family's late patriarch, had sat. Paul had welcomed him into the family as if Nathaniel were one of his own sons.

Nathaniel stared at the men rising from the table. It was startling to see his onetime childhood playmates grown up. He'd known time hadn't stood still for them. Yet the change was greater than he'd guessed. Isaiah wore a beard that was patchy and sparse. He must be married, though Nathaniel hadn't heard about it. All the Stoltzfus brothers were tall, well-muscled from hard work and wore friendly smiles.

Then the twins opened their mouths and asked him how he liked running what they called the Paradise Springs Municipal Zoo. Nothing important had changed, he realized. They enjoyed teasing each other and everyone around them, and he was their chosen target tonight. Nothing they said was cruel. They poked fun as much at themselves as anyone else. Their eyes hadn't lost the mischievous glint that warned another prank was about to begin.

For the first time since he'd returned to Paradise Springs, he didn't feel like a stranger. He was among friends.

Nathaniel sat at the large table. When Esther put a slice of pie and a steaming cup of *kaffi* in front of him, he thanked her. She murmured something before hurrying away to bring more cups to the table. He had no chance to talk to her because her brothers kept him busy with questions. He was amazed to learn that Jeremiah, who'd been all thumbs as a boy, now was a master woodworker, and Isaiah was a blacksmith as well as one of the district's ministers. Amos leaned over to whisper that Isaiah's young bride had died a few months earlier, soon after Isaiah had been chosen by lot to be the new minister.

Saddened by the family's loss, he knew he should wait until he had a chance to talk to Isaiah alone before he expressed his condolences. He sensed how hard Isaiah was trying to join in the *gut* humor around the table.

Nathaniel answered their questions about discovering the alpacas on the farm and explained how he planned to plant the fields in the spring. "Right now, the fields are rented to neighbors, so I can't cut a single blade of grass to feed those silly creatures this winter."

"You're staying in Paradise Springs?" Wanda asked.

"That's my plan." His parents weren't pleased he'd left Indiana, though they'd pulled up roots in Lancaster County ten years ago. He'd already received half a dozen letters from his *mamm* pleading for him to come home. She acted as if he'd left the Amish to join the *Englisch* world.

"*Wunderbaar*, Nate... I mean, Nathaniel." Wanda smiled.

"Call me whichever you wish. It doesn't matter."

"I know your family must be pleased to have you take over the farm that has been in Zook hands for generations. It is *gut* to know it'll continue in the family."

"*Ja.*" He sounded as uncertain as he felt. The generations to come might be a huge problem. He reminded himself to be optimistic and focus on the here and now. Once he made the farm a success, his nephews and nieces would be eager to take it over.

His gaze locked with Esther's. He hadn't meant to let it happen, but he couldn't look away. There was much more to her now than the little girl she'd been. He had a difficult time imagining her at the teacher's desk instead of among the scholars, sending him and her brothers notes filled with plans for after school.

Esther the Pester was what they'd called her then, but he'd been eager to join in with the fun she proposed. He wondered if she were as avid to entertain her scholars. No wonder everyone praised her teaching.

Ezra said his name in a tone suggesting he'd been trying to get Nathaniel's attention. Breaking free of his memories was easier than cutting the link between his eyes and Esther's. He wasn't sure he could have managed it if she hadn't looked away.

Recalling what Ezra had asked, Nathaniel said, "I've got a lot to learn to be a proper farmer. Esther agreed to help me with the alpacas."

"Don't let her tell you Daniel and I tried roping hers,"

Micah said with a laugh. "It was an innocent misunderstanding."

"Misunderstanding? Yes," Esther retorted. "Innocent? I don't think so. Poor Pepe and Delfina were traumatized for weeks."

"The same amount of time it took to get the reek of their spit off me." Micah wrinkled his nose. "Watch out, Nathaniel. They're docile most of the time but they have a secret weapon. Their spit can leave you gagging for days."

Nathaniel grinned. "I'm glad you two learned that disgusting lesson instead of me." He noticed Esther was smiling broadly. "I hope, Ezra, you don't mind me asking you about a thousand questions about working the fields."

"Of course not, though it'd be better to wait to ask until after the first of the year." He reached for another piece of pie.

Nathaniel started to ask why, then saw the family's abruptly bland faces. Ezra must be getting married. His *mamm* and brothers and Esther were keeping the secret until the wedding was announced. They must like his future bride and looked forward to her becoming a part of their family along with any *kinder* she and Ezra might have.

He kept his sigh silent. Assuming he ever found a woman who would consider marrying him, having a single *kind* of his own might be impossible. He'd been thirteen when he was diagnosed with leukemia. That had been after the last summer he'd spent in Paradise Springs with his grandparents. For the next year, he'd undergone treatments and fought to recover. Chemo and radiation had defeated the cancer, but he'd been warned the chemo that had saved his life made it unlikely he'd ever be a *daed*. He thought he'd accepted it as God's will, but, seeing the quiet joy in Ezra Stoltzfus's eyes was a painful reminder of what he would never have. He couldn't imagine a woman agreeing to marry him once she knew the truth.

When the last of the pie was gone, the table cleared and thanks given once more, Nathaniel knew it was time to leave. Everyone had to be up before the sun in the morning.

As he stood, he asked as casually as he could, "Esther, will you walk to my buggy with me?"

Her brothers and *mamm* regarded him with as much astonishment as if he'd announced he wanted to discuss a trip to the moon. Did they think he was planning to court her? He couldn't, not when he couldn't give Esther *kinder*. She loved them. He'd seen that at the school.

"I've got a few questions about your scholars visiting the farm," he hurried to add.

"All right." Esther came to her feet with the grace she hadn't had as a little girl. Walking around the table, she went to the door. She pulled on her black sneakers and bent to tie them.

The night, when they stepped outside, was cool, but crisp in the way fall nights were. The stars seemed closer than during the summer, and the moon was beginning to rise over the horizon. It was a brilliant orange. Huge, it took up most of the eastern sky.

Under his boots, the grass was slippery with dew. It wouldn't be long before the dampness became frost. The seasons were gentler and slower here than in northern Indiana. He needed to become attuned to their pace again.

Esther's steps were soft as she walked beside him while they made arrangements for the scholars' trip. He smiled when she asked if it would be okay for the *kinder* to have their midday meal at the farm.

"That way, we can have time for desk work when we return," she said.

"I'll make sure I have drinks for the *kinder*, so they don't have to bring those."

"That's kind of you, Nathaniel." She offered him another warm smile. "I want to say *danki* again for helping me stop the fight this afternoon."

"Do you have many of them?"

"*Ja*, and Jacob seems to be involved in each one."

He frowned. "Is there something wrong with the boy that he can't settle disagreements other than with his fists?" The wrong question to ask, he realized when she bristled.

"Nothing is *wrong* with him." She took a steadying breath, then said more calmly, "Forgive me. You can't know how it is. Jacob has had a harder time than most kids. He lives with his *onkel*, actually his *daed*'s *onkel*. The man is too old to be taking care of a *kind*, but apparently he's the boy's sole relative. At least Jacob has him. The poor boy has seen things no *kind* should see."

"What do you mean?" He stopped beneath the great maple tree at the edge of the yard.

She explained how Jacob's parents had been killed and the boy badly hurt, physically and emotionally. Nathaniel's heart contracted with the thought of a *kind* suffering such grief.

"After the accident," she said, "we checked everywhere for other family, even putting a letter in *The Budget*."

He knew the newspaper aimed at and written by correspondents in plain communities was read throughout the world. "Nobody came forward?"

"Nobody." Her voice fell to a whisper. "Maybe that's why Jacob is angry. He believes everyone, including God, has abandoned him. He blames God for taking his *mamm* and *daed* right in front of his eyes. Why should he obey Jesus's request that we turn the other cheek and forgive those who treat us badly when, in Jacob's opinion, God has treated him worse than anyone on Earth could?"

"Anger at God eats at your soul. He has time to wait for your fury to run its course and still He forgives you."

"That sounds like the voice of experience."

"It is." He hesitated, wondering if he should tell her about the chemo. It was too personal a subject to share, even with Esther.

She said nothing, clearly expecting him to continue. When he didn't, she bid him good-night and started to turn away.

He put his hand on her arm as he'd done many times when they were kids. She looked at him, and the moonlight washed across her face. Who would have guessed a freckle-faced imp would mature into such a pretty woman? That odd sensation uncurled in his stomach again when she gazed at him, waiting for him to speak. Another change, because the Esther he'd known years ago wouldn't have waited on anything before she plunged headlong into her next adventure.

"*Danki* for agreeing to teach me about alpacas."

He watched her smile return and brighten her face. "I know how busy you are, but without your help I might have to sell the flock."

"Herd," she said with a laugh. "Sheep are a flock. Alpacas are a herd."

"See? I'm learning already."

"You've got much more to learn."

He grinned. "You used to like when I had to listen to you."

"Still do. I'll let you know when I've contacted the scholars' parents, and we'll arrange a day for them to visit." She patted his arm and ran into the house, her skirts fluttering behind her.

With a chuckle, he climbed into his buggy. He might not know a lot about alpacas, but he knew the lessons to come wouldn't be boring as long as Esther was involved.

Chapter Three

Nathaniel stepped down from his wagon and past the pair of mules hooked to it. There would be about twenty-two *kinder* along with, he guessed, at least one or two *mamms* to help oversee the scholars. Add in Esther and her assistant teacher. It was a small load, so it would give the mules, Sal and Gal, some gentle exercise. Tomorrow, he needed them to fetch a large load of hay. He'd store it in the barn to feed the animals during the winter.

The scholars were milling about in front of the school, their excited voices like a flock of blue jays. He was glad he'd left his *mutze* coat, the black wool coat plain men wore to church services, home on the warm morning and had his black vest on over his white shirt. His black felt hat was too hot, and he'd trade it for his straw one as soon as he got to the farm.

A boy ran over to be the first on the wagon. He

halted, and Nathaniel recognized him from the scab on the corner of his mouth. It was the legacy of the punch Benny had taken from Jacob Fisher last week.

"Gute mariye," Nathaniel said with a smile.

The boy watched him with suspicion, saying nothing.

"How's the lip?" Nathaniel asked. "It looks sore."

"It is," Benny replied grudgingly.

"Have your *mamm* put a dab of hand lotion on it to keep the skin soft, so it can heal. Try to limit your talking. You don't want to keep breaking it open."

The boy started to answer, then raised his eyebrows in a question.

"A day or two will allow it to heal. If you've got to say something, think it over first and make sure it's worth the pain that follows."

Benny nodded, then his eyes widened when he understood the true message in Nathaniel's suggestion. Keeping his mouth closed would help prevent him from saying something that could lead to a fight. The boy looked at the ground, then claimed his spot at the very back of the wagon bed where the ride would be the bumpiest.

Hoping what he said would help Esther by preventing another fight, Nathaniel walked toward the school. He was almost there when she stepped out and closed the door behind her. Today she wore a dark blue dress beneath her black apron. The color was the perfect foil for her eyes and her hair, which was the color of spun caramel.

"Right on time, Nathaniel," she said as she came down the steps. He tried to connect the prim woman she was now with the enthusiastic *kind* she'd been. It was almost impossible, and he couldn't help wondering what had quashed her once high spirits.

"I know you don't like to wait," he said instead of asking the questions he wanted to.

"Neither does anyone else." She put her arms around two of the *kinder* closest to her, and they looked at her with wide grins.

He helped her get the smaller ones on the wagon where they'd be watched by the older scholars. He wasn't surprised when Jacob found a place close to the front. The boy sat as stiffly as a cornstalk, making it clear he didn't want anyone near him.

Esther glanced at Nathaniel. He could tell she was frustrated at not being able to reach the *kind*. He'd added Jacob to his prayers and hoped God would bring the boy comfort. As He'd helped Nathaniel during the horrific rounds of chemo and the wait afterward to discover if the cancer had been vanquished.

"I'll keep an eye on him," he whispered.

"Me, too." She smiled again, but it wasn't as bright. After she made sure nobody had forgotten his or her lunch box, she sat on the seat with him.

He'd hoped to get time to chat with Esther during the fifteen minute drive to his farm, but she spent most of the ride looking over her shoulder to remind the scholars not to move close to the edges or to suggest a song for them to sing. Her assistant and the two *mamms* who'd joined them were kept busy with making sure the lunch boxes didn't bounce off. As they passed farmhouses, neighbors waved to them, and the *kinder* shouted they were going to see the alpacas.

"Nobody has any secrets with them around, do they?" Nathaniel grinned as the scholars began singing again.

"None whatsoever." Esther laughed. "It's one of the first lessons I learned. I love my job so I don't mind having everything I do and say at school repeated to parents each night."

"It sounds, from what I've heard, as if the parents are pleased."

A flush climbed her cheeks. "The *kinder* are important to all of us."

He looked past the mules' ears so she couldn't see his smile. Esther was embarrassed by his compliment. If the scholars hadn't been in earshot, he would have teased her about blushing.

Telling the *kinder* to hold on tight, he turned the wagon in at the lane leading to his grandparents' farm. To *his* farm. This morning, he'd received another letter from his *mamm*, begging him to return to Indiana instead of following his dreams in Paradise Springs. He must find a gentle way to let her know, once and for all, that he wanted to remain in Lancaster County. And he'd suggest she find the best words to let Vernita Miller know, as well. He didn't intend to marry Vernita, no matter how often the young woman had hinted he should. She'd find someone else. Perhaps his *gut* friend Dwayne Kempf who was sweet on her.

He shook thoughts of his *mamm*, Indiana and Vernita out of his head as he drew in the reins and stopped the wagon near the barn. Like the house, it needed a new coat of white paint. He'd started on the big project of fixing all the buildings when he could steal time from taking care of the animals, but, so far, only half of one side of the house was done.

"There they are!" came a shout from the back.

Jumping down, Nathaniel smiled when he saw the excited *kinder* pointing at the alpacas near the pasture fence. He heard a girl describe them as "adorable."

Their long legs and neck were tufted with wool. Around their faces, more wool puffed like an aura.

The alpacas raced away when the scholars poured off the wagon.

"Where are they going?" a little girl asked him as he lifted her down.

"To get the others," he replied, though he knew the skittish creatures wanted to flee as far as possible from the noisy *kinder*.

Esther put her finger to her lips. "You must be quiet. Be like little mice sneaking around a sleeping cat."

The youngest scholars giggled. She asked each little one to take the hand of an older child. A few of the boys, including Jacob, which was no surprise, refused to hold anyone else's hand. Esther told them to remain close to the others and not to speak loudly.

"Where do you want us, Nathaniel?" she asked. "By the fence is probably best. What do you think?"

"You're the expert."

She led the *kinder* to the wooden fence backed by chicken wire, making sure the littler ones could see. "Can you name some of the alpacas' cousins?"

"Llamas!" called a boy.

She nodded, but motioned for him to lower his voice as the alpacas shifted nervously. "Llamas are one of their cousins. Can you tell me another?"

"Horses?" asked a girl.

"No."

"Cows?"

"No." She pointed at the herd after letting the scholars make a few more guesses. "Alpacas are actually cousins of camels."

"Like the ones the Wise Men rode?" asked Jacob.

Nathaniel saw Esther's amazement, though it was quickly masked. She was shocked the boy was participating, but he heard no sign of it in her voice when she assured Jacob he was right. That set off a buzz of more questions from the scholars.

The boy turned to look at the pasture, again separating himself from the others though he stood among them. The single breakthrough was a small victory. He could tell by the lilt in Esther's voice how delighted she'd been with Jacob's question.

The scholars' eager whispers followed Nathaniel as he entered the pasture through the barn. He'd try to herd the alpacas closer so the *kinder* could get a better look at them. His hopes were dashed when the alpacas evaded him as they always did. They resisted any attempt to move them closer to the scholars. If he jogged to the right, they went left. If he moved forward, they trotted away and edged around him. He could almost hear alpaca laughter.

"Let me," Esther called. She bunched up her dress and climbed over the fence as if she were one of the *kinder*. She brought a pair of thin branches, each about a yard long. As she crossed the pasture, she motioned for him to stand by the barn.

"Watch the *kinder*," she said. "I'll get an alpaca haltered, so we can bring it closer for them to see."

Curious about how she was going to do that, he watched her walk toward the herd with slow, even steps. She spoke softly, nonsense words from what he could discern.

She held the branches out to either side of her. He realized she was using them like a shepherd's crook to move the alpacas into the small shed at the rear of the pasture. He edged forward to see what she'd do once they were inside. He'd wondered what the shed with its single large pen was for. He hadn't guessed it was to corner the alpacas to make it easier to handle them.

She lifted a halter off a peg once the alpacas were in the pen. She chose a white-and-brown one who was almost as tall as she was. Moving to the animal's left, she gently slid the halter over its nose and behind its ears. The animal stood as docile as a well-trained dog, nodding its head when Esther checked to make sure the buckled halter was high enough on the nose that it wouldn't prevent the animal from breathing.

Latching a rope to the halter, Esther walked the alpaca from the shed. The other animals trotted behind her, watching her. Esther stayed on the alpaca's left side and an arm's length away. The alpaca followed her easily, but shied as she neared the fence where the *kinder* stood.

One *kind* pushed closer to the fence. Jacob! The boy's gaze was riveted on the alpaca. His usual anger was fading into something that wasn't a smile, but close.

Nathaniel wondered if Esther had noticed, but couldn't tell because her back was to him. Again she warned the scholars to be silent. Their eyes were curious but none of them stuck their fingers past the fence.

Esther looked over her shoulder at him. "You can come closer. Stay to her left side."

"You made it look easy," Nathaniel replied with admiration.

"Any task is easy when you know what you're doing." She winked at the scholars. "Like multiplication tables, ain't so?"

The younger ones giggled.

"Be careful it doesn't spit at you," Nathaniel warned the *kinder*.

"It won't." Esther patted the alpaca's head as the scholars edged back.

"Don't be sure. When I put them out this morning, this one started spitting at the others. She hasn't acted like that before."

"Were the males in there, too?"

He nodded. Before he'd gone to the school, he'd spent a long hour separating the males out because he feared they'd be aggressive near the *kinder*.

"Then," Esther said with a smile, "my guess is she's going to have a cria."

"A what?"

She laughed and nudged his shoulder with hers. "A *boppli*, Nathaniel."

The ordinary motion had anything but an ordinary effect on his insides. A ripple of awareness rushed through him like a powerful train. Had she felt it, too? He couldn't be sure because the scholars clapped their hands in delight. She was suddenly busy keeping the alpaca from pulling away in fear at the noise, but she calmed the animal.

"I'm going to need you to tell me what to do," Nathaniel said, glad his voice sounded calmer than he felt as he struggled to regain his equilibrium.

"There's no hurry. An alpaca is pregnant for at least eleven months, but she'll need to be examined by the vet to try to determine how far along she is."

As she continued to talk about the alpacas to her scholars, he sent a grateful prayer to God for Esther's help. His chances of making the farm a success were much greater than they'd been. He wasn't going to waste a bit of the time or the information she shared with him.

No, he assured himself as he watched her. He wasn't going to waste a single second.

* * *

Esther walked to the farmhouse, enjoying the sunshine. The trees along the farm lane were aflame with color against the bright blue sky. Not a single cloud blemished it. Closer to the ground, mums in shades of gold, orange and dark red along the house's foundation bobbed on a breeze that barely teased her nape.

She'd left the scholars with Nathaniel while she checked the alpacas. Though he didn't know much about them, he'd made sure they were eating well. She'd seen no sores on their legs. They hadn't been trying to get out of the pasture, so they must be content with what he provided.

Hearing shouts from the far side of the house, she walked in that direction. She hadn't planned to take so long with the alpacas, but it'd been fun to be with the silly creatures again. Their fleece was exceptionally soft, and their winter coats were growing in well. By the time they were sheared in the spring, Nathaniel would have plenty of wool to sell.

She came around the house and halted. On the sloping yard, Nathaniel was surrounded by the scholars. Jay, the oldest, was helping keep the *kinder* in a line. What were they doing?

Curious, she walked closer. She was amazed to see cardboard boxes torn apart and placed end to end on the grass. Two boxes were intact. As she watched, Nathaniel picked up a little girl and set her in one box. She giggled and gripped the front of it.

"All set?" he asked.

"Ja!" the *kind* shouted.

Nathaniel glanced at Jay and gave the box a slight shove. It sailed down the cardboard "slide" like a toboggan on snow. He kept pace with it on one side while Jay did on the other. They caught the box at the end of the slide before it could tip over and spill the *kind* out.

Picking her up again, Nathaniel swung her around. Giggling, she ran up the hill as a bigger boy jumped into the other box. His legs hung out the front, but he pushed with his hands to send himself down the slide. Nathaniel swung the other box out of the way just in time.

Everyone laughed and motioned for the boxes to be brought back for the next ride. As the older boy climbed out, Esther saw it was Benny. He beamed as he gathered the boxes to carry them to the top. Nathaniel clapped him on the shoulder and grinned.

She went to stand by the porch where she could watch the *kinder* play. She couldn't take her eyes off Nathaniel. He looked as happy as he had when they were *kinder* themselves. He clearly loved being with the youngsters. He'd be a *wunderbaar daed*. Seeing him with her scholars, she could imagine him acting like her own *daed*.

Her most precious memories of *Daed* were when he'd come into the house at midday and pick her up. They'd bounce around the kitchen table singing a silly song until *Mamm* pretended to be irritated about how they were in the way. Then they'd laugh together, and *Daed* would set her in her chair before chasing her brothers around the living room. If he caught them, he'd tickle them until they squealed or *Mamm* called everyone to the table. As they bent their heads in silent grace, their shared joy had been like a glow around them.

Watching Nathaniel with the *kinder*, she wanted that for him. Too bad she and he were just friends. Otherwise—

Where had *that* thought come from? He was her buddy, her partner in crime, her competitor to see who could run the fastest or climb the highest. She *had* told him she'd marry him when they were little kids, something that made her blush when she thought of how outrageously she'd acted, but they weren't *kinder* any longer.

When Nathaniel called a halt to the game, saying it was time for lunch, the youngsters tried not to show their disappointment. They cheered when he said he had fresh cider waiting for them on a picnic table by the kitchen door.

They raced past Esther to get their lunch boxes. She smiled as she went to help Nathaniel collect the pieces of cardboard.

"Quite a game you have here," she said. "Did you make it up?"

As he folded the long cardboard strips and set them upright in one of the boxes, he shook his head. "Not me alone. It's one we played in Indiana. We invented it the summer after I couldn't go sledding all winter."

"Why? Were you sick?"

"Ja."

"All winter?"

"You know how *mamms* can be. Always worrying." He gathered the last bits of cardboard and dropped them into the other box. Brushing dirt off himself, he grimaced as he tapped his left knee. "Grass stains on my *gut* church clothes. *Mamm* wouldn't be happy to see that."

He looked very handsome in his black vest and trousers, which gave his dark hair a ruddy sheen. The white shirt emphasized his strong arms and shoulders. She'd noticed his shoulders when she tumbled against him at school.

"If you want," she said when she realized she was staring. "I'll clean them."

"I can't ask you to do that." He carried the boxes to the porch. "You've got enough to do keeping up with your brothers."

"One more pair of trousers won't make any difference." She smiled as she walked with him toward the kitchen door. "Trust me."

"I do, and my alpacas do, too. It was amazing how you calmed them."

"I'll teach you."

"I don't know if I can convince them to trust me as they do you. It might be impossible. Though obviously not for Esther Stoltzfus, the alpaca whisperer."

She laughed, then halted when she saw a buggy driving at top speed along the farm lane. Even from a distance, she recognized her brother Isaiah driving it. She glanced at Nathaniel, then ran to where the buggy was stopping. Only something extremely important would cause Isaiah to leave his blacksmith shop in the middle of the day.

He climbed out, his face lined with dismay. "Esther, where are the *kinder*?"

"Behind the house having lunch."

"Gut." He looked from her to Nathaniel. "There's no way to soften this news. Titus Fisher has had a massive stroke and is on his way to the hospital."

Esther gasped and pressed her hands to her mouth.

"Are you here to get the boy?" asked Nathaniel.

"I'm not sure he should go to the hospital until Titus is stable." Isaiah turned to her. "What do you think, Esther?"

"I think he needs to be told his *onkel* is sick, but

nothing more now. No need to scare him. Taking him to the hospital can wait until we know more."

"That's what I thought, but you know him better than I do." He sighed. "The poor *kind*. He's already suffered enough. Tonight—"

"He can stay here," Nathaniel said quietly.

"Are you sure?" her brother asked, surprised.

"I've got plenty of room," Nathaniel said, "and the boy seems fascinated by my alpacas."

Isaiah looked at her for confirmation.

She nodded, knowing it was the best solution under the circumstances.

"I'll let Reuben know." He sighed again. "Just in case."

"Tell the bishop that Jacob can stay here as long as he needs to," Nathaniel said.

"That should work out…unless his *onkel* dies. Then the Bureau of Children and Family Services will have to get involved."

Nathaniel frowned, standing as resolute as one of the martyrs of old.

Before he could retort, Esther said, "Let's deal with one problem at a time." She prayed it wouldn't get to that point. And if it did, there must be some plan to give Jacob the family he needed without *Englisch* interference. She had no idea what, but they needed to figure it out fast.

Chapter Four

Esther looked around for Jacob as soon as her brother left. Isaiah was bound for their bishop's house. He and Reuben planned to hire an *Englisch* driver to take them to the hospital where they would check on Titus Fisher.

She wasn't surprised Jacob had left the other scholars and gone to watch the alpacas. The boy stood by the fence, his fingers stuck through the chicken wire in an offer for the shy beasts to come over and sniff them. The alpacas were ignoring him from the far end of the pasture.

The sight almost broke her heart. Jacob, who was small for his age and outwardly fragile, stood alone as he reached out to connect with another creature.

"Are you okay?" asked Nathaniel as he walked beside her toward the pasture.

"Not really." She squared her shoulders, knowing

she must not show the *kind* how sorry she felt for him. Jacob reacted as badly to pity as he did to teasing. He'd endured too much during his short life.

Suddenly she stopped and put out her arm to halt Nathaniel. He frowned at her, but, putting her fingers to her lips, she whispered, "Shhh…"

In the pasture, one of the younger alpacas inched away from the others, clearly curious about the boy who had been standing by the fence for so long. The light brown female stretched out her neck and sniffed the air as if trying to determine what sort of animal Jacob was. Glancing at the rest of the herd, she took one step, then another toward him.

The boy didn't move, but Esther guessed his heart was trying to beat its way out of his chest. A smile tipped his lips, the first one she'd ever seen on his face.

In the distance, the voices of the other scholars fluttered on the air, but Nathaniel and Esther remained as silent as Jacob. The alpaca's curiosity overcame her shyness, and she continued toward the boy. His smile broadened on every step, but he kept his outstretched fingers steady.

The alpaca paused an arm's length away, then took another step. She extended her head toward his fingertips, sniffing and curious.

Beside her, Esther heard Nathaniel whisper, "Keep going, girl. He needs you now."

Her heart was touched by his empathy for the *kind*. Nathaniel's generous spirit hadn't changed. He'd always been someone she could depend on, the very definition of a *gut* friend. He still was, offering kindness to a lonely boy. Her fingers reached out to his arm, wanting to squeeze it gently to let him know how much she appreciated his understanding of what Jacob needed.

Her fingers halted midway between them as a squeal came from near the house where the other scholars must be playing a game. At the sound, the alpaca whirled and loped back to the rest of the herd.

"Almost," Jacob muttered under his breath.

Walking to the boy, Esther fought her instinct to put her hand on his shoulder. That would send him skittering away like the curious alpaca. "It'll take them time to trust you, Jacob, but you've made a *gut* beginning."

When he glanced at her, for once his face wasn't taut with determination to hide his pain. She saw something she'd never seen there before.

Hope.

"Do you think so?" he asked.

She nodded. She must be as cautious with him as she was with the alpacas. "It'll take time and patience on your part, but eventually they learn to trust."

"Eventually?" His face hardened into an expression no *kind* should ever wear. "I guess that's that, then. We'll be leaving for school soon, ain't so?"

He'd given her the opening to tell him the bad news Isaiah had brought. She must tell him the truth now, but she must be careful how she told him until they were sure about Titus Fisher's prognosis.

"Jacob, I need to tell you about something that's happened," she began.

"If Jay said it was my fault, he's lying!" Jacob clenched his hands at his sides. "Benny tipped over Jay's glass, but said I did it. I didn't! I always tell the truth!"

Tears welled in the boy's eyes, and she saw his desperate need for her to believe him. And she did. Unlike some *kinder*, Jacob always admitted what he'd done wrong…if he were caught.

She squatted in front of him, so her eyes were even with his. Aware of Nathaniel behind her, she said quietly, "Nobody has said anything about a glass. This has nothing to do with the other *kinder*."

"Then what?" He was growing more wary by the second.

"I wanted to let you know your *onkel* isn't feeling well, so he went to see some *doktors* who will try to help him."

"Is it his heart?" Jacob's hands loosened, and he folded his arms over his narrow chest. Was he trying to protect himself?

When she glanced at Nathaniel, he looked as shocked as she felt at the forthright question. Clearly the boy was aware of his *onkel*'s deteriorating health. Jacob Fisher was a smart *kind*. She mustn't forget that, as the other scholars did far too often, underestimating his intelligence as well as how brittle his patience was.

"Ja," she answered. "The *doktors* want to observe him. That means—"

"They want to watch what his heart does so they can find out why it's giving him trouble." He gave a careless shrug, but he couldn't hide the fear burning in his eyes. "*Onkel* Titus explained to me the last time he went to the clinic."

She wanted to let him know it was okay to show his distress, but she wouldn't push. *Ja*, he was scared, but Titus had prepared the boy. She reminded herself that Jacob didn't know the full extent of what had happened. For now, it would be better not to frighten him further. She didn't want to think of what would happen if his *onkel* didn't recover. If she did, she wouldn't be able to hold back the tears prickling her eyes.

And that would scare Jacob more.

Nathaniel saw Esther struggling to hold on to her composure. He should have urged her to let him talk to Jacob alone. Unlike him, she knew Titus Fisher, and she must be distressed by the old man's stroke.

He drew her to her feet. He tried to ignore the soft buzz where his palms were spread across her arms. Releasing her because he needed to focus on the boy, he was amazed when the sensation still coursed along his hands.

Trying to ignore it, he said, "Jacob, under the circumstances, I think Esther would agree with me when I say you don't need to go back to school today."

"I don't?" Glee brightened his face for a moment, then it vanished. "Then I'll have to go to my *onkel*'s house by myself."

Nathaniel tried not to imagine what the boy was thinking. The idea of returning to an empty house where he'd be more alone than ever must be horrifying to Jacob. Knowing he must pick his words with care, he said, "I thought you might want to stay here."

"With the alpacas?" Jacob's eyes filled with anticipation.

Nathaniel struggled to keep his smile in place as he wondered if that expression would have been visible on Jacob's face more often if he hadn't watched his parents die and been sent to live with an elderly *onkel*. Titus Fisher had provided him with a *gut* home, or as *gut* as he could. The old man had protected his great-nephew from the realities of his failing health by telling him enough to make this moment easier for the boy.

What would Jacob—or Esther—say if he revealed how his own childhood had been filled with *doktors* and fear? His *mamm* had overreacted any time he got a cold, and his *daed* had withdrawn. If it hadn't been for their *Englisch* neighbor, Reggie O'Donnell, who'd welcomed Nathaniel at his greenhouses whenever he needed an escape, there would have been no break from the drama at home. The retired engineer had let Nathaniel assist and never made him talk or wash his hands endlessly or avoid playing with other *kinder* because he might get some germ that would bring on another bout of what they called "the scourge."

Though the *Englisch doktors* had assured his parents that, upon the completion of the treatments, Nathaniel had no more chance than any other person of contracting cancer again, they never could let go of their fear. He suspected that was one of the reasons his *mamm* insisted he return to Indiana. She wanted to keep an eye on him every second to make sure the scourge didn't return.

Was Titus Fisher a sanctuary for Jacob as Reggie had been for Nathaniel? Someone who didn't talk about the past or what might await in the future? Had he, like Reggie, been someone with a heart big enough to offer a haven for a lonely, lost *kind*?

Grief for the old man and the boy hammered Nathaniel. *"Ja,"* he said, "you can stay here with me and the alpacas, if you'd like."

"And if I don't like?" Jacob asked cautiously.

Esther looked away, and he knew she was having difficulty keeping her feelings from showing. As he was. No *kind* Jacob's age should have to ask such a question. The boy had learned life could change in the blink of an eye. He probably hadn't had any say in where he would go after his parents' funeral.

"Then other arrangements will be made for you, and you can come and visit the alpacas."

Jacob shook his head. "No, I want to stay here. I think I can get one of them to come to me if I've got enough time."

"Then it's settled." Nathaniel tried to curb the sudden disquiet rising in him at the thought of being responsible for the boy. *Dear Lord, help me know the right things to do and say while he's here.* He forced a smile. "We'll work together to convince the alpacas to trust us. It'll be fun."

"It will!" The boy turned to look at the herd again. "Let's start now."

"I have to take everyone back to school."

The boy's shoulders slumped. "Can I stay here? *Onkel* Titus let me stay by myself."

Unsure if Jacob was being truthful or not, in spite of his assertion that he always was honest, Nathaniel hesitated.

Esther didn't. "If it's okay with you, Nathaniel, I can drive everyone to school. I'll take your wagon to our farm tonight. You can come and get it when it's convenient."

Again he hesitated. He'd planned to leave early tomorrow to get the hay for winter feedings, but those plans must change.

"All right," he said. "I'll help you hook Sal and Gal to the wagon. Do you know how to handle mules?"

"*Ja.* A little, but my brothers will know because *Daed* had a team to plow the fields. Ezra will make sure they're taken care of tonight."

He had no choice but to agree or upset Jacob further.

He couldn't blame the boy for not wanting to spend more time with his classmates, especially now.

"I'll be right back," Nathaniel said.

"Can I go into the pasture?" asked Jacob.

"Maybe later tonight when I feed them. Let's see how they're behaving then."

He thought the boy would argue, but Jacob nodded. "I'll wait here for you."

For a moment, Nathaniel wished the boy had protested like a regular kid. He remembered times, especially when he was going through chemo, when he'd found himself trying to be *gut* so he didn't upset the adults around him more. It hadn't been easy to swallow his honest reactions. His respect for Jacob grew, but the boy's maturity also concerned him. A *kind* needed to be a *kind*, not some sort of miniature adult.

When he said as much to Esther as they walked into the barn to get the mules, she sighed and stole a glance at where the boy was gazing at the alpacas once more. "I worry about him when he's cooperative and when he's fighting. It's as if he can't find a middle path."

"He probably can't. When everything inside you is in a turmoil, it's hard to trust your own feelings. Most especially when you've let them loose in the past and people haven't reacted well. Instead they've told you how you should feel so many times you begin to wonder if they're right and you're wrong."

She paused as he kept walking toward where he kept the harnesses for the mules. When he turned to see why she'd stopped, she said, "I hadn't thought about it like that."

Emotions he couldn't decipher scuttled across her face. He wanted to ask what she was thinking, but satisfying his curiosity would have to wait. She hurried past him, murmuring how she'd told the scholars' *mamms* she'd have everyone back by now. They'd spent more than an hour longer at the farm than she'd planned.

As he put Sal and Gal into place and hooked them to the wagon, Nathaniel glanced at Jacob standing by the alpacas' pasture, and then to the other *kinder* racing about by the house. The difference was unsettling, and he wondered if it was possible for Jacob to become carefree again. He had to believe so.

He looked across the mules at Esther, who was checking the reins. "Do you think we should let him continue to believe his *onkel*'s heart is why Titus was taken to the hospital?"

"I don't know." Her expression matched her unsteady words. "Let me talk to Isaiah when he gets back."

"A *gut* idea."

"Are you sure you want Jacob to stay with you? Is that why you asked?"

"No. I'm sure staying here is best for him now. The boy needs something to do to get his mind off the situation, and the alpacas can help."

She nodded. When she called to the other *kinder* to pack their things and prepare to leave, there were the protests Nathaniel had expected to hear. She handled each one with humor and serenity. She was a stark contrast to his *mamm* and his older sisters who saw everything as a potential tragedy.

He smiled as the scholars clambered onto the flatbed. When they passed him, each of them said, *"Danki."* Telling them to have a *gut* ride to school, he held his hand out to assist Esther onto the seat.

She regarded him with surprise, and he had to fight

not to smile. Now *that* reaction reminded him of Esther the Pester, who'd always asserted she could do anything the older boys did...and all by herself.

Despite that, she accepted his help. The scent of her shampoo lingered in his senses. He was tempted to hold on to her soft fingers, but he released them as soon as she was sitting. He was too aware of the *kinder* and other women gathered behind her.

She picked up the reins and leaned toward him. "If it becomes too difficult for you, bring him to our house."

"We'll be fine." At that moment, he meant it. When her bright blue eyes were close to his, he couldn't imagine being anything but fine.

Then she looked away, and the moment was over. She slapped the reins and drove the wagon toward the road. He watched it go. A sudden shiver ran along him. The breeze was damp and chilly, something he hadn't noticed while gazing into Esther's pretty eyes.

The sound of the rattling wagon vanished in the distance, and he turned to see Jacob standing by the fence, his fingers through the chicken wire again in the hope an alpaca would come to him. The *kind* had no idea of what could lie ahead for him.

Take him into Your hands, Lord. He's going to need Your comfort in the days to come. Make him strong to face what the future brings, but let him be weak enough to accept help from us.

Taking a deep breath, Nathaniel walked toward the boy. He'd agreed to take care of Jacob and offer him a haven at the farm. Now he had to prove he could.

Chapter Five

As Jacob helped with the afternoon chores, which included cleaning up after the alpacas and refilling their water troughs, Nathaniel watched closely. He knew Esther would want to know how the boy did in the wake of the news about his *onkel*. She worried about him as if he were her own *kind*. Nathaniel suspected she was that way with each of her scholars.

Jacob didn't say much, but he was comfortable doing hard work. Nathaniel wondered how many of the chores at Titus Fisher's house had become Jacob's responsibility as the old man's health declined. He seemed happy to remain behind, which was no surprise. A chance to skip school was something any kid would enjoy, but Nathaniel couldn't help wondering what the boy was thinking.

One thing he knew from his own childhood. Growing boys were always hungry.

Flashing Jacob a smile and a wink, he asked, "How about grabbing a snack before we feed the alpacas?"

"Whatcha got?"

Nathaniel chuckled as he motioned for the boy to follow him toward the house. Jacob seemed to walk a fine line between being a *kind* and being a wraith who floated through each day, not connecting with anyone else.

"I know there's church spread in the fridge," he answered.

Jacob grinned, and Nathaniel was glad he'd guessed what the boy would like. There weren't too many people who didn't enjoy the combination of peanut butter and marshmallow creme. Keeping it around allowed him to slap together a quick sandwich when he had scant time for dinner or was too tired to cook anything for supper.

"What else do you have to eat with it?" Jacob asked.

"We'll look through the kitchen. A treasure hunt without a map. Who knows what we might find?"

"As long as it's not growing green stuff." Excitement blossomed in Jacob's eyes.

Nathaniel laughed and ruffled the boy's hair. Jacob stiffened for a second, then relaxed with a smile.

The poor kid! Did anyone treat him as a *kind* or did others think of him solely as his sad experiences? The boy needed a chance to be a boy. Nathaniel knew that with every inch of his being. After having his own parents, with their *gut* intentions, nearly deny him his own chance to be a kid, he didn't want to see the same happen to another *kind*.

He wasn't going to let that occur. God had brought Jacob into his life for a reason, and it might be as simple as Nathaniel being able to offer him an escape, temporary though it might be, into a normal childhood. Reggie had given that to him. Now Nathaniel could do the same for Jacob.

With a laugh, he said, "You've got to be tired after tidying up."

"A bit."

"*Gut.* Then you won't be able to beat me to the kitchen door." With no more warning, Nathaniel loped away.

A moment passed, and he wondered if his attempt to get Jacob to play had failed. Then, with a whoop, the boy sped past him. Nathaniel lengthened his stride, but the *kind* reached the door before he could. Whirling to face him, Jacob pumped his arms in a victory dance.

Nathaniel let him cheer for a few moments and didn't remind him it wasn't the Amish way to celebrate beating someone else. There was time enough for those lessons later. For now, Jacob needed to feel like a kid.

"Well done." He clapped the boy on the shoulder. "Next time, I'll beat you."

"Don't be so sure." As Jacob smiled, his brown eyes were filled with humor instead of his usual lost expression.

Nathaniel laughed, thinking how pleased Esther would be when he shared this moment with her tomorrow. He opened the door and ushered the boy into a kitchen that looked the same as it had the day he'd arrived from Indiana for his summer visit so many years ago. The kitchen was a large room, but filled to capacity with furniture, as the living room was. There were enough chairs of all shapes and sizes to host a Sunday church service. His grandparents had been fond of auctions, but he'd been astounded when he arrived to discover the house chock-full of furnishings.

Nathaniel had stored many chairs and two dressers from the living room in an outbuilding, which was now full. He had to find other places to put the rest until there was a charity auction to which he could donate them. Until then he had to wend his way through an obstacle course of chairs every morning and night to reach the stairs.

Jacob walked in and sniffed. "This place smells like *Onkel* Titus's house."

"In what way?" He hoped something familiar would make the boy feel more at home.

"Full of old stuff and dust." He looked at Nathaniel. "Don't grown-ups ever throw anything out?"

He grinned. "Not my grandparents. My *grossmammi* saved the tabs from plastic bags. She always said, 'Use it up, wear it out—'"

"'…make it do or do without,'" finished Jacob with an abrupt grin. "*Onkel* Titus says the same thing. A lot." He glanced around. "Don't you think they could get by with a lot less stuff?"

"I know I could. If you can find an empty chair, bring it to the table while I make some sandwiches."

That brought a snort of something that might have been rusty laughter from the boy, but could have been disgust with the state of the house. Nathaniel didn't look at Jacob to determine which. Getting the boy to smile was *wunderbaar*. As they had an impromptu supper, with Nathaniel eating two sandwiches and Jacob three, he let the boy take the lead in deciding the topics of conversation.

There was only one. The alpacas. Jacob had more

questions than Nathaniel could answer. Time after time, he had to reply that Jacob needed to ask Esther. The boy would nod, then ask another question. That continued while they got the alpacas ready for the night.

Nathaniel hid his smile when he heard Jacob chatter like a regular kid. He thanked God for putting a love for alpacas in his *grossmammi*'s heart, so the creatures could touch a lonely boy's. God's methods were splendid, and Nathaniel sent up a grateful prayer as he walked with Jacob back to the house when their chores were done.

Leading the boy upstairs—where there were yet more chairs—he smiled when Jacob yawned broadly. He opened a door across the hall from his own bedroom. It was a room he'd had some success in clearing out. In the closet were stairs leading to the attic, where he'd hoped there might be room to store furniture. However, like the rest of the house, it was already full.

"Here's where you'll sleep." Nathaniel was glad he'd kept the bed made so the room looked welcoming. He'd slept on the bed with its black and white and blue quilt the time he came to stay with his grandparents. Pegs on the wall waited for clothes, and a small table held the storybooks Nathaniel had read years ago. The single window gave a view of the pasture beyond the main barn.

"I can see them!" crowed Jacob, rushing around the iron bed to peer out the window. "The alpacas! They're right out there."

"They'll be there until I move them to another pasture in a couple of weeks."

The boy whirled. "Why do you have to move them?" His tone suggested Nathaniel was doing that to be cruel to him and the animals.

"If I don't move them, they'll be hungry." He tried to

keep his voice calm. The boy needed to learn that not everything was an attack on him, but how did you teach that to a *kind* who'd seen his parents cut down and killed by a car? "Once the alpacas eat the grass in that field, I must put them in another field so they can graze."

"Oh." Jacob lowered his eyes.

"But they'll be right there in the morning. Why don't you get ready for bed? I'll put an extra toothbrush in the bathroom for you."

The boy nodded, his eyelids drooping. "Can we pray for my *onkel* first?"

"Ja." Nathaniel was actually relieved to hear him speak of Titus. The boy had said very little about his *onkel* since Esther left.

Kneeling by the side of the bed along with Jacob, Nathaniel bowed his head over his folded hands. He listened as Jacob prayed for his *onkel*'s health and thanked God for letting him meet the alpacas. Nathaniel couldn't help grinning when the boy finished his prayers with, "Make the alpacas like me, God, cuz I sure like them."

Nathaniel echoed Jacob's amen and came to his feet. Telling the boy he'd be sleeping on the other side of the hall, he added that Jacob should call if he needed anything.

An hour later, after he'd washed the few supper dishes and put them away, Nathaniel closed his Bible and placed it on a small table in the living room. The words had begun to swim in front of his eyes. He went upstairs and peeked into Jacob's room. The boy was sprawled across the bed in a shaft of moonlight. He'd removed his shoes and socks but not his suspenders. One drooped around his right shoulder, and the other hung loose by his left hip. His shirt had pulled out of his trousers, revealing what looked like a long scar. A legacy of the accident that had taken his parents? He mumbled something in his sleep and turned over to bury his head in the pillow once more. Nathaniel wondered if the boy had nightmares while he slept or if that was the one time he could escape from the blows life had dealt him.

Nathaniel slowly closed the door almost all the way. The evening had gone better than he'd dared to hope. He went into his own room. He left his door open a crack, too, so he'd hear if the boy got up or if someone came to the kitchen door.

He went to the bedroom window and gazed out at the stars overhead. Was Esther looking at the same stars now? Was her heart heavy, as his was, with worries for Jacob and his *onkel*? Was she thinking of Nathaniel as he was of her? Since she'd fallen into his arms at the ball game he'd found it impossible to push her out of his thoughts. Not that he minded. Not a lot, anyhow, because it was fun to think of her sparkling eyes. It was delightful to recall how perfectly she'd fit against him.

He shook the thought from his head. Remembering her softness and the sweet scent of her hair was foolish. No need to torment himself when holding her again would be wrong. He couldn't ignore how much she loved being with *kinder* and how impossible it could be for him to give her *kinder* of her own. He needed to put an end to such thoughts now and concentrate on the one dream he had a chance of making come true: being a success on the farm so it didn't have to be sold.

Esther had just arrived home from school when she heard the rattle of buggy wheels. She looked out the kitchen window in time to see Nathaniel drive into the yard. She went to greet him and Jacob. She hoped letting him skip school had been a *gut* idea.

The afternoon breeze was strengthening, and her apron undulated on top of her dress. Goose bumps rose along her bare arms. She hugged them to her as she rushed to the buggy.

From it, she heard Jacob ask, "Isn't this where Esther lives?"

"Ja" came Nathaniel's reply.

"Why are we coming here? I thought we were going to *Onkel* Titus's house?"

"We are."

Esther kept her smile in place as a wave of sorrow flooded her. Never had she heard Jacob describe Titus's house as his home. Did he see it as another temporary residence?

Calling out a greeting, she pretended not to have heard the exchange. She gave Nathaniel and Jacob a quick appraisal. Both appeared fine, so she guessed their first day together had gone well. That was a great relief, because last night she'd felt guilty for letting Nathaniel take on the obligation of the boy. More than once, she'd considered driving over to his farm and bringing Jacob to her family's house. She was glad to see it hadn't been necessary. At least, not yet.

"Any news about Titus's tests?" Nathaniel asked.

She shook her head, glad he'd selected those words that suggested the elderly man's condition wasn't too serious. "Nothing, and you know what they say."

"No news is good news?"

"Exactly." She motioned toward the bank barn. "Ezra put Gal and Sal on the upper floor. He wasn't sure how they'd be around his cows."

"Is it all right if they stay here a little while longer? We're on our way to Titus's house to get some of Jacob's clothes and other things."

Glancing at Jacob, who hadn't said a word, she replied, "I'll go with you, if you don't mind."

"No, of course we don't mind."

"Jacob?" she asked.

The boy nodded with obvious reluctance.

"Let me get my bonnet." She hurried into the house. After letting *Mamm* know where she was going, she grabbed her black bonnet and her knitted shawl. She threw the shawl over her shoulders and went outside to discover Nathaniel had already turned the buggy toward the road.

Jacob slid over, leaving her room by the door. As soon as she was seated and the buggy was moving, he began asking her questions about the alpacas. She was kept so busy answering his question that the trip, less than two miles long, was over before she realized it.

The buggy rolled to a stop by a house whose weathered boards were a mosaic of peeling paint. The front porch had a definite tilt to the right, and Esther wondered if it remained connected to the house. Cardboard was set into one windowpane where the glass was missing. However, the yard was neat, and the remnants of a large garden out back had at least half a dozen pumpkins peeking from under large leaves.

As they stepped from the buggy, Jacob ran ahead. Nathaniel motioned for Esther to wait for him to come around to her side.

He chuckled quietly. "Blame those questions on me. Yesterday, Jacob asked me a lot of things I didn't know about. I kept telling him to ask you the next time he saw you. I didn't think he'd ask you *all* the questions at once."

"I'm glad to answer what I can, and I'm glad you're here to hear as well, so I don't need to explain them again to you."

He pressed his hand over his heart and struck the pose of a wounded man. "Oh, no! I didn't realize I was supposed to be listening, too."

"You should know anytime you're around a teacher there may be a test at the end."

He laughed again, harder this time, as they walked to the door where Jacob was waiting impatiently. When the boy motioned for them to follow him inside, Nathaniel's laughter vanished along with Esther's smile.

The interior of the house was almost impassable. Boxes and bags were piled haphazardly from floor to ceiling. Esther stared at broken pieces of scooters, parts from *Englisch* cars and farming equipment mixed in with clothing and books and things she couldn't identify. If there was any furniture beneath the heaps it was impossible to see.

She guessed they were in the kitchen, but there were no signs of appliances or a sink. Odors that suggested food was rotting somewhere in the depths of the piles turned her stomach. She pushed the door open again, knowing she couldn't reach a window, even if she knew where one was, to air out the house.

"My room is this way." Jacob gestured again for them to follow him as he threaded a path through the piles with the ease of much practice.

Esther looked around in disbelief. Softly, so her words wouldn't reach Jacob, she said, "I had no idea Titus Fisher was living this way."

"I don't think anyone did other than his nephew." Nathaniel's mouth was a straight line as he walked after the boy.

She hesitated, not wanting to be buried if a mountain of debris cascaded onto her. How could this house have become filled with garbage and useless items? Surely someone came to call on the old man once in a while. She needed to alert the bishop, because other elderly people who were alone might also be living in such deplorable conditions.

Titus couldn't come home to this. Isaiah had said the stroke was a bad one, and if the elderly man survived he would be in a wheelchair. The path from the kitchen was too narrow for one.

Taking a deep breath, Esther plunged into the house. Her shawl brushed the sides of the stacks as she inched forward. How was Nathaniel managing? His shoulders were wider than her own. When she saw him ahead, sidling like a crab, she realized it was the only way he could move through the narrow space.

"Having fun?" he asked as he waited for her to catch up with him.

"Fun? Why would you say that?"

He grinned. "It's like being an explorer in another world. Who knows what lurks in these piles?"

"Mice and squirrels, most likely. Maybe a rat or two. Cockroaches. Do I need to go on?"

"Where's your sense of adventure?"

"Gone."

"I noticed." His face was abruptly serious. Tilting his head and eyeing her as if trying to look within her heart, he said, "You used to see an adventure in everything around us. What happened?"

She didn't want to have this discussion with him, especially not now when Jacob should be their focus. She tried to push aside some of the stacked items so she could move past him. It was as useless as if she were shoving on a concrete wall.

"Esther, tell me why you've changed." His voice had dropped to a husky whisper that seemed to reach deep inside her and uncurl slowly as it peeled away her pretense.

No! She wouldn't reveal the humiliating truth of how she'd been so eager for adventure that she'd gotten involved with Alvin Lee. How could she explain she was supposed to be a respectable daughter and teacher, but she'd ridden in his buggy while he was racing it? What would Nathaniel think of her if he learned how she'd tossed aside common sense in the hope Alvin Lee would develop feelings for her?

Because he reminded me of Nathaniel, who, I believed, was gone forever from my life.

Astonishment froze her. Could that be true? No, she had to be *ferhoodled*. If she wasn't mixed-up, it had to be because she was distressed by the state of Titus's house and knowing Jacob had been living here. That was why she wasn't thinking straight. It had to be!

Nathaniel was regarding her with curiosity because she hadn't answered his question. She raised her chin slightly so she could meet his steady gaze.

"What happened? I grew up," she said before turning and shoving harder on the junk. Items fell on others, and it sounded as if several pieces of glass or china shattered. The path widened enough so she could squeeze past him without touching him. She kept going and didn't look back.

Chapter Six

Esther followed Jacob up the stairs, which were stacked with boxes. She heard Nathaniel's footsteps behind her but didn't turn. She shouldn't have spoken to him like that. It had been rude, and her reply was sure to create more questions. She didn't need those.

The upper hallway was as clogged with rubbish as the first floor. Each room they passed looked exactly like the rest of the house until Jacob opened a door and led them into a neat room.

How often *Mamm* had chided her and her siblings throughout their childhoods to keep their rooms orderly! *Mamm* would have been delighted to see how well Jacob kept his room.

Was it something he'd learned from his own *mamm*, or did he keep the clutter out of his room to have a refuge from his *onkel*'s overpowering collection? She blinked back tears. Either way, it was another sign of a *kind* who'd lost too much and was trying not to let his true feelings show.

Speaking around the clog in her throat, she said, "The first things we're going to need are some bags or a *gut*-sized box."

"I think I know where I can find a box." Nathaniel grinned.

Jacob stepped in front of him to keep him from leaving the room. The boy's eyes were wide with horror. "No! You can't use one of *Onkel* Titus's boxes. Nobody touches anything in *Onkel* Titus's house but *Onkel* Titus."

"Not even you?" asked Esther gently.

The boy shook his head, his expression grim. "I did once, and I got the switch out behind the well house. I learned when *Onkel* Titus says something he means it."

Nathaniel glanced at her over the boy's head, and she saw his closely reined-in anger. A *kind* must learn to heed his elders, but that could be done gently. The idea of Titus striking Jacob for simply moving one of dozens of cardboard boxes set her teeth on edge, as well.

"Wait here." Jacob rushed from the room.

"No *kind* should live as he has here," Nathaniel said.

She squared her shoulders and took a deep breath. "We need to contact Reuben."

"The bishop—" He halted himself as Jacob sprinted into the room.

The boy tossed some cloth grocery bags on the bed. "We can use these. *Onkel* Titus says they're worthless. He'll be glad to get them out of his house."

"Gut." Esther kept her voice light. "Are your clothes in this dresser?"

"*Ja.*"

"Pick out things other than clothes you want to bring and put them on the bed. Nathaniel and you can take them to the buggy." She counted. There were ten bags. "These should be enough to hold your things."

The boy faltered. "How long is *Onkel* Titus going to be in the hospital?"

Esther knew she must not hesitate. She didn't want to cause the boy more worry. "He has to stay there until the *doktors* tell him he can come home. I know you want him home right away, but it's better that the *doktors* are thorough so they know everything about your *onkel*'s health."

Jacob pondered that for several minutes, then nodded. "That makes sense."

"Don't forget your school supplies," she added.

"School?" He looked at Nathaniel. "I thought I didn't have to go to school while I was at your house."

"All *kinder* must go to school." Nathaniel grinned. "Nice try, though."

"When do I have to go back?"

"Monday will be early enough," Esther answered.

Jacob frowned, then began to gather his belongings. For the next ten minutes they worked in silent unison. Jacob set a few books, a baseball and his church Sunday black hat on the bed. Nathaniel put them into bags, making sure nothing was crushed. Esther packed Jacob's work boots and his best pair of shoes into another bag before turning to the dresser.

Like everything else in the room, the drawers were neat. Too neat for an eight-year-old boy.

When she mentioned that to Nathaniel while Jacob was carrying the first bags of clothing downstairs, he said, "Maybe it's his defense against the mess in the rest of the house. I'm glad we're getting him out of here." He picked up the last two cloth bags.

"Has he said anything about going to visit his *onkel*?"

"No."

"You'll let me know if he says something about going to the hospital, won't you?"

"Ja." He gave her a faint smile. "I'm sure he'll ask once he's less fascinated with the alpacas." Before she could add anything else, he asked, "Don't you think it's odd Titus wants to get rid of perfectly *gut* bags when he's stockpiling ripped and torn plastic ones?"

"Everything about him seems to be odder than anyone knows." She walked toward the door. "If I had to guess, I'd say Titus doesn't like cloth bags because you can't see through them. The plastic ones let him keep an eye on his possessions."

"How can he—or anyone else—see into the bags at the bottom of a pile?"

"You're being logical, Nathaniel. I don't think logic visits this house very often."

He led the way down the cramped stairs. When a board creaked threateningly beneath her foot, he turned and grasped her by the waist. He swung her down onto the step beside him. Her skirt brushed against the junk on the stairs. An avalanche tumbled loudly down the stairs and ricocheted off stacks on the ground floor. Things cascaded in every direction.

The noise couldn't conceal the sharp snap of the tread where she'd been standing. It broke and fell into the open space under the stairs.

Nathaniel's arm curved around her, pulling her away from the gap. Her breath burst out of her, and she had trouble drawing another one while she stood so near to him. When she did, it was flavored with the enticing scents of soap and sunshine from his shirt. With her head on his chest, she could hear the rapid beat of his heart. She put her hand on his arm to make sure her wobbly knees didn't collapse beneath her like the boxes and bags. His pulse jumped at her touch, and his arm around her waist tightened, keeping her close, exactly where her heart wanted her to be.

"Are you okay?" he whispered, his breath swirling along her neck in a gentle caress.

More than okay. She bit back the words before they could seep past her lips. At the same time, she eased away from him. Glancing at the hole in the staircase, she rushed the rest of the way down the stairs, past half-open bags spilling their reeking contents onto the steps.

She couldn't stay there with him. She'd been a fool to linger and let her heart overrule her head. Hadn't she learned that was stupid? Every time she gave in to her heart's yearnings for something it wanted—whether it was to let a much younger Nathaniel know how much he meant to her or to chase adventure with Alvin Lee— she'd ended up humiliated and hurt.

Esther hurried through the barely passable room, not slowing when Nathaniel called after her to make sure she wasn't hurt. She was, but not in the way he meant. It hurt to realize she still couldn't trust her heart.

Nitwit! Nitwit! Nitwit!

The accusation followed her, sounding on every step, as she found her way out of the horrible house. Fresh air struck her, and she drew in a deep, satisfying breath. Maybe it would clear her mind as well as her lungs.

Seeing Jacob trying to close the rear of the buggy,

Esther went to help him. It took the two of them shoving down the panel to shut it after he'd squeezed the bags in there.

"All set," she said with a strained smile.

"If you say so…" His voice was taut, and she shoved her problems aside. "I don't think I need all that."

"If you're worried about Nathaniel making room for your things at his house, don't be."

Jacob surprised her by giving her a saucy grin. "I guess you've never been inside the house."

"I was years ago when I was about your age."

"That's a *long* time ago."

She smiled when she realized she was talking about a time before he was born. "Quite a long time ago. His *grossmammi* liked to quilt, so there were always partially finished projects in the living room."

"Not any longer. There wouldn't be room for a quilt!" He started to add more, then halted when Nathaniel pushed his way out of the house and gave the pair of bags to Jacob.

"These are the last of your clothes," he said. "You may have to hold them on your lap because I'm sure the storage area behind the seat is full."

"Let me check to see. I think I can fit these in there."

"Make sure the rear door closes. I don't want a trail of your things from here to Esther's house."

The boy smiled and opened the back. Bags started to spill out, but he shoved them back inside. Tossing the other two on top, he managed to close the door again.

Jacob chattered steadily on the way to the Stoltzfus farm. That allowed Esther to avoid saying anything. Nathaniel was, she noticed, as quiet, though he replied when Jacob posed a question to him. Unlike the swift ride to Titus Fisher's house, the one back seemed too long.

As soon as the buggy stopped in front of the white barn, Esther jumped out. She was surprised when Nathaniel did, too. He told Jacob to wait while he hooked up the mules before Jacob drove the buggy to his farm. She'd assumed Nathaniel would tie the horse and buggy to the rear of his wagon.

"He'll be fine," Nathaniel said, and she knew her thoughts were on her face. "I've had him show me how he drives, and he's better than kids twice his age. From what he's told me, he's been driving his *onkel* to appointments with *doktors* and on other errands for the past six months or more."

She hesitated, then went with him into the barn. "Are you sure? I could drive him."

"Then we'll need to get you back here, and chores won't wait." He smiled. "I'll be right behind him, so he won't get any idea about racing my buggy. Not that he's foolish! The boy has a *gut* head on his shoulders."

His words silenced her. She'd thought she had a *gut* head on her shoulders, too, but she'd let herself get caught up in racing buggies on deserted roads late at night.

Nathaniel must have taken her silence for agreement because he went to the stall where the mules watched them.

As he led Gal out to the wagon, Esther asked, "Have you noticed Jacob never calls Titus's house his home? Only his *onkel*'s?"

"Now that you mention it, I have noticed that. I wonder why."

"He lost one home and one family." She watched Nathaniel put the patient mule into place, checking each strap and buckle to make sure it was right.

Straightening, he said, "Maybe he's afraid of losing another."

"That's sad. No *kind* should have to worry about such things."

"No *kind* should, but many don't have the happy and comfortable childhood you did, Esther." His mouth grew taut, and she got the feeling he'd said something he hadn't intended to.

"But he seems happier and less weighted down since you've taken him under your wing."

"Jacob has had too much sorrow and responsibility." Picking up the reins, he put his hand on the wagon's seat. "*Danki* for your help today, Esther. Let me know what Reuben says."

"I will." She drew in a deep breath, then said something she needed to say. Something that would be for the best for Nathaniel and for her. Something to prevent any misunderstandings between them. The words were bitter on her tongue, but she hurried to say, "I'm glad you're my friend. You've been my friend since we were *kinder*, and I hope you'll be my friend for the rest of our lives." She put her hand out and clasped his. Giving it a squeeze, she started to release it and turn away.

His fingers closed over hers, keeping her where she stood. She looked at him, astonished. Her shock became uncertainty when she saw the intensity in his gaze. Slowly, he brought her one step, then another toward him until they stood no more than a hand's breadth apart. She couldn't look away from his eyes. She longed to discover what he was thinking.

Suddenly she stiffened. What was *she* thinking?

Hadn't she decided she needed to make sure he knew friendship was all they should share? She drew her arm away, and after a moment's hesitation he lifted his fingers from hers. At the same moment his eyes shuttered.

"Ja," he said, his voice sounding as if he were waking from a dream. Or maybe her ears made it sound that way because the moment when they'd stood face-to-face had been like something out of time.

"Ja?" Had she missed something else he'd said?

"I mean, I'm glad, too. We're always going to be friends." Now he was avoiding her eyes. "It's for the best."

"For us and for Jacob."

"Of course, for Jacob, too." A cool smile settled on his lips. "That's what I meant."

"I know." She took another step away. She couldn't remember ever being less than honest with Nathaniel before.

But it was for his own *gut*.

Right?

That's right, God, isn't it? She had to believe that, but she hadn't guessed facing the truth would be so painful.

"What a sad way for a *kind* to live!" *Mamm* clicked her tongue in dismay as she set her cup of tea on a section of the kitchen table where Esther wasn't working. "I don't know why none of us wondered about the state of the house before. An old bachelor and a young boy. Neither of them knows a lick about keeping a house."

Esther raised her eyes from where she was kneading dough for cinnamon rolls for tomorrow's breakfast. She'd added a cup of raisins to the treat she hadn't made for the family since spring. Now she chased the raisins across the table when they popped out as she folded the dough over and pressed it down. Dusting her hands with more flour so they didn't get stickier, she continued working the dough.

"Jacob never gave us any reason to think his *onkel* wasn't taking *gut* care of him." She beat the dough harder. "He comes to school in clean clothes, and he never smells as if he's skipped a bath."

"Don't take out your frustration on that poor dough." *Mamm* chuckled. "Don't blame yourself for not knowing the truth. None of us did, but now you have the responsibility of letting Reuben know."

"I plan to speak to Reuben. I'll go over once I get the bread finished." She was certain the bishop would know a way to help Jacob and his *onkel* without making either of them feel ashamed. She was as sure the *Leit*, the members of their district, would offer their help.

But where? At Titus's house or Nathaniel's? Jacob had mentioned in passing that the Zook farmhouse was as cluttered as his *onkel*'s. She was astonished. When she'd visited Nathaniel's grandparents during her childhood, the house had been pristine. In fact, he'd joked that no dust mote ever entered because it would die of loneliness. Sometime between then and now, the condition of the house had changed.

"Going to talk to Reuben is a *gut* idea," *Mamm* said, "but I don't think that's necessary."

"What?" Esther looked up quickly and flour exploded from the table in a white cloud. Waving it away, she said, "*Mamm*, we need to do something. Nobody should be living in there." *Or at Nathaniel's if it is also in such a sorry state.*

"You don't need to visit Reuben, because he just pulled into the dooryard."

"Oh." Esther punched the dough a couple more times and then dropped it into the greased bowl she had ready. Putting a towel over it, she opened the oven she'd set to preheat at its lowest temperature. A shallow pan of water sat on the bottom rack, so the dough would stay moist in the gas oven. She put the bowl with the bread dough on the upper rack, checked the kitchen clock and closed the door. The dough needed to rise for an hour.

She began to wash the flour off her hands as her *mamm* went to the back door.

"Reuben, *komm* in," *Mamm* said. "We were talking about Esther paying you a call later today."

The bishop entered and took off the black wool hat he wore when he was on official business. He hung it on one of the empty pegs near *Mamm*'s bonnet. His gray eyebrows matched his hair and were as bushy as his long beard. He wasn't wearing the black coat he used on church Sunday. Instead he was dressed in his everyday work clothes, patched from where he'd snagged them while working on his farm.

"A cup of *kaffi*?" Esther asked as she took another cup from the cupboard. Everyone in the district knew the bishop's weakness for strong *kaffi*.

"Ja," he said in his deep voice. "That sounds *gut*."

She filled a cup for him from the pot on top of the stove. She set it in front of where he sat at the kitchen table where the top was clean. Taking her *mamm*'s cup, she poured more hot water into it before placing it on the table, as well. She arranged a selection of cookies on a plate for Reuben, who had a sweet tooth.

"Pull up a chair, Esther," Reuben said with a smile. When she did, he said, "Tell me how the boy is doing."

"He seems as happy as he can be under the circumstances." She was amazed she could add with a genuine smile, "Jacob has fallen in love with the alpacas at Nathaniel Zook's farm, and they're pretty much all he thinks about."

"He needs to return to school."

"*Ja.* He'll be back on Monday. I wanted to give him a bit of time to become accustomed to the changes in his life. That also gives me time to work with the other scholars so they understand they need to treat him with extra kindness."

The bishop nodded. "An excellent plan. So tell me what you want to talk to me about."

"When we took Jacob to his *onkel*'s house, Nathaniel and I were disturbed by what we saw there." Esther quickly explained the piles of papers and boxes and everything anyone could collect. She told him about the narrow walkways through the rooms, even the bathroom. "The only place not filled to overflowing is Jacob's bedroom."

Reuben sighed and clasped his fingers around his cup. Letting the steam wash his face, he said, "I shouldn't be surprised. Titus is a *gut* man, but he's never been able to part with a single thing. I understand his *daed* was much the same, so the hoarding is not all his doing. *Danki*, Esther, for caring enough about the Fishers to want to help them. However, I'm not sure if we should do anything until we know what's going to happen with Titus. If it's God's will that he comes home, having his house cleaned out will upset him too much."

"How is he?" *Mamm* asked.

The bishop's face seemed to grow longer. "The *doktors* aren't optimistic. At this point, they can't be sure what his condition will be if he comes out of his coma. One told me he hadn't expected Titus to last through the first night, but he's breathing on his own and his heart remains strong. Is there anything of the man himself left? Nobody can know unless he awakens."

"Jacob will want to know how his *onkel* is doing," Esther said.

"Having the boy visit the hospital now might not be a *gut* idea. I'd rather wait until there's some change in Titus's condition before we inflict the sight of his *onkel*, small and ill in a hospital bed, on the boy."

"Can I tell him nothing's changed?"

"Ja." He took a deep sip of his *kaffi*. "I don't like not telling Jacob the whole truth, but having him worry won't help."

Mamm stared down into her cup. "While we're waiting, we'll pray."

Reuben smiled and patted *Mamm*'s arm. "Putting Titus in God's hands is the best place for him."

"And Jacob, too," Esther said softly around the tears welling in her throat.

"And Jacob, too," repeated the bishop. "We'll need God's guidance in helping him as he faces the days to come."

Chapter Seven

Nathaniel ignored the chilly rain coursing down the kitchen windows as he tapped his pencil against the table. In front of him were columns of numbers he'd written. No matter how he added them, his expenses almost matched his income. The money from the rents on the fields was supposed to tide him over until he could bring in his own harvest next fall.

He wasn't going to have enough. He didn't want to start selling fields to keep from losing everything. If he sold more than one or two, he wouldn't have enough land to keep the farm going.

He could look for someone to loan him enough to get through the winter, spring and summer. Someone in Paradise Springs. He wouldn't ask his parents. They had money put away, but he knew they'd pinched pennies for years hoping his *daed* could retire from the factory in a few years.

There was another reason he couldn't ask his family for help. An unopened envelope sat on the table beside his account book. He didn't need to read it, because he knew his *mamm* was pleading with him again to return to Indiana where *doktors* would be able to help him if "the scourge" returned. He'd told her so many times that he hadn't needed to see an oncologist in six years. She refused to listen to the facts, still too shaken by what he'd gone through to believe the battle against his cancer had been won.

He pushed back his chair, something he was able to do now that he and Jacob had moved more of them into the barn. Leaning on the chair's two rear legs, he raked his fingers through his hair. There must be some way to keep the farm going until the fields produced enough that he didn't have to keep buying feed for the animals.

His *grossmammi* had bought the alpacas. Her mind had not been as muddled at the end of her life as his *grossdawdi*'s apparently had been. She'd intended the herd to be more than pets.

Hadn't she?

Looking across the kitchen, he stood. He paused when he heard footsteps upstairs. He was still getting accustomed to having someone else in the house, but he was glad Jacob was settling in well. Today would be the last school day he was skipping. On Monday, Nathaniel would have him there before Esther rang the bell.

Esther…everything led to her. When he'd held her close as the stair splintered, any thought of Esther the Pester disappeared as he savored the warmth of the woman she'd become. If she hadn't pulled away then—

and again at her house—he wasn't sure if he could have resisted the temptation to kiss her. Just once. To see what it would be like. He should be grateful she'd stepped away, because when he was honest with himself, he doubted a single kiss would have been enough.

He couldn't kiss her when he couldn't offer to marry her. Assuming she'd be willing to be his wife, he couldn't ask her. He'd first have to tell her the truth about his inability to give her *kinder*, and he didn't want to see pity in her expressive eyes.

Hochmut. Pride was what it was, and he wasn't ready to admit he wasn't the man he'd hoped to be: a man with dreams—no, expectations—of a home filled with *kinder*.

You could tell her the truth. His conscience spoke with his *grossmammi*'s voice. When he was young, she'd been the one to sit and talk to him about why things were right or wrong. Everyone else laid down the rules and expected him to obey them. Because of that, he shouldn't be surprised her voice was in his head, telling him that he was trying to fool himself.

Nathaniel grumbled under his breath. God had given him this path to walk. *Forgive me, Lord. You have blessed me with life, and I'm grateful.*

He went into the living room and to the bookcase next to his *grossmammi*'s quilting frame. Scanning the lower of the two shelves, he smiled as he drew out a thin black book. It was the accounts book his *grossmammi* had kept until she became ill. When he'd first arrived, he'd scanned its pages and seen something about income from the alpacas in it.

Returning to the kitchen table, he began to flip through it. His eyes narrowed when he noticed a listing for income from the alpacas' wool. He'd assumed they were sheared in the spring, and the dates of the entries in the account book confirmed that.

How did someone shear an alpaca? He'd seen demonstrations of sheepshearing at fairs, but had never seen anyone shear an alpaca. The beasts were bigger and stronger—and more intelligent—than sheep. Three factors that warned it'd be more difficult to shear them.

Jacob came into the kitchen and went to the refrigerator. He pulled out the jar of church spread and reached for the loaf of bread.

"Hungry already?" Nathaniel asked.

"It's noon."

"Really?" Nathaniel glanced at the clock, startled to see the morning had ended while he was poring over his accounts...and thinking of Esther.

Closing the account book, he stuck his mother's letter in *Grossmammi*'s book to mark the page with the entry about the alpacas' wool. He'd deal with writing back to *Mamm* later, and he'd ask Esther about shearing the alpacas when he and Jacob attended services in her district on Sunday.

"Do you want a sandwich?" asked Jacob as he slathered a generous portion of the sticky, sweet spread on two slices of bread.

Before Nathaniel could reply, a knock came at the kitchen door. Who was out on such a nasty day? Dread sank through him like a boulder in a pool. Was it Reuben or Isaiah with news about Jacob's *onkel*?

Please, God, hold Jacob close to You.

His feet felt as if they had drying concrete clinging to them as he went to the door. He couldn't keep from glancing at the boy. Jacob was moving his knife back and forth on the bread, making patterns in the church spread. The boy tried to look nonchalant, but Nathaniel knew Jacob's thoughts were identical to his own.

Be with him, Lord. He needs You more than ever right now.

Hoping no sign of his thoughts was visible, Nathaniel opened the door. So sure was he that a messenger with bad news would be there that he could only stare at Esther. Her blue eyes sparkled with amusement, and it was as if the clouds had been swept from the sky. A warmth like bright summer sunshine draped over him, easing the bands around his heart, a tautness that had become so familiar he'd forgotten it was there until it loosened. Suddenly he felt as if he could draw a deep breath for the first time in more years than he wanted to count.

"Hi." Esther smiled. "We're here for a sister day."

"You want to have a sister day *here*?" Nathaniel's voice came out in a startled squeak as he looked past Esther, noticing for the first time that she wasn't alone. Behind her were two other women.

They crowded under the small overhang as they tried to get out of the rain. Each carried cleaning supplies, and he heard rain falling into at least one of the plastic buckets. Looking more closely, he realized one of the other women was Esther's older sister Ruth. She hadn't changed much because she'd been pretty much grown when he left Paradise Springs. She was more than a decade older than Esther and very pregnant.

He didn't recognize the younger blonde who was also several years older than Esther. When the woman smiled and introduced herself as Leah Beiler, he wondered why she was involved in a sister day with Esther and Ruth. He didn't want to embarrass her by asking.

"It's a school day," he managed to blurt out.

"Neva is teaching today. I decided I was needed here more than there."

"I don't understand."

"May we come in?" Esther asked, her smile never wavering. "I'll explain once we're out of the rain."

"Of course." He stepped aside so she and the other two women could enter. Hearing footsteps rushing into the front room, he knew Jacob was making himself and his sandwich scarce. Did the boy think his teacher was there to bring the schoolwork he'd missed?

"Do you remember Ruth?" Esther motioned for her sister to come forward. "She offered to help when she heard what I planned to do."

"Danki," he said, not sure why. It seemed the right thing to say.

Ruth, who resembled their *mamm* more than any of the other Stoltzfus *kinder*, nodded as she walked through the kitchen into the even more cluttered living room.

"Leah's already told you her name." Esther put her arm around the blonde's shoulders. "I don't know if you two ever met. The Beilers live on the farm next to ours." Without a pause, she went on, "We thought you could use a little help getting settled in here, Nathaniel."

Her sister grumbled, "It'll take more than a little help."

Esther ignored her and lowered her voice. "Jacob mentioned when we were at Titus's house that yours didn't look much better. I'm glad to see he was exaggerating."

"Not much." He put his hands on the backs of two chairs he'd pushed to one side. "My grandparents accumulated lots of things. I don't remember so many chairs when I came to visit."

"That, as Jacob reminded me the last time we talked, was a very long time ago. How were you to know what was going on while you were far away?"

Was she accusing him of staying away on purpose? When he saw her gentle smile, he knew he was allowing his own guilt at not returning to Paradise Springs while his grandparents were alive trick him into hearing a rebuke where there wasn't one. Except from within himself. For so long his parents had insisted he do nothing to jeopardize his health. He'd begun to feel as if he lived in a cage. The chance to try to make his dream come true had thrown a door open for him, and he'd left for Pennsylvania as soon as he could purchase a ticket.

"Where would you like us to start?" Esther's question yanked him out of his uncomfortable thoughts.

"You really don't need to do this. The boy and I are doing okay."

"I know we don't need to, but we'd like to."

"Really—"

He was halted when Leah smiled and said, "I've known Esther most of her life, and I can tell you that you're not going to change her mind."

"True." He laughed, wondering why he was making such a big deal out of a kindness. "I've noticed that about her, too."

"I'm sure you have." Leah chuckled before taking off her black bonnet and putting it on a chair. Instead of a *kapp*, she wore a dark kerchief over her pale hair.

Esther and her sister had work kerchiefs on, as well. He wasn't surprised when Esther toed off her shoes and stuffed her socks into them. She left them by the door when she picked up her bucket and a mop.

"You need a wife, Nathaniel Zook!" announced Ruth from the living room in her no-nonsense voice. "If you cook as poorly as you keep house, you and the boy will starve."

"I'm an adequate cook. Jacob is fond of church spread sandwiches."

Ruth rolled her eyes. "You can't feed a boy only peanut butter and marshmallow sandwiches."

"I know. Sometimes we have apple butter sandwiches, instead."

When her sister drew in a deep breath to retort, Esther interjected, "He's teasing you." She and Leah laughed, but Ruth frowned at them before she began pushing chairs toward the walls so she could sweep the floor.

Esther went to the sink. Sticking the bucket under the faucet, she started to fill it.

"You'll have to let it run a bit to get hot," he called over the splash of water in the bucket.

She tilted the bucket to let the water flow out. Holding her fingers under the faucet to gauge the temperature, she gave him a cheeky grin. "You need to have Micah come over and put a solar panel or two on your roof. You'll have hot water whenever you want it."

"Are you trying to drum up business for your brother?"

"You know how we Stoltzfuses stick together." She laughed lightly.

He did know that. It had been one of the things he'd first noticed about the family when he was young. Esther and her brothers might spat with each other, but they were a united front if anyone else confronted them. That they'd included him in their bond had been a precious part of his childhood in Paradise Springs.

Esther shooed him out of the kitchen so she and the others could get to work. He paused long enough to collect the sandwich Jacob must have made for him. Not wanting to leave the boy alone in the house with women determined to chase every speck of dirt from it, he called up the stairs. Jacob came running, and they made a hasty retreat to the barn.

"I hope they leave my things alone," the boy said when they walked into the barn and out of the rain.

"Don't worry." Nathaniel winked. "Your bedroom and mine should pass their inspection without them doing any work."

Jacob looked dubious, and Nathaniel swallowed his laugh. After he set the boy to work breaking a bale of hay to feed the horses and the mules, he went to get water for the animals. He stood under the barn's overhang and used the hand pump to fill a pair of buckets.

Hearing feminine laughter through a window opened enough to let air in but not the rain, he easily picked out Esther's lyrical laugh. He couldn't help imagining how it would be to hear such a sound coming from the house day after day. Listening to it would certainly make any work in the barn a lighter task.

"Hey, stop pumping!" cried Jacob from the doorway.

Nathaniel looked down to see water running from the bucket under the spout and washing over his work boots. He quickly released the pump's handle. Pulling the bucket aside, he sloshed more water out.

"Are you okay?" Jacob asked.

"Fine. Just daydreaming."

"About what?"

"Nothing important," he replied, knowing it wasn't a lie because what he'd been imagining wasn't ever going to come true. He needed to work on the dream he could make a reality—saving the farm from being sold. Otherwise, he'd have no choice but to return to Indiana and a life of working at the RV plant. He couldn't envision a much worse fate. He'd be stuck inside and never have the chance to bring plants out of nourishing soil.

And he wouldn't see Esther again.

He tried to pay no attention to the pulse of pain throbbing through him. Picking up the bucket, he walked into the barn. The boy followed, chattering about the alpacas, but Nathaniel didn't hear a single word other than the ones playing through his head. *You've got to make this farm a success.*

Esther wasn't surprised that the attic with its sharply slanting roof was filled with more chairs. What about them had fascinated Nathaniel's grandparents so much?

She wasn't sitting on one. Instead, she perched on a small stool so she could go through the boxes stacked beside her. Ruth and Leah had gone home an hour ago after leaving the house's two main floors sparkling and clean. Esther had remained behind, because she'd suspected the attic would be overflowing with forgotten things.

She'd found two baseball bats and a well-used glove that needed to be oiled because the leather was cracking. Jacob might put the items to *gut* use. In addition, she'd set a nice propane light to one side for Nathaniel to take downstairs, because it was too heavy for her to carry. If he put it by the small table in the living room,

Jacob would have light to do one of the puzzles she'd stacked by the top of the attic stairs. As the weather grew colder and the days shorter, the boy would be confined more and more to the house.

Opening the next box, she peered into it with the help of a small flashlight. She wanted to make sure, before she plunged her hands into it that no spiders had taken up residence inside.

"Finding anything interesting?"

Esther glanced over her shoulder and smiled when she saw Nathaniel on the stairs. His hair was drying unevenly, strands springing out in every direction. He looked as rumpled and dusty as she felt, but she had to admit that looked *gut* on him. And she liked looking.

The thought startled her. Nathaniel was a handsome man, as he'd been a *gut*-looking boy. But she wanted his friendship now. Nothing more. She didn't want to make another mistake with her heart. It hadn't seemed wrong at the time when she discovered that Alvin Lee had loved racing. She'd been seeking an adventure. Exactly as Nathaniel was with his all-or-nothing attitude toward the farm.

She never again wanted the insecurity of wondering if the next dare to race a buggy or have a drink would lead to more trouble than she could get out of. Or of suspecting Alvin Lee might not be honest about being in love with her, despite his glib comments about how she was the one and only girl for him. Or of realizing, almost too late, how much her sense of her self-worth was in jeopardy.

No, she must not be foolish and risk her heart again.

She and Nathaniel must remain just friends.

Right?

She tightened her clasped fingers until she heard her knuckles creak. Why did she have to keep convincing herself?

Making sure she had an innocuous smile in place, she raised her eyes to meet Nathaniel's. "I've found a couple of useful things. I'm not sure I'd describe them as interesting."

"Useful is *gut*." He stepped into the attic but had to bend so he didn't bump his head on the low ceiling. Glancing around, he said, "I've been meaning to come up here to sort things out since I moved back, but somehow the day flies past and I haven't gotten around to it."

"Where's Jacob?"

"In the barn. He's hoping to coax an alpaca to come to him. He's determined. I'll give him that."

"He's patient. One of these days, he'll succeed."

"If anyone can, it'll be him." Nathaniel looked into the box in front of her and grinned. Reaching in, he pulled out a pair of roller skates. He set the pairs of wheels spinning. "I remember these. *Grossdawdi* bought them for me when my parents refused to let us have roller skates. *Mamm* feared we'd break our necks—or get used to going fast so we'd never be content driving a buggy instead of a fast *Englisch* car."

"She thought you'd get what the *kinder* call the need for speed."

He laughed. "*Ja*. My grandparents kept the skates here and never told my folks about them, though I suspect *Mamm* grew suspicious when I returned home from visits too often with the knees on my trousers ripped. She never asked how I'd torn them, so the skates remained a secret."

"I remember you bringing them to our farm. You

and my brothers used to have a great time skating in the barn."

"The only place smooth enough for the wheels other than the road, and your *mamm* wisely wouldn't allow us to play there." He set the skates on the floor beside the box. "Did you ever get a pair of your own?"

"I did. Hand-me-downs from one of my brothers, but I was thrilled to have them so I didn't have to walk to school in the fall and spring." She picked up one skate and appraised it. The black leather shoe wasn't in much better shape than the baseball glove, but with some saddle soap and attention it could be made useful again. "These look close to Jacob's size."

"I'll give them to him if you'll skate with us next Saturday."

"What?"

His eyes twinkled. "Don't pretend you didn't hear me promise your brother—our preacher—I'd make sure Jacob was kept safe. If I'm going to give him these skates, then we should make sure the boy has a place to enjoy them and someone to watch over him so he doesn't get hurt." He grinned. "I'll need someone to show me how to patch his trousers when he tears the knees out of them, too."

"You don't have any skates, do you?"

"I can get a pair. Does your brother sell them at his store?"

She shook her head. "Amos mostly sells food and household goods."

"There must be a shop nearby that sells them. I've seen quite a few boys and at least three or four men using Rollerblades to get around."

"Why don't you ask Amos? He usually knows where

to send his customers for items he doesn't carry." She set the wheels on the skate spinning and grinned. "I used to love roller skating."

"Do you still have your skates?"

"Not the ones from back then. They were about the same size as these." She laughed as she held one against her foot. "My feet have grown since then. Besides, I don't skate any longer."

"Too grown-up?" he asked with a teasing smile, but she heard an undertone of serious curiosity in the question.

"Too busy to stay in practice."

He took the skate from her and set it next to the baseball bat. When he looked at her, his smile was gone. "I should have said this first thing. *Danki* for having your sister day here. I'm amazed at what you did downstairs in a few hours. Everything is clean, and many of the chairs are gone. Where did you put them?"

"Leah and I took most down to the cellar. We stacked the ones that would stack. The rest are out of the way behind the racks where your *grossmammi* stored her canned goods."

"*Danki.* That's a *gut* place for them until I can start donating them to mud sales in the spring."

"You may be able to get rid of them before then. Isaiah mentioned at supper last night that plans are being made for a community fund-raiser to help pay for Titus's hospital bills."

"I'd be glad to give the chairs to such a *gut* cause."

"I'll let him know."

He studied the attic again. "I should have known you'd be up here. You always liked poking around here when you and your brothers came over to play."

"Your *grossmammi* enjoyed having someone who'd listen to her stories about your ancestors who lived here long before she was born."

He squatted beside her. "Do you remember those stories?"

"A few."

"Would you share them with me?"

"Now?"

"No." His voice softened, drawing her eyes toward him. "Sometime when I can write down what you remember."

"You don't remember her stories?"

"I didn't listen." His mouth twisted in a wry grin. "I was too busy thinking of the mischief I could get into next to worry about long-dead relatives." His gaze swept the attic before meeting hers. "Now I'd give almost anything to hear her tell those stories again."

Her hand reached out to his damp cheek. He leaned against it, but his eyes continued to search hers. What did he hope to see? The answers to his questions? She doubted she recalled enough of his *grossmammi*'s stories to ease his curiosity.

"We learn too late to value what we have," he whispered. "By then, it may be lost to us forever."

Were they still talking about his *grossmammi*'s stories? She wasn't sure, and when he ran a single fingertip along her cheek, she quivered beneath his questioning touch. His finger slid down her neck, setting her skin trembling in anticipation of his caress. When his hand curved around her nape, he tilted her lips toward his.

A warning voice in her mind shouted for her to pull back, stand, leave, anything but move closer to him.

She heard it as if from a great distance. All that existed were his dark eyes and warm breath enticing her nearer.

"Nathaniel, *komm* now!" Jacob exploded into the attic. He bounced from one foot to the other in his anxiety. Water pooled on the floor beneath him.

Esther drew away, blinking as if waking from a *wunderbaar* dream. She came to her feet when Nathaniel did. He glanced at her, but she looked away. She wasn't sure if she was more distressed because she'd almost succumbed to his touch or because they'd been interrupted.

Jacob's face was as gray as the storm clouds. What was wrong? She peered out the attic window. Through the thick curtain of rain, no other buggies were in sight, so Jacob couldn't have received any news about his *onkel*.

Nathaniel asked what was wrong in a voice far calmer than she could have managed, and the boy began to talk so quickly his words tumbled over one another, making his answer unintelligible. She thought she picked out a few phrases, but they didn't make sense.

...in the side of the barn...

...just missed...

Hurry!

The last he repeated over and over as they followed him downstairs and outside.

What had happened?

Chapter Eight

Wind-driven rain struck her face like dozens of icy needles, but Esther didn't return to the house for her bonnet or shawl. She ran to keep up with Jacob and Nathaniel. The boy didn't slow as he reached the barn. Throwing open the door, he vanished inside.

The interior of the barn was darker than the rainy day. Scents of hay and animals were thick, but not unpleasant. She blinked to get her eyes to adjust to the dimness, glad the roof didn't leak. Seeing Jacob rush through the door leading outside toward the pasture where the alpacas were kept, she swallowed a groan, ducked her head and followed.

The rain seemed chillier and the wind more ferocious. It tugged at her bandanna, and she put a hand on it to keep the square from flying off.

Looking over his shoulder, Jacob motioned for them

to hurry. He ran toward the alpacas, for the first time not being cautious with them. The frightened creatures scattered like a group of marbles struck at the beginning of a game. At the far end of the field, they gathered together so closely they looked like a single multiheaded creature. Something must be horribly wrong for Jacob to act like this.

Her foot slipped on the wet grass, and she slowed to get her balance. Ahead of her, Nathaniel had caught up with the boy.

"Here! See it?" Jacob pointed at the side of the alpacas' shed.

She heard Nathaniel gasp. She ran faster and slid to a stop when she saw what the boy was pointing to.

An arrow! An arrow was protruding from the side of the small building. She choked on a gasp of her own.

Whirling, she ran into the shed. The steel point of the arrowhead protruded from the wall. She didn't touch it, knowing the point would be as sharp as a freshly honed razor.

She came back outside to see Nathaniel pulling the arrow out of the shed. He held it carefully and scanned the fields around the house and barn. She did, too, squinting through the rain trying to blind her.

"Where did it come from?" Nathaniel mused aloud.

"Probably a deer hunter," she said.

"They shouldn't be firing close to the alpacas."

She scowled. "I doubt it was *close* to the alpacas. More likely, someone was aiming *at* your herd. The light brown ones are fairly close to the color of a deer."

When Jacob cried out in horror, she regretted her words. Why hadn't she thought before she'd spoken?

"They don't have antlers, and they're not the same

shape or size as a deer." Jacob looked at Nathaniel for him to back up his assertion.

She selected her words carefully, not wanting to upset the boy—or Nathaniel—more. "At this time of year, archers can shoot does as well as bucks. Irresponsible, over-eager hunters have been known to shoot at anything that moves. Ezra always has his Brown Swiss cows in a pasture next to the barn during archery season. Once the hunters can use guns, he brings the whole herd inside for the winter."

"You're joking." Nathaniel put his arm around Jacob's shoulders, and she noticed how the boy was shaking.

With fear or fury? Maybe both.

"No," she replied with a sad smile. "Some hunters shouldn't be allowed to hunt because they don't take the proper precautions when they're in the woods or traipsing across the fields. They ignore farmland posted No Trespassing. They're a danger to themselves and everyone else. Don't you remember how it was when you lived here years ago? Every fall someone loses a dog or some other animal because of clueless hunters."

"I remember."

"To be honest, we count ourselves blessed when no *person* is hurt or killed." With a sigh, she wiped rain out of her hair. "Right now, we need to check the herd and make sure none of them was hit. As frightened as they are, clumped together, it's impossible to tell if one is bleeding."

"Bleeding?" cried Jacob. "No!"

Nathaniel put his hand on the boy's shoulder. "Let's pray they're fine. But we need to check them. Do you remember how Esther got the alpacas into the shed?"

Jacob nodded.

"*Gut.* I'll need your help and Esther's, so we can examine them. They'll have to stay in until…" He looked at her.

"Until mid-December," she said. "I'm not exactly sure when hunting season is over, but I can check with Ezra. He'll know."

"That's a long time," Jacob grumbled. "The alpacas like being outside."

"When they can come out again, it'll be nice and cool." Nathaniel smiled. "With their wool getting thicker, they'll be more comfortable then."

Jacob jumped to another subject with the innocence of a *kind.* He pointed to the arrow Nathaniel still held. "Can I have that?"

Nathaniel didn't wait for Esther to reply. Though she'd be cautious with the boy—after all, she seemed to be cautious with everything now—he didn't want to delay getting the alpacas into the barn. Not just the herd, but Esther and Jacob, too. The hunter might still be nearby and decide to try another shot at the "deer."

With a smile, he said, "I'll give you its feathers, Jacob. How's that?"

"Great!" His grin reappeared as if nothing out of the ordinary had happened.

"Let's get the alpacas inside first."

"Okay." He ran to get the two branches Nathaniel used to move the alpacas.

"Well done," Esther said quietly, and he knew she didn't want Jacob to overhear. "He can't hurt himself with feathers. If he had the arrow, he'd be sure to nick himself."

"I'll make sure it gets disposed of where no *kinder* can find it."

"*Gut.* There can't be any chance Jacob will decide to see if he can make it fly."

"As we would have?"

She scowled. "We were foolish *kinder* back then. I've learned it's better to err on the side of caution."

"You?" He began to laugh, then halted when she didn't join in.

"*Ja.* I don't know why you find it hard to believe."

He could have given her a dozen reasons, but she walked away before he could speak. Pushing his wet hair out of his eyes, he watched as she took the branches from Jacob and sent the boy running to open the barn door.

What had changed Esther so much? It was more than the fact that she'd grown up. He had, too, especially after facing cancer, but he hadn't lost his love of the occasional adventure. Yet whenever he hinted at fun, she acted as if he'd suggested something scandalous. What had happened to her, and why was she keeping it a secret?

Her shout for him to get inside with Jacob so the alpacas didn't see them spurred him to action. As he went into the barn, making sure the door was propped open, he saw the alpacas milling about, frightened and more uncooperative than they'd been since he'd arrived at the farm.

More quickly than he'd have guessed she could, she moved the herd into the pen at one side of the barn. He closed the door and dropped the bar, locking it into place so the alpacas couldn't push against the door and escape.

Esther moved among them, talking softly. She might be perturbed with him, but she was gentle with the terrified beasts. While she checked the alpacas in the center of the herd, he and Jacob walked around the outside, keeping the creatures from fleeing to the corners of the pen before she could look at them.

Nearly a half hour later, she edged out of the herd and motioned for him and Jacob to step back. The alpacas turned as one. They rushed toward the door, halting when they realized the opening was gone. Moving along the wall, they searched for it.

"They'll calm down soon." Esther wiped her apron. It was covered with bits of wool and debris that had been twisted into the alpacas' coats. "Are you going to let the police know what happened?"

Nathaniel couldn't hide his shock because the Amish didn't involve outsiders unless it was a true emergency. "Why? Nobody was hurt."

"This time."

He shook his head. "I won't go to the police without alerting Reuben and my district's preachers first."

"Talk to them. No one was hurt this time, but someone fired off an arrow without thinking of where it could fly." She glanced at Jacob, who was watching the alpacas intently, but didn't speak his name.

There was no need. He understood what she hadn't said. Jacob was near the alpacas whenever he could be. A careless shot could strike him. Nathaniel needed to protect the boy who was his responsibility while his *onkel* was in the hospital.

As if the boy had guessed the course of his thoughts, Jacob asked, "Can I take the feathers and show them to *Onkel* Titus?"

This time, Nathaniel didn't have a swift answer. He thanked God that Esther spoke in a tone suggesting it was a question she'd expected, "As soon as the *doktors* say we can visit the hospital, you can take the feathers and tell your *onkel* about today."

"He'll be proud of me for not pulling out the arrow myself." The boy grinned.

"*Ja*, he will."

"He says no one should handle any weapon until they've learned how to use it the right way."

"Your *onkel* is a wise man." She returned his smile, and Nathaniel tried to do the same, though the expression felt like a gruesome mask.

"Because he's old." Jacob spoke with the certainty of his eight years. "He's had lots of time to learn." He pulled his gaze from the alpacas, which were already less frantic, and glanced over his shoulder. "That's what he tells me when I make a mistake or touch his stuff when I know I shouldn't."

Esther's smile grew taut, and Nathaniel gave up any attempt at one. Every time the boy mentioned his *onkel*'s obsession with those piles of junk, Nathaniel was torn between hugging the boy and wishing he could remind Titus that Jacob was more important than any metal or broken wood.

Jacob began to croon to the animals, but they wouldn't come closer to him. He whirled in frustration, his fists tight by his sides, and stomped his foot. At the sound, the alpacas turned and fled to the farthest corner of the barn. The boy's face fell from annoyance to dismay.

"Why don't they like me?" he asked.

Esther gave him a gentle smile. "They don't know you yet."

"I come out here every day. I help Nathaniel feed them. I make sure they have plenty of water. Why can't they see I won't hurt them?"

"Alpacas take a long time to trust someone. You have to be patient, Jacob."

"I have been."

"They still don't trust me completely," said Nathaniel, "and I was taking care of them for more than a month before you came here."

Crestfallen, Jacob nodded. "I wish they liked me."

"If you give them time, they may," Esther said.

"I want her to like me." He pointed to a light brown female. "I want her to like me before she has her *boppli*."

"How do you know she's pregnant?"

"She told me." He grinned. "Not with words. I'm not out of my mind, no matter what other kids say. She told me by the way she looks. Like our dog did when she was going to have puppies."

"How is that?" Nathaniel asked.

"Her belly moves, and I know it's the *boppli* waiting to be born."

Esther patted Jacob's shoulder. "You're right, but you need to know one thing. Newborn alpacas are called crias."

"Why?"

"From what I've read, it's because the little ones make a sound like a human *boppli*. The word is based on a Spanish one, which explorers used when they first visited the mountains in South America where alpacas come from."

He nodded and said the word slowly as if testing out how it felt. "Cria. I like that. She's not the only one going to have a cria, is she?"

"I'd say there are at least five pregnant females."

"Are you sure?" Nathaniel looked from the boy to her. How would he ever make the farm a success if he'd failed to see something obvious to an eight-year-old boy?

"Not completely." Esther put her hand on the wall. "You should have Doc Anstine stop by and look at them. He provided *gut* care for my alpacas, so he's familiar with their health needs."

Jacob grinned at Nathaniel. "Can I have one to raise by myself?"

"You need to see if the *mamm* alpacas are willing to let us near their crias."

"But if they will…?"

Nathaniel wanted to say *ja*, but he couldn't think of the alpacas and their offspring as pets. They might be the single way to save his grandparents' farm. On the other hand, he didn't want to crush Jacob's hopes.

Slender fingers settled on his sleeve, and he saw Esther shake her head slightly. How could what he was thinking be transparent to her, when he had no idea what secrets she was keeping from him?

You're keeping a big secret from her, too. His conscience refused to be silent, and he knew the futility of trying to ignore it. Now it was warning him of the dangers of ferreting out secrets better left alone.

"Let's talk about this later," Esther said, breaking into his thoughts. "Right now, will you watch the alpacas for Nathaniel?"

Jacob nodded, a brilliant smile on his face. "*Ja*. Maybe if they see me here, they'll know they're okay."

"You're right. What they need right now is what's familiar to them." She patted the boy's arm. "Stay with them ten or fifteen minutes, then come to the house. By the time you return later to make sure they're settled for the night, they should be fine. They may not know you kept them safe today, Jacob, but I know Nathaniel is grateful for your quick thinking."

"I am," Nathaniel said as the boy positively glowed. "The alpacas are important to me."

"Because they belonged to your *grossmammi*?" The boy hesitated, then reached into a pocket in his trousers. He pulled out a round disk. A yo-yo, Nathaniel realized. "This belonged to my *grossmammi*, and she gave it to my *daed* when he was a little boy. That's what my *mamm* told me." He stroked the wood that once had been painted a bright red. Only a few hints of paint remained. "My *onkel* owns a lot of stuff. He gave me some stuff of my own like my baseball and books. This is all I have that once belonged to my *grossmammi* and my *daed*."

The sight of the boy holding his single connection to the parents who had been taken from him by a drunk driver twisted Nathaniel's heart. Beside him, he heard Esther make a soft sound that might have been a smothered sob.

Knowing he must say something to the boy who had allowed them to see a portion of his pain, Nathaniel asked, "Do you always carry it in your pocket?"

"Not always." He shot a guilty glance at Esther. "I don't like others touching it, and I didn't know how much cleaning would be done in my room."

"Why don't you run and put it in your dresser drawer, so it doesn't get lost?"

"But the alpacas—"

"I'll stay here until you get back." He forced a grin. "I'll try not to upset them too much."

Jacob shoved the yo-yo into his pocket and bolted out of the barn.

By the pen, Esther wiped away tears she'd tried to hide from the boy. She gave Nathaniel a watery smile. "He'll be right back. I don't think he trusts you with *his* alpacas."

"I think you're right."

"He trusts you." She pushed away from the railing. Walking toward him, she said, "He showed you his most precious possession."

"And you, too."

She shook her head, and several light brown strands of her hair tumbled from beneath her kerchief. "No. If he trusted me, he wouldn't have put the toy in his pocket to make sure it was safe. Besides, I'm his teacher. You're his friend. He's learned he can depend on you."

"He'll come to see you're someone he can rely on, too." He stared at the long, damp curls along her neck. They appeared as silken as the alpacas' wool, and his fingers tingled at the thought of winding those vagrant tresses around them.

Pulling his gaze from them, he found his eyes lock with her pretty blue ones. They glistened with residual tears for the boy, but he saw other emotions, as well. Would she ever look at him with the longing he felt whenever she was close, a longing to hold her? Suddenly he found himself wondering if her eyes would close, brushing her long lashes on her soft cheeks, as he bent to kiss her.

No! He couldn't take advantage of her. She was unsteady in the wake of Jacob's confession…as he was.

He clasped his hands behind him before he pulled her close as he'd started to do in the attic before Jacob intruded. "One thing I can rely on is you. You're a *gut* friend, Esther Stoltzfus."

She didn't look at him as she said, "*Danki*. So are you." She stuffed her hair under her kerchief and headed toward the barn's main door. She didn't add anything else before she opened the door and was gone, leaving him more confused than ever.

When Nathaniel walked into Amos Stoltzfus's store, it was busy. Amos's customers hurried to get their errands and chores done before day's end. Tomorrow would be a day of worship, and no work, other than the necessary tasks of caring for farm animals, could be done.

In the midst of all the activity, Amos moved with a purposeful calm. He lifted a box down from a high shelf for an elderly man, who'd been standing on tiptoe to try to reach it on his own, though a pair of box grippers hung from a brad at the end of the aisle. He answered a *kind*'s question as if it were the most important thing he'd do all day.

Nathaniel smiled. There was no doubt Amos was a Stoltzfus. Not only did he have the brothers' height, something they didn't share with petite Esther, but he had the same sense of humor. He left everyone he spoke with either smiling or laughing. The Stoltzfus brothers seemed to have an ability to make others feel better…

as Esther did, too. Nathaniel doubted any of them realized what a special gift they'd been given. It was simply a part of them.

"Nate—Nathaniel!" Amos grinned. "I'll get it right one of these days."

"As I told your *mamm*, it doesn't matter which name you use."

"What can I help you with?" He wiped his hands on his apron that was stained with a multitude of colors.

"I'm looking for roller skates." He'd planned to buy a pair last week, but the days had hurried past, each one busier than the preceding one. Between caring for his animals, trying to keep the house in some sort of order and taking Jacob to school, he hadn't had a second to call his own. Only because Neva, Esther's assistant teacher, had come over to the house today to help Jacob with the schoolwork he'd missed had Nathaniel been able to come to the Stoltzfus Family Shops alone. "Do you sell them?"

He shook his head. "You might try the bicycle shop on Route 30. It's not far from the post office. Someone told me they had a small selection. Otherwise, the closest place I know of is an *Englisch* shop near the Rockvale Outlets in Lancaster, and that'll take you about a half hour drive with heavy traffic each way. The *Englischers* are already swarming on the outlets for Christmas shopping."

"It's only October."

"I know." Amos shrugged and then chuckled. "Apparently they want bragging rights to being the first one done. Traffic is really hectic this time of year."

"*Danki* for the warning. I think I'll check the bicycle shop." He started to turn to leave, so Amos could assist his other customers. When Amos spoke his name, Nathaniel paused.

"Esther tells me the boy has settled in well at your farm. If you ever need some time to yourself, he's welcome to stay at our house."

"I know, but right now some stability is the best thing for him."

"If you change your mind—"

"Danki." He let a smile spread across his face. "But think about it, Amos. Would you have wanted to stay at your teacher's house?"

With a roar of laughter, Amos clapped him on the shoulder. "That's putting it in perspective." He was kept chuckling as he turned to help a woman Nathaniel didn't recognize find a particular spice she needed.

Nathaniel walked out, hoping he had enough time to get to the other shop and back to the farm before Neva had to leave. His life was hectic now, but he wouldn't have it any other way. He still needed to talk to Esther about shearing the alpacas so he could have cash to keep the farm going until next fall's harvest. If the alpacas' wool wasn't the solution, he wasn't sure where he'd turn next. He knew he couldn't return defeated to Indiana. Not only would his parents again smother him in an attempt to protect him, but he'd have to say goodbye to Esther.

He didn't want to face either.

Chapter Nine

The Sunday service was almost over. Esther saw two *mamms* with new *bopplin* slip back into the room. Little ones seldom could remain quiet for the full three hours of the service. The *mamms* had to inch through to sit among the other women because the church benches were closer together than usual. It was always a tight squeeze at the Huyard house.

Marlin Wagler, the district's deacon, stood to make announcements. First, as he did each church Sunday, he announced which family would be hosting the district's next service. Then he paused and glanced around the room.

Esther held her breath as the room grew so silent breathing would have seemed loud. This time of year there was an air of suspense during announcements. Secret engagements were made public along with let-

ting the *Leit* know the couple's wedding date and who
would be invited. She glanced around the room, trying to see who, besides her brother Ezra, wasn't there.
When Ezra had stuttered over an excuse not to drive
them to the Huyards' this morning, she'd guessed his
and Leah's wedding plans were going to be published
today. That was confirmed when Esther noticed Leah
was missing, as well. It was traditional that an engaged
couple didn't attend the service when their wedding
was announced.

Anyone else?

Her search of the room came to an abrupt halt when
her gaze was caught by Nathaniel's. Dressed in his Sunday *mutze*, he looked more handsome than usual. The
black frock coat made his hair appear darker, something she hadn't guessed was possible. She noticed how
the coat strained across his shoulders and guessed the
hard work he was doing on the farm was adding to his
already sturdy muscles.

She looked hastily away, not wanting anyone to notice how she was staring at him. But she couldn't keep
from peeking out from beneath her lashes to watch him.
He was scanning the rows where the women sat. Was
he trying to figure out who was missing, too?

Or was he considering which single woman he might
choose as a bride? That thought sliced through her like
a well-honed knife, but she couldn't ignore the truth. He
was in Paradise Springs to rebuild the family's farm.
Why would he do that unless he planned to marry in
the hopes of having a son to take over the farm when
he was ready to retire? He needed someone who loved
adventures and challenges, because she knew every day
with him would be one.

That woman wasn't Esther Stoltzfus. When she told him she no longer roller-skated, Nathaniel had seemed to get the idea her days of seeking out adventures were in the past. Warmth crawled up her face when she recalled how the conversation between them in the attic ended. She shouldn't have touched him. That was too bold for the woman she wanted to be, but was it wrong to reach out when a friend was troubled? It was when thoughts of friendship had vanished as his fingers danced along her skin, setting it to sparkling like stars in a moonless sky. Then she'd watched his mouth coming closer to hers for a kiss.

In the open area between the benches, the deacon cleared his throat. The sound cut through Esther's reverie and brought her back to reality. A reality where she and Nathaniel were friends.

"Ezra Stoltzfus and Leah Beiler have come to me with their intention to marry," Marlin boomed over a *boppli*'s cries. "They've asked to be in our prayers, so please keep them in yours today and from this day forward."

Esther watched as *Mamm* stood to announce the date of the wedding. Her eyes were bright with tears, but Esther couldn't be sure if they were happy ones or if *Mamm* was thinking that it should have been *Daed* sharing the information today.

"Everyone is invited," *Mamm* said with a broad smile as she looked around the room, "no matter their age. Please pray the weather will be fine so we don't have to hold the wedding dinner in the barn."

That brought laughter from the adults and eager grins from the *kinder*. Many weddings restricted the age of the guests because there wasn't enough room for youngsters to be served along with the adults. Then some people couldn't attend because they had to stay home with the *kinder*.

Two other weddings were published, both for two days after Ezra and Leah's. There weren't enough Tuesdays and Thursdays, the days when the ceremonies were held, during the wedding season, so there were always conflicts. Esther was delighted there wouldn't be another wedding in their district on the day of her brother's wedding.

With a final prayer, the service came to a close. She went to the kitchen with half a dozen women to help serve the cold meats and sandwiches that had been prepared for their midday meal. The men and older boys rearranged the church benches as tables and seats for lunch. They would eat first, and then the women, girls and younger *kinder* would have their turn. The girls were watching the smaller kids run around while they got rid of some of the energy that had been bottled up during the long service.

Esther grinned as her *mamm* accepted *gut* wishes on the upcoming wedding. Volunteers came forward to promise to help with cooking and serving as well as cleaning up. Everyone enjoyed playing a part in a wedding, no matter how big or small the task might be.

By the time she'd eaten and helped wash the dishes, Esther suspected she'd heard about every possible amusing story of past weddings. She wiped her hands on a damp towel and went outside for some fresh air.

The afternoon was surprisingly balmy after the chill of the previous week. Not needing her shawl, she draped it over her arm as she walked toward a picnic table beneath a pair of large maples. In the summer, their broad branches offered shade for half the yard.

She sat, leaning against the table as she stretched out her legs. Hearing childish shouts, she smiled when she saw a trio of boys running toward the barn. Two were the younger Huyard boys, and the third was Jacob. He was joining in their game as if he always played with other *kinder*. They were laughing and calling to each other as they disappeared around the far side of the barn.

She closed her eyes, sending up a grateful prayer. Today, at least for now, Jacob was being a *kind*. It was a gift from God who was bringing him healing.

Even that simple prayer was difficult to complete, though it came directly from her heart, because her mind was filled with the work needing to be done before the wedding day. Perhaps Neva could fill in for her afternoons, so Esther could help *Mamm* and Leah and Leah's *mamm* get everything prepared. She'd been much younger when her oldest siblings married, and when her brother Joshua had wed for the second time earlier in the year it had been a simpler celebration.

Would it be her turn one day? She almost laughed at the question. When she considered the single men in the district, she couldn't imagine one she'd want to marry and spend the rest of her life with. Most of them thought of her as "one of the boys," as they had when they were *kinder*. They laughed with her and talked about the mischief they'd shared, but when it came time to select a girl to walk out with, they looked at the girls who'd spent their childhoods learning a wife's skills instead of climbing trees and racing across fields.

Was that why she'd fallen hard for Alvin Lee when

he asked her to ride in his buggy the first time? He'd come to Paradise Springs about five years ago, so he hadn't known her as a *kind*. She'd been flattered by his attention, but when he raced his buggy she knew she should tell him she wanted no part of such sport. Instead she'd remained silent, telling herself she didn't want to look like a coward. The truth was she hadn't wanted to lose the one boy who might be able to look past her tomboy past.

She'd learned her lesson. It'd be better to remain a *maedel* the rest of her life than to offer her heart to someone who didn't want it. If she could find someone who could love her as she was...

Nathaniel's face filled her mind, but she pushed it away. He was risking everything on making his family's farm prosperous once again. Though she admired his dream, as she'd discovered with Alvin Lee, when a man focused obsessively on a goal—whether it was a successful farm or the best racing buggy in the county—everything and everyone else was dispensable.

She wouldn't let herself be cast off like the junk in Titus Fisher's house. Not ever again.

Nathaniel walked back from helping Jacob and the other boys set up a temporary ball field behind the barn. He saw Esther sitting alone at the picnic table. During the meal, she and Wanda had been asked question after question about the upcoming wedding. Esther had answered many of them, giving her *mamm* a slight respite.

Now she was alone.

He sat on the other end of the bench. It shifted beneath him, and her eyes popped open. She looked at him in surprise, and he wondered how far away her thoughts had been.

"Hiding?" he asked with a grin.

"In plain sight?" She half turned on the bench to face him, her elbow resting on the table. "Just thinking. Mostly about the things we need to get done before the wedding."

"Nobody seemed surprised by the announcement."

She chuckled. "It's hardly unexpected. I'm happy it's finally coming to pass."

"*Gut* things come to those who wait."

"I can't believe that's coming out of *your* mouth! You never were willing to wait for anything."

"Look who's talking!" He grinned. "Esther the Pester never waited for anything, either."

"Oh!" she gasped, her blue eyes widening. "I'd forgotten that horrible name! Don't mention it in front of Micah and Daniel. They'll start using it again."

With an easy grin, he said, "I won't, but it's not such a bad nickname."

"It is when you're trying to keep up with three older boys who sometimes didn't want you around."

"Not true." His voice deepened, and his smile faded. "I liked having you around, Esther. When I went to Indiana, you were what I missed most. Not my home, not my grandparents, not the twins. You."

"I missed you, too." Her gaze shifted, and he wondered what she was trying to hide. "You're here now, and you're helping Jacob. I saw him playing with the other *kinder*."

"I may have let him assume the alpacas might get along with him better if he could get along with his schoolmates."

"You didn't!" She laughed, the disquiet fading from her eyes. "Whatever he assumed, it's *gut* to see him acting like a normal *kind*."

Nathaniel grimaced. "Wouldn't a normal *kind* be curious about how his *onkel* is doing? It's been more than two weeks since Titus was taken to the hospital, and Jacob has barely expressed interest in going there. He speaks fondly of his *onkel*, so I'm surprised he doesn't want to see him."

"Don't forget Jacob was in the hospital for almost a month in the wake of the accident."

"I hadn't considered that."

"I don't know any way you could use his determination to have the alpacas accept him ease *that* problem."

He smiled, then said, "Speaking of the alpacas, what can you tell me about shearing them?"

"Only what I've read and observed. I've got a book at home that explains how an alpaca is sheared." She gave him a wry grin and folded her fingers on her lap. "Not that I ever attempted it myself. I took mine to a neighbor's farm when their sheep were sheared, and the men handled it when they were done with the flock. I let them keep the wool in exchange for their work. They seemed to think it was a fair exchange."

"How long did it take them to shear your alpacas?"

"Not long. Maybe ten minutes each or less."

"So quickly?" His hopes that the alpacas' wool might be the way to fund the farm until the harvest deflated. "I guess the wool isn't worth much."

"I didn't have enough to make it worthwhile to try to sell it on my own. With your herd of alpacas, you should be able to do well. This past spring, the best wool was selling for over twenty dollars a pound. The next quality level down sells for around fifteen dollars a pound."

He stared at her in amazement. "How do you know that?"

"I'd been thinking of getting a small herd of my own. Ezra has pastures I can use. I'd started collecting information about income and expenses, but I had to set it aside to begin the school year."

"You've never said anything about that."

"You never asked." She grinned the slow, slightly mischievous smile that always made his heart beat quickly.

"True." He tapped his chin with his forefinger. "I never guessed their wool would be so valuable."

"Alpaca's wool doesn't contain lanolin, so people who are allergic to sheep's wool can wear it. The cleaner the wool, the better price you can get for it."

"How do I keep it clean?"

"Some people put thin blankets over their alpacas to keep the wool as clean as possible."

"Like a horse's blanket?" He tried to imagine buckling a blanket around a skittish alpaca.

"*Ja*, but smaller and lighter. The covers have to be adjusted as the wool grows, so the fibers stay straight and strong."

"I should have guessed a teacher would have done her reading on this."

She raised her hands and shrugged. With a laugh, she rested her elbow on the table again. That left her fingers only inches from him. If he put his hand over hers, how would she react?

Stop it! he ordered himself. *How many more ways*

can she make it clear she wants to be friends and nothing more?

"Looking up things in books is as natural to me as breathing," she said, drawing his attention from her slender fingers to her words. "I saw a bunch of books behind the chairs at your house. Could any of them help you?"

"I never noticed them until the chairs were moved, but I didn't find anything about alpacas."

"You're welcome to borrow the few I've collected."

"*Danki*. I—"

"Nathaniel! Esther! *Komm!*" called one of the Huyard boys. He, his younger brother and Jacob raced toward them, their faces alight with excitement.

The boy who'd shouted grabbed Esther's hand, and Jacob and the other boy seized Nathaniel's. Pleading with them to join in the softball game because the *kinder* needed more players, they tugged on the two adults.

She laughed and said, "You want us to play so you can strike me out again, Clarence."

The older boy grinned. "We'll take it easy on you."

"No, we won't," asserted his younger brother. "That wouldn't be fair, and we have to be fair. That's what you always say, Esther."

"*Ja*, I do. Milo is very, very serious about playing ball," Esther said with another chuckle as she stood. "Do you want to play, too, Nathaniel?" She held out her hand to him.

For a second, he was transported to the days when the Stoltzfus *kinder* had been his playmates. How many times had Esther stood as she was now, her hand stretched out to him as she asked him to take part in a game or an exploration in the woods or an adventure born from her imagination?

"Of course," he said as he would have then, but now it was because he wanted to see the excitement remain in her scintillating eyes.

When the two boys grabbed his hands again and pulled him to his feet, he walked with them and Esther to where other *kinder* were choosing teams. Soon the game began with Esther pitching for one side and he for the other. Nobody bothered to keep score as laughter and cheers filled the afternoon air.

One of the girls on his team hit a ball long enough for a home run. When she ran around the bases and to home plate, he held up his hand to give her a high five. Instead she threw her arms around him and hugged him in her excitement.

"This is the best day ever!" she shouted.

"Ja," he replied, looking at where Esther was bouncing the ball and getting ready for the next batter. Her smile was warm as she urged her team not to get discouraged. When her gaze focused again on home plate, his eyes caught it and held it. Her expression grew softer as if it were especially for him. More to himself than the girl, he repeated, *"Ja.* It's a *gut* day. The very best day ever."

Chapter Ten

Esther had planned to go home from the Huyards' with *Mamm*, but stayed for the evening's singing when *Mamm* insisted she wanted some time to talk with Ezra and Leah about the wedding alone. They were waiting at the house.

"You'll be able to get a ride home with someone else," *Mamm* said, her eyes twinkling. "The Huyards have invited Jacob to stay with them and their *kinder* tonight, so Nathaniel doesn't have to bring him to school in the morning. Jacob is excited, and Nathaniel can have an evening without worrying about the boy. See how well that's working out?"

"Ja." She didn't add anything else. Telling *Mamm* to stop her matchmaking would be rude. Her *mamm* wanted all her *kinder* to be happily married.

She didn't want to be matched with Nathaniel. Right?

Why did she keep thinking about riding in his buggy without Jacob sitting between them? The quiet night with only the sound of buggy wheels and horseshoes to intrude, a blanket over their laps to ward off the cold... his arm around her. She could lean her head against his shoulder and listen to his voice echo in his chest as he spoke.

She ejected those too-enticing thoughts from her mind. It'd be better if she just thought about the singing that had already started. From across the yard she could hear voices, which didn't sing as slow as during the church service. Going to a singing was the perfect way to end a church Sunday. As the weather worsened with the coming of winter, many singings would be canceled so people could get home before dark.

The barn doors were thrown wide open. Inside, propane lights set on long tables and on the floor sent bright light in every direction. A trio of tables to one side held snacks. Most of the singers had chosen a place on either side of the long tables. Couples who were walking out together sat across from each other so they could flirt during the songs.

Esther paused outside the crescent of light by the doorway, not wanting to intrude on the song. She wrapped her arms around herself as the breeze blew a chill across her skin.

"Are you going in or not?" asked Nathaniel as he stopped next to her.

"I could ask you the same thing."

"*Ja*, you could. They don't need me croaking like a dying frog in time with the music." He rubbed his right shoulder and grinned. "I'm not sure I want to show off how throwing a ball the whole afternoon for the *kinder* has left my shoulder aching."

"Only *half* the afternoon," she replied, wagging her finger. "The other half I was throwing the ball."

"You look as fresh as if you'd gotten a *gut* night's sleep. Don't rub it in."

She closed her eyes as the voices swelled out of the barn and surrounded them with "Amazing Grace." It was one of her favorite songs.

"You look pensive. Singings are supposed to be fun." He leaned against the wall by the door.

"Just listening," she said quietly. "A joyous noise unto the Lord."

"The hundredth psalm."

She nodded. "One of my *mamm*'s favorite verses, and whenever she reads it aloud, I imagine a grand parade entering the Lord's presence, everyone joyous and filled with music they couldn't keep inside."

"I know what you mean."

He did. He almost always had understood her without long explanations. Not once had he tried to make her into something she wasn't. When she looked at him, his face was half-lit by the lamps in the barn. His eyes burned through her, searing her with sweetness. He moved toward her.

She held her breath. His face neared hers, and she closed her eyes. Had time slowed to a crawl? What other explanation was there for his lips taking so long to reach hers? Her hands began to move toward his shoulders when someone stepped out of the barn and called to her.

Micah. If her brother discovered her about to kiss Nathaniel, she'd hear no end to the teasing.

Her eyes popped open. Nathaniel wasn't slanting

toward her. Had she only imagined he intended to kiss her? Especially in such a public place with many witnesses? Perhaps she'd imagined his intentions in the attic, too.

As the song came to an end, Micah called, "Why are you loitering out here? The more the merrier." With a wave of his arm, he went inside.

Nathaniel glanced into the barn as dozens of conversations began among the singers. "Shall we go in? You can sing, and I can croak."

He must not have noticed her silly anticipation of his kiss. Doing her best to laugh at his jest, she walked in with him. The singers rose to help themselves to the cider and lemonade waiting among the snacks. In the busy crowd, she was separated from Nathaniel.

Esther thanked someone who handed her a cup of cider. She didn't notice who it was as she looked for Nathaniel. Not seeing him, she let herself get drawn into a conversation with Neva, Celeste Barkman and Katie Kay Lapp, the bishop's daughter. She realized Celeste and Katie Kay were peppering Neva with questions about Nathaniel.

"I don't know," her assistant teacher said in a tone that suggested she'd repeated the same words over and over. "Ask Esther. She's spent more time with Nathaniel and Jacob than I have."

The two young women whirled to Esther. She couldn't miss the relief on Neva's face. Katie Kay and Celeste were known as *blabbermauls*, and both of them fired a question at Esther. They exchanged a glance, then looked at her again...and both at the same time again.

Esther tried not to smile at the exasperated look they

shot each other. Before they could speak a third time, someone clapped his hands and called for everyone to take a seat.

As the others rushed to the table, she drained the cup and put it beside others on a tray that would be returned to the kitchen later. She realized her mistake when she turned and saw Nathaniel at the far end with Katie Kay across from him and Celeste to his left. Katie Kay giggled as if what he'd said was the funniest thing she'd ever heard.

I doubt he's talking about alpacas with her. The ill-mannered thought burst through Esther's mind before she could halt it. Why was she acting oddly? Friendship was all she'd told Nathaniel they should share. It *was* all she wanted. Right? Right! If she ever offered her heart again, the man would be stolid and settled with the quiet dignity her *daed* had possessed. Watching Katie Kay flirt with Nathaniel made Esther's stomach cramp, as if she'd eaten too many green apples.

She looked away and saw her brother Micah leaning against some bales of hay by the snack tables. His arms were crossed in front of his chest and his face was blank. Except for his eyes. They narrowed slightly when Katie Kay giggled again at something Nathaniel said.

Esther had suspected for several months that her brother had a crush on the bishop's daughter, though, as far as she knew, Micah had never asked Katie Kay if he could drive her home from a singing. It wasn't easy to think of her jovial, outgoing brother as shy, but he was around the tall blonde. That, as much as anything, told her how much he liked Katie Kay.

Now the girl he liked was flirting openly with Nathaniel, his *gut* friend.

Walking over to him, Esther said, "Micah, if—"

"Everything is fine," he retorted sharply. "I want to stand over here. Okay?"

"Okay." She wasn't going to argue with him when she could see how distressed he was. "Do you mind if I stand here, too?"

"Ja."

His answer surprised her, but she simply nodded before she took one of the last empty seats at the table. It was on the end of a bench with nobody sitting across from her. She smiled at the people sitting near her and joined in the singing as each new song was chosen. Her eyes swiveled from Nathaniel to Micah and back. Her brother was growing more dismayed, but Nathaniel was grinning as if he were having the best night of his life.

When the last song was sung, the pitchers were empty and the last cookie was gone, the participants stood. Some, including Esther, carried empty plates and cups to the house. The men hooked their horses to their buggies and waited for the girls who'd agreed to ride home with them. Though nobody was supposed to take note of who rode with whom, Esther knew hers weren't the only eyes noticing how Katie Kay claimed a spot in Nathaniel's buggy before he gave the command to his horse to start. Certainly Celeste saw, because she pouted for a moment before setting her sights on someone else. Soon she was perched on a seat and heading down the farm lane toward the main road, as well.

Esther stood by the barn door and watched the buggies roll away. Several of the men had mentioned how much their younger sisters and brothers had enjoyed playing ball with her, but not one asked if she needed a ride home.

Even Nathaniel, it seemed. She'd thought—twice—he was about to kiss her, but now he drove away with another girl. *Don't blame him for your overactive imagination.* She sighed, knowing her conscience was right.

"It looks as if we both struck out tonight." Micah jammed his hands into his pockets and frowned in the direction of the departing buggies. "I figured you'd ride home with Nathaniel."

"He didn't ask me." The words burst out of her before she could halt them.

"Oh." Micah put his arm around her shoulders and gave them a squeeze. "Let's go home."

She nodded, not trusting her voice.

The next evening, Esther was putting a casserole in the oven when the door opened. As she straightened, Leah Beiler entered. Leah wore a kerchief over her hair, and like Esther, her feet were bare. Her dress was black because she was still in mourning for her brother who'd died earlier in the year, but her eyes glistened with happiness. That, as much as the fact that Ezra was always whistling a cheerful tune, had been signs of how they'd fallen in love again after years apart, separated by miles and misunderstandings.

Would Esther offer her heart again to Alvin Lee if she had the chance? No! Not even if he put an end to his wild life and made a commitment to live according to the rules of the *Ordnung*. He needed to care about something other than drinking and racing. He must start looking toward the future.

As Nathaniel clearly was, because he'd asked Katie Kay to ride home with him. She shouldn't be bothered, but she was. Pretending she wasn't was lying to herself.

Help me remember what's best for both of us, she prayed.

She put a smile on her face. "Perfect timing, Leah. I can't make any other preparations for supper until after the casserole has cooked for half an hour. Would you like something to drink?"

"Do you have lemonade or cider?" asked Leah. "It's too hot for anything else."

"I know." Esther opened the fridge and took out a pitcher of cool cider. Moisture immediately formed on its sides and around the bottom when she set it on the counter. "It feels more like August than October."

Leah took two glasses out of the cupboard and picked up the pitcher, then gave Esther a shy smile because she'd acted as if she already lived in the farmhouse.

With a laugh, Esther asked, "If you hold that pitcher all afternoon, the cider will get warm."

"Oh, *ja*." Leah poured two glasses before handing Esther the pitcher.

She put it in the fridge. "Let's sit on the porch. Maybe there's a breath of air out there." She gave Leah another teasing grin. "And who knows? You might catch sight of your future husband."

"I like how you think."

Esther kept her smile in place by exerting all her willpower. If Leah had any idea of the course of Esther's endless circle of thoughts about Nathaniel and Katie Kay, she'd know Esther's teasing was only an act.

They sat on the porch and sipped their drinks. Few insects could be seen in the wake of overnight frosts the previous week, so there were no distractions as the sun fell slowly toward the western horizon.

Leah put her emptied glass on the floor by her chair.

"Would you be one of my *Newehockers*? Unless Ezra has already asked you."

"He hasn't, and I'd be honored." The four attendants to the bride and groom needed to be available throughout the wedding day to help with everything from emotional support to running errands.

"Gut!" Leah's smile became bashful. "I can't believe this is finally happening."

"I can. Ezra never looked at another girl until you came back."

Leah flushed. "You shouldn't say such things."

"I'm only being honest."

"Esther, will you be as honest when I ask you what I have to ask you?"

"I'm always honest."

"Except when you think you might hurt someone's feelings with the truth. Don't deny it. I've seen you skirt the truth, though I've never heard you lie." She looked steadily at Esther. "Tell me the truth. Are you going to be okay with me taking over the household chores?" Before Esther could answer, Leah hurried on, "I know you've been in charge of the household since Wanda moved into the *dawdi haus*. Your brothers tell me what a *gut* job you've been doing."

"I'll be more than okay with you taking over the house."

"I'm glad that's cleared up. I didn't want to step on your toes."

She took Leah's hand and squeezed it. "Please feel free to step on my toes. I'll be glad to hand over anything you prefer to do yourself. It'll give me more time to focus on my scholars."

"How are the lessons going?"

"What do you mean?" she asked.

Leah's twinkling eyes warned she wasn't talking about school. She laughed. "Just teasing. How's Nathaniel doing with learning to take care of his alpacas?"

"I've taught him pretty much all I know until one of the pregnant females is ready to deliver. Once one of them has its cria, he'll know everything I know about them."

"I'm sure you'll find some other reason to visit the farm and make sure he's doing things right." With a wink, Leah stood. She picked up her empty glass and went into the house.

Esther didn't move. She should have been accustomed to the matchmaking now, and Leah hadn't been at the singing to see Nathaniel drive away with Katie Kay. Why hadn't Esther given her soon-to-be sister-in-law a teasing answer in return, as she had when Leah talked about taking over the household chores?

Because, she knew too well, she didn't care who did the cooking and cleaning, but she cared far too much about Nathaniel. The worrisome part was she didn't know how to change that.

Or if she wanted to, and that troubled her the most.

Nathaniel turned his buggy onto the lane leading to the Stoltzfus farm. Beside him, Jacob was almost jumping in his excitement and anticipation. The boy held his skates, the ones Esther had found in the attic, on his lap. He'd wanted to wear them in the buggy, but Nathaniel had refused. The boy could slip and fall getting in or out.

As he drew the buggy around the back of the house, he smiled. Esther was outside hanging up laundry. The clothes flapped around her in the gentle breeze, sending the fragrance of detergent spilling through the air.

She paused and looked around the shirt she held. Her eyes widened, and he knew she was surprised to see him and Jacob. After she finished pinning the shirt, she picked up the empty laundry basket and walked toward the buggy.

Nathaniel had already climbed out, and Jacob was jumping down beside him, his roller skates thumping against its side.

"Ready?" Nathaniel called to her.

"For what?"

He heard the note of caution in her voice that never had been there when they were younger. What—or who—had stolen Esther's daring attitude? It couldn't be just growing up and becoming a teacher and wanting to be a role model for her scholars.

He lifted two pairs of Rollerblades out of the buggy. One was black and his perfect size. The other pair was a garish pink, the only ones he'd seen in what he guessed was her size. "It's past time to prove you've still got your skating skills. These should fit you."

"I've got some, too!" piped up Jacob.

Esther put the basket on the grass. Her gaze riveted on the bright pink skates. "Where did you find *those*?"

"At a sports store Amos recommended." Nathaniel grinned. "They didn't have any black or white ones in your size on the shelves, so I got these."

When he held them out to her, she took the Rollerblades, examining them with curiosity. "I've never used these kinds of skates."

"You've been ice skating, right?"

She nodded. "Years ago. The pond seldom freezes hard enough."

"This is supposed to be like ice skating."

"Supposed to be?" Her eyes widened again. "Don't you know?"

"I haven't tried mine yet."

She pressed the pink skates into his hand. "Let me know how it goes."

"You don't want to try?"

"Even if I did, those are so—so—"

"Pink?" He chuckled. "If it makes you feel better, get some black shoe polish and cover the color. We'll wait."

Jacob frowned. "I want to skate now. You said as soon as we got here, we'd skate."

Nathaniel motioned toward the boy with the hand holding the pink skates. "You heard him. Are you going to disappoint him because of the color of a pair of skates?" He leaned toward her. "Don't you want to try them?"

He could see she was torn as she looked from where Jacob sat on the buggy's step lacing on his skates. Maybe the daring young girl hadn't vanished completely.

She grabbed the basket and said, "Have fun." She started toward the house.

"I dare you to try them," he called to her back.

He half expected her to keep walking as she ignored his soft words. Esther the Pester wouldn't have been able to, but this far more cautious woman probably could.

When she faced him, he made sure he wasn't grinning in triumph. She wagged a finger toward him. "I don't take dares any longer. I'm not a *kind*."

"I can see that, but if you don't take dares, do you still have fun?"

"In bright pink Rollerblades?"

"Don't you at least want to try them?" He raised his brows in an expression he hoped said he was daring her again.

With a mutter of something he didn't quite get and knew he'd be wise not to ask her to repeat, she dropped the basket and snatched the Rollerblades out of his hand. She sat, pulling the skates onto her bare feet.

Nathaniel yanked off his workboots and secured his skates tightly. He hadn't been ice-skating in years, but he remembered the boots needed to be secure or he was more likely to fall.

Esther stood beside him, rocking gently in every direction. She raised her arms to try to keep her balance. She almost fell when she laughed as Jacob couldn't stop before hitting the grass and dropped to his knees in it. The boy laughed, but Nathaniel's eyes were focused on her face.

It glowed with an excitement he'd seen only when she was playing ball with her scholars or working with the alpacas. This, he was convinced, was the real Esther, the one she struggled to submerge behind a cloak of utter respectability.

Why? he ached to shout. *Why can't you be yourself all the time?*

He didn't ask the question. Instead, he got to his feet. He took her hands and struggled not to wobble. The man at the shop had assured him anyone who had experience with ice-skating would have no trouble with inline skates. Nathaniel had had plenty of practice during the long, cold winters in Indiana. Now he wondered if the man had said that in hopes of making a sale.

As he drew Esther with slow, unsteady steps into the middle of the paved area between the house and the barn, he admitted to himself that the real reason he'd bought her the skates was for the opportunity to hold her hands as they had fun. She laughed when he struck the grass at the far end of the pavement and collapsed as Jacob had. Somehow she managed to remain on her feet.

Pushing himself back up, he dusted off his trousers. "You could have warned me how close I was to the edge."

"You could have found me skates that aren't bright pink." She folded her arms in front of her, but her scowl didn't match her sparkling eyes.

"I told you they were the only ones in your size."

"On the shelves. Did you ask what was stored in the back?"

He shook his head, unable to keep from grinning. "Probably should have."

"*Ja.* You probably should have." Her feigned frown fell away, and she chuckled. "Let's see if we can go a little farther."

She pushed off and was gliding across the pavement before he could grasp her hands again. With the skill she'd always had as a *kind*, she quickly mastered the Rollerblades and was spinning forward and backward.

More slowly, Nathaniel figured out how to remain on his feet. He doubted he'd ever be able to go backward, as she was, but he enjoyed skating with her and Jacob. The boy didn't seem to be bothered by his falls. He bounced up after each one, including one that left his trousers with a ripped knee.

"Someone's coming," called Jacob.

Nathaniel looped one arm around Jacob and another around Esther as a buggy came at a fast pace up the farm lane. He saw Reuben holding the reins. When Esther tensed beside him, he knew she'd recognized the bishop, too. There could be only one reason for Reuben to be driving with such a determined expression on his face.

"Esther," he began.

She didn't let him finish. Sitting, she began to unhook the bright pink skates as she said, "Jacob, let's go inside and get some cookies and cider."

"Are there any of your *mamm*'s chocolate chip cookies?"

"Let's see." She had the skates off and was herding the boy ahead of her toward the house by the time the bishop's buggy stopped next to Nathaniel's. She glanced back, and Nathaniel saw anxiety on her face.

Reuben didn't waste time with a greeting as he stepped out of his buggy. "I don't think we can wait any longer. The *doktors* are concerned because Titus seems to be taking a turn for the worse. They told me if the boy wants to see his *onkel* alive, he should come soon."

"We'll arrange for him to go tomorrow."

The bishop nodded, his face lined with exhaustion and sorrow. "*Danki*, Nathaniel. You and Esther have been a blessing for that boy." He glanced at the pink Rollerblades she'd left in the grass and smiled. "Though I can't say I would have approved of those if I'd been asked. *Gut* neither of you asked me." He turned to his buggy. "Let me know how the visit to the hospital goes."

"If Jacob wants to go."

Reuben halted. "You don't think he'll want to go?"

"He's been reluctant when I've asked him. Esther believes it's because he was in the hospital so long himself."

The bishop considered Nathaniel's words, then nodded. "We're blessed to have Esther as our teacher. She understands *kinder* well. Someday, she'll be a fine *mamm*."

Nathaniel must have said something sensible because the bishop continued on to his buggy. He had no idea what he'd said. Reuben's words were a cold slap of reality. *Ja*, Esther would be an excellent *mamm*. She deserved a man who could give her *kinder*. That couldn't be Nathaniel Zook.

The thought followed him into the house as he gently broke the news to Jacob, who was enjoying some cookies, that his *onkel* wasn't doing well. He didn't have details, because he realized he hadn't gotten them from Reuben.

"Do you want to go to the hospital to see your *onkel*?" he asked.

"Why can't I wait until he comes home? I hate hospitals!"

He looked over the boy's head to Esther whose face had lost all color. She comprehended, as the boy didn't, what it meant for the *doktors* to suggest he visit.

She sat beside Jacob. "I don't like hospitals either, but I think it's important you visit your *onkel*."

"Will you come with me, Esther?"

Surprise filled her eyes, and Nathaniel couldn't fault her. He hadn't expected Jacob to ask her to join them at the hospital that was on the western edge of the city of Lancaster.

She didn't hesitate. "If you want me to, I will."

Her response didn't surprise Nathaniel. Esther would always be there for her scholars or any *kind*. Another sign that he needed to spend less time with her because he was the wrong man for her.

So, why did life feel perfect when they were together?

Chapter Eleven

Esther didn't regret agreeing to go with Nathaniel and Jacob to the hospital, but that did nothing to lessen her dread about what they'd find there. In the weeks since Titus Fisher had his stroke, no *gut* news had come from the hospital. The reports she'd heard from Reuben and from Isaiah were the same—the old man showed no signs of recovery. His heart remained strong, but it was as if his mind had already departed.

She made arrangements for an *Englisch* driver, Gerry, to take them to the hospital the next morning in his white van. Also, she alerted her assistant teacher that Neva would be the sole teacher today.

When Gerry's van pulled into the farm lane, Esther hurried outside. The day promised to be another unseasonably warm one, so she didn't bring a coat or a shawl. She wore her cranberry dress and her best black apron. Beneath her black bonnet, her *kapp* was crisply pressed, and she wore unsnagged black stockings and her sneakers.

She watched while Gerry turned his van around so it was headed toward the road. The white van with a dent in its rear left bumper beside a Phillies bumper sticker was a familiar sight in Paradise Springs. The retired *Englischer*, who always wore a baseball cap, no matter the season, provided a vital service to the plain communities. He was available to drive anyone to places too far to travel to in a buggy. Also he'd drop passengers off and pick them up at the train station and the bus station in Lancaster. *Englischers* could leave their cars in the parking lot, but that wouldn't work with a horse and buggy. Though he claimed not to understand *Deitsch*, Esther suspected Gerry knew quite a few basic phrases after spending so much time with Amish and Mennonites.

"Good morning, Esther," he said when he opened the door to let her climb in. "It's good to see you again."

"How are you, Gerry?" She sat on the middle bench.

"Good enough for an old coot." He winked and closed the door as she pulled the seat belt over her shoulder. As she locked it in place, he slid behind the wheel. "Did your students like those colored pencils you bought for them before school started?"

"Ja." The *Englisch* driver had a sharp memory, another sign he cared about his passengers.

While Gerry chattered about baseball, his favorite topic even when the Philadelphia team wasn't in the playoffs, Esther sat with her purse on her lap and stared straight ahead. If she looked out the side windows at the landscape racing past at a speed no buggy could ever obtain, her stomach would rebel. She was already distressed enough about how Jacob would handle the upcoming visit. She didn't need to add nausea to the situation.

Gerry flipped the turn signal and pulled into the lane to Nathaniel's farm more quickly than she'd expected. She took a steadying breath when the van slowed to a stop between the house and the barn. Glancing at the empty field where the alpacas had been, she wondered how they were faring inside. They'd be as eager to return outdoors as she was to have the visit to the hospital over.

As if he were bound for the circus rather than the hospital, Jacob bounced out of the house. He would have examined every inch of the van if Nathaniel hadn't told him that they needed to get in because Gerry might have other people waiting for a ride. As he climbed in, the boy noticed Gerry's Phillies cap. He edged past Esther and perched behind their driver. Nathaniel sat on the back bench and reminded Jacob to latch his seat belt. When she realized he didn't know how, Esther helped him.

Jacob peppered Gerry with questions about postseason baseball games as they drove to the hospital. Soon they were talking as if they were the best of friends, arguing the strengths and weaknesses of the various teams.

"How are you doing?" Nathaniel whispered from the seat behind her.

She turned to see him leaning forward. Their faces were only inches from each other. She backed away. Or tried to, because her seat belt caught, holding her in place. When he grinned, she did, as well. It would be silly to try to hide her reaction when it must have been obvious on her face.

"I'll be glad when this is over," she murmured, though she needn't have worried about Jacob. He was too enthralled with Gerry's opinion of the upcoming World Series to notice anything else.

"Me, too." His eyes shifted toward the boy. "He hasn't asked a single question."

She nodded, knowing he was worried about Jacob. She was, too. Jacob was holding so much inside himself. He must release some of it, or...she wasn't sure what would happen, but it couldn't be *gut* for the boy.

Neither she nor Nathaniel said anything else while the van headed along Route 30 toward Lancaster. When Gerry pulled into a parking lot in front of a four-story white building, she saw a sign pointing ambulances to the emergency room. She looked at the rows of windows that reflected a metallic blue shine, and she wondered if Jacob's *onkel* was behind one of them.

Gerry stopped in a parking spot that would have been shaded by some spindly trees in the summer. Now sunlight pushed past empty branches to spill onto the asphalt. He shut off the engine.

"When will you want to return?" Gerry asked, reaching to turn on the radio. The sounds of voices discussing the upcoming baseball games filled the van.

"We shouldn't be more than an hour," Nathaniel said.

"Take all the time you need. I don't have anywhere else to be the rest of the afternoon."

"Danki," he said, then quickly added, "Thank you."

"Anytime." Gerry folded his arms on the wheel and looked at where Jacob was staring at the hospital. "Like I said, take all the time you and the boy need."

Nathaniel got out first. Esther was glad for his help, and she had to force herself to relinquish his hand before they walked through the automatic doors. Jacob was delighted with how they worked with a soft whoosh, and she guessed he would have liked to go in and out a few more times. Instead, Nathaniel herded him toward a reception desk.

Esther followed. She was uneasy in hospitals, but found them fascinating at the same time. People who came to them were often sick to the point of dying, and she despised how they must be suffering. On the other hand, she was impressed and intrigued by the easy efficiency and skill the staff showed as they handled emergencies and wielded the machinery that saved lives.

The receptionist looked over her dark-rimmed glasses as they approached. "May I help you?"

"We're here to visit Titus Fisher," Esther said quietly. "Can you tell us which room he's in?"

"Are you family?"

"Jacob is." She glanced at the boy who was watching people go in and out the doors.

"Let me see which room Mr. Fisher is in." She typed on the keyboard in front of her, then said, "Mr. Fisher is in the ICU."

Jacob, who clearly had been listening, frowned. "I see you, too, but what about my *onkel*?"

"ICU means the intensive care unit," Esther explained.

"Oh." The boy tapped his toe against the floor, embarrassed at his mistake.

"Don't worry, young man," the receptionist said with a compassionate smile. "We've got lots of strange names for things here. It takes a doctor almost ten years to learn them, and they keep inventing new ones."

That brought up Jacob's head. "*Doktors* are really smart, ain't so?"

"Very, so the rest of us can't be expected to know the words they use right away." Turning to Nathaniel and Esther, she said, "The ICU is on the third floor." She pointed to her right. "The elevator is that way. When you reach the third floor, follow the signs marked ICU."

"*Danki,*" Esther said, and hoped the receptionist understood she was more grateful for her kindness than for the directions.

Nathaniel led the way toward where three elevators were set on either side of the hallway. He told Jacob which button to push, and the boy did, his eyes glowing with excitement as the elevator went smoothly to the third floor.

Jacob faltered when it came time to step out. Esther looked at him and saw his face was ashen. The full impact of where they were was hitting him. Did he remember similar hallways and equipment from his long stay in the hospital? She wanted to take him in her arms and assure him everything would be all right. She couldn't.

"Let's go," Nathaniel said, his arm draped around Jacob's shoulders.

When Jacob reached out and gripped her hand, Esther matched her steps to the boy's. She glanced at Nathaniel. His jaw was tight, and he stared straight ahead.

The ICU didn't have rooms with doors like the other ones they'd passed. Instead, one side of each room was completely open, so anyone at the nurses' desk could see into it. Some had curtains drawn partway, but the curtains on most were shoved to one side. Monitors beeped in a variety of rhythms and pitches. Outside each room, a television monitor displayed rows of numbers as well as the ragged line she knew was a person's heartbeat. Everything smelled of disinfectant, but it couldn't hide the odors of illness.

A nurse dressed in scrubs almost the exact same shade as the pink Rollerblades came toward them. "May I help you?"

"This is Jacob. He's Titus Fisher's great-nephew," Nathaniel explained.

Sadness rippled swiftly across the woman's face before her professional mask fell into place. "Follow me," she said. As she walked past the nurses' station, she explained to the other staff members the visitors were for Titus Fisher. When she continued toward the far end of the ICU, she added over her shoulder, "Usually we allow only two visitors at a time in here, but when children visit, we like having both parents here."

Esther opened her mouth to reply, then shut it. If the nurse discovered they weren't Jacob's parents, they might not be able to stay with him. She glanced at the boy. He was intently watching the monitors, his face scrunched as he tried to figure out what each line of information meant.

"Here you go," said the nurse as she pulled aside a curtain.

Stepping into the shadowed room, because there was no window, Esther looked at the bed. She'd rarely seen Titus as he seldom attended a church Sunday, but she hadn't expected to see him appearing withered on the pristine sheets. Tubes and other equipment connected him to bags of various colored solutions as well as the monitors.

Jacob's hold tightened on her hand. She winced but didn't pull away. He needed her now. When his lower lip began to quiver, Nathaniel put his arm around the boy's shoulders again. They stood on either side of him, and she guessed Nathaniel's thoughts matched hers. They wished they could protect Jacob from pain and grief and fear.

"Your *onkel* is asleep," she said in not much more than a whisper. If she spoke more loudly, she feared her voice would break. She didn't want to frighten the *kind* more.

"He sleeps a lot," the boy said.

"This is a special kind of sleep where you can talk to him, if you want."

Jacob's brow furrowed. "What kind of sleep is that?"

Before she could answer, Nathaniel asked, "You know how you talk to the alpacas and they understand you, though they can't talk to you?"

The boy nodded, his eyes beginning to glisten as they did whenever the conversation turned to the alpacas.

"It's like that," Nathaniel said. "Right now, your *onkel* isn't able to answer you, but he can hear you. Why don't you talk to him?"

"What should I say?"

"You could tell him how much you love him," Esther suggested.

"That's mushy stuff." His nose wrinkled.

Esther smiled as she hadn't expected she'd do in the ICU. "Then tell him about the alpacas. That's not mushy."

The boy inched toward the bed and grasped the very edge of it. He was careful not to jar any of the wires or tubes, and he gave the IV stands a scowl. Again she wondered what he'd endured when he'd been in the hospital after his parents were killed.

"*Onkel* Titus," he began, "I got my stuff and took it to Nathaniel's, and some things fell into the hole when a stair broke. Otherwise, nothing's been touched. All your bags and boxes—except for the ones that fell in the hole—are there just as you like them."

He glanced over his shoulder at her and Nathaniel, then went on. "I'm staying with Nathaniel Zook. Do you remember him? He used to live in Paradise Springs when he was a kid. He's back now, and he's got alpacas!" The boy's voice filled with excitement as he began to outline in excruciating detail how he was helping take care of the herd and his efforts to get them to trust him.

Esther was glad for the shadows in the room so nobody could see the tears filling her eyes as she gazed at the boy who was brave and loving and compassionate. She wished she had his courage and ability to forgive. Maybe…

She kept herself from looking at Nathaniel. If things had been different. If things *were* different.

Things weren't different. He was walking out with Katie Kay, and he was her friend…just as she'd asked him to be.

But she knew it wouldn't be enough, and she'd thrown away her chance at love by ignoring her heart.

Nathaniel said nothing as he held the curtain open for Esther and Jacob. The boy was once again holding on tightly to her hand. Esther's taut jaw was set, and he couldn't ignore the tears shimmering in her eyes.

He couldn't say anything about them, either. He didn't want to bring Jacob's attention to them or embarrass her in the ICU.

What he truly wanted to do was draw her into his arms and hold her until they both stopped shaking. Until he'd stepped into that room, he'd harbored the hope Titus would recover. Now he knew it was impossible. The elderly man hadn't reacted to anything while they were there, and Nathaniel knew that while Titus's body might be alive, his mind was beyond recovery.

In the elevator going down to the main floor, he sought words to comfort Jacob and Esther. He couldn't find any. He wasn't sure there were any, so he remained silent as they walked out of the hospital and toward the white van.

Gerry must have read their faces because he got out and opened the doors without any comment. Jacob claimed the middle bench, and Esther sat with Nathaniel. As soon as they were buckled in, the van started for Paradise Springs.

They hadn't gone more than a mile before Jacob curled up on the seat. The emotions he hadn't shown in the ICU were like a shadow over him. When Esther began to talk to him, Jacob cut her off more sharply than Nathaniel had ever heard him speak to her. Shortly after, the boy fell asleep, exhausted from the visit.

Nathaniel turned to Esther whose gaze was focused on the boy. "*Danki* for coming with us," he whispered. "I wasn't sure how he'd handle seeing the old man."

As he did, she chose words that wouldn't intrude on Jacob's slumber. "He handled it better than either of us." Her voice caught. "He's too familiar with how quickly life can be snuffed out like a candle."

"Yet he knows when the old man dies, he'll have no place to go."

She faced him. "He does have a place to go. He's with you."

"He's welcome to stay at the farm for as long as he wishes, but he needs someone who knows how to be a parent. That's not me."

"You're doing a great job."

He gave a soft snort to disagree. "I depend on those witless beasts my *grossmammi* bought to keep him entertained. Otherwise, I don't know what I'd do. He's becoming more skilled with them than I'll probably ever be."

"You'd have managed to help without the herd."

"You've got a lot of faith in me."

"I do, but I also have a lot of faith God arranged for him to be at the best possible place when his *on*—the old man was taken to be monitored." She corrected herself with a glance at the boy. "God's plans for us are only *gut*."

This time, he managed to silence his disagreement. If God's plans for His *kinder* were only *gut*, then why had Nathaniel lost his hope of being a *daed*? He appreciated every day he'd been given, and he enjoyed having Jacob living with him in that big farmhouse. He was grateful the boy had found happiness as well as frustration with the alpacas. However, the boy was also a reminder of everything Nathaniel wouldn't have in the future.

Chapter Twelve

The day of Ezra and Leah's wedding dawned with the threat of clouds on the horizon, but by the time the service was over shortly before noon, the sun was shining on the bride and groom. Almost everyone in the district had come to the farm for the wedding, as *Mamm* had hoped.

After the service, Esther sat with her brother and new sister-in-law at a corner table among those set in front of the house. Everyone was excited to celebrate the first wedding of the season, especially one so long in the making. She smiled as she watched Ezra and Leah together. They were in love, and her brother had waited for ten years for Leah to return from the *Englisch* world. They deserved every ounce of happiness they could find together.

It was delightful to sit with them as food was served.

Stories ran up and down the tables as the guests shared fond and fun memories of the newlyweds. Leah's niece Mandy and Esther's niece Debbie could barely sit still in their excitement, and more than one glass of milk was tipped over among the younger guests.

Mamm was just as happy. She'd had a broken arm and couldn't do much when Joshua, Esther's oldest brother, had married for the second time earlier in the year. She was trying to make up for that with Ezra's wedding as she talked to the many guests and made sure everyone had plenty to eat.

The day sped past, and Esther saw Nathaniel and Jacob in the distance several times. When she noticed Jacob joining other *kinder* for games in the meadow beyond the barn, she was relieved. She hadn't seen him since they went to the hospital. She'd agreed with Nathaniel that a few more days skipping school might help the boy. Now she was glad to discover he hadn't become traumatized and withdrawn again.

Jacob wasn't the only subject she wanted to discuss with Nathaniel, but she never had a chance to talk to him. During the afternoon singing, she'd been in the kitchen with *Mamm*, her sister and other volunteers while they washed plates from the midday meal and readied leftover food for dinner. The married or widowed women had urged her to join the singles for the singing, but she'd demurred after seeing Nathaniel walk into the barn with Katie Kay and Celeste. She didn't want to watch him flirting with them while they flirted with him.

Now the guests were leaving, and she hadn't even said hello to him. She stepped out of the kitchen and huddled into her shawl as the breeze struck her face. It was going to be cold tonight. Looking around the yard, she spotted several men standing near the barn where the buggies were parked.

Through the darkness, she could pick out Nathaniel. Her gaze riveted on him as if a beam of light shone upon his head. There was something about how he stood, straight and sure of himself, that always caught her eyes. Her heart danced at the thought of having a few minutes with him. Just the two of them. She waited for her conscience to remind her that friendship should be all she longed for from him.

It was silent, and her heart rejoiced as if it'd won a great battle.

Esther hesitated. Maybe she should stay away from him while her brain was being overruled by her heart. She might say the wrong thing or suggest she'd changed her mind.

But you have!

Ignoring that small voice of reason, she came down off the steps, but had to jump aside as a trio of young women burst out of the night. They were giggling and talking about the men who were taking them home. When she recognized them as Katie Kay, Celeste and her own cousin Virginia, she greeted them.

They waved with quick smiles, but were intent on their own conversation. Esther flinched when she heard Nathaniel's name, but she couldn't tell which one spoke it because they'd opened the door and the multitude of voices from the kitchen drowned out their words. She assumed it was Katie Kay. She squared her shoulders and crossed the yard. Clearly, if she wanted to speak with Nathaniel she needed to do so before he drove away with the bishop's daughter.

Again she faltered. Should she skip talking with him? No, she needed to know how Jacob was doing because he would be returning to school tomorrow. Because she was racked with jealousy—and she couldn't pretend it was anything else—didn't mean she could relinquish her obligations to her scholars.

The thought added strength to her steps as she left the house lights behind and strode toward the barn. She'd reached the edge of the yard when she heard a voice.

"Guten owed," said someone from the shadows.

Esther peered through the dark, wondering who'd called a "good evening" to her. Her eyes widened when Alvin Lee stepped out into the light flowing from the barn door in front of her. He hadn't attended church services or any other community function since the last time she'd spoken with him, the night she refused to be part of his reckless racing any longer.

There was no mistaking his bright red hair and his sneer. He used that expression most of the time. He had on the simple clothes every Amish man wore, but everything was slightly off. His suspenders had shiny clips peeking out from where he'd loosened his shirt over them. His hair was very short in the style *Englischers* found stylish and the faint lettering of a T-shirt was visible beneath his light blue shirt. She couldn't read the words, but the picture showed men wearing odd makeup and sticking out their tongues. She guessed they belonged to some *Englisch* rock-and-roll band.

She waited for her heart to give a leap as it used to whenever he appeared. Nothing happened. Her heart maintained its steady beat. She murmured a quick prayer of praise that God had helped it heal after Alvin

Lee had turned his back on her because she didn't want to go along with his idea of fun and games.

"Heading toward the singing?" He leaned one elbow nonchalantly against the tree. He thought such poses made him look cool.

Cool was the best compliment he could give anyone or anything. In retrospect, she realized he'd never used it while describing her. Not that she needed compliments, then or now. They led to *hochmut*, something Alvin Lee had too much of. He was inordinately proud of his fancy buggy and his unbeaten record in buggy races. Though he'd never admitted it, she'd heard he'd begun wagering money with friends, Amish and *Englisch*, on his driving skills and his horse's speed. That would explain how he could afford to decorate his buggy so wildly.

"The singing was earlier today," Esther said, selecting her words with care. What did he want?

"Glad I missed it. Singings are boring, and nobody ever wants to sing music I like." He flexed his arm, and she saw the unmistakable outline of a package of cigarettes beneath his shirt. Smoking wasn't forbidden by the *Ordnung*, and some older farmers in the area grew tobacco, but it wasn't looked upon favorably, either. "I'm sure it was boring as death." He pushed away from the tree. "Attending singings is for the kids, anyhow. Why don't you come with me, and we'll have some real excitement?"

At last, she realized why he'd shown up after dark. He was looking for people to race with and drink with, and she didn't want to think what else he had in mind. She didn't want any part of it. Not any longer.

"I'm not interested." She turned to walk away.

He stepped in front of her again, blocking her way. "Hey, Essie, are you mad at me?"

"No." She didn't feel anger at him any longer. Nor did she feel special, as she used to when he called her by that nickname. She didn't feel anything but dismay at how he was risking his life for a few minutes of excitement.

"Are you sure? You act like you're mad." His ruddy brows dropped in a frown. "Is it because I asked Luella to ride with me one time?"

"No," she answered, glad she could be honest when he wasn't. New reports of him and Luella riding together in his garish buggy were whispered almost every weekend. Esther had to be grateful that Alvin Lee hadn't decked out his buggy when *she* was riding with him. Otherwise, rumors would have flown about her and him, as well. "I'm not interested tonight."

"Sure you are, Essie. You've always been interested in fun."

"Not your kind of fun. Not anymore."

His eyes narrowed. "You're serious, aren't you?"

"How many different ways do I have to tell you I'm not interested?"

"They got to you, didn't they? Broke your spirit and made you a Goody Two-shoes."

She wasn't quite sure who "Goody Two-shoes" was, but the insult was blatant. "Nobody's broken my spirit. I've simply grown up." She flinched when she remembered uttering those same words to Nathaniel after they'd gone to Titus Fisher's house.

She hurried away, leaving Alvin Lee to grumble behind her. Relief flooded her. She'd spoken with him for the first time since he'd crushed her heart, and she hadn't broken down into tears or been drawn into being a participant in his dangerous races. Maybe she was, as she'd told him and Nathaniel, finally putting her child-ish ways behind her.

Esther heard him stomp away in the opposite di-rection. He hadn't pulled his buggy into the barnyard as the others had. With a shudder of dismay, she real-ized he'd cut himself off from the community as surely as Jacob once had. Would Alvin Lee see the error of his ways and reach out to others again as the boy was doing? Or was he too much a victim of *hochmut* to admit he was wrong?

She continued toward the barn. She wanted to talk to Nathaniel more than ever. She needed to listen to him. He didn't focus completely on himself. Even his idea of adventure was doing something important for his family, not something to give him a few moments of triumph over someone else.

As she neared the men, they were laughing together. She started to call out, but paused when she heard Na-thaniel say, "Ah, I understand you now, Daniel. Playing the field is *gut* in more than baseball."

Her twin brothers roared in appreciative laughter before Micah replied, "Now there will be two of you leaving a trail of broken hearts in your wake."

"No, I wouldn't do that," Daniel said with a chuckle.

"No?" challenged Micah.

"No, and nobody seems to wonder if *I've* got a broken heart."

His twin snorted. "Because nobody's seen any sign of it."

"I like to enjoy the company of lots of girls, and they enjoy my company."

"Because they think you're serious about them." Mi-cah's voice lost all humor. "I got a truly ferocious look this afternoon from Celeste Barkman until she realized I wasn't you, baby brother."

Nathaniel laughed along with Daniel before changing the subject to the upcoming World Series.

Esther knew she should leave. None of them had noticed her yet, and she shouldn't stand there eavesdropping. Yet, if she moved away, they would see her and realize she'd been listening.

The quandary was resolved when Nathaniel and her brothers walked toward the parked buggies. They didn't glance in her direction.

She turned and hurried toward the house. She was a short distance from the kitchen door when it opened, and Celeste and Katie Kay rushed out. They were giggling together as they told her *gut nacht*.

Thin arms were flung around her waist, and she smiled as Jacob hugged her.

"Are you leaving now?" she asked.

"*Ja*. Will you be coming to visit the alpacas soon?"

"I hope to."

"You could drive me home after school tomorrow, and you could see them then." He looked at her with expectation.

She hid her astonishment when he called Nathaniel's farm "home." Not once had he described Titus's place as anything other than his *onkel*'s house. It was a tribute to Nathaniel that the boy had changed. She was grateful to him for helping Jacob, but she shouldn't be surprised. Nathaniel had welcomed the boy as if he were a member of his own family from the very first. Though she was disturbed by how contemptuous Nathaniel had sounded about courting, she had to admit he'd done a *wunderbaar* job with Jacob.

Why had Nathaniel talked about playing the field as her brother Daniel did? She'd heard what sounded like admiration and perhaps envy in his voice at her brother's easy way with the girls.

"Esther?"

Jacob's voice broke into her thoughts, and Esther smiled at the boy. "*Ja.* I'd like to check on the alpacas." She refused to admit she'd accepted the invitation so she could see Nathaniel without everyone else around to distract him.

"I'll tell Nathaniel!" With a wave, he ran toward where the buggies were beginning to leave.

Esther didn't follow. She stayed in the shadows beneath a tree as buggy after buggy drove past. Some contained families or married couples. Others were courting buggies, some with one passenger but most with two. Only one held three crowded in it: Nathaniel's.

She turned to watched Nathaniel's courting buggy head down the farm lane. From where she stood, she could hear Celeste's laugh drifting on the night air. That Jacob was riding with them, acting as a pint-size chaperone, didn't lessen the tightness in her chest or the burning in her eyes.

Nathaniel couldn't ask to drive Esther when she was already home, but why did he have to ask flirtatious Celeste, who hadn't made any secret of her interest in him? Why hadn't he spoken a single word to Esther all day?

Because you avoided him. Oh, how she despised the small voice of honesty in her mind! *Ja*, she'd found ways to stay away from him, but what would it have mattered if she'd shadowed him as Katie Kay and Celeste had? He was enjoying playing the field, an *Englisch* term for enjoying the company of many single girls. *And you told him you weren't interested.*

She'd been sincere when she said that, but was beginning to see her attempts to protect her heart by not risking it had been futile. Her heart ached now more than it had when Alvin Lee pushed her out of his life. God had led her away from that dangerous life, and she should be grateful He'd been wiser than she was. She was, but that did nothing to ease her heart's grief.

God, help me know what to feel. She longed to pray for God to give her insight into why Nathaniel had gazed at her with such strong emotions while they rode from the hospital…and days later blithely drove past her with another woman by his side.

Abruptly the night had become far colder—and lonelier—than she'd guessed it ever could.

Nathaniel turned his buggy onto a shortcut between the Barkman farm and his own. He hadn't planned to go so far out of his way when Jacob needed to be at school tomorrow. However, at this time of night, the winding, hilly road was deserted and the drive was pleasant. As the moonlight shone down on the shorn fields, he was alone save for his thoughts because Jacob was asleep.

He'd enjoyed the wedding more than he'd expected he would. Seeing friends whom he'd known as a *kind* had been fun, and he was glad they hadn't jumped the fence and gone to live among the *Englischers*. Several had married someone he never would have guessed they would. Time had changed them, and he knew they'd faced challenges, too, because they spoke easily of what life had thrown at them since the last time Nathaniel had visited his grandparents. Among the conversations that were often interrupted when someone else recognized him, nobody seemed to notice he said very little about his own youth.

He'd deflected the few questions with answers like, "Things aren't different in Indiana from here," or "Ancient history now. My brain is full of what I need to do at the farm. There isn't room for anything else." Both answers were received with laughter and commiserating nods, which made it easy to change the conversation to anyone other than himself.

However, he hadn't had a chance to spend any time with Esther. He'd known she'd be busy in her role as a *Newehocker*, but he'd hoped to have some time with her. She hadn't come to the singing, though he wouldn't have had much time to talk with her. The singing had gone almost like the one after church. Katie Kay Lapp had monopolized his time that day, not giving him a chance to speak to anyone else. At this afternoon's singing, she'd been flirting with a young man who was a distant cousin of the Stoltzfus family.

He'd been greatly relieved, until Celeste Barkman had pushed past several other people and lamented to him that her brother was going home with someone else and she didn't have a ride. As the Barkman farm wasn't too far out of his way, Nathaniel had felt duty-bound to give her a ride. He hadn't thought much about it until he happened to glance at the Stoltzfuses' house and saw Esther standing alone beneath one of the big trees.

She'd looked upset, though the shadows playing across her face could have masked her true expression. If she'd been disconcerted, was it because he was giving Celeste a ride? An unsettling thought, especially when Esther had stressed over and over she wanted his friendship and nothing more. Why wasn't she being honest with him?

Shouts came behind him, and Nathaniel tightened his hold on the reins. He'd been letting the horse find its own way, but the raucous voices were mixed with loud music coming toward him at a high speed. As Jacob stirred, Nathaniel glanced in his rearview mirror. He was surprised not to see an *Englischer*'s car or truck.

Instead, it was a buggy decked out with more lights and decals than any district's *Ordnung* would have sanctioned. What looked like *Englisch* Christmas lights were strung around the top of the buggy, draped as if on the branches of a pine tree. He wondered how either the driver or the horse could see past the large beacons hooked to the front of the buggy. Twin beams cut through the darkness more brilliantly than an automobile's headlights. The whole configuration reminded him of decked-out tractor-trailers he'd seen on the journey from Indiana to Paradise Springs.

Who was driving such a rig? He couldn't see into the vehicle as it sped past him on the other side of the road, though they were approaching a rise and a sharp corner. Large, too-bright lights were set next to the turn signals at the back, blinding him. When he could see again, it was gone.

He continued to blink, trying to get his eyes accustomed to the darkness again. What a fool that driver was! He prayed God would infuse the driver with some caution.

"What was that?" asked Jacob in a sleepy tone.

"Nothing important. We'll be home soon."

"*Gut.* I want to make sure the alpacas' pen is clean before Esther comes tomorrow."

Nathaniel's hands tightened on the reins, but he loosened his grip before he frightened Bumper. The horse was responsive to the lightest touch.

Trying to keep his voice even, Nathaniel asked, "Esther said she was coming over tomorrow?"

"I asked her. She needs to check the alpacas."

"The veterinarian did."

Jacob yawned. "She knows more about them than Doc Anstine does."

Nathaniel had to admit that was true. She had a rare gift for convincing the shy creatures to trust her as she had with Jacob…and with him. He'd trusted her to tell him the truth, but he wasn't sure she had.

But you haven't been exactly honest with her, ain't so? Again his conscience spoke to him in his *grossmammi*'s voice.

He pushed those thoughts aside as his buggy crested the hill. He frowned. The flashy vehicle was stopped on the shoulder of the road. Slowing, he drew alongside it.

"Is there a problem?" he asked, bringing Bumper to a halt.

"Not with us." Laughter followed the raucous reply.

For the first time, Nathaniel realized that, in addition to the driver, there were a woman and two men in the buggy that had been built to hold two people. He wondered how they managed to stay inside when the buggy hit a bump. Two men were dressed in *Englisch* clothes, but he couldn't tell if they were *Englischer* or young Amish exploiting their *rumspringa* by wearing such styles.

"Nice buggy," the driver said. In the bright light, his red hair glowed like a fire. "It looks as if it were made by Joshua Stoltzfus."

"I guess so." He really hadn't given the matter any

thought. It had been in the barn when he arrived at his grandparents' farm.

"He builds a *gut* buggy."

"I can't imagine any Stoltzfus not doing a *gut* job with anything one of them sets his or her mind to."

"Prove it."

Nathaniel frowned. "Pardon me?"

"Prove it's *gut*. We'll have a race."

He shook his head, aware Jacob was listening. "I don't want to race you."

"Scared I'll beat you?"

The driver's companions began making clucking sounds, something Nathaniel had heard young *Englischers* do when they called someone a coward.

"It doesn't matter why I don't want to race," he said, giving Bumper the command to start again. "I don't want to."

The outrageous buggy matched his pace. "But we do."

"Then you're going to have to find someone else." He kept his horse at a walk.

"We will." The driver leaned out of the buggy and snarled, "One other thing. Stay away from my girl."

He frowned. The red-haired man was trying to pick a fight, futile because Nathaniel wouldn't quarrel with him.

When Nathaniel didn't answer, the driver hissed, "Stay away from Esther Stoltzfus. She's my girl."

"Does she know that?" he retorted before he could halt himself.

The other men in the buggy crowed with laughter, and the driver threw them a furious glare.

"*Komm* on, Alvin Lee," grumbled one of the men. "He's not worth it. Let's go find someone else who's not afraid."

The buggy sped away, and Nathaniel wasn't sorry to see its silly lights vanish over another hill. Beside him, Jacob muttered under his breath.

When Nathaniel asked him what was wrong, Jacob stated, "Racing could hurt Bumper. That would be wrong."

"Very wrong."

"So why do they do it?"

He shrugged. "I don't know. Boredom? Pride? Whatever the reason is, it isn't enough to risk a horse and passengers."

"Would you have raced him if I hadn't been here?"

"No. I'm not bored, and I know *hochmut* is wrong." He grinned at the boy. "I know Bumper is a *gut* horse. I know I don't need to prove it to anyone."

Jacob's eyes grew round, and Nathaniel realized the boy was startled by his words. He waited for the boy to ask another question, but Jacob seemed lost in thought. The boy didn't speak again until they came over the top of another hill only a few miles from home and saw bright lights in front of them.

"What's that?" Jacob pointed along the road.

Nathaniel was about to reply that it must be the redhead's buggy, then realized the bright lights weren't on the road. They looked as if they'd fallen off it.

"Hold on!" he called to Jacob. "Go!" He slapped the reins on Bumper.

As they got closer, he could see the buggy was lying on its side in the ditch. The sound of a horse thrashing and crying out in pain was louder than Bumper's iron shoes on the asphalt. He couldn't hear any other sounds.

After pulling his buggy to the side of the road, taking care not to steer into the ditch, he jumped out.

"Stay here, Jacob."

"The horse—"

"No, stay here. There's nothing you can do for the horse now."

The boy nodded, and Nathaniel ran to the broken buggy. He had to leap over a wheel that had fallen off. Pulling some of the lights forward, he aimed them within the vehicle. One look was enough to show him the two passengers inside were unconscious. Where were the others?

Running to his own buggy, he pulled out a flashlight. He sprayed its light across the ground and saw one crumpled form, then another. He took a step toward them, then paused at the sound of metal wheels in the distance.

Nathaniel looked past the covered bridge on a road intersecting this one. He saw another buggy rushing away into the night. Had it been racing this one? How could the other buggy flee when these people were hurt?

No time for answers now. He scanned the area and breathed a prayer of gratitude when he saw lights from an *Englisch* home less than a quarter mile up the road. He'd send Jacob to have the *Englischers* call 911.

He halted in midstep. He couldn't do that. The boy had seen his parents killed along a country road like this one.

Knowing his rudimentary first aid skills might not be enough to help now, he moved his own buggy far off the road. He told Jacob to remain where he was. Sure the frightened boy would obey, he ran toward the house. He hoped help wouldn't come too late.

Chapter Thirteen

Esther was on time for school the next morning, but several of her scholars were late. She guessed they'd stayed in bed later, as she'd longed to do. It hadn't been easy to face the day…and the fact Nathaniel had left with Celeste from the wedding. He seemed to be doing as he'd discussed with her brothers: playing the field.

She should be pleased he didn't include her in his fun and adventures, but it hurt. A lot. Alvin Lee had dumped her without a backward glance when she urged him to stop his racing. He'd called her a stick-in-the-mud, though he'd tried to convince her to join him again.

Telling herself to concentrate on her job, she looked around her classroom. Jacob wasn't at his desk. She wondered why he hadn't come to school. The other scholars were toiling on worksheets, and the school-room was unusually quiet.

Maybe that was why she heard the clatter of buggy wheels in the school's driveway. So did the scholars, because their heads popped up like rows of woodchucks in a field.

She rose and was about to urge the *kinder* to finish their work when the door opened. In astonishment, she met her brother Joshua's brown eyes. Whatever had brought him to the schoolhouse must be very important because he hadn't taken time to change the greasy shirt and trousers he wore at his buggy shop.

Her niece and nephew jumped to their feet and cried as one, *"Daed!"*

He gave them a quick smile and said, "Everything is fine at home and at the shop. I need to speak to Esther for a moment."

"Once you're done with your numbers," Esther said to the scholars, pleased her voice sounded calm, "start reading the next chapter in your textbooks. Neva and I'll have questions for you on those chapters later." She gave her assistant teacher a tight smile as a couple of the boys groaned.

Neva nodded, and Esther was relieved she could leave the *kinder* with her. Next year she wouldn't have that luxury, because Neva would have a school of her own.

As she walked to the door, Esther saw the scholars exchange worried glances. Apparently neither she nor Joshua had concealed their uneasiness as well as she'd hoped.

Her brother waited until she stepped out of the schoolroom and closed the door. She motioned for him to remain silent as she led him down the steps. He followed her to the swing set.

"*Was iss letz*, Joshua?" She could imagine too many answers, but pushed those thoughts aside.

"Alvin Lee is in the hospital."

She sank to one of the swings because her knees were about to buckle. Holding it steady, she whispered, "The hospital?"

"*Ja*. I thought you'd want to know." Joshua didn't meet her eyes, and she wondered how much about Alvin Lee courting her the family had guessed.

"What happened?" she asked, though her twisting gut already warned her the answer would be bad.

"He crashed his buggy last night while racing."

"How is he?" A stupid question. Alvin Lee would only be in the hospital if he was badly hurt. Otherwise, he'd be recovering at home.

"It's not *gut*, Esther. I don't know the details."

"What do you know? Was he alone?" The questions were coming from her automatically, because every sense she had was numb. Alvin Lee had wounded her deeply, but she'd believed she loved him.

"I know Alvin Lee is in the hospital because Isaiah was alerted and came to tell me before he left for the hospital. Luella Hartz was one of the passengers with Alvin Lee. She was treated in the emergency room and released to her parents. From what Isaiah heard, she's pretty badly scraped, and she has a broken leg and some cracked ribs. Two *Englisch* men were in the buggy, too, and they were banged up but nothing is broken." His mouth drew into a straight line. "The buggy was too small for four adults. No wonder it rolled when Alvin Lee couldn't make the corner. If a car had come along…" He shook his head.

Sickness ate through her. Alvin Lee had asked her to

ride with him last night. If she had, she'd be the one with broken bones and humiliation. Or it could have been worse. She might be in the hospital, as Alvin Lee was.

God, danki *for putting enough sense in my head to save me from my own foolishness.* She added a prayer that all involved would recover as swiftly as possible.

"I hate to think of what might have happened if help hadn't arrived quickly," Joshua continued when she didn't reply. "They should be grateful Nathaniel went to a nearby *Englisch* house and called 911."

Her stomach dropped more. "Nathaniel? He was there?"

"Ja."

Esther wasn't able to answer. She felt as if someone had struck her. She couldn't catch her breath. Nathaniel? He'd been racing last night? With Alvin Lee? She was rocked by the realization she must have misjudged Nathaniel as she had Alvin Lee. Many times, Nathaniel had spoken of having a *gut* time. Was he—what did *Englischers* call it?—an adrenaline junkie like Alvin Lee?

Jacob had been with him. She asked her brother about the boy, but Joshua couldn't tell her anything. How could Nathaniel have been so careless? Blinding anger rose through her as she jumped to her feet.

"I want to go to the hospital and find out how Alvin Lee is doing," she said.

"They may not tell you." Joshua rubbed his hands together. "*Englisch* hospitals have a lot of rules about protecting a patient's privacy. When Tildie was in the hospital toward the end of her life, I had to argue with the nurses to let some of our friends come there to pray for her."

Esther blinked on searing tears. Though her brother was happy with his new wife and their melded family, the grief of those difficult months when his first wife had been dying of cancer would never leave him completely.

"I know they may not tell me anything, but I should go," she said.

"You know what you need to do, Esther." He gave her a faint grin. "I know better than to try to stand in your way. From what Isaiah told me, Nathaniel is still at the hospital."

She glanced at the schoolhouse. "What about Jacob?"

"I don't know. Isaiah didn't say anything about him." He put his hand on her shoulder. "What can I do to help, Esther?"

"Call Gerry and tell him I need him to take me to the hospital as soon as he can. He can pick me up here."

"I'll call from the shop." He squeezed her shoulder gently, then strode away to his buggy.

Esther hurried into the school. She had a lot of things to go over with Neva before she left. If Gerry wasn't busy, his white van would be pulling up in front of the school shortly. She needed to be ready.

What a joke! How could she ever be ready to go to the hospital where Alvin Lee was badly injured? As well, she'd see Nathaniel to whom her heart desperately longed to belong…and who clearly wasn't the man she'd believed him to be. One fact remained clear—she had to be there for Jacob because she couldn't trust Nathaniel with him any longer.

Gerry's white van arrived in fewer than fifteen minutes. Esther knew she must have spoken to him on the trip to the same hospital where Jacob's *onkel* was. She must have made arrangements for him to take her home. She must have crossed the parking lot and entered the hospital and gotten directions to Alvin Lee's room. She must have taken the elevator to the proper floor and walked past other rooms and hospital staff.

All of it was a blur as she stood in the doorway of the room where Alvin Lee was. She resisted the urge to run away and looked into the room. Her breath caught as the beeping machines created a strange cacophony in the small room where the curtains were pulled over the window.

For a moment, she wasn't sure if the unmoving patient on the bed was Alvin Lee. She hadn't imagined how many tubes could be used on a single person. One leg was raised in a sling, and she saw metal bolts sticking out of either side. Each was connected to lines and pulleys. Bandages covered his ashen face except where a breathing tube kept raising and lowering his chest. Sprigs of bright red hair sprouted out between layers of gauze. That, as much as his name on the chart in the holder outside his room, told her the man who looked more like a mummy than a living being was Alvin Lee Peachy.

"Oh, Alvin Lee," she murmured, her fingers against her lips. "Why couldn't you be sensible?"

She received no answer as she walked to his bedside. She didn't expect one. A nurse, she wasn't sure which one because everything between her stepping into Gerry's van and this moment seemed like a half-remembered nightmare, had told her Alvin Lee was in what was called a medically induced coma. It had something to do with letting his brain heal from its trauma while keeping his heart beating. Everything else was being done for him by a machine or drugs.

She bowed her head and whispered a prayer. She'd have put her hand on his, except his had an IV taped to it.

Footsteps paused by the door, and she looked over her shoulder, expecting to see a doctor or nurse. Instead Nathaniel stood there. He was almost as haggard as Alvin Lee. A low mat of whiskers darkened his jaw and cheeks, and his eyes looked haunted by what he'd seen.

Suddenly she whirled and flung herself against him. His arms enfolded her, and his hand on her head gently held it to his chest. Her *kapp* crinkled beneath her bonnet as he leaned his cheek against it.

The tears she'd held in flooded down her cheeks and dampened the black vest he'd worn to the wedding. Safe in his arms—and she knew she'd always be safe there—she could surrender to fear and sorrow. She remained in his arms until her weeping faded to hiccupping sobs.

"I'm done," she whispered, raising her head. "Where's Jacob?" She was caught by his wounded gaze, and she wished he'd free his pain as she had. She'd gladly hold him while he wept.

Esther stiffened and pulled away as she recalled what Joshua had told her. Nathaniel had been the one to call an ambulance last night. He'd been there when Alvin Lee was racing. Had they been competing against each other?

Nathaniel put his arm around her shoulders and drew her out of the room. The beeping sound of the machines followed them down the hall to a waiting area. After she'd entered, he followed, closing the door. She looked at Jacob who stood up from where he'd been sitting on what looked like an uncomfortable chair. He appeared as exhausted as Nathaniel, and she realized the boy had been at the hospital since last night.

Jacob threw his arms around her as he had after the wedding last night. Just last night? It seemed more like a decade ago now.

She hugged the boy and kissed his hair, which needed to be brushed. As she looked over his head toward Nathaniel, she had to bite her tongue to halt her furious words. How could he endanger this boy?

Nathaniel's brows lowered, but his voice remained steady as he said, "It was nice of you to come and see him, Esther."

"He didn't know I was there."

"According to his parents, the *doktors* say he can hear us, but he can't speak to us right now."

"Like my *onkel*," Jacob said as he rocked from one foot to the other. "*Onkel* Titus can't talk to us because he's listening to God now. God knows what he needs more than any of us, including the *doktors*. He can't talk to us because it's not easy to listen to God and to us at the same time."

Her eyes burned with new tears. What a simple and beautiful faith he had! Nathaniel's eyes glistened, too, and she knew he was as touched by Jacob's words as she was.

Not looking away from her, Nathaniel said, "Jacob, you remember where the cafeteria is, don't you?"

"*Ja.*"

"Go and get yourself a soda." He pulled several bills out of his pocket. "There should be enough here for some chips, as well."

The boy grinned at the unexpected treat. When Nathaniel told him he'd stay in the waiting room with Esther, Jacob left.

"Go ahead," Nathaniel said. "Tell me what's got you so upset you're practically spitting."

"You."

"Me?" He seemed genuinely puzzled. "Why?"

"I thought you were smarter than this, Nathaniel. I thought you meant it when you said making the farm a success was the great adventure you wanted. And Jacob...how could you risk him?"

Anger honed his voice. "What are you talking about?"

"Racing! How could you race Alvin Lee when a *kind* was in your buggy? Was Celeste in there, too? Were you trying to show off for her?"

"I wouldn't ever do anything that might hurt Jacob or anyone else." His gaze drilled into her. "I thought you knew me better."

"I thought I did, too." Her shoulders sagged. "But when I heard how you were racing Alvin Lee—"

"I didn't race him! He tried to get me to, but I refused."

"I was told—"

"I was the one who went to find a phone to call 911? *Ja*, that's true, but it was because I was the first one to come upon the accident." He dropped to sit on a blue plastic sofa. "After I told him I wouldn't race him, he took off. He must have found someone else to race because we came upon the buggy on its side only a little farther ahead. I don't know whom he was racing because the other buggy was more than a mile away on the far side of the covered bridge out by Lambrights' farm."

She sank to another sofa, facing him as she untied

her bonnet and set it beside her on the cushion. "The other driver just left?"

"I told the police I saw a buggy driving away beyond the covered bridge, and they're going to investigate. Of course, it could be someone who wasn't involved. Maybe Alvin Lee was simply driving too fast."

"No. He's too skilled a driver to make such a mistake."

His brows lowered. "How do you know?"

"We all know each other in our district, Nathaniel."

"Be honest with me. You seem to have more knowledge of racing buggies than I'd thought you would."

Esther gnawed on her bottom lip. Why hadn't she kept quiet? She should have pretended she didn't know anything about the young fools who challenged one another.

He reached across the space separating them and took her hand. He clasped it between his. "I'm your friend, Esther. Tell me the truth about how you know so much about Alvin Lee's racing. Did you watch him?"

"Okay, if you want the truth, here it is." She doubted he'd think the same of her once she divulged what she'd hidden from everyone. "I know about racing. Not because I watched it, but because I was in buggies during races."

He pulled back, releasing her hands. "You could have been killed!"

"I wasn't. By God's *gut* grace, I know now, but at the time it was only meant to be a fun competition." She put up her hands when he opened his mouth to argue. "I learned it's dangerous. When I realized that, I didn't take part in any more races."

"Why did you start?"

Heat rose up her face, and she prayed she wasn't blushing. "Alvin Lee asked me to ride with him in one race. I didn't want to look like a coward."

"Oh."

Esther watched Nathaniel stand and walk toward the hallway. Was he looking for Jacob, or was he eager to get away from a woman who'd been silly?

"Is this why you're cautious about everything now?" he asked without facing her.

"I'm sure that's part of it. When we're young, we can't imagine anything truly terrible happening."

"Some do."

She waited for him to explain his cryptic comment. Silence stretched between them until the faint sounds from beyond the door seemed to grow louder and louder with each breath she took.

Slowly she stood. "Nathaniel, I was foolish, but please don't shut me out."

"I'm not shutting you out." He turned to look at her, his face as blank as the door behind him.

"No? I don't have any idea what you're thinking."

"You don't?" A faint smile tickled the corners of his mouth. "That's a change. You almost always have known what I'm thinking."

"I don't now. I wish I did."

He closed the distance between them with a pair of steps. Gently he framed her face between his work-roughened hands and tilted it as he whispered, "You're curious what I'm thinking? Do you really want to know?"

"Nathaniel—"

He silenced her as his mouth found hers. She froze, fearing she'd forgotten how to breathe. Then she soft-

ened against his broad chest as he deepened the kiss.
She slid her arms up his back, wanting to hold on to him
and this *wunderbaar* moment. All thoughts of being
only his friend were banished from her mind as well
as her heart.

He raised his head far enough so his lips could form
the words, "*That* was what I was thinking. How much
fun it would be to kiss you."

Fun? Was that all their kiss was to him? Fun? Another adventure? She didn't want to think of his jesting words with her brothers, but they rang through her
mind.

Playing the field is gut *in more than baseball.*

"Esther..." he began.

The door opened, and Jacob came in. His grin was
ringed with chocolate from the candy he'd been eating.
He held a half-finished cup of soda in one hand and a
crinkled bag of chips in the other.

"I should go," she said, grateful for the interruption.

She picked up her bonnet. If Nathaniel noticed how
her hands trembled, he didn't mention it. Somehow,
she managed to tell him and Jacob goodbye without
stumbling over her words. She didn't wait to hear their
replies.

What a mess he'd made of everything!

Nathaniel took off his straw hat and hung it by the
kitchen door. The alpacas and the other animals were
fed and watered and settled for the night. He checked
the door out of the barn and the gate to the alpacas' pen
to make sure they were locked. They constantly tested
every possible spot to find a way out.

As Esther had at the hospital after he'd kissed her.

He couldn't guess why she'd retreated quickly, but he should be relieved she had. What had he been thinking to give in to his yearning to kiss her? A woman considered a man's kiss a prelude to a proposal, and he wouldn't ask her to be his wife. He cared about her too much—he *loved* her too much—to ask her to marry him when he couldn't give her *kinder*. The memory of one perfect kiss would have to be enough for him for the rest of his days.

God, You know I want her in my life. To watch her wed another man, knowing her husband will savor her kisses that set my soul alight, would be the greatest torment I can imagine.

He made himself a glass of warm milk and went into the living room, glad Jacob was upstairs. Sitting in the chair that had been his *grossdawdi*'s, he didn't light a lamp. Instead he stared out into the deepening darkness. It was silent save for the distant yapping of a dog. Not even the sound of a car intruded.

How could he stay in Paradise Springs where he'd see Esther and her husband and their *kinder*? He was realizing now that becoming a farmer and making his grandparents' farm a success had been in large part a cover for his desire to return to Lancaster County and to her. Something he hadn't realized himself until he understood he could have lost her forever in a buggy accident.

Should he give in to his *mamm*'s frequent requests and return home? He could sell the farm and the animals. Ironically, Esther would be his best chance of finding a home for the alpacas. She wanted a herd of her own. He couldn't imagine a better home for his animals—or for himself—than with her.

Stop it! Feeling sorry for himself was a waste of time and energy. The facts were unalterable.

Another thought burst into his head. *All you have to do is tell her the truth.* He needed to, because kissing her had changed everything. She might think he wanted to court her.

He did.

But he couldn't. Not without telling her the truth. He wasn't the man for her.

He needed to think of something else. He'd been shocked when she told him she'd taken part in buggy races. He wondered how many of those friends living a fast life she'd estranged when she came to her senses. Some important ones, he'd guess, by how dim her eyes had become as she spoke.

Abruptly he understood what she was *not* saying. One of those people who'd turned away from her must have been a suitor. It would explain why she'd lost much of her daring, turning into a shadow of the girl he'd known. She needed someone special to bring forth her high spirits again. Someone who understood Esther the Pester resided somewhere deep within her.

Someone like Nathaniel Zook.

He growled a wordless argument with his own thoughts, but halted when Jacob came down the stairs.

"Why are you sitting in the dark?" Jacob asked.

He held out his glass of lukewarm milk to the boy. "Sometimes a man likes to have some quiet time to think."

"*Onkel* Titus used to say that." Taking the glass, Jacob sat on the sofa. He swallowed half the milk in a big gulp.

"Your *onkel* sounds as if he's a very wise man."

"You'll see for yourself when he comes home from the hospital." Sipping more slowly, Jacob grinned. "I'm going to ask *Onkel* Titus if we can get some alpacas to raise on our farm. He's going to like them as much as we do, ain't so?"

Nathaniel let him continue to outline his plans for fixing his *onkel's* outbuildings for alpacas and how he'd teach Titus what Esther had helped him and Nathaniel learn. There was no reason to dash the boy's dreams tonight, simply because his own had been decimated.

At last, Nathaniel said, "Time for you to get to bed, Jacob. You didn't sleep much last night, and you don't want to fall asleep while they're making cider tomorrow, do you?" Before the wedding, Jacob had told him about a trip the scholars were taking to a neighboring farm to watch windfall apples being squeezed into cider.

"No!" He jumped to his feet, ran out to the sink, rinsed out the glass and put it near the others to be washed after breakfast. With a cheerful wave, Jacob rushed up the stairs. His bedroom door closed with a distant click.

Nathaniel was left in the dark to try to figure out what he'd do and say the next time he saw Esther. As long as he was in Paradise Springs, he couldn't avoid her forever.

Chapter Fourteen

Nathaniel stepped out of his buggy and let the reins drop to the ground. Bumper would stay put until he returned. If the horse thought it was strange they'd returned to the place they'd left ten minutes before, he kept his thoughts to himself as he chomped on dried grass.

Hearing excited voices and a heavy metallic clunk, Nathaniel walked toward an outbuilding at the rear of the Gingerichs' farm where he'd been told the cider press was kept. The aroma of apples reached him long before he stood in the doorway.

Sunlight burst between the planks in the walls and seemed to focus on the large cider press in the middle of the barn. It was a simple contraption. Tall, thick wooden beams stood upright on either side. Stacked on a metal table with narrow gutters across it were planks with apples sandwiched between them. Heavier beams had been set on top of the uppermost plank and a heavy metal weight had been lowered onto them. From between the planks and running down the gutters to a hole in the side of the table were steady streams of the juice being squeezed out slowly by the weight.

Nathaniel noticed that in a single glance as his eyes adjusted to the dim interior of the barn. His gaze went to where Esther stood with her hands on the shoulders of two smaller scholars. She was making sure they could see the great press and the juice.

It'd been two weeks since he'd said more than hello or goodbye to her when he dropped off Jacob at school or picked him up at the end of the day. He'd known he would see her at services on Sunday if he attended in her district, but he hadn't made up his mind about going or not.

During that time, Alvin Lee Peachy had been released from the hospital into a rehab facility. The community was planning several fund-raising events to help pay for his care, which likely would continue for months, if not years. Nathaniel had seen flyers for a supper to be held next week as well as an auction after the first of the year. He planned to donate the extra furniture his grandparents had collected. If he did decide to sell the farm, the new owners wouldn't have to deal with the chairs.

But that wasn't the reason he'd returned to the Gingerichs' farm shortly after he'd brought Jacob to join the other scholars. He'd met the bishop on way home, and Reuben had shared news with him that he needed to deliver to Esther and the boy immediately.

He took a step into the barn, and Esther's head snapped up as if he'd pulled a string. Her smile evaporated. She bent to whisper to the two scholars beside her. Walking toward him, she caught her assistant's eye and pointed toward him and the door. Neva glanced at him and nodded.

Nathaniel went outside to wait for Esther. As she emerged from the barn, three apples in her hands, he saw wisps of cobwebs clinging to her dark blue dress. It was the same one she'd worn to her brother's wedding, and its color was a perfect complement to her eyes. His heart did somersaults, but he tried to ignore it.

"I thought you'd already left," Esther said in the cool, polite voice she'd used since the night he'd kissed her.

Not now, he ordered those memories that were both *wunderbaar* and sad. Squaring his shoulders, he said, "I did, but I have some news I didn't want you to hear from anyone else."

His face must have displayed the truth, because she clutched the apples close to her as she whispered, "Jacob's *onkel*?"

"He died this morning."

Tears rushed into her eyes, and he had to fight his hands that immediately wanted to pull her to him so he could offer her what sparse comfort there was. When she glanced at the barn, she asked, "What will happen to Jacob now?"

"I don't know." He swallowed hard. "I need to tell him."

"*We* will tell him. After school." A single tear fell down her cheek. "He's having such a *gut* time, and there's nothing he can do now, anyhow."

"I agree. Let him enjoy the day. I can stay here until…"

She shook her head. "No. We must make this seem like a normal day until we tell him what's happened. If you'd like to help—"

"You know I do."

"Bring Reuben with you," she finished as if he hadn't interrupted.

"*Gut* idea. I'll talk to him." He hesitated, wanting to add that he needed to talk with Esther as well, to clear the air between them. He missed their friendship. How could a single kiss—a single splendid kiss meant to show her how much he cared for her—drive such a wedge between them? He hoped she wanted to recover their friendship as much as he did.

"*Danki.*" She took a step back and wiped away her tears with the back of her hand. "I'll see you and Reuben after school."

He didn't have a chance to reply as she rushed into the barn. No sign of her dismay would be visible on her face when she was among the *kinder*. She'd make sure each of the scholars enjoyed the day. What strength she possessed! Exactly as she had when she was a little girl and kept up with and then surpassed him and her brothers. He'd loved her then, and his childish love had grown into what he wanted to offer her now.

Turning away, he went to his buggy. He'd drive to Reuben's farm and talk to the bishop before going to his own farm to tend to the animals. It was going to be a long, difficult day.

Esther didn't pretend to do work at her desk when the other *kinder* left after school. Jacob stood by a window and watched for Nathaniel's buggy.

"I'm sorry he's late," the boy said for the fourth time in as many minutes. "He's usually on time. Do you think the alpacas are okay?"

"I'm sure they're fine." It wasn't easy to speak past the lump filling her throat.

"What if one is having her cria?"

"Nathaniel knows you don't want to miss that."

"But—" He halted himself, then laughed. "Here he comes now. He won't be able to tease me about being slow in the morning!"

She smiled, but her heart was breaking at the sight of his easy grin. Jacob had become a cheerful *kind* during his time with Nathaniel. Everything was about to change for the boy again, and she wished she could spare him the sorrow.

God, give us the right words and let him know we are here for him, though everyone in his family has gone away.

"Someone's with him," Jacob called from by the window. "It's Reuben. What's he doing here?"

"I'm sure he'll tell us."

"I haven't been fighting again. I'm being honest." His face flushed. "Most of the time, and always when it matters."

She put her arm around his shoulders. Was he trembling hard or was she? "Jacob, you know the bishop doesn't discipline members of our community. You don't need to worry, anyhow." She forced another smile. "You've been a very *gut* boy lately."

His shoulders drooped beneath her arm, and she realized how tense he'd been. She couldn't help recall how he'd mentioned his *onkel* punishing him harshly for the slightest transgression.

The door opened, bringing chilly air into the classroom. Reuben entered first, taking off his straw hat and hanging it where the scholars usually did. Nathaniel followed. As he set his hat on the shelf above the pegs, he looked everywhere but at her and Jacob. His face was drawn and looked years older than it had that morning. The day had been as painful for him as it had for her. Such news shouldn't ever be held as a secret within a heart because it burned like a wildfire, without thought or compassion.

She fought her feet that wanted to speed her across the room so she could draw his arms around her. She stayed where she was.

"Are the alpacas okay?" asked the boy before anyone else could speak.

"They're fine." Nathaniel gave him a gentle smile. "You can see for yourself as soon as we get there."

"Gut!" Jacob shrugged off Esther's arm and sprinted toward the door. "I'm ready. Let's go home now."

She saw the glance the two men exchanged, and she wondered if it was the first time they'd heard Jacob describe Nathaniel's farm as home.

Reuben cleared his throat. "Jacob, can we talk for a minute?"

"Ja," the boy answered, though it was clear from his expression he wished he had any excuse to say no.

The bishop motioned toward the nearest desk. "Why don't you sit down?"

"What's happened?" Jacob's eyes grew wild with fear, and his face became a sickish shade of gray. "They told me to sit down when they told me *Mamm* and *Daed* were dead. Is it *Onkel* Titus? Is he dead?"

Esther knew she should leave the answer to the bishop, but she couldn't bear the pain in the *kind*'s voice. Putting her arms around Jacob, she drew him close to her. He resisted for a moment, then clung to her as if she were a lifesaver in a turbulent sea.

"I'm sorry," she whispered against his hair.

"Danki." His voice was steadier than hers. As he

stepped away and looked at Reuben and Nathaniel, he asked in his normal tone, "Can we go home now?"

"Go on out and turn the buggy around, so it'll be ready when we leave," Nathaniel said quietly.

The boy grabbed his hat, coat and lunch box before racing out of the schoolroom. Esther went to the window to watch him scurry to the buggy. He patted Bumper and spoke to him before climbing in and picking up the reins. Except for a brief moment when he'd held on to her, he acted as if nothing had occurred.

"We grieve in different ways," Reuben murmured, as if she'd spoken aloud. Turning to Nathaniel, he added, "You must watch for his moods to change abruptly. He understands more than most *kinder* his age about death and loss, but he's still only eight years old."

Walking away from the window, Esther asked, "What will happen to him now? Titus Fisher was, as far as we could find out, his only living relative."

"He's welcome to stay with me," Nathaniel replied quietly. "For as long as he needs to."

The tears that had scorched her eyes all day threatened to fall when she heard the genuine emotion in his words. Not only had Nathaniel made a positive change in Jacob, but the boy had done the same for him. Nathaniel had become more confident in handling the animals at the farm and had a clear vision of how he could make the farm a success.

If only he wasn't playing the field like Daniel, I could...

She silenced the thoughts. This was neither the time nor the place for them. She should be grateful she knew his intentions.

"That is *gut* of you, Nathaniel," Reuben said. "However, the choice isn't ours. With his *onkel*'s death, Jacob is now a ward of the Commonwealth of Pennsylvania. I received a call earlier today. An *Englisch* social worker named Chloe Lambert will be visiting you at your farm once the funeral is over."

"Is it just a formality?" Esther asked.

The bishop raked his fingers through his beard as he did often when he was distressed. "I wish I could say it was, but Nathaniel isn't related to Jacob, so there will need to be supervision by a social worker."

"What can we do?" Nathaniel asked.

"I'll be talking to the *Leit* about making a plan for taking care of the boy. I suggest you do the same. He has done well at your farm, Nathaniel." Reuben sighed and looked at Esther. "The two of you need to think about the ways you have helped the boy and ways you can in the future."

"We will," Esther said at the same time Nathaniel did. "Will that be enough to convince an *Englisch* social worker Jacob's place is here among us?"

The bishop looked steadily from her to Nathaniel. "We must heed the lesson in the Book of Proverbs. 'Trust in the Lord with all thine heart; and lean not unto thine own understanding. In all thy ways acknowledge Him, and He shall direct thy paths.' He knows what lies ahead and is here to guide us."

"What else can we do?"

She expected Reuben to answer, but instead Nathaniel did. "We must believe our combined efforts and prayer are enough to touch an *Englisch* woman's heart and open her eyes to the truth that Jacob's home is with us."

Chapter Fifteen

Esther closed the teacher's edition of the fifth graders' textbook. She rubbed her tired eyes and looked out at the star-strewn sky. It wasn't late, just after supper, but sunset was so early this time of year. As the weather grew colder, the stars became brighter and somehow felt closer to her window. She leaned back in her chair and turned out the propane light hissing on her bedroom table.

Instantly the sky seemed a richer black, and the stars burned more fiercely. She sat straighter when a shooting star raced across the sky. *Englischers* made wishes on them, but that was a *kind*'s game.

What would she wish if she believed in such silliness? For hearts to be healed, most especially Jacob's. The boy had been stoic during his *onkel*'s funeral, but she'd seen the anger in his eyes when he didn't think anyone was looking at him. He'd started getting into fights at school again and seemed to think everyone was against him. Nothing Esther said made a difference.

You should discuss this with Nathaniel. The thought had nagged her every day for the past week. She'd spoken with him a few times during the funeral, but otherwise she'd avoided him. It was cowardly, she knew, but allowing herself to be drawn to him again would be foolish. He wanted to play the field.

She heard her name shouted up the stairs. "Esther, a call came at the barn for you."

"For me?" She had no idea who'd use the phone to contact her.

Micah answered, "*Ja.* Jacob Fisher called. A cria is coming, and they could use your help."

Esther didn't hesitate. Jumping to her feet, she grabbed a thick wool shawl from the chest by her bed and picked up the bag of supplies she'd packed. She ran down the stairs, barely missing Micah who stood at the bottom.

"Jeremiah is getting your buggy ready," he said.

"*Danki.*" She didn't add anything else as she raced into the kitchen, snatched her bonnet and set it on her head with one hand while opening the door with the other.

The ride to Nathaniel's farm seemed longer in the darkness. There wasn't much traffic, but she slowed at the crest of each hill in case a vehicle was coming. She wasn't worried solely about *Englisch* cars. Despite Alvin Lee's accident, others might foolishly be racing their buggies tonight.

She breathed a sigh of relief when she pulled into Nathaniel's farm lane. The house was dark, but light shone from the barn. She jumped from her buggy, collected her bag and ran in. She started to call out to Nathaniel and Jacob, but clamped her lips closed when she saw the astounding sight in front of her.

In the glow of several lanterns arranged around the barn, Nathaniel stood inside the alpacas' pen, his back to her. He was staring at Jacob. The boy was surrounded by the herd, which seemed to be seeking his attention. He stroked one, then another. None of them shied from his touch. His face was glowing with happiness.

She wanted to praise him for his patience in letting the alpacas come to him. She stayed silent because the sound of her voice might send the excitable creatures fleeing, and that could be dangerous for the one in labor.

Crossing the barn, she opened the gate so she could stand beside Nathaniel. He glanced at her with a wide grin before looking at the boy.

Jacob pushed his way through the herd and loped over to the gate. "Did you see that?"

"You're a *wunderbaar* friend to the alpacas," Esther said, then laughed when one of the braver ones trotted after him, clearly hoping he had something for her to eat. "They've discovered that."

"*Ja.* I like them, and they like me." His eyes glowed with joy.

"Well done," Nathaniel said, clapping his hand on the boy's shoulder with the respect one man showed another.

Esther looked at one corner of the pen where a young alpaca was lying on her side. Nathaniel started to give her a report on the alpaca's labor. She waved him to silence.

"Let the *mamm* alpaca do what she needs to," she said as she knelt in the hay by the gate.

"Shouldn't we do something?" asked Jacob.

"She should do well by herself. If she needs help, we'll be here to offer it. Otherwise, we'll watch and cheer when her cria comes."

"That's it?" asked Nathaniel.

"Alpacas have been giving birth on their own in the wild forever. She'll do fine."

Though Esther saw doubt on their faces, the alpaca proved her right when, about ten minutes later, the cria made its entrance, nose and front legs first. Within moments of its head's appearance, the cria was born. It sniffed the world, trying to find out more about it. The alpaca stretched to nose her newborn. A couple of the other alpacas came over to do the same, but she stood and got between them and her cria.

"Wait here," Esther whispered as she carried her bag closer to the *boppli*.

The *mamm* shied away, but not too far, her eyes remaining on the cria. Speaking in a low, steady voice, Esther opened the bag and withdrew a sling hooked to a handheld scale. She carefully lifted the unsteady cria into the sling and held it up.

"She's sixteen pounds," Esther said with a smile. "A *gut* size for a female cria." Lowering the *boppli* to the hay, she crooked a finger at Jacob. "Come over and see her."

"The *mamm* won't care?"

"They trust you now. Move slowly and don't get between her and the cria."

The boy crept closer. "She's cute."

"Would you like to pick out a name for her?" Nathaniel asked.

"Me?" His grin stretched his cheeks. "You want me to name the cria?"

"If you want to. Take a few days and think it over."

"Ja," Esther said. "Right now, the cria isn't going to do much other than eat and sleep. Her *mamm* will take care of her, but in a few days, the cria will be running about and playing."

Jacob considered that, then asked, "What if something happens to her *mamm*?"

Esther wiped her hands on the towel Nathaniel held out to her. "She's healthy, and she should live a long time. Some live until they're twenty years old."

"My *mamm* wasn't much older when she died."

Esther couldn't move as she stared at the *kind* who was regarding her and Nathaniel with an acceptance beyond his years. Yet she saw the pain he was again trying to hide. Jacob seldom spoke of his parents and never this directly.

"We'll watch over the cria," she replied, "and we won't be the only ones. God keeps a loving eye on all of us."

"Not me."

Nathaniel started to say, "Of course He—"

Esther halted him. One thing she'd learned as a teacher and as an *aenti*, trying to tell *kinder* their feelings were wrong got her nowhere.

"Why do you think God doesn't look out for you?" she asked.

"Why would He? He knows how furious I am with Him. He let my *mamm* and *daed* die, and He let me live so I can't be with them."

Squatting in front of the *kind*, she put her hands on his shoulders. "We have to believe, no matter what happens, God loves us."

"But if He loved me, why…?" His voice cracked as tears filled his eyes that had been joyous moments before.

"Why did He take your parents? I can't give you an answer, Jacob. There are things we can't know now. That's what faith is. Believing in God's *gut* and loving ways when our own hearts are broken."

"I miss them." He leaned into her, reforming his body to fit against hers.

"I know. I miss my *daed*, too."

Jacob raised his head. "You have your *mamm*."

"For which I'm grateful, but that doesn't lessen my sorrow when I think of my *daed* and how he used to make me laugh when I was a little girl." She wiped one of his tears away with the crook of her finger. "If he were here, he'd be in great pain, and I don't want him to suffer."

"My parents would have suffered, too. Really bad. *Onkel* Titus told me I shouldn't want them to stay here."

"It's okay to miss them and want to be with them."

"It is?"

"*Ja*, but we have to believe God has His reasons for healing some of us and for releasing others from their pain by bringing them home to Him. We have to see His grace either way and realize mere humans can't understand what He chooses. But we know God grieves along with us because He loves us."

"Does God cry, too?"

"When we turn away from Him," Nathaniel said. Pointing to the alpaca that had given birth, he added, "Look at her. She's glad because her *boppli* is alive. She wants to keep her cria close to her, to protect and nourish it. That's what makes her happy. Just as God is happy when we are close to Him."

"Oh." Jacob didn't say more as he watched the alpaca and the cria.

"When the cria is old enough to go off on her own," Esther whispered, "the alpaca won't be angry. She knows that is how life is intended to be, and to be angry at her daughter would be as useless as being angry at a piece of hay. That's how parents think, and God is our heavenly Father. He knows sometimes we have to make mistakes, but His love for us never falters. Even if you're angry with Him, He isn't angry with you."

The boy searched their faces, then looked at the alpacas. "He loves me like I love the alpacas." The tension slowly slid from his shoulders. Without another word, he went to the rest of the herd and let them surround him as he petted them.

Nathaniel smiled at Esther, and she saw the same pure happiness in his eyes as the boy's. It was a perfect moment.

And a moment was all it lasted. One moment, because before she could say anything, gravel crunched beneath rubber tires in the driveway. Someone was coming. Someone who wasn't driving in on metal wheels.

Her stomach cramped as the late model *Englisch* car stopped by the house and the driver turned off the engine. Through the windshield in the lights from the dashboard, she could see it was a young woman.

"The social worker." Esther didn't make it a question.

She heard the same uncertainty and dismay in his voice when he said, "We knew the state would be sending someone."

"But why now?"

* * *

Nathaniel glanced over his shoulder to where Jacob was relishing his chance to pet the alpacas and feed them by hand. Esther did the same. He knew what she was thinking. It'd been such a *wunderbaar* moment, and it was sad to have it interrupted by the outside world. But the outside world was there, and they must deal with it.

Putting his arm around Esther's shoulders and picking up a lantern, he told Jacob they'd be back in a few minutes. He wasn't sure if the boy heard them because he was enthralled by the alpacas nuzzling him.

The *Englisch* woman was stepping out of the car as they emerged from the barn. Chloe Lambert was nothing like he'd expected. Nothing like he'd feared. Instead of wearing a fancy business suit, the young woman had on khaki pants and a simple blouse. She wore sneakers like Esther's, and her dark hair was short and flattered her round face. One thing was as he'd anticipated. Chloe Lambert carried a briefcase with a long strap to allow it to hang from her shoulder.

"I'm Nathaniel Zook," he said.

She nodded and looked at Esther. "Where's Jacob Fisher?"

"He's feeding the alpacas. I'm Esther, by the way."

"Very nice to meet you, Esther. Is Jacob safe with those animals?"

Esther laughed, but the sound was laced with anxiety. "He's very safe. He's been trying to convince the herd for almost a month to let him get close to them. Tonight that happened just before a new one was born."

She glanced down at Esther's feet. "Is he wearing sneakers, too? Does he need to wear boots?"

"He's fine," Nathaniel said. "Why don't you come in and see for yourself?"

"Thank you. I'd like that." Chloe took a step, then looked steadily at them. "Please understand we want the same thing. What's best for the boy. I'm not your enemy or his."

Nathaniel nodded. "I'm sorry if we gave you that impression."

Miss Lambert smiled kindly. "You haven't. I wanted to make that clear. Now please show me where the boy is."

Esther began talking with the social worker as if they were longtime friends and with an ease Nathaniel couldn't have managed. He remembered the social workers who'd spoken with his parents at the hospital, outlining programs available to him and them. Some had sounded interesting and probably would have been approved by their bishop, but his parents wanted nothing more to do with *Englischers* and hospitals and *doktors* and tests.

Had they been right to distrust the *Englisch* system, or had it been only the unrelenting fear and guilt driving them? He hadn't known then, and he didn't know now. At last he understood how intrusive it was to have someone examining every aspect of his life and how little control he had over the situation.

I can hand control over to You, Lord, and trust You'll direct our paths in a direction where we can travel toward You together.

The prayer eased the initial panic he hadn't been able to submerge. No wonder Miss Lambert thought he saw her as an enemy. As he watched Esther introducing Miss Lambert to Jacob and listened while the social worker spoke to the boy about the alpacas as if they were the most important thing in the world, he relaxed further. He doubted the social worker was as interested in the herd as she acted, but she was allowing Jacob to tell her every detail about the cria's birth. She oohed and aahed over the adorable *boppli*. It was a *gut* way for her to get insight into the boy's life.

A half hour later, they were sitting in Nathaniel's living room. Miss Lambert got out her computer and put it on a chair she'd drawn near where she sat.

"Do you mind?" she asked as she opened her laptop. "I'd like to take notes while we're talking. It'll make it easier for me later to transfer the information to the department's forms."

"Of course not," Nathaniel replied. What else could he say? He hated everything about this situation where each word he spoke could be the wrong one. *Lord, be with us today and guide our words and actions so Miss Lambert sees Jacob belongs here with this community. Here with me!* The last came directly from his heart.

"Let me say again how much I appreciate you being willing to let me come and visit like this, Mr. Zook."

"Please call me Nathaniel."

"Thank you. I appreciate that, and I think it'll be simpler if you call me Chloe."

"*Danki.* I mean, thank you."

She smiled, obviously trying to put them at ease. "I understand enough of the language of the plain folk to know what *danki* means. I've worked with other plain families, which is why I was assigned as Jacob's social worker. If you say something I don't understand, I'll ask you to explain. Please do the same if I say something you don't understand."

Nathaniel nodded and watched Esther do the same. Jacob was hunched on his chair, trying to make himself as small as possible. Did he have any idea why the social worker was there? Probably not. It was more likely he wanted to return to the alpacas.

Chloe looked at Esther. "I understand you are Jacob's teacher."

"I am."

She typed a few keys on her computer, then said, "I know it'll be an imposition, but I'll need to see Jacob at school. I can't let you know before I arrive." She gave Esther a wry smile. "We're supposed to drop in so we see what's really going on. I hope that won't be a problem."

"The scholars—our students are accustomed to having parents come to the school to help. You're welcome to come anytime you need to, but I must ask you not to talk to the *kinder* without their parents' permission."

"That is fair. Will you arrange for me to obtain the permission if I need it?"

"It will be for the best if our bishop does."

"That's Reuben Lapp, right?"

"Ja."

Chloe smiled as she continued typing. "I've already spoken with Bishop Lapp. He expressed his concerns about the situation, and I told him—as I'm telling you— those concerns will be taken into consideration before any decision will be made."

"Gut." Relief was evident in Esther's voice.

When she looked at him, Nathaniel gave her what he hoped she'd see as a bolstering smile. The situation between them might be tenuous now, but she was his greatest ally...as she'd always been. It wasn't a *kind*'s game they were caught up in now, but he knew he could trust she'd be there for him and for Jacob. Her heart was steadfast, and in spite of her trepidation now, he knew she had the courage of the Old Testament woman whose name she shared. That Esther had done all she could to save her people, and Esther Stoltzfus would do no less for an orphaned boy.

His attention was pulled back to the social worker when Chloe said, "Now, Nathaniel, I've got a few questions for you."

When she saw Nathaniel's shoulders stiffen, Esther wanted to put her hand out to him as she had in the schoolroom on the day they'd told Jacob of his *onkel*'s passing. She wasn't sure how Chloe would react, so she clasped her fingers together on her lap.

She listened to questions about Jacob's schedule, what he ate, and where he slept. The boy began to squirm with boredom, and she asked if he could be excused. Her respect for the *Englisch* woman rose when Chloe gave him a warm smile and told him to enjoy his time with the alpacas, but not to spend so much time with them he didn't get his homework done.

"I don't give the *kinder* homework," Esther said when Jacob regarded the social worker with bafflement. "They've got chores, so the scholars complete their work at school. Besides, they need some time to play and be *kinder*."

Chloe's smile broadened as Jacob made his escape. "I wish more people felt that way. Children need to be children, but too many find themselves in situations where that's impossible." She looked at Nathaniel. "Just a few more questions. I know this must seem like the whole world poking its nose into your business, but we must be certain being here is the best place for Jacob."

"It is." Not a hint of doubt was in his voice or on his face.

"I hope you're right." Glancing at the screen, she asked, "Do you have family in the area, Nathaniel?"

"Not any longer. This farm belonged to my grandparents, and when they died, it became mine."

"So your parents are deceased, too?"

"No. They're in Indiana with my four sisters and younger brother. Two of my sisters are married, and I have several nephews and nieces. They live near my parents."

"So there's nobody here to help you with Jacob?"

"Our community is here to help if we need it." His smile was so tight it looked painful. "So far, we haven't. Jacob and I have gotten along well."

As she'd promised, the social worker had only a few more questions. Esther listened as Nathaniel answered thoughtfully and without hesitation or evasion. When Chloe asked to see the boy's room, Esther didn't follow them upstairs. She remained in the living room, listening to the hiss of the propane lamp and staring at the computer. If she peeked at the screen, would she be able to see what Chloe had written?

She couldn't do that. If the social worker found her snooping, it might be a mark against Nathaniel. What did Chloe think about Jacob's situation? Would she recommend he stay with Nathaniel?

The social worker and Nathaniel returned to the lower floor. They spoke easily before Nathaniel said he'd go and get Jacob to have a few words with the social worker.

As he went outside, Chloe closed her computer and put it in her bag. "Thank you for taking time to speak with me." She straightened. "I appreciate you being forthcoming. Some people aren't, but you and your husband—"

"Nathaniel isn't my husband."

The social worker stared at her, astonished. "I'm sorry. When I saw you together, I assumed you were married. I know I shouldn't assume anything about anyone, but you two seem like a perfectly matched set…" She turned away, embarrassed.

"Would it make a difference in your recommendation for where Jacob will live?" Esther asked before she could halt herself.

"What?" Chloe faced her.

"If Nathaniel and I were married?"

"Maybe. Maybe not. I can't give you a definite answer. Without any blood relationship between either of you and the boy, it's far more complicated."

"Jacob having a *mamm* and a *daed*…" She halted and amended, "Having a mother and a father would make a difference, wouldn't it?"

"It could." The social worker put the bag's strap over her shoulder. "Don't worry that my mistake will have any impact on this case, Esther. I can see both of you care deeply about the boy. However, sometimes the best thing for a child isn't what the adults around him want. We have to think first and foremost of what will give him the stable home he's never had. We prefer that to be with two parents."

Esther felt her insides turn to ice. She couldn't doubt Chloe's earnestness, but were her words a warning the state would take Jacob away? Somehow she managed to choke out a goodbye as the social worker left to speak to Jacob once more.

Groping for a chair, she sat and stared at the spot

where Jacob had been curled up. She didn't move and couldn't think of anything other than watching the boy being taken away from his community and his heritage.

She wasn't sure how long she sat there before Nathaniel returned. He strode into the living room. When she turned her gaze toward him, his face grew grayer.

"What is it?" he asked. "Did she say something to you?"

She explained the short conversation before saying, "Chloe suggested her superiors would prefer Jacob being in a family with two parents who can help him try to overcome the pain he has suffered. We can't offer him that now unless…"

"It sounds as if you want me to ask you to be my wife."

"I don't know what I'm saying, Nathaniel." She surged to her feet. "All I know for sure is Jacob needs to stay here. He's begun to heal, and if he's taken away, he'll lose any progress he's made."

"Did you tell her that?"

"No." Her eyes swam in tears. "I don't think I needed to. She looked dismayed when she found out we aren't married."

"Esther, you're probably the best friend I've ever had. Now and when we were kids, but—"

"That's all we'll ever be." Why did the words taste bitter? She'd told him many times friendship was what she wanted from him. She'd been lying. Not just to him, but to herself. Maybe not at the beginning when she first learned he'd come back to Paradise Springs, but as the days went on and she spent time with him and Jacob. Sometime, during those weeks in spite of her assertions, she'd begun to believe she and Nathaniel might be able to build a life together.

Then he'd kissed her…and her old fears of taking a risk had returned.

His broad hands framed her face and tilted it toward him so his gaze met hers. She saw his sorrow. Did he regret their agreement to be friends, too? Or was his grief focused on Jacob?

"I can't marry you, Esther. Not now." His voice broke. "Not ever."

She pulled away before her tears fell and betrayed her. "*Danki* for telling me that. You've made yourself really clear."

"Esther, wait!" he called as she started to walk away. "I've got a *gut* reason for saying that. I should have told you this right from the beginning, but I was ashamed."

"Of what? Most young men like to play the field, as you put it so tersely."

"What?"

"I heard you and Micah and Daniel laughing at the wedding about how you weren't going to settle down."

"Esther, look at me."

She slowly faced him. "Don't tell me you didn't say that, because I heard you."

"I'm sure you did. What you didn't hear were the words before those. Micah and I were teasing Daniel about his habits of bringing a different girl home from every event. I was repeating his words to him in jest."

"If that's not the reason—"

"The truth is I may never be able to be a *daed*." The resignation in his voice was vivid on his face. It was the expression of a man who had fought long and hard for a goal, but it was still beyond his reach, and it might be forever.

"I don't understand," she whispered.

"After we left Paradise Springs, I came back the next summer."

"I remember." She did. That year she'd been too bold and told him she planned to marry him. How ironic that sounded now!

"I didn't return the next summer because I was ill." He took a deep breath and said, "I had leukemia."

"Cancer?" she choked out. "I never knew."

"I know. My parents wanted to keep it quiet, even from our neighbors in Indiana. They sold off most of their farmland to pay the bills for my treatment." He rubbed his hands together as if he didn't know what else to do with them. "They were horrified one of their children was weak enough to succumb to such a disease."

"Weakness or strength has nothing to do with it." She pulled his hands apart, folding one between hers. "You know that, don't you?"

"*I* do, but I don't think they've ever accepted the truth. They always believed they or I had done something wrong. Something to call the scourge down on me." His mouth tightened into a straight line. "That's what they call it. The scourge."

"I'm sorry." She was beginning to understand his compassion for Jacob and why it went beyond the simple kindness of helping a *kind* who was alone in the world. He knew too well how it was to be different.

"I appreciate that, Esther."

"You are all right now?"

"As *gut* as if I'd never had cancer. With chemotherapy and radiation, the *Englisch doktors* saved my life from the disease. That's how they saw it. A disease that strikes indiscriminately, not a scourge sent to punish my family." He sighed. "However, the *Englisch dok-*

tors warned me that the treatments probably had made it impossible for me ever to father a *boppli.*"

Tears flooding her eyes blurred his face, but she doubted she'd ever be able to erase his desolate expression from her memory.

"Oh, Nathaniel, I'm sorry. I know how you love *kinder.*" She pressed her hands over her heart. "Now you have to worry about losing Jacob. If you think it'll make a difference—"

"Don't say it, Esther. I won't do that to you. I won't ask you to take the risk. How many times have you told me you aren't the same person you were when we were little? That you like to consider all aspects of an issue before you make a decision, that you no longer leap before you look around you."

"Nathaniel—"

"No, Esther, I'm sure of this. I've seen you with your scholars. You love *kinder.* You light up when they're around, whether at school or at home with your nieces and nephews. Or with Jacob who, despite his grumbling, appreciates the time you spend with him."

"So I have nothing to say about this?"

"What do you mean?"

She stood on tiptoe and pressed her lips against his. When his arms came around her, they didn't enfold her. They drew her away but not before she saw the regret in his eyes.

"Stop it, Esther. My *daed* warned me I must be stronger than I was when I contracted cancer." He groaned. "I never imagined I'd have to be this strong and push you away."

"Your *daed* is wrong." She took his hand again and folded it between her fingers as if in prayer. "I was wrong, Nathaniel, when I let myself believe it's a *gut* idea to hide from my adult pain by putting aside my childhood love of adventure. Remember what it was like then? We never questioned if something was worth the risk. We simply went with our hearts."

"And ended up bruised and battered."

"And happy." She hesitated, then realized if she hoped for him to open his heart to her, she must be willing to do the same to him. With a tentative smile, she said, "Well, except for one time I've never forgotten."

"Which time?"

"You don't remember?" She was astonished.

"I'm not sure what you're referring to. We got into a lot of scrapes together, so you'll need to be more specific."

She looked down at their hands. "I'm talking about the day when you were visiting from Indiana and I came over to your grandparents' farm, and I took your hand...like this."

He smiled as he put one finger under her chin and tipped it so her gaze met his. "I do remember. I thought you were the most *wunderbaar* girl I'd ever known." He chuckled. "That hasn't changed."

"I told you I was going to marry you as soon as we were old enough. Remember that?"

"*Ja.* I thought you were joking."

"*I* thought I was going to die of embarrassment."

He put his hands on her shoulders and smiled. "Never be embarrassed, Esther, to tell someone how you feel. You were brave enough to be honest. If more of us were like that, the world would be a better place."

"It didn't feel like that at the time." She took a deep breath, knowing if she backed away from risking her heart now, she'd never be able to risk it again. "I'm not going to be embarrassed now when I tell you I love you. I always have, and I always will. Get that through your thick head, Nathaniel Zook. I love you. Not some *kinder* we might be blessed with some day. You. I'm not saying this because of Jacob. I'm saying this because I can't keep the truth to myself any longer. If you don't love me, tell me, but don't push me away because you're trying to protect me from what God has planned for the future."

She held her breath as he stared at her. Had she been too blunt? Had she pushed too hard?

"That was quite a speech," he said with a grin.

"Don't ask me to repeat it."

"Not even the part when you said you love me?" His arm around her waist drew her to him. As he bent toward her, he whispered, "I want to hear you repeat that every day of our lives, and I'll tell you how much I've always loved you, Esther Stoltzfus. I don't need to be like your brother and play the field." He chuckled. "Actually I was in the outfield when you tumbled into my arms. From that moment, I knew it was where I wanted you always to be. But—"

She put her finger to his lips. "Let's leave our future in God's hands."

"As long as you're in mine." He captured her lips, and she softened against him.

Savoring his kiss and combing her fingers through his thick hair, letting its silk sift between her fingers, she wondered why she'd resisted telling him the truth until now. Some things were worth any amount of risk.

Epilogue

"Hurry, hurry!" called Chloe as she motioned for them to enter a small room beside one of the fancy court-rooms. "You should have been here ten minutes ago so we could review everything before we go before the judge."

"We're sorry. We were delayed." Nathaniel, dressed in his church Sunday *mutze* and white shirt, smiled at Esther. In fact, he hadn't stopped smiling the whole time they rode in Gerry's van from Paradise Springs into the city of Lancaster.

She put her hand on his arm, still a bit unsteady after her bout of sickness that morning. When it first had afflicted her last week, she'd thought she'd contracted some bug. However, the illness came only in the first couple of hours of each morning before easing to a general queasiness the rest of the day. It had continued day after day for nearly ten days now.

This morning, she'd told Nathaniel she believed she was pregnant. His shock had been endearing. She'd warned him that she must go to the midwife and have a test to confirm her pregnancy tomorrow, but she was certain what the test would show. They'd been married only three months, taking their vows barely a month after Ezra and Leah had, and already God had blessed them with a *boppli*.

"As long as you're here now." Chloe smiled at them. "Any questions before we go in?"

Jacob tugged on Nathaniel's sleeve. When Nathaniel bent down, the boy whispered frantically in his ear.

The social worker smiled and answered before Nathaniel spoke. "Down the hall on your right. Don't forget to wash your hands, Jacob. The judge will want to shake your hand when she finalizes your adoption."

As the boy scurried away, Nathaniel put his arm around Esther. They listened while Chloe explained again what would happen when they went into the courtroom. Official paperwork and recommendations from social services would be presented to the judge, who'd already reviewed copies of them. The judge might ask Jacob a few questions, but the procedure was simple and quick.

Jacob rushed into the room as another door opened, and a woman invited them into the courtroom. As they walked in, Jacob took Nathaniel's hand and then Esther's. They went together to a table where they sat facing a lady judge on her high seat behind a sign that read Judge Eloise Probert.

The paperwork was placed in front of the judge who

barely glanced at it. She smiled at Jacob and asked him if he understood what was going on.

"*Ja*... I mean, yes, your honor," he replied as he'd been instructed. "Once you say so, I won't be Jacob Fisher any longer. I'll be Jacob Zook, and Nathaniel and Esther will be my new *daed* and *mamm*." He gulped. "I mean, dad and mom."

"That's right, Jacob." Judge Probert had a nice smile and a gentle voice. "So this is what you want? To be Nathaniel and Esther's son?"

Jacob nodded so hard Esther had to bite her lip not to laugh. She heard a smothered sound from either side of her and saw Nathaniel and Chloe trying not to laugh, too.

"More than anything else in the whole world," Jacob answered. "Except maybe a couple more alpacas for our herd."

This time, nobody restrained their laughter, including the judge. "Well, I'll leave that decision to your new parents. Congratulations, Zook family. From this day forward, you *are* a forever family. All three of you."

Esther hugged Jacob and Nathaniel at the same time. She felt so happy and blessed.

After the paperwork was checked and they signed a few more papers and shook the judge's hand as well as Chloe's, Esther walked out of the courtroom with her husband and their son. They smiled at other families awaiting their turn to go before the judge. Congratulations were called to them, and her face hurt from smiling so widely.

They stepped through the doors and walked toward the tall columns edging the front of the courthouse,

Nathaniel said, "You know, the judge got almost everything right."

"Almost?" she asked.

"She said the three of us are a forever family. It's the *four* of us."

Tapping his nose, she said, "So far. Who knows how often God will bless us?"

With a laugh, he spun her into his arms and kissed her soundly. Then, each of them grabbing one of Jacob's hands, they walked toward where the white van was parked. The van that would take their family home.

* * * * *

HARLEQUIN
PLUS

Try the best multimedia subscription service for romance readers like you!

Read, Watch and Play.

Experience the easiest way to get the romance content you crave.

Start your **FREE TRIAL** at
www.harlequinplus.com/freetrial.